CORMAC McCARTHY

SUTTREE

The novels of the American writer Cormac McCarthy have
received a number of literary awards, including the Pulitzer
Prize, the National Book Award, and the National Book
Critics Circle Award. His works adapted to film include
All the Pretty Horses, The Road, and *No Country for Old
Men*—the latter film receiving four Academy Awards,
including the award for Best Picture. McCarthy died in
2023.

INTERNATIONAL

Praise for
CORMAC McCARTHY

"McCarthy is a writer to be read, to be admired, and quite honestly—envied."
—Ralph Ellison

"McCarthy is a born narrator, and his writing has, line by line, the stab of actuality. He is here to stay."
—Robert Penn Warren

"Mr. McCarthy has the best kind of Southern style, one that fuses risky eloquence, intricate rhythms and dead-to-rights accuracy."
—*The New York Times*

"Cormac McCarthy is a Southerner, a born storyteller, a writer of natural, impeccable dialogue, a literary child of Faulkner...capable of black, reasonable comedy at the heart of his tragedy."
—*New Republic*

"[McCarthy's] lyrical prose never sacrifices necessary economies [and his] sense of the tragic is almost unerring."
—*Times Literary Supplement* (London)

Books by CORMAC McCARTHY

Stella Maris
The Passenger
The Counselor (a screenplay)
The Road
The Sunset Limited (a novel in dramatic form)
No Country for Old Men
Cities of the Plain
The Crossing
All the Pretty Horses
The Stonemason (a play)
The Gardener's Son (a screenplay)
Blood Meridian
Suttree
Child of God
Outer Dark
The Orchard Keeper

SUTTREE

CORMAC McCARTHY

Vintage International
Vintage Books
A Division of Penguin Random House LLC
New York

The author wishes to express his gratitude to
The American Academy of Arts and Letters, The
Rockefeller Foundation, and The John Simon
Guggenheim Memorial Foundation.

FIRST VINTAGE INTERNATIONAL EDITION, MAY 1992

Library of Congress Cataloging-in-Publication Data
McCarthy, Cormac, 1933–
Suttree.
Reprint. Originally published: New York: Random House, 1979.
(Vintage contemporaries)
I. Title.
[PS3563.A258S9   1986   813'.54   91–50743
Vintage International Trade Paperback ISBN: 978-0-679-73632-5
eBook ISBN: 978-0-307-76247-4

The author and publisher gratefully acknowledge the assistance of
the Lyndhurst Foundation.

Author photograph © Marion Ettlinger

Manufactured in the United States of America
3579F8642

SUTTREE

*D*ear friend now in the dusty clockless hours of the town when the streets lie black and steaming in the wake of the watertrucks and now when the drunk and the homeless have washed up in the lee of walls in alleys or abandoned lots and cats go forth highshouldered and lean in the grim perimeters about, now in these sootblacked brick or cobbled corridors where lightwire shadows make a gothic harp of cellar doors no soul shall walk save you.

Old stone walls unplumbed by weathers, lodged in their striae fossil bones, limestone scarabs rucked in the floor of this once inland sea. Thin dark trees through yon iron palings where the dead keep their own small metropolis. Curious marble architecture, stele and obelisk and cross and little rainworn stones where names grow dim with years. Earth packed with samples of the casketmaker's trade, the dusty bones and rotted silk, the deathwear stained with carrion. Out there under the blue lamplight the trolleytracks run on to darkness, curved like cockheels in the pinchbeck dusk. The steel leaks back the day's heat, you can feel it through the floors of your shoes. Past these corrugated warehouse walls down little sandy streets where blownout autos sulk on pedestals of cinderblock. Through warrens of sumac and pokeweed and withered honeysuckle giving onto the scored clay banks of the railway. Gray vines coiled leftward in this northern hemisphere, what winds them shapes the dogwhelk's shell. Weeds sprouted from cinder and brick. A steamshovel reared in solitary abandonment against the night sky. Cross here. By frograils and fishplates where engines cough like lions in the dark of the yard. To a darker town, past lamps stoned blind, past smoking oblique shacks and china dogs and painted tires where dirty flowers grow. Down pavings rent with ruin, the slow cataclysm of neglect, the wires that belly pole to pole across the constellations hung with kitestring, with bolos composed of hobbled bottles or the toys of the smaller children. Encampment of the damned. Precincts perhaps where dripping lepers prowl unbelled. Above the heat and the improbable skyline of the city a brass moon has risen and the clouds run before it like watered ink. The buildings stamped against the night are like a rampart to a farther world forsaken, old purposes forgot. Countrymen come for miles with the earth clinging to their shoes and sit all day like mutes in the marketplace. This city constructed on no known paradigm, a mongrel architecture reading back through the works of man in a brief delineation of the aberrant disordered and mad. A carnival *of shapes upreared on the river plain that has dried up the sap of the earth for miles about.*

Factory walls of old dark brick, tracks of a spur line grown with weeds, a course of foul blue drainage where dark filaments of nameless dross sway in the current. Tin panes among the glass in the rusted window frames. There is a moonshaped rictus in the streetlamp's globe where a stone has gone and from this aperture there drifts down through the constant helix of aspiring insects a faint and steady rain of the same forms burnt and lifeless.

Here at the creek mouth the fields run on to the river, the mud deltaed and baring out of its rich alluvial harbored bones and dread waste, a wrack of cratewood and condoms and fruitrinds. Old tins and jars and ruined household artifacts that rear from the fecal mire of the flats like landmarks in the trackless vales of dementia praecox. A world beyond all fantasy, malevolent and tactile and dissociate, the blown lightbulbs like shorn polyps semitranslucent and skullcolored bobbing blindly down and spectral eyes of oil and now and again the beached and stinking forms of foetal humans bloated like young birds mooneyed and bluish or stale gray. Beyond in the dark the river flows in a sluggard ooze toward southern seas, running down out of the rainflattened corn and petty crops and riverloam gardens of upcountry landkeepers, grating along like bonedust, afreight with the past, dreams dispersed in the water someway, nothing ever lost. Houseboats ride at their hawsers. The neap mud along the shore lies ribbed and slick like the cavernous flitch of some beast hugely foundered and beyond the country rolls away to the south and the mountains. Where hunters and woodcutters once slept in their boots by the dying light of their thousand fires and went on, old teutonic forebears with eyes incandesced by the visionary light of a massive rapacity, wave on wave of the violent and the insane, their brains stoked with spoorless analogues of all that was, lean aryans with their abrogate semitic chapbook reenacting the dramas and parables therein and mindless and pale with a longing that nothing save dark's total restitution could appease.

We are come to a world within the world. In these alien reaches, these maugre sinks and interstitial wastes that the righteous see from carriage and car another life dreams. Illshapen or black or deranged, fugitive of all order, strangers in everyland.

The night is quiet. Like a camp before battle. The city beset by a thing unknown and will it come from forest or sea? The murengers have walled the pale, the gates are shut, but lo the thing's inside and can you

4

guess his shape? Where he's kept or what's the counter of his face? Is he a weaver, bloody shuttle shot through a timewarp, a carder of souls from the world's nap? Or a hunter with hounds or do bone horses draw his deadcart through the streets and does he call his trade to each? Dear friend he is not to be dwelt upon for it is by just suchwise that he's invited in.

The rest indeed is silence. It has begun to rain. Light summer rain, you can see it falling slant in the town lights. The river lies in a grail of quietude. Here from the bridge the world below seems a gift of simplicity. Curious, no more. Down there in grots of fallen light a cat transpires from stone to stone across the cobbles liquid black and sewn in rapid antipodes over the raindark street to vanish cat and countercat in the rifted works beyond. Faint summer lightning far downriver. A curtain is rising on the western world. A fine rain of soot, dead beetles, anonymous small bones. The audience sits webbed in dust. Within the gutted sockets of the interlocutor's skull a spider sleeps and the jointed ruins of the hanged fool dangle from the flies, bone pendulum in motley. Fourfooted shapes go to and fro over the boards. Ruder forms survive.

Peering down into the water where the morning sun fashioned wheels of light, coronets fanwise in which lay trapped each twig, each grain of sediment, long flakes and blades of light in the dusty water sliding away like optic strobes where motes sifted and spun. A hand trails over the gunwale and he lies athwart the skiff, the toe of one sneaker plucking periodic dimples in the river with the boat's slight cradling, drifting down beneath the bridge and slowly past the mud-stained stanchions. Under the high cool arches and dark keeps of the span's undercarriage where pigeons babble and the hollow flap of their wings echoes in stark applause. Glancing up at these cathedraled vaultings with their fossil woodknots and pseudomorphic nailheads in gray concrete, drifting, the bridge's slant shadow leaning the width of the river with that headlong illusion postulate in old cupracers frozen on photoplates, their wheels elliptic with speed. These shadows form over the skiff, accommodate his prone figure and pass on.

With his jaw cradled in the crook of his arm he watched idly surface phenomena, gouts of sewage faintly working, gray clots of nameless waste and yellow condoms roiling slowly out of the murk like some giant form of fluke or tapeworm. The watcher's face rode beside the boat, a sepia visage yawing in the scum, eyes veering and watery grimace. A welt curled sluggishly on the river's surface as if something unseen had stirred in the deeps and small bubbles of gas erupted in oily spectra.

Below the bridge he eased himself erect, took up the oars and began to row toward the south bank. There he brought the skiff about, swinging the stern into a clump of willows, and going aft he raised up a heavy cord that ran into the water from an iron pipe driven into the mud of the bank. This he relayed through an open oarlock mounted on the skiff's transom. Now he set out again, rowing slowly, the cord coming up wet and smooth through the lock and dipping into the river again. When he was some thirty feet from shore the first dropper came up, doubling the line until he reached and cast it off. He went on, the skiff lightly quartered against the river's drift, the hooks riding up one by one into the oarlock with their leached and tattered gobbets of flesh. When he felt the weight of the first fish he shipped the dripping oars and took hold of the line and brought it in by hand. A large carp broke water, a coarse mailed flank dull bronze and glinting. He braced himself with one knee and hefted it into the boat and cut the line and tied on a fresh hook with a chunk of cutbait and dropped it over the side and went on, sculling with one oar, the carp warping heavily against the floorboards.

When he had finished running the line he was on the other side of the river. He rebaited the last drop and let the heavy cord go, watching it sink in the muddy water among a spangled nimbus of sunmotes, a broken corona up through which flared for a moment the last pale chunk of rancid meat. Shifting the oars aboard he sprawled himself over the seats again to take the sun. The skiff swung gently, drifting in the current. He undid his shirt to the waist and put one forearm to his eyes. He could hear the river talking softly beneath him, heavy old river with wrinkled face. Beneath the sliding water cannons and carriages, trunnions seized and rusting in the mud, keelboats rotted to the consistency of mucilage. Fabled sturgeons with their horny pentagonal bodies, the cupreous and dacebright carp and catfish with their pale and sprueless underbellies, a thick muck shot with broken glass, with bones and rusted tins and bits of crockery reticulate with mudblack crazings. Across the river the limestone cliffs reared gray and roughly faceted and strung with grass across their face in thin green faults. Where they overhung the water they made a cool shade and the surface lay calm and dark and reflected like a small white star the form of a plover hovering on the updrafts off the edge of the bluff. Under the seat of the skiff a catfish swam dry and intransigent with his broad face pressed to the bulkhead.

Passing the creek mouth he raised one hand and waved slowly, the old blacks all flowered and bonneted coming about like a windtilted garden with their canes bobbing and their arms lifting dark and random into the air and their gaudy and barbaric costumes billowing with the movement. Beyond them the shape of the city rising wore a wrought, a jaded look, hammered out dark and smoking against a china sky. The grimy river littoral lay warped and shimmering in the heat and there was no sound in all this lonely summer forenoon.

Below the railway trestle he set to running his other line. The water was warm to the touch and had a granular lubricity like graphite. It was full noon when he finished and he stood in the skiff for a moment looking over the catch. He came back upriver rowing slowly, the fish struggling in a thin gray bilge in the floor of the boat, their soft barbels fingering with dull wonder the slimed boards and their backs where they bowed into the sunlight already bleached a bloodless pale. The brass oarlocks creaked in their blocks and the riverwater curled from the bowplanks with a viscid quality and lay behind the skiff in a wake like plowed mire.

He rowed up from under the shadow of the bluffs and past the sand and gravel company and then along by barren and dusty lots where rails ran on cinder beds and boxcars oxidized on blind sidings, past warehouses of galvanized and corrugated tin set in flats gouged from the brickcolored earth where rhomboid and volute shapes of limestone jutted all brindled with mud like great bones washed out. He had already started across the river when he saw the rescue boats against the bank. They were trolling in the channel while a small crowd watched from the shore. Two white boats lightly veiled in the heat and the slow blue smoke of their exhaust, a faint chug of motors carrying the calm of the river. He crossed and rowed up the edge of the channel. The boats had come alongside each other and one of them had cut the engine. The rescue workers wore yachting caps and moved gravely at their task. As the fisherman passed they were taking aboard a dead man. He was very stiff and he looked like a window-dummy save for his face. The face seemed soft and bloated and wore a grappling hook in the side of it and a crazed grin. They raised him so, gambreled up by the bones of his cheek. A pale incruent wound. He seemed to protest woodenly, his head awry. They lifted him onto the deck where he lay in his wet seersucker suit and his lemoncolored socks, leering walleyed up at the workers with the hook in his face like some gross water homunculus taken in trolling that the light of God's day had stricken dead instanter.

The fisherman went past and pulled the skiff into the bank upriver from the crowd. He rolled a stone over the rope and walked down to watch. The rescue boat was coming in and one of the workers was kneeling over the corpse trying to pry the grapnel loose. The crowd was watching him and he was sweating and working at the hook. Finally he set his shoe against the dead man's skull and wrenched the hook with both hands until it came away trailing a stringy piece of blanched flesh.

They brought him ashore on a canvas litter and laid him in the grass where he stared at the sun with his drained eyes and his smile. A snarling clot of flies had already accrued out of the vapid air. The workers covered the dead man with a coarse gray blanket. His feet stuck out.

The fisherman had made to go when someone in the crowd took his elbow. Hey Suttree.

He turned. Hey Joe, he said. Did you see it?

No. They say he jumped last night. They found his shoes on the bridge.

They stood looking at the dead man. The squad workers were coiling their ropes and seeing to their tackle. The crowd had come to press about like mourners and the fisherman and his friend found themselves going past the dead man as if they'd pay respects. He lay there in his yellow socks with the flies crawling on the blanket and one hand stretched out on the grass. He wore his watch on the inside of his wrist as some folks do or used to and as Suttree passed he noticed with a feeling he could not name that the dead man's watch was still running.

That's a bad way to check out, said Joe.

Let's go.

They walked along the cinders by the edge of the railroad. Suttree rubbed the gently pulsing muscle in his speculative jaw.

Which way do you go? said Joe.

Right here. I've got my boat.

Are you still fishin?

Yeah.

What made you take that up?

I dont know, Suttree said. It seemed like a good idea at the time.

You ever get uptown?

Sometimes.

Why dont you come out to the Corner some evenin and we'll drink a beer.

I'll get out there one of these days.

You fishin today?

Yeah. A little.

Joe was watching him. Listen, he said. You could get on up at Miller's. Brother said they needed somebody in men's shoes.

Suttree looked at the ground and smiled and wiped his mouth with the back of his wrist and looked up again. Well, he said. I guess I'll just stick to the river for a while yet.

Well come out some evenin.

I will.

They lifted each a hand in farewell and he watched the boy go on up the tracks and then across the fields toward the road. Then he went down to the skiff and pulled the rope up and tossed it in and pushed off into the river again. The dead man was still lying on the bank under his blanket but the crowd had begun to drift away. He rowed on across the river.

He swung the skiff in beneath the bridge and shipped the oars and sat looking down at the fish. He selected a blue cat and fetched it up by the gillslots, his thumb resting in the soft yellow throat. It flexed once and was still. The oars dripped in the river. He climbed from the skiff and tied up at a stob and labored up the slick grassless bank toward the arches where the bridge went to earth. Here a dark cavern beneath the vaulted concrete with rocks piled about the entrance and a crudely lettered keep out sign slashed in yellow paint across a boulder. A fire burned in a stone cairn on the rank and sunless clay and there was an old man squatting before it. The old man looked up at him and looked back at the fire again.

I brought you a catfish, Suttree said.

He mumbled and waved his hand about. Suttree laid the fish down and the old man squinted at it and then poked among the ashes of the fire. Set down, he said.

He squatted.

The old man watched the thin flames. Slow traffic passed above them in a muted rumble. In the fire potatoes blistered and split their charred jackets with low hissing sounds like small organisms expiring on the coals. The old man speared them from the ashes, one, two, three black stones smoking. He grouped them in a rusty hubcap. Get ye a tater, he said.

Suttree lifted a hand. He did not answer because he knew that the old man would offer three times and he must parcel out his words of refusal. The old man had tilted a steaming can and was peering inside. A handful of beans boiled in riverwater. He raised his ruined eyes and looked out from under the beam of tufted bone that shaded them. I remember you now, he said. From when you was just little. Suttree didnt think so but he nodded. The old man used to go from door to door and he could make the dolls and bears to talk.

Go on and get ye a tater, he said.

Thanks, said Suttree. I've already eaten.

Raw steam rose from the mealy pith of the potato he broke in his hands. Suttree looked out toward the river.

I like a hot dinner, dont you? the old man said.

Suttree nodded. Arched sumac fronds quivered in the noon warmth and pigeons squabbled and crooned in the bridge's ribbed spandrels.

The shadowed earth in which he squatted bore the stale odor of a crypt.

You didnt see that man jump, did you? Suttree said.

He shook his head. An old ragpicker, his thin chops wobbling. I seen em draggin, he said. Did they find him?

Yes.

What did he jump for?

I dont guess he said.

I wouldnt do it. Would you?

I hope not. Did you go over in town this morning?

No, I never went. I been too poorly to go.

What's the matter?

Lord I dont know. They say death comes like a thief in the night, where is he? I'll hug his neck.

Well dont jump off the bridge.

I wouldnt do it for nothin.

They always seem to jump in hot weather.

They's worse weather to come, said the ragpicker. Hard weather. Be foretold.

Did that girl come out to see you?

Aint been nobody to see me.

He was eating the beans from the tin with a brass spoon.

I'll talk to her again, said Suttree.

Well. I wish ye'd get ye one of these here taters.

Suttree rose. I've got to get on, he said.

Dont rush off.

Got to go.

Come back.

All right.

A slight wind had come up and going back across the river he braced his feet against the uprights in the stern and pulled hard. The skiff had shipped enough water through her illjoined planks to float the morning's catch and they wandered over the cupped and paint-chipped floorboards colliding dumbly. Rag ends of caulkingstring flared from the seams and ebbed in the dirty water among bits of bait and paper and the sweeps dipped and rose and a constant sipe of riverwater sang from under the tin of one patched blade. Half awash as she was the skiff wallowed with a mercurial inertia and made heavy going. He turned upriver close to shore and went on. Black families in bright Sunday clothes fishing at the river's brim watched somberly his passage. Dinner pails and baskets adorned the grass and dark infants were displayed on blankets kept at their corners by stones against the wind.

When he reached the houseboat he shipped the oars and the skiff slewed to a stall and settled ponderously against the tirecasings nailed there. He swung himself up with the rope in one hand and made fast. The skiff bobbed and slid heavily and the bilgewater surged. The fish sculled sluggishly. Suttree stretched and rubbed his back and eyed the sun. It was already very hot. He went along the deck and pushed open the door and entered. Inside the shanty the boards seemed buckled with the heat and beads of pitch were dripping from the beams under the tin roof.

He crossed the cabin and stretched himself out on the cot. Closing his eyes. A faint breeze from the window stirring his hair. The shantyboat trembled slightly in the river and one of the steel drums beneath the floor expanded in the heat with a melancholy bong. Eyes resting. This hushed and mazy Sunday. The heart beneath the breastbone pumping. The blood on its appointed rounds. Life in small places, narrow crannies. In the leaves, the toad's pulse. The delicate cellular warfare in a waterdrop. A dextrocardiac, said the smiling doctor. Your heart's in the right place. Weathershrunk and loveless. The skin drawn and split like an overripe fruit.

He turned heavily on the cot and put one eye to a space in the rough board wall. The river flowing past out there. Cloaca Maxima. Death by drowning, the ticking of a dead man's watch. The old tin clock on Grandfather's table hammered like a foundry. Leaning to say goodbye in the little yellow room, reek of lilies and incense. He arched his neck to tell to me some thing. I never heard. He wheezed my name, his grip belied the frailty of him. His caved and wasted face. The dead would take the living with them if they could, I pulled away. Sat in an ivy garden that lizards kept with constant leathery slitherings. Hutched hares ghost pale in the shade of the carriagehouse wall. Flagstones in a rosegarden, the terraced slope of the lawn above the river, odor of boxwood and mossmold and old brick in the shadow of the springhouse. Under the watercress stones in the clear flowage cluttered with periwinkles. A salamander, troutspeckled. Leaning to suck the cold and mossy water. A rimpled child's face watching back, a watery isomer agoggle in the rings.

In my father's last letter he said that the world is run by those willing to take the responsibility for the running of it. If it is life that you feel you are missing I can tell you where to find it. In the law courts, in business, in government. There is nothing occurring in the streets. Nothing but a dumbshow composed of the helpless and the impotent.

From all old seamy throats of elders, musty books, I've salvaged not a word. In a dream I walked with my grandfather by a dark lake and the old man's talk was filled with incertitude. I saw how all things false fall from the dead. We spoke easily and I was humbly honored to walk with him deep in that world where he was a man like all men. From the small end of a corridor in the autumn woods he watched me go away to the world of the waking. If our dead kin are sainted we may rightly pray to them. Mother Church tells us so. She does not say that they'll speak back, in dreams or out. Or in what tongue the stillborn might be spoken. More common visitor. Silent. The infant's ossature, the thin and brindled bones along whose sulcate facets clove old shreds of flesh and cerements of tattered swaddle. Bones that would no more than fill a shoebox, a bulbous skull. On the right temple a mauve halfmoon.

Suttree turned and lay staring at the ceiling, touching a like mark on his own left temple gently with his fingertips. The ordinary of the second son. Mirror image. Gauche carbon. He lies in Woodlawn, whatever be left of the child with whom you shared your mother's belly. He neither spoke nor saw nor does he now. Perhaps his skull held seawater. Born dead and witless both or a terratoma grisly in form. No, for we were like to the last hair. I followed him into the world, me. A breech birth. Hind end fore in common with whales and bats, life forms meant for other mediums than the earth and having no affinity for it. And used to pray for his soul days past. Believing this ghastly circus reconvened elsewhere for alltime. He in the limbo of the Christless righteous, I in a terrestrial hell.

Through the thin and riven wall sounds of fish surging in the sinking skiff. The sign of faith. Twelfth house of the heavens. Ushering in the western church. St Peter patron of fishmongers. St Fiacre that of piles. Suttree placed one arm across his eyes. He said that he might have been a fisher of men in another time but these fish now seemed task enough for him.

It was late evening before he woke. He did not stir, lying there on the rough army blanket watching the licking shapes of light from the river's face lapse and flare over the ceiling. He felt the shanty tilt slightly, steps on the catwalk and a low trundling sound among the barrels. No shade, this. Through the cracks he could see someone coming along the walk. A timorous tapping, once again.

Come in, he said.

Buddy?

He turned his head. His uncle was standing in the doorway. He looked back at the ceiling, blinked, sat up and swung his feet to the floor. Come in, John, he said.

The uncle came through the door, looking about, hesitant. He stopped in the center of the room, arrested in the quadrate bar of dusty light davited between the window and its skewed replica on the far wall, a barren countenance cruelly lit, eyes watery and half closed with their slack pendules of flesh hanging down his cheeks. His hands moved slightly with the wooden smile he managed. Hey boy, he said.

Suttree sat looking at his shoes. He folded his hands together, opened them again and looked up. Sit down, he said.

The uncle looked about, pulled the one chair back and sat carefully in it. Well, he said. How are you Buddy?

Like you see. How are you?

Fine. Fine. How is everything going?

All right. How did you find me?

I saw John Clancy up at the Eagles and he said that you were living in a houseboat or something so I looked along the river here and found you.

He was smiling uncertainly. Suttree looked at him. Did you tell them where I was?

He stopped smiling. No no, he said. No. That's your business.

All right.

How long have you been down here?

Suttree studied with a cold face the tolerant amusement his uncle affected. Since I got out, he said.

Well, we hadnt heard anything. How long has it been?

Who's we?

I hadnt heard. I mean I didnt know for sure if you were even out or not.

I got out in January.

Good, good. What, do you rent this or what?

I bought it.

Well good. He was looking about. Not bad. Stove and all.

How have you been John?

Oh, I cant complain. You know.

Suttree watched him. He looked made up for an older part, hair streaked with chalk, his face a clay mask cracked in a footman's smile.

You're looking well, said Suttree. A tic jerked his mouthcorner.

Well thanks, thanks. Try to keep fit you know. Old liver not the best. He put the flat of his hand to his abdomen, looked up toward the ceiling, out the window where the shadows had grown long toward night. Had an operation back in the winter. I guess you didnt know.

No.

I'm pulling out of it, of course.

Suttree could smell him in the heat of the little room, the rank odor of his clothes touched with a faint reek of whiskey. Sweet smell of death at the edges. Behind him in the western wall the candled woodknots shone blood red and incandescent like the eyes of watching fiends.

I dont have a drink or I'd offer you one.

The uncle raised a palm. No, no, he said. Not for me, thanks.

He lowered one brow at Suttree. I saw your mother, he said.

Suttree didnt answer. The uncle was pulling at his cigarettes. He held out the pack. Cigarette? he said.

No thanks.

He shook the pack. Go ahead.

I dont smoke.

You used to.

I quit.

The uncle lit up and blew smoke in a thin blue viper's breath toward the window. It coiled and diffused in the yellow light. He smiled. I'd like to have a dollar for every time I quit, he said. Anyway, they're all fine. Thought I'd let you know.

I didnt think you saw them.

I saw your mother uptown.

You said.

Well. I dont get out there much, of course. I went at Christmas. You know. They left word at the Eagles for me to call one time and I dont know. Come to dinner sometime. You know. I didnt want to go out there.

I dont blame you for that.

The uncle shifted a little in his chair. Well, it's not that I dont get along with them really. I just . . .

You just cant stand them nor them you.

A funny little smile crossed the uncle's face. Well, he said. I dont think I'd go so far as to say that. Now of course they've never done me any favors.

Tell me about it, said Suttree dryly.

I guess that's right, the uncle said, nodding his head. He sucked deeply on his cigarette, reflecting. I guess you and me have a little in common there, eh boy?

He thinks so.

You should have known my father. He was a fine man. The uncle was looking down at his hands uncertainly. Yes, he said. A fine man.

I remember him.

He died when you were a baby.

I know.

The uncle took another tack. You ought to come up to the Eagles some night, he said. I could get you in. They have a dance on Saturday night. They have some goodlooking women come up there. You'd be surprised.

I guess I would.

Suttree had leaned back against the raw plank wall. A blue dusk filled the little cabin. He was looking out the window where nighthawks had come forth and swifts shied chittering over the river.

You're a funny fella, Buddy. I cant imagine anyone being more different from your brother.

Which one?

What?

I said which one.

Which what?

Which brother.

The uncle chuckled uneasily. Why, he said, you've just got the one. Carl.

Couldnt they think of a name for the other one?

What other one? What in the hell are you talking about?

The one that was born dead.

Who told you that?

I remembered it.

Who told you?

You did.

I never. When did I?

Years ago. You were drunk.

I never did.

All right. You didnt.

What difference does it make?

I dont know. I just wondered why it was supposed to be a secret. What did he die of?

He was stillborn.

I know that.

I dont know why. He just was. You were both premature. You swear I told you?

It's not important.

You wont say anything will you?

No. I was just wondering about it. What the doctor says for instance. I mean, you have to take them both home, only one you take in a bag or a box. I guess they have people to take care of these things.

Just dont say anything.

Suttree was leaning forward looking down at his cheap and rotting shoes where they lay crossed on the floor. God, John, dont worry about it. I wont.

Okay.

Dont tell them you saw me.

Okay. Fair enough. That's a deal.

Right John. A deal.

I dont see them anyway.

So you said.

The uncle shifted in the chair and pulled at his collar with a long yellow forefinger. He could have helped me, you know. I never asked him for anything. Never did, by God. He could have helped me.

Well, said Suttree, he didnt.

The uncle nodded, watching the floor. You know, he said, you and me are a lot alike.

I dont think so.

In some ways.

No, said Suttree. We're not alike.

Well, I mean . . . the uncle waved his hand.

That's his thesis. But I'm not like you.

Well, you know what I mean.

I do know what you mean. But I'm not like you. I'm not like him. I'm not like Carl. I'm like me. Dont tell me who I'm like.

Well now look, Buddy, there's no need . . .

I think there is a need. I dont want you down here either. I know they dont like you, he doesnt. I dont blame you. It's not your fault. I cant do anything.

The uncle narrowed his eyes at Suttree. No need to get on your high horse with me, he said. At least I was never in the goddamned penitentiary.

Suttree smiled. The workhouse, John. It's a little different. But I am what I am. I dont go around telling people that I've been in a T B sanitarium.

So? I dont claim to be a teetotaler, if that's what you're getting at.

Are you an alcoholic?

No. What are you smiling at? I'm no goddamned alcoholic.

He always called you a rummy. I guess that's not quite as bad.

I dont give a damn what he says. He can . . .

Go ahead.

The uncle looked at him warily. He flipped the tiny stub of his cigarette out the door. Well, he said. He dont know everything.

Look, said Suttree, leaning forward. When a man marries beneath him his children are beneath him. If he thinks that way at all. If you werent a drunk he might see me with different eyes. As it is, my case was always doubtful. I was expected to turn out badly. My grandfather used to say Blood will tell. It was his favorite saying. What are you looking at? Look at me.

I dont know what you're talking about.

Yes you do. I'm saying that my father is contemptuous of me because I'm related to you. Dont you think that's a fair statement?

I dont know why you try and blame me for your troubles. You and your crackpot theories.

Suttree reached across the little space and took his uncle's willowing hands and composed them. I dont blame you, he said. I just want to tell you how some people are.

I know how people are. I should know.

Why should you? You think my father and his kind are a race apart. You can laugh at their pretensions, but you never question their right to the way of life they maintain.

He puts his pants on the same way I do mine.

Bullshit, John. You dont even believe that.

I said it didnt I?

What do you suppose he thinks of his wife?

They get along okay.

They get along okay.

Yeah.

John, she's a housekeeper. He has no real belief even in her goodness. Cant you guess that he sees in her traces of the same sorriness he sees in you? An innocent gesture can call you to mind.

Dont call me sorry, said the uncle.

He probably believes that only his own benevolent guidance kept her out of the whorehouse.

That's my sister you're talking about, boy.

She's my mother, you maudlin sot.

Sudden quiet in the little cabin. The uncle rose shaking, his voice was low. They were right, he said. What they told me. They were right about you. You're a vicious person. A nasty vicious person.

Suttree sat with his forehead in his hands. The uncle moved warily to the door. His shadow fell across Suttree and Suttree raised his head.

Maybe it's like colorblindness, he said. The women are just carriers. You are colorblind, arent you?

At least I'm not crazy.

No, Suttree said. Not crazy.

The uncle's narrowed eyes seemed to soften. God help you, he said. He turned and stepped onto the catwalk and went down the boards. Suttree rose and went to the door. The uncle was crossing the fields in the last of the day's light toward the darkening city.

John, he called.

He looked back. But that old man seemed so glassed away in worlds of his own contrivance that Suttree only raised his hand. The uncle nodded like a man who understood and then went on.

The cabin was almost dark and Suttree walked around on the little deck and kicked up a stool and sat leaning back against the wall of the houseboat with his feet propped on the railing. A breeze was coming off the river bearing a faint odor of oil and fish. Night sounds and laughter drifted from the yellow shacks beyond the railspur and the river spooled past highbacked and hissing in the dark at his feet like the seething of sand in a glass, wind in a desert, the slow voice of ruin. He wedged his knuckles in his eyesockets and rested his head against the boards. They were still warm from the sun, like a faint breath at his nape. Across the river the lights of the lumber company lay foreshort and dismembered in the black water and downriver the strung bridgelamps hung in catenary replica shore to shore and softly guttering under the wind's faint chop. The tower clock in the courthouse tolled the half hour. Lonely bell in the city. A firefly there. And there. He rose and spat into the river and went down the catwalk to the shore and across the field toward the road.

He walked up Front Street breathing in the cool of the evening, the western sky before him still a deep cyanic blue shot through with the shapes of bats crossing blind and spastic like spores on a slide. A rank smell of boiled greens hung in the night and a thread of radio music followed him house by house. He went by yards and cinder gardens rank with the mutes of roosting fowls and by dark grottoes among the shacks where the music flared and died again and past dim window-lights where shadows reeled down cracked and yellowed paper shades. Through reeking clapboard warrens where children cried and craven halfbald watchdogs yapped and slank.

He climbed the hill toward the edge of the city, past the open door of the negro meetinghouse. Softly lit within. A preacher that looked like a storybook blackbird in his suit and goldwire spectacles. Suttree coming up out of this hot and funky netherworld attended by gospel music. Dusky throats tilted and veined like the welted flanks of horses. He has watched them summer nights, a pale pagan sat on the curb without. One rainy night nearby he heard news in his toothfillings, music softly. He was stayed in a peace that drained his mind, for even a false adumbration of the world of the spirit is better than none at all.

Up these steep walkways cannelured for footpurchase, the free passage of roaches. To tap at this latched door leaning. Jimmy Smith's brown rodent teeth just beyond the screen. There is a hole in the rotten fabric which perhaps his breath has made over the years. Down a long hallway lit by a single sulphurcolored lightbulb hung from a cord in the ceiling. Smith's shuffling slippers rasp over the linoleum. He turns at the end of the hall, holding the door there. The slack yellow skin of his shoulders and chest so bloodless and lined that he appears patched up out of odd scraps and remnants of flesh, tacked with lap seams and carefully bound in the insubstantial and foul gray web of his undershirt. In the little kitchen two men are sitting at a table drinking whiskey. A third leans against a stained refrigerator. There is an open door giving onto a porch, a small buckled portico of gray boards that hangs in the dark above the river. The rise and fall of cigarettes tells the occupants. There are sounds of laughter and a bloated whore looks out into the kitchen and goes away again.

What'll you have, Sut.

A beer.

The man leaning against the refrigerator moves slightly to one side. What say Bud, he says.

Hey Junior.

Jimmy Smith has opened a can of beer and holds it toward Suttree. He pays and the owner deals up change out of his loathsome breeks and counts the coins into Suttree's palm and shuffles away.

Who's back in the back?

Bunch of drunks. Brother's back there.

Suttree tipped a swallow of the beer against the back of his throat. It was cold and good. Well, he said. Let me go back there and see him.

He nodded to the two men at the table and went past and down the corridor and entered an enormous old drawing room with high sliding doors long painted fast in their tracks. Five men sat at a card table, none looked up. The room was otherwise barren, a white marble fireplace masked with a sheet of tin, old varnished wainscoting and a high stamped rococo ceiling with parget scrolls and beaded drops of brazing about the gasjet where a lightbulb now burned.

Surrounded as they were in this crazed austerity by the remnants of a former grandeur the poker players seemed themselves like shades of older times or rude imposters on a stage set. They drank and bet and muttered in an air of electric transiency, old men in gaitered sleeves galvanized from some stained sepia, posting time at cards prevenient of their dimly augured doom. Suttree passed on through.

In the front room was a broken sofa propped on bricks, nothing more. One wonky spring reared from the back with a beercan seized in its coils and deeply couched in the mousecolored and napless upholstery sat a row of drunks.

Hey Suttree, they called.

Goddamn, said J-Bone, surging from the bowels of the couch. He threw an arm around Suttree's shoulders. Here's my old buddy, he said. Where's the whiskey? Give him a drink of that old crazy shit.

How you doing, Jim?

I'm doin everybody I can, where you been? Where's the whiskey? Here ye go. Get ye a drink, Bud.

What is it?

Early Times. Best little old drink in the world. Get ye a drink, Sut.

Suttree held it to the light. Small twigs, debris, matter, coiled in the oily liquid. He shook it. Smoke rose from the yellow floor of the bottle. Shit almighty, he said.

Best little old drink in the world, sang out J-Bone. Have a drink, Bud.

He unthreaded the cap, sniffed, shivered, drank.

J-Bone hugged the drinking figure. Watch old Suttree take a drink, he called out.

Suttree's eyes were squeezed shut and he was holding the bottle out to whoever would take it. Goddamn. What is that shit?

Early Times, called J-Bone. Best little old drink they is. Drink that and you wont feel a thing the next mornin.

Or any morning.

Whoo lord, give it here. Hello Early, come to your old daddy.

Here, pour some of it in this cup and let me cut it with Coca-Cola.

Cant do it, Bud.

Why not?

We done tried it. It eats the bottom out.

Watch it Suttree. Dont spill none on your shoes.

Hey Bobbyjohn.

When's old Callahan gettin out? said Bobbyjohn.

I dont know. Sometime this month. When have you seen Bucket?

He's moved to Burlington, the Bucket has. He dont come round no more.

Come set with us, Sut.

J-Bone steered him by the arm. Set down, Bud. Set down.

Suttree eased himself down on the arm of the sofa and sipped his beer. He patted J-Bone on the back. The voices seemed to fade. He waved away the whiskeybottle with a smile. In this tall room, the cracked plaster sootstreaked with the shapes of laths beneath, this barrenness, this fellowship of the doomed. Where life pulsed obscenely fecund. In the drift of voices and the laughter and the reek of stale beer the Sunday loneliness seeped away.

Aint that right Suttree?

What's that?

About there bein caves all in under the city.

That's right.

What all's down there in em?

Blind slime. As above, so it is below. Suttree shrugged. Nothing that I know of, he said. They're just some caves.

They say there's one that runs plumb underneath the river.

That's the one that comes out over in Chilhowee Park. They was supposed to of used it in the Civil War to hide stuff down there.

Wonder what all's down in there now.

Shit if I know. Ast Suttree.

You reckon you can still get down in them Civil War caves, Sut?

I dont know. I always heard there was one ran under the river but I never heard of anybody that was ever in it.

There might be them Civil War relics down there.

Here comes one of them now, said J-Bone. What say, Nigger.

Suttree looked toward the door. A graylooking man in glasses was watching them. I caint say, he said. How you boys? What are ye drinkin?

Early Times, Jim says it is.

Get ye a drink, Nig.

He shuffled toward the bottle, nodding to all, small eyes moving rapidly behind the glasses. He seized the whiskey and drank, his slack gullet jerking. When he lowered it his eyes were closed and his face a twisted mask. Pooh! He blew a volatile mist toward the smiling watchers. Lord God what is that?

Early Times, Nig, cried J-Bone.

Early tombs is more like it.

Lord honey I know they make that old splo in the bathtub but this here is made in the toilet. He was looking at the bottle, shaking it. Bubbles the size of gooseshot veered greasily up through the smoky fuel it held.

It'll make ye drunk, said J-Bone.

Nig shook his head and blew and took another drink and handed over the bottle with his face averted in agony. When he could speak he said: Boys, I've fought some bad whiskey but I'm a dirty nigger if that there aint almost too sorry to drink.

J-Bone waved the bottle toward the door where Junior stood grinning. Brother, dont you want a drink?

Junior shook his head.

Boys, scoot over and let the old Nigger set down.

Here Nig, set here. Scoot over some, Bearhunter.

Lord boys if I aint plumb give out. He took off his glasses and wiped his weepy eyes.

What you been up to, Nig?

I been tryin to raise some money about Bobby. He turned and looked up at Suttree. Dont I know you? he said.

We drank a few beers together.

I thought I remembered ye. Did you not know Bobby?

I saw him a time or two.

Nigger shook his head reflectively. I raised four boys and damned if they aint all in the penitentiary cept Ralph. Of course we all went to Jordonia. And they did have me up here in the workhouse one time but I slipped off. Old Blackburn was guard up there knowed me but he never would say nothin. Was you in Jordonia? Clarence says they aint nothin to it now. Boys, when I was in there it was rougher'n a old cob. Course they didnt send ye there for singin in a choir. I done three year for stealin. Tried to get sent to T S I where they learn ye a trade but you had to be tardy to get in down there and they said I wasnt tardy. I was eighteen when I come out of Jordonia and that was in nineteen and sixteen. I wisht I could understand them boys of mine. They have costed me. I spent eighteen thousand dollars gettin them boys out. Their grandaddy was never in the least trouble that you could think of and he lived to be eighty-seven year old. Now he'd take a drink. Which I do myself. But he was never in no trouble with the law.

Get ye a drink, Sut.

Nigger intercepted the bottle. You know Jim? He's a fine boy. Dont think he aint. I wisht McAnally Flats was full of em just like him. I knowed his daddy. He was smaller than Junior yonder. Just a minute. Whew. Damn if that aint some whiskey. He wouldnt take nothin off nobody, Irish Long wouldnt. I remember he come over on what they used to call Woolen Mill Corners there one time. You know where it's at Jim. Where Workers Cafe is at. Come over there one Sunday mornin huntin a man and they was a bunch of tush hogs all standin around out there under a shed used to be there, you boys wouldnt remember it, drinkin whiskey and was friends of this old boy's, and Irish Long walked up to em and wanted to know where he's at. Well, they wouldnt say, but they wasnt a one of them tush hogs ast what he wanted with him. He would mortally whip your ass if you messed with him, Irish Long would. And they wasnt nobody in McAnally no betterhearted. He give away everthing he owned. He'd of been rich if he wanted. Had them stores. Nobody didnt have no money, people couldnt buy their groceries. You boys dont remember the depression. He'd tell em just go on and get what they needed. Flour and taters. Milk for the babies. He never turned down nobody, Irish Long never. They is people livin in this town today in big houses that would of starved plumb to death cept for him but they aint big enough to own it.

Better get ye a drink there Sut, fore Nigger drinks it all.

Give Bearhunter a drink, Suttree said.

How about givin Bobbyjohn a drink, said Bobbyjohn.

There's a man'll take a drink, said Nigger. Dont think he wont.

Which I will myself, said J-Bone.

Which I will my damnself, said Nigger.

Jimmy Smith was moving through the room like an enormous trained mole collecting the empty cans. He shuffled out, his small eyes blinking. Kenneth Hazelwood stood in the doorframe watching them all with a sardonic smile.

Come in here, Worm, called J-Bone. Get ye a drink of this good whiskey.

Hazelwood entered smiling and took the bottle. He tilted it and sniffed and gave it back.

The last time I drank some of that shit I like to died. I stunk from the inside out. I laid in a tub of hot water all day and climbed out and dried and you could still smell it. I had to burn my clothes. I had the dry heaves, the drizzlin shits, the cold shakes and the jakeleg. I can think about it now and feel bad.

Hell Worm, this is good whusk.

I pass.

Worm's put down my whiskey, Bud.

I think you better put it down before it puts you down. You'll find your liver in your sock some morning.

But J-Bone had turned away with a whoop. Early Times, he called. Make your liver quiver.

Hazelwood grinned and turned to Suttree. Cant you take no better care of him than that? he said.

Suttree shook his head.

Me and Katherine's goin out to the Trocadero. Come on go with us.

I better get home, Kenneth.

Come ride out there with us. We'll bring you back.

I remember the last time I went for a ride with you. You got us in three fights, kicked some woman's door in, and got in jail. I ran through some yards and like to hung myself on a clothesline and got a bunch of dogs after me and spotlights zippin around and cops all over the place and I wound up spendin the night in a corrugated conduit with a cat.

Worm grinned. Come on, he said. We'll just have a drink and see what all's goin on out there.

I cant, Kenneth. I'm broke anyway.

I didnt ast ye if you had any money.

Hey Worm, did you see old Crumbliss in the paper this mornin?

What's he done now?

They found him about six oclock this mornin under a tree in a big alfalfa field. He found the only tree in the whole field and run into it. They said when the cops come and opened the door old Crumbliss fell out and just laid there. Directly he looked up and seen them blue suits and he jumped up and hollered, said: Where is that man I hired to drive me home?

Suttree rose grinning.

Dont run off, Sut.

I've got to go.

Where you goin?

I've got to get something to eat. I'll see you all later.

Jimmy Smith fell in with him to see him to the door, down the long corridor, mole and guest, an unlatching of the screendoor and so into the night.

It is overcast with impending rain and the lights of the city wash against the curdled heavens, lie puddled in the wet black streets. The watertruck recedes down Locust with its footmen in their tattered oilskins wielding brooms in the flooded gutters and the air is rich with the odor of damp paving. Through the midnight emptiness the few sounds carry with amphoric hollow and the city in its quietude seems to lie under edict. The buildings lean upon the dim and muted corridors where the watchman's heels click away the minutes. Past black and padlocked shopfronts. A poultrydresser's window where half-naked cockerels nod in a constant blue dawn. Clockchime and belltoll lonely in the brooding sleepfast town. The gutted rusting trucks on Market Street with their splayed tires pooling on the tar. The flowers and fruit are gone and the sewer grates festooned with wilted greens. Under the fanned light of a streetlamp a white china cuphandle curled like a sleeping slug.

In the lobbies of the slattern hotels the porters and bellmen are napping in the chairs and lounges, dark faces jerking in their sleep down the worn wine plush. In the rooms lie drunken homecome soldiers sprawled in painless crucifixion on the rumpled counterpanes and the whores are sleeping now. Small tropic fish start and check in the mossgreen deeps of the eyedoctor's shopwindow. A lynx rampant with a waxen snarl. Gouts of shredded wood sprout from the sutures in his leather belly and his glass eyes bulge in agony. Dim tavern, an alleymouth where ashcans gape and where in a dream I was stopped by a man I took to be my father, dark figure against the shadowed brick. I would go by but he has stayed me with his hand. I have been looking for you, he said. The wind was cold, dreamwinds are so, I had been hurrying. I would draw back from him and his bone grip. The knife he held severed the pallid lamplight like a thin blue fish and our footsteps amplified themselves in the emptiness of the streets to an echo of routed multitudes. Yet it was not my father but my son who accosted me with such rancorless intent.

On Gay Street the traffic lights are stilled. The trolleyrails gleam in their beds and a late car passes with a long slish of tires. In the long arcade of the bus station footfalls come back like laughter. He marches darkly toward his darkly marching shape in the glass of the depot door. His fetch come up from life's other side like an autoscopic hallucination, Suttree and Antisuttree, hand reaching to the hand. The door swung back and he entered the waiting room. The shapes of figures sleeping on the wooden benches lay like laundry. In the men's room an elderly pederast leaning against a wall.

Suttree washed his hands and went out past the pinball machines to the grill. He took a stool and studied the menu. The waitress stood tapping her pencil against the pad of tickets she held.

Suttree looked up. Grilled cheese and coffee.

She wrote. He watched.

She tore off the ticket and placed it facedown on the marble counter and moved away. He watched the shape of her underclothes through the thin white uniform. In the rear of the cafe a young black labored in a clatter of steaming crockery. Suttree rubbed his eyes.

She came with the coffee, setting it down with a click and the coffee tilting up the side of the pink plastic cup and flooding the saucer. He poured it back and sipped. Acridity of burnt socks. She returned with napkin, spoon. Ring of gold orangeblossoms constricting her puffy finger. He took another sip of the coffee. In a few minutes she came with the sandwich. He held the first wedge of it to his nose for a minute, rich odor of toast and butter and melting cheese. He bit off an enormous mouthful, sucked the pickle from the toothpick and closed his eyes, chewing.

When he had finished he took the quarter from his pocket and laid it on the counter and rose. She was watching him from beyond the coffee urn.

You want some more coffee? she said.

No thank you.

Come back, she said.

Suttree shoved the door with his shoulder, one hand in his pocket, the other working the toothpick. A face rose from a near bench and looked at him blearily and subsided.

He walked along Gay Street, pausing by storewindows, fine goods kept in glass. A police cruiser passed slowly. He moved on, from out of his eyecorner watching them watch. Past Woodruff's, Clark and Jones, the theatres. Corners emptied of their newspedlars and trash scuttling in the wind. He went down to the end of the town and walked out on the bridge and placed his hands on the cool iron rail and looked at the river below. The bridgelights trembled in the black eddywater like chained and burning supplicants and along the riverfront a gray mist moved in over the ashen fields of sedge and went ferreting among the dwellings. He folded his arms on the rail. Out there a jumbled shackstrewn waste dimly lit. Kindlingwood cottages, gardens of rue. A patchwork of roofs canted under the pale blue cones of lamplight where moths aspire in giddy coils. Little plots of corn, warped purlieus of tillage in the dead spaces shaped by constriction and want like the lives of the dark and bitter husbandsmen who have this sparse harvest for their own out of all the wide earth's keeping.

Small spills of rain had started, cold on his arm. Downstream recurving shore currents chased in deckle light wave on wave like silver spawn. To fall through dark to darkness. Struggle in those opaque and fecal deeps, which way is up. Till the lungs suck brown sewage and funny lights go down the final corridors of the brain, small watchmen to see that all is quiet for the advent of eternal night.

The courthouse clock tolled two. He raised his face. There you can see the illumined dial suspended above the town with not even a shadow to mark the tower. A cheshire clock hung in the void like a strange hieroglyphic moon. Suttree palmed the water from his face. The smoky yellow windowlight in the houseboat of Abednego Jones went dark. Below he could make out the shape of his own place where he must go. High over the downriver land lightning quaked soundlessly and ceased. Far clouds rimlit. A brimstone light. Are there dragons in the wings of the world? The rain was falling harder, falling past him toward the river. Steep rain leaning in the lamplight, across the clock's face. Hard weather, says the old man. So may it be. Wrap me in the weathers of the earth, I will be hard and hard. My face will turn rain like the stones.

He came up from the back lot threading his way among the shapes of castoff and broken and useless debris rotting under the late summer sun. Old tires and bricks and broken jars. A rusty chickenfeeder. He squinched his nose at the rank odor of washwater in the air and he threw a rock he was carrying at the tethered goat. The goat raised its chin from the grass and looked at him with its strange goat's eyes and lowered its head to graze again. He went on around the corner of the house to the front porch where a green and white washingmachine shuddered and churned and over which stood a young woman with a soapy paddle clubbed in her hands as if defying the first insurgent rag to rear from the slateblue and foamless water in which the week's wash moiled.

Hidy, he said.

She moved, her weight bringing up out of the spongy boards beneath her shoes a black seepage. She did not look nor answer.

Old Orville aint been by is he?

She laid the paddle across the washer where it slurred into concatenate images with the motion of the machine and began to slide off slowly. She wiped her forehead with the hem of her apron. No, she said. He aint been here.

He looked toward the open door of the house. What does she want now? he said.

What do you care?

I just ast.

She didnt answer. He propped his foot on the porch and spat, watching out across the dead clay yard at nothing at all.

The paddle dropped to the floor and she stooped and got it and began to dig at the clothes, her breasts pendulous and bobbing with the movement of her shoulders. Blue curded washwater dripped from the end of the porch into a puddle of gray scum. When she looked at him he had not moved. She tossed her hair and tilted one shoulder forward, blotting the sweat from her upper lip. She pouted and blew the hair from her eyes. Why dont you grub some of them weeds out of the tomatoes for me if you aint got nothin else to do, she said.

He sat down facing out across the yard. He put one finger in his ear and jiggled it and she bent to the washer again.

After a while a thin voice came again from the rear of the house. She stopped and looked at him. See what she wants, will ye?

He spat. I didnt take her to raise, he said.

She lifted her bleached and wrinkled hands from the water and wiped them on the front of her dress. All right, Mama, she called. Just a minute.

When she came back out he was hanging by his elbows in the wire fence that ran along the little lane the house faced and he was talking to another boy. They left together. He came back for his supper and went out again and stayed until past dark. Just before midnight she heard him leave the house again.

He listened at her door and then went on to the front room where he sat on the daybed and donned his shoes. Then he was out in the warm August night, lush and tactile, the door set shut with a faint cry of the keeperspring, down the path through the gate and into the lane. When he came out on the pike he could feel the day's warmth from the macadam through his thin shoesoles and he could smell it, musky and faintly antiseptic. He went up the pike at a jog.

He went solitary and starlit through the sleepfast countryside, trotting soundlessly on his softworn shoes, past dead houses and dark land with the odor of ripe and humid fruits breathing in the fields and nightbirds crying in the keep of enormous trees. The road climbed up out of the woods and went on through farmland and he slowed to a walk, his hands slung in his hippockets and his elbows flapping, taking a dirt road down to the right, padding along soft as a dog, sniffing the rank grass and the odor of dust the dew had laid.

He crossed the tracks of the railway and loped into the growth on the far side wiping his nose with his sleeve as he went and casting his eyes about, passing along a high revetment of honeysuckle and then through a patch of cane and coming at last along the edge of a field where his old tracks had packed the clay in a furrow you could follow in the dark and his shape washed shadowless across a backdrop of sumac and sassafras. He could see the house beyond in darkness against the starblown sky and the barn behind it rising outsize and stark. He was going along the troughs in the heavy turned earth, past cornrows, the shellbrown spears on his arms with fine teeth, into the open field where the melons lay.

There were no more than a quarteracre of them, a long black rectangle set along the edge of the corn in which by the meager starlight of late summer he could see the plump forms supine and dormant in spaced rows. He listened. In the distance a dog was yapping and in his keen ears the blind passage of gnats sounded incessantly. He knelt in the rich and steaming earth, his nostrils filled with the winey smell of ruptured melons. To steal upon them where they lay, his hand on their warm ripe shapes, his pocketknife open. He lifted one, a pale jade underbelly turning up. He pulled it between his knees and sank the blade of the knife into its nether end. He shucked off the straps of his overalls. His pale shanks kneeling in a pool of denim.

A whippoorwill had begun to call and with his ear to the ground this way he began to hear the train too. A star arced long and dying down the sky. He raised his head and looked toward the house. Nothing moved. The train had come on and her harpiethroated highball wailed down the lonely summer night. He could hear the wheels shucking along the rails and he could feel the ground shudder and he could hear the tone of the trucks shift at the crossing and the huffing breath of the boiler and the rattle and clank and wheelclick and couplingclacking and then the last long shunting on the downgrade drawing on toward the distance and the low moan bawling across the sleeping land and fading and the caboose clicking away to final silence. He rose and adjusted his clothes and went back along the rows of corn to the woods and to the road and set himself toward home again.

Brogans stood in the tracks he left. Walking up, back, turning. Toeing the bunged melons lying in the sun. A slow spout of black ants pluming forth. A yellowjacket.

He came again that night. In a persimmon tree at the edge of the field a mockingbird whistled him back but he would not hear. Down past the corn he came and into the dark of the melonpatch with stark wooden lubricity, looking once toward the lightless house and then going to his knees in the rich and wineslaked loam.

When the light of the sealedbeam cut over the field he was lying prone upon a watermelon with his overalls about his knees. The beam swept past, stopped, returned to fix upon his alabaster nates looming moonlike out of the dark. He rose vertically, pale, weightless, like some grim tellurian wraith, up over the violated fruit with arms horrible and off across the fields hauling wildly at the folds of old rank denim that hobbled him.

Hold it, a voice called.

He had no ear for such news. The dry bracken that rimmed the field crashed about him. He crossed the stand of cane in a series of diminishing reports and went over the top of the honeysuckle in graceful levitation and lit in the road in the lights of a car rounding the curve. The car braked and slewed in the gravel. A crazed figure dressing on the run blown out of the dark wall of summer green and into the road. In the distance the train called for the crossing.

Two pairs of brogans went along the rows.

You aint goin to believe this.

Knowin you for a born liar I most probably wont.

Somebody has been fuckin my watermelons.

What?

I said somebody has been . . .

No. No. Hell no. Damn you if you aint got a warped mind.

I'm tellin you . . .

I dont want to hear it.

Looky here.

And here.

They went along the outer row of the melonpatch. He stopped to nudge a melon with his toe. Yellowjackets snarled in the seepage. Some were ruined a good time past and lay soft with rot, wrinkled with imminent collapse.

It does look like it, dont it?

I'm tellin ye I seen him. I didnt know what the hell was goin on when he dropped his drawers. Then when I seen what he was up to I still didnt believe it. But yonder they lay.

What do you aim to do?

Hell, I dont know. It's about too late to do anything. He's damn near screwed the whole patch. I dont see why he couldnt of stuck to just one. Or a few.

Well, I guess he takes himself for a lover. Sort of like a sailor in a whorehouse.

I reckon what it was he didnt take to the idea of gettin bit on the head of his pecker by one of them waspers. I suppose he showed good judgment there.

What was he, just a young feller?

I dont know about how young he was but he was as active a feller as I've seen in a good while.

Well. I dont reckon he'll be back.

I dont know. A man fast as he is ought not to be qualmy about goin anywheres he took a notion. To steal or whatever.

What if he does come back?

I'll catch him if he does.

And then what?

Well. I dont know. Be kindly embarrassin now I think about it. I'd get some work out of him is what I'd do.

Ought to, I reckon. I dont know.

You reckon to call the sheriff?

And tell him what?

They were walking slowly along the rows.

It's just the damndest thing I ever heard of. Aint it you? What are you grinnin at? It aint funny. A thing like that. To me it aint.

Once she had moved beyond the shadow of the smokehouse he could not see her anymore. He could hear the dull chop of the hoe among the withered yardflowers as she progressed with bland patience along the little garden she had planted there, her and the hoe in shadow oblique and thin. And the chop and clink of the shadow blade in the stony ground. Or she came up from the springhouse lugging a shrunken bucket that sprayed thin fans of water from between the slats and left a damp and trampled swath out to the flowerbeds and back. He sat on the porch with his feet crossed and fashioned knots in weedstems.

Finally it rained. It rained all one afternoon and at dusk the burnt grass stood in water and it rained on into the night. By the time he left the house it had quit and the sky was clearing but he would not turn back.

He waited and waited at the field's edge watching the house and listening. From the dark of the corn they saw him pass, lean and angular, a slavering nightshade among the moonsprung vines, over the shadowed blue and furrowed summer land. They gripped each other's arm.

It's him.

I hope it is. I'd hate to think of there bein two of em.

Before them in the field there appeared sudden and apparitional a starkly pale set of legs galvanized out of the night like a pair of white flannel drawers.

34

Thow the light to him.

He aint mounted.

Thow it to him.

He was standing in the middle of the patch facing them, blinking, his overalls about his ankles.

Hold it right there, old buddy. Dont move.

But he did. He caught up the bib of his overalls in both hands and turned to run. The voice called out again. He had the straps clenched in his fist, making for the field's edge. The train bawled twice out there in the darkness. Now beg God's mercy, lecher. Unnatural. Finger coiled, blind sight, a shadow. Smooth choked oiled pipe pointing judgment and guilt. Done in a burst of flame. Could I call back that skeltering lead.

He was lying on the ground with his legs trapped in his overalls and he was screaming Oh God, Oh God. The man still holding the smoking gun stood about him like a harried bird. The blood oozing from that tender puckered skin in the gray moonlight undid him. Shit, he said. Aw shit. He knelt, flinging the gun away from him. The other man picked it up and stood by. Hush now, he said. Goddamn. Hush.

Lights from the house limn them and their sorry tableau. The boy is rolling in the rich damp earth screaming and the man keeps saying for him to hush, kneeling there, not touching him.

The deputy held the car door and he climbed out and they entered a building of solid concrete. The first deputy handed Harrogate's papers to a man at a small window. The man looked through the papers and signed them. Harrogate stood in the hall.

Harrogate, the man said.

Yessir.

He looked him over. Goddamn if you aint a sadsack, he said. Walk on down to that door.

Harrogate walked down the corridor to an iron barred door. The other deputy had emerged from a side door with a cup of coffee. He had his thumb stuck in his belt and he blew on the coffee and sipped at it. He did not look at Harrogate.

After a while the man came down the hall with a big brass ring of keys. He opened the gate and pointed for Harrogate to enter. He shut the gate behind them and locked it and turned and went up a flight of concrete stairs. There were two men in striped pants and jumpers sitting there smoking. They scooted against the wall to let the man pass. Harrogate had started up the stairs when one of them spoke to him.

You better not go up there if he aint said to.

He came back down again.

When the man reappeared he had a young black with him. The black wore stripes too. The man opened the door to a large cell and they entered. The black looked at Harrogate and shook his head and went on through to a door at the rear. There was a little window in the wall and Harrogate could see him in there thumbing through stacks of clothing on a shelf.

Strip out of them clothes and take a shower yonder, said the man.

Harrogate looked around. In the center of the room was a stained porcelain trough with a row of dripping taps hung from a pipe. In each corner at the front of the cell was a concrete wall about as high as Harrogate. Behind one wall there were three toilets and behind the other there were two showers. While he was looking at the showers a dry towel hit him in the back of the head and fell to the floor.

You better get on some kind of time, the man said. Harrogate picked up the towel and put it around his neck and undid his shirt and peeled out of it and laid it on a bench by the wall. Then he unbuttoned his trousers and stepped out of them and laid them across the shirt. He looked like a dressed chicken, his skin puckered with the shotwounds still red and fresh looking. He raised his shoes each and slid them from his feet without untying the laces. The concrete floor was cold. He crossed to the showers and peered at them, their valves and spouts.

I aint goin to tell you again, said the man.

I dont know how, said Harrogate.

The black boy at the window turned his face away.

The man looked up at this news with what seemed to be real interest. You dont know how to what? he said.

How to run a shower.

What are you, a fuckin smart-ass?

No sir.

You mean to tell me you aint never took a shower?

I aint never even seen one.

The man turned and looked back down the hall. Hey, George?

Yeah.

Come in here a minute.

A second man looked in. What is it? he said.

Tell him what you just told me.

I aint never even seen one? said Harrogate.

Seen what?

A shower. He dont know how to take a shower.

The second man looked him over. Does he know where he shit last? he said.

I doubt it.

It was down at the county jail, said Harrogate.

I think you got a smart-ass on your hands.

I think I got a dumb-ass is what I got. You see them there handles? These here?

Them there. You turn em and water comes out of that there pipe.

Harrogate stepped into the shower stall and turned the taps. He picked a slab of used soap from a niche in the wall and soaped himself and adjusted the taps, stepping under the shower carefully so as not to wet his hair. When he was done he turned off the shower and took the towel down from where he'd hung it over the top of the partition and dried himself and crossed the floor to where he'd left his clothes. He had one leg in his trousers when the black spoke to him.

Hold it, little buddy.

He paused on one leg.

Bring them over here.

Harrogate collected his clothes and carried them to the window. The black took them and hung them on a hanger gingerly with two fingers. The man was sorting about behind him.

It's hangin on the nail yonder, the black said.

Harrogate was sitting naked on the bench. The man came out with a longhandled spraygun. He stood up.

Raise your arms.

He did. The man pumped the sprayer and squirted his armpit.

Shoo, said Harrogate. What's that for?

Bugs, said the guard. Turn around.

I aint got no bugs.

You aint now, said the man. He sprayed under the other arm and then gave Harrogate a good spraying over his sparse pubic hair. Get them crotch crickets too, he said. When he was done he stepped back. Harrogate stood with his arms aloft like a robbery victim.

Damn if you aint just barely feathered, said the man. How old are you?

Eighteen, said Harrogate.

Eighteen.

Yessir.

You just did get in under the wire, didnt ye?

I reckon.

What's these here?

That's where I's shot.

The man looked from his skinny body to his face again. Shot, eh? he said. He handed the spraygun through the window to the black and the black hung the gun back up behind him and pushed a folded set of stripes through the window at Harrogate.

Harrogate unfolded the suit and looked at it. He held the shirt in his teeth while he flapped the trousers out and started to step into them.

Aint you got no underwear? said the man.

No.

The man shook his head. Harrogate stood on one leg. He took a little hop to capture his balance.

Go on, said the man. If you aint got any you aint got any.

He dressed and stood barefoot. The trousers ran down over his feet and onto the floor and just his fingertips hung from the sleeves of the jumper. He looked at the black in the window.

Dont look at me, said the black. Them's the smallest they come. Roll them sleeves and pants up. You'll be all right.

Harrogate rolled the sleeves back two turns. The clothes were clean and rough against his skin. Do I wear my own shoes? he said.

You wear your own shoes.

The smallest prisoner crossed the floor and stepped into his shoes and clattered back to the window. The man looked him over sadly and handed him a blanket. Let's go, he said.

Harrogate followed him out and up the stairs, shuffling along, a slight limp. At the top of the stairs they turned down a hall past huge barred cages like the one they'd left. At the end of the hall sat a man at a table reading a magazine. He rose smiling and placed the magazine facedown on the table.

The man was sorting through the keys. I think they ought to've thrown thisn back, Ed, what do you think?

Ed looked at Harrogate and smiled.

The man opened the iron door and Harrogate entered alone. A concrete room painted pea green. He walked past the sink, the taps each tied with little tobaccosacks hanging from their mouths. Pale winter light fell through the welded iron windows. The door clanked shut behind him and the guard's footsteps receded in the corridor.

With his blanket he went down the room past rows of iron beds in blocks of four all painted green, some with sacklike mattresses, some with nothing but the woven bare iron straps that served for springs. He went along the aisle looking left and right. A few figures lay motionless in the cots he passed. He went to the end of the room and stood on tiptoe and peered out the window. Rolling hills. Stark winter trees. He came back up the aisle and nudged a sleeper by the foot. Hey, he said.

The man on the pallet opened one eye and looked at Harrogate. What the fuck do you want? he said.

Where am I supposed to sleep?

The man groaned and closed his eyes. Harrogate waited for him to open them again but he did not. After a while he jostled the foot again. Hey, he said.

The man did not open his eyes. He said: If you dont get the fuck away from me I'm going to kick the shit out of you.

I just wanted to know where I'm supposed to sleep.

Anywhere you like you squirrely son of a bitch now get the hell away from here.

Harrogate wandered on up the aisle. Some of the bunks had pillows as well as blankets. He picked one out that had only a bare tick and climbed up and spread his blanket and sat in the middle of it. He sat there for a while and then he climbed down again and went to the bars and peered out. Someone in a suit like his was coming backward down the hallway towing a bucket on wheels by a mop submerged in the black froth it held. He glanced at Harrogate as he went past, a cigarette in the corner of his mouth. He didnt look friendly. Across the hall another prisoner was peering from his cage. Harrogate studied him for a minute. Then he gave sort of a crazy little wave at him. Hidy, he said.

Sure, said the other prisoner.

Harrogate turned and went back and climbed into his bunk and lay staring at the ceiling. Concrete beams painted green. A few half blackened lightbulbs screwed into the masonry. It had grown dim within the room, the early winter twilight closing down the day. He slept.

When he woke it was dark out and the bulbs in the ceiling suffused the room with a sulphurous light. Harrogate sat up. Men were filing into the cell with a sort of constrained rowdiness, not quite jostling one another, lighting or rolling cigarettes, speaking only once they were inside. A rising exchange of repartee and shaded insult. One spied Harrogate where he sat up in his cot like a groundsquirrel and pointed him out.

Looky here, new blood.

They filed past. Toward the end came men hobbling with what looked like the heads of pickaxes welded about one ankle. The door clanged, keys rattled. Two men turned in at the bunks beneath Harrogate. One of them lay down and closed his eyes for a minute and then sat up and shucked off his shoes and lay back and closed his eyes again. The other stood with his head bent a few inches from Harrogate's knee and began to unload his pockets of various things. A pencil stub, matchbooks, a beercan opener. A flat black stone. A sack of tobacco. He saw Harrogate watching him and looked up. Hey, he said.

Hey, said Harrogate.

You dont piss in the bed do you?

No sir.

You smoke?

I used to some. Fore I got thowed in the jailhouse and couldnt get nary.

Here.

He pitched the sack of tobacco up onto Harrogate's blanket.

Harrogate immediately opened the sack and took a paper from the little pocket under the label and began to roll a cigarette.

You get one of those every week, the man said.

When do I get mine?

Next week.

You aint got no match have ye?

Here.

Harrogate lit the cigarette and sucked deeply and blew out the match and put it in his cuff.

Keep em.

He put the matches in his pocket.

How old are you?

Eighteen.

Eighteen?

Yessir.

You just made it didnt you?

That's what they keep tellin me.

What's your name?

Gene Harrogate.

Harrogate, the man said. He had one elbow on the upper bunk and was holding his chin in his fingers, studying the new prisoner with a rather detached air. Well, he said. My name's Suttree.

Howdy Mr Suttree.

Just Suttree. What are you in for?

Stealin watermelons.

That's bullshit. What are you in for.

I got caught in a watermelon patch.

What with, a tractor and trailer? They dont send people to the workhouse for stealing a few watermelons. What else did you do?

Harrogate sucked on his cigarette and looked at the green walls. Well, he said. I got shot.

Got shot?

Yeah.

Whereabouts? Yeah, I know. In the watermelon patch. Where did you get hit.

Pret near all over.

What with, a shotgun?

Yeah.

For stealing watermelons.

Yeah.

Suttree sat down on the lower bunk and put one foot up and began to rub his ankle. After a while he looked up. Harrogate was lying on his stomach looking down over the edge of his bunk.

Let's see where you got shot, said Suttree.

Harrogate knelt up in the bed and lifted his jumper. Little mauve tucks in his pale flesh all down the side of him like pox scars.

I got em all down my leg too. I still caint walk good.

Suttree looked up at the boy's eyes. Bright with a kind of animal cognizance, with incipient good will. Well, he said. It's getting rough out there, isnt it?

Boy I thought I was dead.

I guess you're lucky you're not.

That's what they said at the hospital.

Suttree leaned back in his bunk. What kind of son of a bitch would shoot somebody for stealing a few watermelons? he said.

I dont know. He come out to the hospital and brung me a ice cream. I didnt much blame him. He said hisself he wished he'd not done it.

Didnt keep him from pressing charges though, did it?

Well, I guess seein as he'd done shot me he couldnt back out.

Suttree looked at the boy again with this remark but the boy's face was bland and without device. He wanted to know when supper was served.

Five oclock. Should be in a few minutes.

Do they feed good?

You'll have time to get used to it. What did you draw anyway?

Eleven twenty-nine.

Old eleven twenty-nine.

Boy they feed good in that hospital. Best you ever ate.

Couldnt you have run off from there?

I never had no clothes. I thought about it but I didnt have stitch one nor no way to come by any. I'd rather to be in the workhouse than get caught out wearin one of them old crazy nightshirts they make ye wear. Wouldnt you?

No.

Well. That's you.

That's me.

Harrogate looked down at him but he had his eyes closed. He rolled back over and stared at the ceiling. Someone had written a few sentiments there but they were lost in the glare of the lightbulbs. After a while he heard a bell clang somewhere. A guard came to the door and opened it and when Harrogate sat up he saw that the prisoners were shaping up ready to leave and he hopped from the bunk and shaped up with them.

They marched down the concrete stairs and turned through a door and filed through a messhall where picnic tables ran the length of the room. They were cobbled up out of oak flooring and had the benches bolted to them. At the end of the messhall the prisoners turned into the kitchen where each man got a tin plate and a large spoon. They filed past a steamtable where the kitchen help likewise in stripes ladled up smoking pinto beans, cabbage, potatoes, hot rounds of cornbread. Harrogate had his thumb in his plate and got hot cabbage spooned over it by a smiling black man. He said: Yeeow. Swapped hands and stuck the thumb in his mouth. A guard came over and looked down at him. Was that you? he said.

Yessir.

One more holler out of you and you get no supper.

Yessir.

Nearby prisoners wore pinched faces, apparently in pain, eyes half shut with joy constrained. Harrogate followed on into a messhall like the one they'd come through. The benches and tables were filling up with prisoners. He sought out Suttree and sat next to him and fell to with his spoon. A great clanking and scraping throughout the hall and no word spoke. The table across from them was taken by black prisoners and Harrogate eyed them narrowly from under his brows, his head bent over his plate and the spoon he gripped like a trowel rising and falling woodenly.

When his group had all done eating the guard walked along behind them to the head of the table and rapped and they rose and filed back through the kitchen, scraping their plates into a slopcan and stacking them on a table, dropping their spoons into a bucket. Then they filed out through the other messhall, now partly filled with prisoners eating, and into the hall and up the stairs to their cell again.

They wasnt no meat, said Harrogate.

That's right, said Suttree.

Do they ever have meat?

I dont know.

Have you ever eat any meat here?

You mean other than breakfast bacon?

Yeah. Other than breakfast bacon.

No.

Harrogate leaned against the bunk. After a while he said: How long you been here?

About five months.

They hell fire, said Harrogate.

It was dark when they rose in the morning and dark when they filed into the kitchen to get their plates and spoons and still dark when they turned out in the dewfall and grainy mist of the yard. He stood there with his sleeves and cuffs rolled two turns each and watched the men climb into the trucks. He looked for Suttree but by the time he saw him he was already in a truck and the door was shut. Some of the trucks started to pull away. A guard came over and looked down at him. He stooped with his hands on knees to see into his face. Who the hell are you? he said.

Harrogate.

The guard nodded his head as if this was the right answer.

Did you get your breakfast?

Sure did.

Feel like you're ready for a day's work do you?

I reckon.

Well we have a truck over here for you to ride in if that's all right with you.

Thisn here?

Yeah. You dont care do you?

Harrogate grinned. Shoot, he said. I reckon that's what all I'm here for. I'll do just whatever.

Well we're mighty pleased about that. We like for everbody to be happy.

Shoot, said Harrogate over his shoulder as he slouched toward the waiting truck. I aint hard to get along with.

As he reached the rear of the truck and put up one hand to help himself the guard fetched him a kick from behind that lifted him through the door and dropped him among the boots and shoes of the other prisoners. They looked down at him with crazed grins and someone jerked him forward by the collar in time to keep the door from slamming on his foot. A redheaded man leaned down and said: Get in here, idjit. You make that son of a bitch mad this early of the mornin and I'll kick your ass myself.

I didnt know which truck I was supposed to go to.

Well no truck was the wrong one. Set over here. This son of a bitch drives like a drunk indian goin after more whiskey.

The truck coughed up gouts of white smoke and they lurched off into the fog down the hill and down the winding workhouse road to the highway where the taillights of the other trucks went by twos like eyes before them in the cool October dawn. The prisoners sat in rows facing each other, jiggling and rolling, some trying to sleep. Harrogate crouched on the bench with his hands beneath his thin legs and watched the floor. There was no conversation. The truck gained speed and the tires sang on the black road.

At the first stoplight a young girl was waiting for a bus at the edge of the road. The prisoners shoved and crowded at the wiremesh door of the truck. She turned to stare out over the barren lots toward houses swimming in the mist. A cold light was leaking across the landscape from the east. Harrogate watched two birds come out of the colorless heavens and alight upon a wire and look down into the truck and fly again. They went on, the driver's eyes in a car come up behind them somewhat uneasy at the sight of these striped miscreants.

By good daylight they had crossed the north end of the county and were pulled up at a roadside where sewerpipe lay unjointed along a selvedge of red mud and where riders from the first truck had already descended into ditches and begun to swing picks. The sun rose and warmed them where they stood waiting tools and orders. A man handed Harrogate a pick, stepped back and studied him with it and took it away again. A few cars eased past, faces at the glass. Men bound for work in the city looking out with no expression at all. The prisoners shuffled and milled about until all had tools and Harrogate stood alone. He had started down into the ditch with naked hands when a guard called to him.

Wait here a minute, he said.

The guard went away and returned with another man who looked down at Harrogate suspiciously.

How old are you son?

I'm still eighteen, said Harrogate. He had one black tooth in the front of his mouth and he sucked at it nervously.

The two men looked at each other. The younger one shrugged. I dont know, he said.

Well hell. Take him on back and let Coatney have him. You. You go on back with Mr Williams. You hear?

Yessir.

Get in that pickup over yonder and wait, the other man said.

Harrogate nodded and hobbled up the road to the truck and climbed up into the bed and sat there in his outsized togs watching the men in the ditch. He saw Suttree shoveling dirt up over the rim of the excavation and Suttree looked his way once sitting there alone in the truck but he did not nod or gesture. After a while the guard came up. He motioned to him and opened the door of the truck. Get up front, he said.

Harrogate climbed over the side of the truck and opened the door and got in. There was a speaker hanging by a cord from the dashboard and there was a pumpaction shotgun hung in a rack over the rear window. The guard started the truck, glanced down at Harrogate and pulled away shaking his head.

When Suttree came in that night the smallest prisoner was not in the cell. He saw him at supper. Half obscured behind tottering tiers of pans smoking a homerolled cigarette and firing thin pipes of smoke from his nostrils in disgust. He was moved that night to the kitchen cell. When he came to get his blanket Suttree was lying stretched on his cot with his shoes off. His socks were streaked with red clay.

Guess what, said Harrogate.

What.

They got me warshin fuckin dishes.

I know. I saw you.

Shit, said Harrogate.

Hell, that's no bad shake. It beats swinging a pick all day.

It dont to me. I'd rather to do anything as to warsh dishes.

You'll appreciate it more when the weather turns colder.

Shit.

Harrogate gathered up his blanket in his arms. Someone down the cell called up to Suttree was he through with the newspaper.

Yeah, said Suttree. Come and get it.

Fold it and pitch it here.

Suttree folded the paper and tried to remember how you tucked them in for throwing.

Goddamn Suttree, was you not ever a paperboy?

No.

I guess you was on a allowance.

The man had turned out of his cot and come up the hall.

I used to know how to roll them but I've forgotten.

Here. Let me have it. Fuckin educated pisswillies. He goes to college but he cant roll a newspaper. What do you think of that, little buddy?

The man was standing alongside the bunk. Redheaded, freckled, pumpkintoothed. The nose he talked through spread all over his face.

Howdy Mr Callahan, said Harrogate.

Suttree poked his head out from under the bunk. Mr Callahan? he said.

You heard him.

Oh boy, said Suttree, lying back down.

Callahan grinned his gaptooth grin.

Mr. Callahan's got a lot of pull around here, said Suttree. Ask him if he can do something for you.

Do what?

He wants to get out of the kitchen. He thinks washing dishes is beneath his dignity.

Hell fire little buddy. You got the best job in the joint.

I dont like it, said Harrogate sullenly. They got me workin with a bunch of old crippled fuckers and I dont know what all.

Specially in the guard's mess, said Callahan.

Guard's mess? Goddamn, said Suttree.

That's what they promised him, said Callahan. I guess he dont like steak and gravy. Ham. Eggs ever mornin.

Shit, said Harrogate.

It's true, said Suttree.

Hell Suttree, I dont want to be no goddamned dishwarsher. I got to get up at four oclock in the mornin.

Yeah. We sleep in here till five thirty.

You get to fuck around in the afternoon, said Callahan.

Well we dont get done till seven at night.

Well if you dont want to work in the guard's mess ask if they'll put you back on the trucks.

What if they say no?

Say yes.

What happens then? I guess they beat the shit out of ye.

No they wont. Will they, Red?

Nah. Put ye in the hole. Less you get real shitty. Then you go in the box.

Well that's where they'd put me. What is it?

Just a concrete box about four feet square.

You ever been in there Suttree?

No. You're talking to a man that has though.

What did they put you in there for Mr Callahan?

Aw, slappin a little old guard.

He slapped a vertebra loose in his neck, said Suttree.

Goddamn, said Harrogate. When was this?

When was it Red? Two years ago?

Somethin like that.

They hell fire, how long you been in here Mr. Callahan?

That was another offense, said Suttree. He's been in and out.

They dont give ye nothin to eat but bread and water, said Callahan. In the box they dont.

I believe you'll like the guard's mess better than the box.

I aint warshin no more goddamned dishes.

Well, said Suttree, that's you.

That's me, said Harrogate.

I think you've lost your rabbitassed mind, said Callahan.

Maybe. But I'll tell ye one thing. I ever get out of here I sure to shit aint comin back again.

I think I even heard Bromo say that one time.

Who's Bromo?

The old guy. He's been in and out of here since nineteen thirty-six.

He was in fore that, said Callahan. He was in the other workhouse fore this one was built.

Well, said Harrogate. That's him.

Suttree grinned. That's him, he said.

The crimes of the moonlight melonmounter followed him as crimes will. Truth of his doings came in at the door and up the stairs in the dark. Come morning the prisoners were seeing this half fool in a new light. To his elbows in dishwater and wreathed in steam he watched them file across the kitchen with their plates of biscuits and gravy, nodding, gesturing. He smiled back. They saw him again that night, lost in his stained and shapeless suit. He appeared not to have moved the day long nor the stacked pans diminished. After supper he was returned to them clutching his blanket before him.

Well, said Suttree, you back?

Yep.

What happened.

I told em I was done fuckin with em. They want a dishwarsher they can hunt somebody else cause I aint it.

What did they say.

They asked me did I want to be hallboy. Said you make a few dollars sellin coffee.

A few dollars a year.

That's just what I figured. I told em I didnt want no hallboy bullshit.

So what happened?

Nothin. They just sent me on up.

He stood there with his rat's face in a kind of smug smirk. Suttree shook his head.

Yonder he is, called Callahan.

Watermelon man.

Punkins wasnt it?

Punkins? Godamighty.

Yeah, sang out Callahan, we get out we goin to open a combination fruitstand and whorehouse.

Harrogate smiled nervously.

Callahan was sketching for them a portrait of his brothel. Melons in black negligees.

Watch out the niggers dont hear of it.

The niggers is liable to lynch ye.

Other fruits discussed. A cantaloupe turned queer. Do you buy them a drink.

Worst of it is havin gnats swarm around the head of ye dick.

Fruitflies.

Stealing watermelons eh? said Suttree.

Harrogate grinned uneasily. They tried to get me for beast, beast . . .

Bestiality?

Yeah. But my lawyer told em a watermelon wasnt no beast. He was a smart son of a bitch.

Oh boy, said Suttree.

In the morning he went with them on the trucks. Rising in the rank cold, faint odor of bathless sleepers all about. People stirring in the dull yellow bulblight, stumbling into clothes and shoes. The warmth of the kitchen and the smell of coffee. Cooks and potwashers aged or maimed all hovered by the stove with hot crockery mugs in their hands. Harrogate nodded to them distantly, holding his thumbs wide of his plate.

In the long days of fall they went like dreamers. Watching the sky for rain. When it came it rained for days. They sat in groups and watched the rain fall over the deserted fairgrounds. Pools of mud and dark sawdust and wet trodden papers. The painted canvas funhouse walls and the stark skeletons of amusement rides against a gray and barren sky.

A sad and bitter season. Barrenness of heart and gothic loneliness. Suttree dreamed old dreams of fairgrounds where young girls with flowered hair and wide child's eyes watched by flarelight sequined aerialists aloft. Visions of unspeakable loveliness from a world lost. To make you ache with want. In the afternoon the riggers came and set about taking down a spiderlike centrifuge and loading it on a float. As the prisoners shuffled over the grounds filling their crokersacks with bottles and trash the workers backhanded to them packs of cigarettes. Suttree was given a pack and passed it on to an old man with a goiter who took it without a word. The old man was a smokehound, a drinker of shaving lotion, stove fuel, cleaning fluid. Suttree watched him shuffle on. Scowling at the world from under his wild thatched brows. His thin and rimpled mouth working very faintly as he spoke with himself. He took up each paper, each bottle, with something like solicitude, looking about as if he would discover who had put it there. Suttree never heard him speak aloud, this elder child of sorrow. He crouched on the truck bench opposite going home, jostled and nodding. He saw Suttree watching him and lowered his eyes and fell to talking to himself with a kind of secretive viciousness.

Sundays a female evangelist from Knoxville would come out to hold service in the chapel downstairs. Concrete tabernacle, small wooden podium. The prisoners who went seemed stricken nigh insensate by this word of God strained distaff they were hearing. Lounging in the wooden folding chairs, heads lolling. She seemed unaware of their presence. She told old tales from bible days that might have come down orally, so altered were they from their origins. In the afternoon visitors arrived. Family scenes, mothers and fathers, wives, anonymous kinfolk gathered at the long tables in the dining hall. They'd call the names back down the hall and up the stairs and the guard would let them out. To return laden with candy, fruit, cigarettes. No one came for Suttree. None for Harrogate. Callahan's friends from McAnally Flats brought brownlooking apples, sacks of halfspoiled oranges. Callahan would peel these and slice them into a lardpail and cover them with water, adding a little yeast from the kitchen, covering it over with a cloth and storing it under his bed. In a few days a yeasty orange wine would work up and he'd strain it off and invite friends to take a cup with him. They called it julep and it kicked and spewed in the stomach all night. Callahan would get slightly drunk and look about goodnaturedly to see was there thing or body worth destroying.

Byrd Slusser came back, clumping sullenly down the aisle with his blanket, a pick about his ankle. When the workers returned in the evening he was asleep nor did he rise for supper.

In these tranquil evening hours before lights out Harrogate would sit up in his bunk and work on his jailhouse ring. They were made from silver coins and Harrogate had gotten a guard to bore a hole in his and he sat for hours on end with a messhall spoon and beat the coin's rim. The edges of the piece would flare out and come at last to a shape much like a wedding band. Now as he sat tapping Slusser turned in his bunk, raising his leg to clear the rear tine of the pick, and sought out the source of the noise. Harrogate squatted above him in the bunk opposite, bent over his coin, the spoon tapping steadily. Much like a little old cobbler crouched there half lost in his clothes.

Hey, said Slusser.

Harrogate looked down benignly. Hidy, he said.

Knock off that fuckin tappin.

He fixed Harrogate with a fearful look and rolled back over.

Harrogate sat with the coin in one hand and the spoon in the other. He looked down at the man. He took a tentative click at the coinrim. Click. He pulled up the blanket from the edge of the bunk and folded it over his hands, muffling the work between his knees. Click click click. He looked down at the man. The man lay as before. Click click click.

Slusser rose from the bunk slowly like a man bored. He came around the end of the bunk and reached his hand up to Harrogate. Give me that, he said.

Harrogate clutched the blanket to his chest.

You little fistfucker you better hand me that goddamned spoon before I jerk you out of there.

Suttree who'd been half asleep below had a failing sensation in the pit of his stomach. He said: Leave him alone, Byrd.

The boy's tormentor lost interest in him instantly and his eyes swung toward Suttree with a schizoid's alacrity. Well now, he said. I didnt know he was yours.

He's not anybody's.

He's a punk.

I dont believe he is.

Maybe you're one yourself.

Maybe—said Suttree, on whose forehead small beads of sweat had begun to glisten—you've been pulling your pud too much.

Slusser reached and seized him by the front of his jumper and dragged him upright. Suttree gripped his arm, coming out onto the floor. Turn loose of my shirt, Byrd, he said.

Byrd twisted the cloth in his fist. There was no sound in the cell. Suttree could see himself twinned in the cool brown eyes and he didnt like what he saw. He swung at Slusser's face. Immediately a fist crashed against the side of his head. He heard the sea roll. He swung again. His shirt came loose with a loud rip but he did not hear it. He pushed himself forward, his head ducked, and caromed off the side of the bunk. When he looked up he could not see Slusser. Some prisoners were standing between him and the hall and he heard grunts and the meaty sound of fists. Callahan's face went past smiling, beyond the shoulders of the watching men.

Suttree elbowed his way through the spectators. The fight crashed into the bunks and went to the wall and back down the cell, Slusser standing flatfooted because of the pick on his ankle, cursing. Callahan smiling. He was backing Slusser down along the wall in the narrow space behind the bunks. In turning between the bunks Slusser's pick got hung. Callahan stepped forward and slammed him broadside in the head. Slusser lashed out blindly, then kicked out with the pick. It stung a starshaped pock in the concrete and Slusser's eyes rolled with pain. He was still trying to kick Callahan with the pick when the iron door swung and two guards rushed in with slapsticks.

The first person to get clobbered was a country boy from Brown's Mountain named Leithal King. He sat down in the floor holding his head with both hands. Goddamn, he said.

Callahan had leaped back, holding up his hands. He's gone crazy, he said.

Slusser turned. He looked crazy. Eyes wild, a blue swelling at his temple giving his face an asymmetrical twist. The prisoners had fallen away. Slusser turned toward the guards in a half crouch and they fell upon him with slapsticks flailing. Callahan lowered his hands and leaned forward to see better. The slapsticks were going whop whop whop, Slusser on the floor with just the pick sticking out, the guards hammering away from kneeling positions like carpenters on a roof.

When they raised him up he was limp and bleeding from the mouth and ears and his face was his face seen through bad glass. Leithal had risen from the floor and Blackburn pointed his cudgel at him and said: You. Get this man. Callahan you son of a bitch. You get his other side.

I aint done nothin, said Leithal, coming forward uncertainly.

Callahan already had Slusser's arm draped around his neck and was bearing him up. He wiped a thin trickle of blood from his own mouth with a freckled fist and turned and gave the prisoners a pinched grimace of idiotic triumph which sent such a plague of grins among them that the other guard turned at the door. What the hell are you doing, Callahan?

Just holdin this man up. Where you want him?

They followed the guards out the door and Blackburn slammed the gate and locked it and they followed them down the hall and down the stairs, Slusser's pick dragging along behind until the other guard fell back and raised it up and they went on like that, bearing Slusser on toward the box with his hindleg aloft like a wounded iceskater.

The guard returned with Leithal and Callahan and when he unlocked the door Callahan started through it.

Hold it Callahan, said the guard.

Callahan held it.

The guard shut the door behind Leithal and locked it and motioned Callahan down the hall. The prisoners could hear him protesting. Hell fire, what for? I aint done a goddamned thing. Hell fire.

Suttree went back to his bunk, touching his swollen ear with his fingertips. Harrogate was still crouching in the top of his bunk with the spoon in his hand.

Where are they goin with Mr Callahan? he said.

To the hole. Blackburn's wise to his bullshit.

How long will they keep him in there?

I dont know. A week maybe.

Goddamn, said Harrogate. We sure stirred up some shit, didnt we?

Suttree looked at him. Gene, he said.

What.

Nothing. Just Gene.

Yeah. Well . . .

You better hope they keep Slusser in the box.

What about you?

He's already punched me.

Well. As long as they let Mr Callahan out before they do him.

Suttree looked at him. He was not lovable. This adenoidal leptosome that crouched above his bed like a wizened bird, his razorous shoulderblades jutting in the thin cloth of his striped shirt. Sly, rat-faced, a convicted pervert of a botanical bent. Who would do worse when in the world again. Bet on it. But something in him so transparent, something vulnerable. As he looked back at Suttree with his almost witless equanimity his naked face was suddenly taken away in darkness.

Some of the prisoners called out complaining. The hall guard told them to knock it off.

Hell fire, it aint but eight oclock.

Knock it off in there.

Bodies undressing in the dark. The hall light made a puppet show of them. Suttree sat on his bunk and eased off his clothes and laid them across the foot of the bed and crawled under the blanket in his underwear. Voices died in the room. Rustlings. The light from the yardlamps falling through the windows like a cold blue winter moon that never waned. He was drifting. He could hear a truck's tires on the pike a half mile away. He heard the chair leg squeak in the hall where the guard shifted. He could hear . . . He leaned out of the bunk. I will be goddamned, he said. Harrogate?

Yeah. Hoarse whisper in the dark.

Will you knock off that goddamned clicking?

There was a brief pause. Okay, said Harrogate.

When they came in from work the next evening Harrogate had a couple of small jars he'd found in the roadside. Suttree saw him descend from his bunk after lights out. He seemed to disappear somewhere in the vicinity of the floor. When he reappeared he camped on the floor at the head of Suttree's bed and Suttree could hear a tin set down on the concrete and the clink of glass.

What the fuck are you doing? he whispered.

Shhh, said Harrogate.

He heard liquid pouring.

Whew, said a voice in the dark.

A whiff of rank ferment crossed Suttree's nostrils.

Harrogate.

Yeah.

What are you up to?

Shhh. Here.

A hand came toward him from the gloom offering a jar. Suttree sat up and took it and sniffed and tasted. A thick and sourish wine of unknown origins. Where'd you get this? he said.

Shhh. It's Mr Callahan's julep he had workin. You reckon it's ready?

If it'd been ready he'd of drunk it.

That's what I thought.

Why dont you put it up and let it work some more and we'll drink it Saturday night.

You reckon it'll tear your head up?

Suttree reckoned it would tear your head up.

They lay there in the dark.

Hey Sut?

What.

What you aim to do when you get out?

I dont know.

What was you doin fore you got in?

Nothing. Laying drunk.

A deep wheezing of sleepers rose and fell about them.

Hey Sut?

Go to sleep Gene.

By morning a heavy rain had set in and they did not go out. They sat in small groups in the dimly lit cell and played cards. It was cold in the room and some wore their blankets shawled about their shoulders. They looked like detained refugees.

At noon a gimplegged prisoner brought up sandwiches from the kitchen. Thin slices of rat cheese on thin slices of white bread. The prisoners bought matchboxes of coffee from the hallboy for a nickel and he poured hot water in their cups. Harrogate came awake from a deep nap and hopped to the floor to get his lunch. He drank plain water with his sandwich, crouched up there in his bunk, his cheeks jammed. Outside the cold gray winter rain fell across the county. By nightfall it would turn to snow.

He'd finished his sandwiches and was back to tapping at his ring when a new thought changed his face. He put aside his work and climbed down to the floor and crawled under Suttree's bunk. Then he crawled out and back up topside where he fell to work again. In a little while he crawled down again.

Toward dusk a few prisoners looked his way to see what went, the smallest prisoner sitting in the top of his bunk suddenly going whooo whoo like a chimpanzee and lapsing silent again.

When the triangle rang for dinner all fell out save he. Suttree came by from his cardgame and shook him by the shoulder. Hey hotshot. Let's go.

Harrogate raised up with one eye shut, his face matted where it had lain crushed in the blanket. Aaangh? he said.

Let's go to supper.

He swung his legs over the side of the bed and pitched out onto the floor face down.

Suttree had turned to go when he heard the crash. He looked and saw Harrogate struggling in the floor and came back and helped him up. What the fuck's wrong with you?

Yeeegh yeegh, said Harrogate.

Shit, said Suttree. You better stay here. Can you get back in the bunk?

Harrogate fended him away and focused one eye toward the cell door. Sup sup, he said.

You crazy fucker. You cant even walk.

Harrogate started across the tilted floor listing badly. The other prisoners were jammed at the door, filing out by twos and down the stairs. Some looked back.

Look comin here.

What's happened to him?

Looks like one leg's grown longer'n the other one.

Harrogate crashed into the end of a set of bunks and reeled away.

Damned if the country mouse aint drunker'n hell.

Them eyes look like two pissholes in the snow.

He veered toward them like a misfired android. One caught him up by the sleeve.

You goin to supper, Countrymouse?

You fuckin ay, said Countrymouse.

They covered for him in line, holding him erect, shielding him from the guards. The cook's helper who loaded his plate looked at his face probably because it was the only one in the line passing at that diminished altitude. Shit a brick, he said.

Bet your ass, said Harrogate, winking profoundly.

They went on to the messhall. Harrogate stepped over the bench and misbalanced and stepped back. He raised his foot to try again. One of the prisoners grabbed his leg and pulled it down and caught his tilting plate and jerked him into the bench alongside him.

Hee hee, said Harrogate.

Someone kicked him under the table. He peered about at nearby faces for the culprit. The blacks filing in at the table opposite seemed to have wind of him already and were ogling and grinning.

Harrogate spooned up a load of pinto beans and shoved them toward his jaw. Some fell down the front of him. He looked after them. He began to spoon beans from his lap. Several guards were watching. He was having difficulty sitting on the bench. He was tottering about. The guard at the head of the table, a man named Wilson, walked down to get a better look. Harrogate sensed him standing there above him and turned to see, falling against the prisoner at his side as he did so. Wilson looked down into the thin face, now slightly green. Harrogate turned back to his food, holding onto the edge of the table with one hand.

This man's drunk, said Wilson.

Somewhere down the table someone muttered No shit and a ripple of tittering passed through the messhall. Wilson glared. All right, he said. Knock it off. You. Get up.

Harrogate put down his spoon and took another grip on the table and raised himself up. But since the bench would not push back from the table he remained in a sort of crouched position, finally losing his balance and sitting down again. Now he turned in his seat and tried to get one foot over the bench, lifting his leg up by the cuff of his trousers, one elbow resting in his food.

The clanking and scraping of spoons had ceased altogether. The only sound in the messhall was Harrogate struggling to free himself from the table. Wilson standing over him like a faith healer over a paraplegic. Until he actually raised up astraddle the bench, creamed corn dripping from his sleeve. Ick, he said.

What? said Wilson menacingly.

The country mouse closed his eyes, belched, opened them again. Sick, he said. He was trying to raise his other leg. The prisoner alongside looked up at him and leaned away. Harrogate lurched and his neck gave a sort of chickenlike jerk and he vomited on Wilson's shoes.

The prisoners on either side of Harrogate leaped up. Wilson's slapstick was out. He was looking at his shoes. He couldnt believe it. Harrogate wore a look of terror. He seized hold of the table, looking about wildly, his gorge swollen. He spied his plate. He leaned toward it. He vomited on the table.

You nasty little bastard, screamed Wilson. He was doing little kicks, trying to shake the puke from his shoes. The prisoners who'd been sitting opposite Harrogate had risen from the table and were watching the country mouse in awe. Harrogate looked up at them with weeping eyes and managed just the smallest blacktooth grin before he puked again.

They did not see him for ten days. Then one morning as they filed through the kitchen with their plates there he was, grinning sheepishly, ladling up gravy for their biscuits. Beyond him through the steam, on a can with a cigarette in his mouth, sat Red Callahan. No one asked where Slusser was.

That night when they came in he must have been showering in the kitchen cell because when they went past on their way to their own quarters silently in twos, exuding the aura of cold they'd brought in with them, Harrogate suddenly appeared naked at the bars, his thin face, his hands clutching, like a skinned spidermonkey.

Sut, he called out softly. Hey Sut.

Suttree heard his name. As he came abreast of the smallest prisoner he dropped out of the line. When will the phantom puker strike again, he said. What the fuck are you doing bare assed?

Listen Sut, that fuckin Wilson's got it in for me. I got to get out of here.

Out of where?

Here. The joint.

You mean run off?

Yeah.

Suttree shook his head. That's crazy, Gene, he said.

I need you to help me.

Suttree fell back in at the tail of the line. You're nuts, Gene, he said.

He saw him again a week later on Thursday when he was assigned to the indigent food detail. The needy trooping through in rags, their eyes rheumy, snuffling, showing their papers at the desk and going on to where the prisoners unloaded bags of cornmeal from pallets or scooped dried beans into grocery bags. Suttree sought their eyes but few looked up. They took their dole and passed on. Old shapeless women in thin summer dresses, socks collapsed about their pale and naked ankles, shoes opened at the side with knives to ease their feet. The seams of their lower faces stained with snuff, their drawstrung mouths. To Suttree they seemed hardly real. Like pictureshow paupers costumed for a scene. At the noon dinner break he and Harrogate fell in together. They crouched with others among the palleted beans and unwrapped their sandwiches.

What we got?

Baloney.

Anybody got a cheese?

They aint no cheese.

Sut.

Yeah.

Shhh. Do you know where we're at?

Where we're at?

I mean which way is town?

Harrogate speaking in loud hoarse whispers, spewing bits of bread. Suttree jerked a thumb over his shoulders. It's thataway, he said.

Harrogate motioned his thumb down and looked about. What I figure to do, he said . . .

Gene.

Yeah.

If you run off from here you'll wind up like Slusser.

You mean with a pick on my leg?

I mean you'll be in and out of institutions for the rest of your life. Save for one thing.

What's that.

They aint goin to catch me.

Where will you go?

Go to Knoxville.

Knoxville.

Hell yes.

What makes you think they wont find you in Knoxville?

Hell fire Sut. Big a place as Knoxville is? They never would find ye there. Why you wouldnt even know where to start huntin somebody.

Suttree looked at Harrogate and shook his head.

How far you reckon it is to town? said Harrogate.

It's six or eight miles. Listen. If you've got to run off why dont you wait and slip off from the county garage some evening?

What for?

Hell, you're practically in town. Besides it would be dark or damn near it.

Harrogate paused from his chewing, his eyes fixed on his shoe. Then he commenced chewing again. You might be right, he said.

Suttree was unwrapping his other sandwich. It dont make all that much difference actually, he said.

Why's that?

Cause they'll catch your skinny ass anyway.

They aint no way.

What do you aim to do about clothes? What do you think people are going to say when they see you wandering around in that outfit?

I'll get me some clothes first thing.

Suttree shook his head.

Hell Sut. I can slip around.

Gene.

Yeah.

You look wrong. You will always look wrong.

Harrogate looked at the floor. He had stopped chewing. No I wont, he said.

The weather turned colder and they did not go out. Wilson put Harrogate to work painting the black borders along the lower hallway walls that served for baseboards. The workhouse smelled of paint and so did the country mouse when he came up in the evening with the smears of black on his face like a guerrilla fighter.

One night Suttree said to him: Dont you have any family?

The lights were out. A few bodies shifted in the dark. Dont you? said the small voice overhead.

Christmas came and some of the married prisoners were furloughed home to holiday with their families. A few were released. Slusser came from solitary, the pick still on his leg. He entered with his blanket and went down the aisle without speaking to anyone.

There was a lighted tree in the recreation room downstairs and on Christmas day they had turkey with all the trimmings. Callahan in the kitchen drunk making pumpkin pies out of old sweet potatoes and carrots. Sots loose from the drunk tank wandering about crazed with thirst. An air of wary joy, like Christmas in some arctic outpost.

The following day was Sunday. Suttree was playing poker when his name was called. He played on.

That's you, Suttree.

He folded his cards. He glanced toward the door and rose heavily, handing the cards down to Harrogate. Dont lose all my money, he said.

The hall guard opened the door and he went out and down the stairs.

The messhall was filled with families. Enormous baskets of fruit. Country people, some bewildered, some in tears. Old men who had been here themselves perhaps.

Over yonder, said Blackburn.

She was sitting at the table at the far end of the hall. Quietly in her good clothes. He turned to go back but Blackburn gripped him by his sleeve and pulled him around. You get your ass over there, he said.

He made his way along the edge of the table. She had her purse in her lap and she was looking down. She was still wearing her hat from church. He sat down on the bench across the table from her and she looked up at him. She looked old, he could not remember her looking so. Her slack and pleated throat, the flesh beneath her jaws. Her eyes paler.

Hello Mother, he said.

Her lower chin began to dimple and quiver. Buddy, she said. Buddy . . .

But the son she addressed was hardly there at all. Numbly he watched himself fold his hands on the table. He heard his voice, remote, adrift. Please dont start crying, he said.

See the hand that nursed the serpent. The fine hasped pipes of her fingerbones. The skin bewenned and speckled. The veins are milkblue and bulby. A thin gold ring set with diamonds. That raised the once child's heart of her to agonies of passion before I was. Here is the anguish of mortality. Hopes wrecked, love sundered. See the mother sorrowing. How everything that I was warned of's come to pass.

Suttree began to cry nor could he stop it. People were looking. He rose. The room swam.

Buddy, she said. Buddy.

I cant, he said. Hot salt strangled him. He wheeled away. Blackburn would have stopped him at the door but when he saw his face he let him go. Suttree jerked his arm away and went through the gate and up the stairs.

He was released a few days later on order from Judge Kelly. The country mouse had run off from a work detail the morning before and as Suttree came from the supply room dressed in the clothes he'd worn through the slam seven months earlier Harrogate was being led clumping along the hall with a pick on his leg. They exchanged glances as they passed but you couldnt say it in words. Suttree was taken back to town in the same car that had brought him out. It was snowing but the roads were clear.

He woke in the logy heat of full summer noon with the sun beating on the tin roof above him and raising a sour smell out of the old wood of the cabin. He could hear the howl of the saws in the lumbermill across the river and he could hear the intermittent scream of swine come under the knacker's hand at the packing company. He turned his face to the wall and opened one eye. Watched through a split in the sunriven boards the slow brown neap of the passing river. After a while he struggled up, blinking in the dusty slats of sunlight that sliced through the hot murk. He tottered erect onto the floor in the trousers he'd slept in and made his way to the door and stepped out, scratching his naked belly, watching the boards for stray fish hooks as he went barefoot toward the rail. He leaned on his elbows and looked out over the river. The skiff had sunk to the gunwales and lay quietly awash in the current. He propped up one foot and studied his toes. He could hear everywhere in the hot summer air the drone of machinery, the lonely industry of the city. He blinked and stretched. A graveldredger was moving upriver, her pipes and tackle slung up in the trucks. He watched it pass. A figure on the pilot deck waved and he waved back.

Suttree took the rope loose from the rail and began to haul the skiff along the side of the houseboat. It yawed and wallowed in the river. He threw the rope ashore and went down the plank and retrieved it from the mud and miring to his anklebones he eased the skiff in. He got hold of the ring in the prow and braced himself and lifted. Mud spurted between his toes. He hoisted the front of the skiff and watched the water sluice heavily over the transom into the river. Tails flared and subsided. He hauled the skiff partly up the bank and lifted it sideways. The trapped fish milled and surged. He tilted with care, their shapes riding up along the overflow and dropping back again. When he lowered the skiff they lay gaping on the boards under a sun that withered them visibly.

Suttree gripped his forepockets, searching. He rose and went to the shanty and returned with a large claspknife. He reached into the bottom of the boat and brought up a catfish by the lower jaw. It quivered slightly and curled its tail. Suttree turned it and sank the point of his knife into its throat and opened its wet and pale blue belly with a clean slicing motion that dumped forth the living viscera down his forearm in a welter of dark blood. He seized these entrails and hauled them from the fish and slung them, a wet anneloid mass writhing brightly in the sun and dropping through the placid face of the river with a light splash that sucked away almost at once. He laid the cleaned fish by and seized the next. They were seven in all and he had them dressed in minutes and aligned in the shade under the skiff's seat. He cut the leaders from the hooks he'd salvaged and he rinsed the blood and mucus from his hands and cleaned the knife and folded the blade away and returned to the shanty.

When he came out again he wore a shirt loosely unbuttoned and he had a towel over one shoulder and he carried a small porcelained basin and a leather shavingbag. He came down the plankwalk and went across the field toward the warehouse still barefoot and stepping carefully, emerging onto the railbed and walking three tentative steps on the hot steel before hopping off again. He did a little hotfoot dance and went on among the cinders and rough ties. Passing through a landscape of old tires and castoff watertanks rusting in the weeds and bottomless buckets and broken slabs of concrete. When he left the roadbed he turned up along the side of the warehouse, the new tin brightly galvanized and reeling in the enormous heat and his shadow wincing blackly across the corrugated glare of it like a crepepaper player in a shadowshow. At the far end of the warehouse was a brass spigot. Beneath it the cracked red clay lay shaped in a basin centered by a dark ocherous eye where the water dripped. Suttree knelt and laid out his things, hung his small mirror from a nail, set his washbasin under the tap and turned on the water. Squinting, he inspected his beard, testing the water idly with one finger. It came hot from the tap in this weather and he laved a palmful over his cheeks and wet his brush and lathered carefully. Then he opened his razor and stropped it briefly on the side of his shavingbag and commenced to shave, pulling the skin taut with his fingers.

When he was finished he flung away the water in a beaded explosion of vapor under the scorching wall of the warehouse, a brief rainbow. He filled the basin again and took off his shirt and splashed himself wet and soaped and rinsed and dried himself with the towel. He put away the razor and brushed his teeth, squatting on his heels there in the raw clay, looking about. A hot silence hung over the riverfront. Over the stained and leaning clapboard shacks, over the barren rubble lots and the fields of wirecolored sedge, over the cratered wastes of hardpan and the railway road. And silence among these broiling colossi of tin and down by the stones and bracken and mud that marked the river shore. Something that looked like a mouse save it had no tail came out of the weeds below him and crossed the open like a windup toy and scuttled from sight beneath the warehouse wall. Suttree spat and rinsed his mouth. A black witch known as Mother She was going along Front Street toward the store, a frail bent shape in black partlet with cane laboring brokenly through the heat. He rose and collected his things and went back down the dry clay gutter by the edge of the warehouse and along the tracks and across the fields.

As he neared the shanty he saw a long gray cat struggling toward the weeds towing its own length of fish. He shouted and waved at it. He scooped and shied a rock. Hobbling along gingerfooted through the stubble. When he came up the cat squared off at him, a starved and snarling thing with the hackles reared along its razorous spine. It did not let go the fish. Suttree threw a rock at it. The cat's ears lay flat along its head and its tail kept jerking. He threw another rock that caromed off its stark ribs. It dropped the fish and yowled at him, still crouched there cocked on its bony elbows.

Why goddamn you, said Suttree. He cast about until he found a huge clod of dried mud and going close he broke it over the animal. It squalled and scrabbled away, shaking its head. Suttree retrieved the fish and looked it over. He rinsed it in the river and gathered up the other fish and piled them in his washbasin, a tottery load, and went on to the shanty. The cat was already back in the skiff, searching.

With the day's sun full on the tin roof the heat in the houseboat was unendurable. He put away his things and got a clean shirt and trousers from his cardboard bureau and dressed and took his shoes and socks and towel and went out onto the deck. There he sat looking out through the rails with his feet hanging in the river. Down near the bridge an old man poled a skiff by the shore. Standing precarious and daring. Wielding a longhandled hook. A fellow worker in these cloacal reaches, plying the trade he has devised for himself. The old man's name was Maggeson and Suttree smiled to see him at his work, going slow, shaded by the fronds of a huge and raveled fiber hatbrim.

He dried his feet and put on his socks and shoes and combed his hair. Inside the shanty he wrapped the fish in a newspaper and tied them with a string and took the coaloil can from its corner. At the door he looked to see had he forgotten anything and then he left.

When he reached the street he walked along until he found a flat place at the paving's edge and under the weeds and here he stopped and poured the kerosene over the warm tar. Then he set the can from sight in the weeds and went on.

Gravely, gravely, small chocolate children nodded or lifted pale brown palms. Hello. Hidy. He climbed up from the river and went toward the city with his fish.

Early in his living by the river Suttree had found a shortcut through old gardens on the river bluff, a winding path with cinder paving that angled up behind old homes of blackened boarding and old porches where rusted skeins of screening fell down the rotting facades. But passing under one high window always he heard a dull mutter of invective and sullen oaths and he no longer took the near path but went the longer way round by the streets. The invector however had moved to a new window so large was the house that he shared with his soul and he could still watch for the fisherman to pass. In these later years he had become confined altogether and this was hard for one accustomed to tottering daily abroad and dripping vitriol on passing strangers. He keeps his watch with fidelity. An old man dimly seen in upper windowcorners.

Market Street on Monday morning, Knoxville Tennessee. In this year nineteen fifty-one. Suttree with his parcel of fish going past the rows of derelict trucks piled with produce and flowers, an atmosphere rank with country commerce, a reek of farmgoods in the air tending off into a light surmise of putrefaction and decay. Pariahs adorned the walk and blind singers and organists and psalmists with mouth harps wandered up and down. Past hardware stores and meatmarkets and little tobacco shops. A strong smell of feed in the hot noon like working mash. Mute and roosting pedlars watching from their wagonbeds and flower ladies in their bonnets like cowled gnomes, driftwood hands composed in their apron laps and their underlips swollen with snuff.

He went among vendors and beggars and wild street preachers haranguing a lost world with a vigor unknown to the sane. Suttree admired them with their hot eyes and dogeared bibles, God's barkers gone forth into the world like the prophets of old. He'd often stood along the edges of the crowd for some stray scrap of news from beyond the pale.

He crossed the street, stepping gutters clogged with greenstuff. Coming from behind the trucks a beggarlady's splotched and marcid arm barred his way, a palsied claw that gibbered at his chest. He slid past. Stale nunlike smell of her clothes, dry flesh within. The old almstress's eyes floated by in a mist of bitterness but he had nothing but his fish.

He passed under the shade of the markethouse where brick the color of dried blood rose turreted and cupolaed and crazed into the heat of the day form on form in demented accretion without precedent or counterpart in the annals of architecture. Pigeons bobbed and preened in the high barbicans or shat from the blackened parapets. Suttree pushed through the gray doors below.

He went over the cool tiles, his heels muted by sawdust and wood-shavings. A halfman on a skatecart oared past with leather chocks. Huge fans wheeled slowly in the upper murk and marketers shoul-dered past with baskets, eyes stunned by the plenty through which they moved, shy women in wrappers of gingham print with the arm-pits eaten out and trailing small streaked children in tennis shoes. They milled and turned and shuffled by. Suttree wandering among the stalls where little grandmothers offered flowers or berries or eggs. Rows of faded farmers hunched at the lunchcounters. This lazaret of comestibles and flora and maimed humanity. Every other face goit-ered, twisted, tubered with some excrescence. Teeth black with rot, eyes rheumed and vacuous. Dour and diminutive people framed by paper cones of blossoms, hawkers of esoteric wares, curious electuar-ies ordered up in jars and elixirs decocted in the moon's dark. He went by stacks of crated pullets, plump hares with ruby eyes. Butter tubbed in ice and brown or alabaster eggs in ordered rows. Along by the meatcounters shuffling up flies out of the bloodstained sawdust. Where a calf's head rested pink and scalded on a tray and butchers honed their knives. Great cleavers and bonesaws hung overhead and truncate beeves in stark abbatoir by cambreled hams blueflocced with mold. At the fishmarket cold gray shapes dimly limned in troughs of powdered ice.

Suttree eased past the cool glass cases with their piscean wares and went on to the rear of the stall.

Hello Mr Turner.

Howdy Suttree, said the old man. What have you got?

Two nice cats and some carp. He unrolled the paper and laid them out on the block. Mr Turner thumbed one of the catfish over. Bits of newsprint clung to it. He felt the flesh, picked up the two fish and laid them in the scales.

Call it seven pounds.

All right. What about the carp?

He regarded the dull placoid shapes with doubt. Well, he said. I could maybe take one of them.

Well.

He lifted out the catfish and selected a small carp. They watched the needle swing. The old jowter twisted up his apron in his hands. Two and a half, he said.

Okay.

He nodded and went to his till and rang open the drawer. He came back with a dollar bill and four cents and handed the money to Suttree.

When are you going to bring me some of them little channel cats?

Suttree had slid the folded dollar into his pocket and was rewrapping the remaining fish. He shrugged. I dont know, he said. When I get a chance.

Turner watched him. Windchimes belled thinly, a flutter of glass above them stirred by the fans. I get people askin all the time, he said.

Well. Maybe later on this week. I have to go up on the French Broad for them. This hot weather is bad.

Well, you bring me some quick as you get a chance.

All right.

He slid the other fish under one arm and nodded.

Mr Turner wiped his hands again. Come back, he said.

Suttree went on through the markethouse and out the double doors to Wall Avenue. A blind black man was fretting a dobro with a broken bottleneck and picking out an old blues run. Suttree let the four pennies into the tin cup taped to the box. Get em, Walter, he said.

Hey Sut, said the player.

He crossed the street toward Moser's to admire the boots in the window. A graylooking cripple sat on the walk with a hatful of pencils trapped in his wasted kneecrooks. His head lay sunken on his chest. As if he were trying to read the sign hung from his neck. I AM A POOR BOY. His grizzled wool tiaraed with smoked glasses worn gogglewise. Suttree went on. He crossed Gay Street with the shoppers and went up the long cool tunnel of the bus station arcade and through the doors.

A nasal voice called out through a megaphone the names of southern cities in this cavern of stale smoke and boredom. Suttree adjusted his fish and went through the doors at the far side of the waiting room and down the concrete steps, along the platform past idling buses and into State Street. He went past the firehouse where the inmates sat tilted in cane chairs along a shaded wall and he went down the hill past dolorous small taverns and cafes and down Vine Avenue by secondhand furniture stores among throngs of blacks and along Central where loud and shoddy commerce erupted out of the dim shops into the streets and packs of scarred dogs wandered. Shouldering his way through dark shoppers in a market ripe with sweat and the incendiary breath of splo drinkers, wide white teeth and laughter and cupshot eyeballs. Beyond the grocery cases a long trestle of beerdrinkers. An old woman thickly mantled in rags mumbled something incoherent at his ear in passing. He leaned on the meatcase and waited.

A pocked black face peered at him over the top of the counter through racks of packaged sausage and porkskins.

I've got four fresh buglemouth, Suttree said.

Lessee.

He handed up the limp package. The dark butcher unrolled it and looked the fish over and placed them in his bloodstained balance. Foteen pound, he said.

All right.

How come you aint never got no catfish?

I'll try and get you some.

Folks astin all the time: Where yo catfish at? Aint none, that's all.

I'll see if I can get you some.

Dollar twelve.

Suttree held out his hand for the money.

Out in the baking street with the bills wadded together in the toe of his pocket he swung along whistling. He went up Vine to Gay Street and along the walk by pawnshop windows. Wares to find a thousand trades. Consulting with his image in the glass he studied a display of knives. Come in, come in. A round and shirtsleeved merchant from the doorway. Suttree moved along. Late noon traffic pushed sluggishly through the heat and trolleys clicked past dimly dragging sparks from the wires overhead.

He cruised the cool wooden dimestore aisles, eyeing the salesgirls. He revolved into the perfumed and airconditioned sanctuary of Miller's. A cool opulence available to the most pauperized. Up the escalator to the second floor. Holt was standing with his hands clasped in the small of his back like an usher at a funeral. He wore a shoehorn in his waistband and a small grin.

He didnt make it today.

Thanks, said Suttree.

He went down the escalator and into the street again.

Jake the rack stood with his hands in the change of his apron, tilling the coins. He spat enormously and dark brown toward a steel spittoon and stepped to a table where the balls were being shucked up from the pockets and a player was pounding the floor with his cue. He called back over his shoulder: He just left, him and Boneyard. I think they went to eat. Jim's drunk.

He saw them in the rear of the Sanitary Lunch, J-Bone and Boneyard and Hoghead all three, bleary figures gesturing beyond the fogged glass. He went in.

Jimmy the Greek speared up meat from his gasping trypots and forked the slabs onto thick white plates. He adjusted salads with his thumb and wiped away drips of gravy with his apronskirt. Suttree waited at the counter. The fans that hung from the stamped tin ceiling labored in a backwash of smoke and steam.

The Greek was blinking at him.

Two hamburgers and a chocolate milk, Suttree said.

He nodded and scratched the order on a pad and Suttree went on to the back of the cafe.

Here's old Suttree.

Come here and set down, Sut.

Scoot over, Hoghead.

Suttree looked them over. What are you all doing?

I'm tryin to get well, said J-Bone.

How do you feel?

I feel like I need a drink.

Suttree looked at Hoghead. A halfcrazed grin spread over Hoghead's freckled face. Suttree looked from one to the other of them. They were all drunk.

You sons of bitches havent been to bed.

Early Times, called out J-Bone.

J-Bone's crazy, Hoghead said.

Boneyard's black eyes darted about from one to the other.

The Greek set down a glass of water and a carton of milk and an empty glass.

Bring us another Coke, Jimmy, J-Bone said.

He nodded, collecting dishes.

Suttree took a drink of the water and poured the water into the empty glass and opened the milk and poured it into the cold glass and sipped it. J-Bone was fumbling around under the seat. When the Greek came back he straightened up and cleared his throat loudly. The Greek set down a plate with two hamburgers and a Coke with a glass of ice and shuffled off again. Suttree lifted the sandwiches open and poured salt and pepper. The meat was seasoned and thinned with meal and there were scoops of coleslaw on top.

J-Bone had come up with a bottle from under the booth and was pouring whiskey over the ice, holding the glass in his lap and looking about cunningly. He slid the bottle partly from the sweatwrinkled bag that held it and checked the level of the contents and slid it back.

We're on that good stuff now, Sut. Here. Have a little drink.

Suttree shook his head, his mouth full of hamburger.

Go on.

No thanks.

J-Bone was looking at him crazily. He leaned a little, as if to lift one leg. His eyes wandered in his head. An enormous fart ripped through the lunchroom, stilling the muted noontime clink of cutlery and cup clatter, stunning the patrons, rattling the cafe to silence. Boneyard rose instantly and took a stool at the counter, looking back wildly. The Greek at his steamtable tottered backwards, one hand to his forehead. Hoghead staggered into the aisle, strangling, his face a mask of anguish and the lady in the next booth rose and looked down at them with a drained face and made her way to the cash register.

Hee, crooned J-Bone into cupped hands.

Goddamn, said Suttree, rising with his plate and glass.

Hurt yourself Jim? called Boneyard past the back of his hand.

Whew, said Hoghead, sitting at the counter. I believe somethin's crawled up in you and died.

The Greek was glaring toward the rear of the cafe. J-Bone, in the booth alone, wrinkled his face. After a minute he climbed out into the aisle. Lordy, he said. I dont believe I can stand it my ownself.

Get away from here.

I'm trying to eat, Jim.

Lord, said J-Bone. I believe it's settled in my hair.

Let's get out of here, said Boneyard.

Suttree looked at the grinning faces. Just a minute and let me finish this, he said.

The interior of the Huddle was cool and dark, the door ajar. They came down the steep street and turned in two by two.

Dont bring no whiskey in here, said Mr Hatmaker, pointing.

J-Bone turned and went out and took the near empty bottle from under his shirt and drained it and threw it across the street where it exploded against the wall of the hotel. A few faces appeared at the windows and J-Bone waved to them and went in again.

The light from the door fell upon the long mahogany bar. A pedestal fan rocked in its cage and huge flies droned back and forth beneath the plumbing hung from the ceiling. Whores lounged in a near booth and light in dim smoked palings sloped in through the dusty windowpanes. Blind Richard was sitting at the corner of the bar with a mug of beer before him and the wet duck end of a cigarette smoldering in his thin lips, his blownout eyeballs shifting behind squint lids, his head tilted for news of these arrivals. J-Bone walloped him on the back.

What say, Richard.

Richard unleashed his wet green teeth in the semidark. Hey Jim. I been lookin for you.

J-Bone pinched his sad dry cheek. You sly rascal, you found me, he said.

Suttree tapped him on the elbow. You want a fishbowl? Give us three, Mr Hatmaker.

At a table in the rear a group of dubious gender watched them with soulful eyes. They tucked their elbows and their hands hung from the upturned stems of their wrists like broken lilies. They stirred and subsided with enormous lassitude. Suttree looked away from their hot eyes. Mr Hatmaker was drawing off beer into frozen bowls. Suttree handed back the first of them beaded and dripping and dolloped with thick foam. Richard's nose twitched.

How are you, Richard?

Richard smiled and fondled the facets of his empty mug. He said that he was only fair.

Well, said Suttree, give us one more. Mr Hatmaker.

Watch old Suttree spring, said Hoghead.

You want a Coca-Cola?

What for? Jim drank all the whiskey didnt he?

Ask Jim.

Here you go Richard.

Looky here, said Jim.

What?

Look what's loose.

They turned. Billy Ray Callahan was standing in the door smiling. Hey Hatmaker, he said.

Mr Hatmaker raised his head, whitehaired and venerable.

Is Worm barred?

The barkeeper nodded dourly that he was.

How about lettin him back in?

He set the last schooner on the bar and wiped his hands and took the money. He stood looking toward the door, weighing the bill in his hand. All right, he said. You can tell him he's not barred no more.

What about Cabbage and Bearhunter?

They aint barred that I know of.

Come on, assholes.

They entered grinning and squinting in the gloom.

Red On The Head like the dick on a dog, sang out J-Bone.

Callahan whacked him in the belly with the back of his hand. Hey Jim, he said. How's your hammer hangin? He glanced about. The whores looked up nervously. He bequeathed upon them collectively his gaptoothed grin. Ladies, he said. He crouched slightly to peer toward the back of the room. Hey, he called. The queers is back. He punched Worm playfully on the shoulder and pointed toward the group at the table. They turned to one another in elaborate indignation, drawing their wandlike arms to their breasts. With the unison of the movement those pale and slender limbs mimed dancing egrets in the gloom. Callahan extended a hand into the air. Hidy queers, he said.

Suttree was standing against the bar watching all this with something like amusement. When Callahan saw him he gathered his head into the crook of his arm. Goddamned old Suttree, he said.

How's it feel to be on the street again?

Feels thirsty. You holdin anything?

Give us another fishbowl, Mr Hatmaker.

Callahan reached past Suttree and gave Blind Richard a great whack on the shoulders. Richard's cigarette hopped from his mouth and expired in his beer. What say Richard old buddy! screamed Callahan.

The blind man raised up coughing. He put one finger to his ear. Goddamn, Red. I aint deaf. He was groping about on the bar with long yellow fingers.

Where'd my cigarette get to, Jim?

Red got it, Richard.

Give me my cigarette, Red.

Suttree passed the mug of beer from the bar and Callahan sucked down about half of it and belched and looked about. Someone had put a coin in the jukebox and pastel lights exchanged within the plastic fascia. Bearhunter and Cabbage composed a light impromptu dance. Boneyard watched, his anthracite eyes shining.

Tell him to give me my cigarette, Jim.

An enormous whore had come to the bar with empty mugs for filling. She stood against Suttree and gave him a sidelong look of porcine lechery.

Watch out, Suttree, called Cabbage.

Your buddy was supposed to of got out with us, said Red.

Harrogate?

Yeah. They couldnt find him no clothes. He says he's comin to the big city to make his fortune.

He's as crazy as a shithouse rat.

That old big gal's after you, called Cabbage, punching buttons at the jukebox.

The whore grinned and took the filled mugs to the table.

J-Bone turned to the room with outspread hands. All right now. Who got Richard's cigarette?

Richard tugged at his sleeve. Here, Jim. Let it go.

Hell no. Nobody leaves the room.

Callahan leaned and called to a thin woman among the whores. Hey Ethel. How's that rabbit hole?

Somebody told me you were a fisherman now, said Bearhunter.

Damn right he is, said Cabbage. Catches them *big ones.*

Piss on you, Cabbage.

Cabbage put one hand to his mouth. That old Suttree, he called. He knows where the good holes is at.

Listen at old Cabbage hammer, said J-Bone.

Old Cabbage, said Red, he beat that morals charge they had him on. They caught him and this girl parked in a car buck naked but old Cabbage, he ate the evidence.

Aw shit, said Richard. Who put a danged old cigarette out in my danged beer?

Who done that? called J-Bone.

A small owlfaced man was trying to get up a game on the bowling machine. Here's my horse, said Boneyard, raising J-Bone's arm aloft.

I'm too drunk. Who was it put a duck out in Richard's beer when he wasnt lookin?

Bill, you and me partners, said Worm.

Here's my horse, said Red, hugging Richard's thin shoulders.

Where's Ethel? She'll play. Get her.

Ethel was at the end of the bar with her empty mug. She snapped her fingers and pointed at her crotch with her thumb. Get this, she said.

Suttree studied her. Her bony sootstreaked arms were bare to the shoulder and one bore a slaverous and blueblack panther. He could see part of a peacock, a wreath with the name Wanda and the words Rest In Peace 1942. He had his head tilted studying the blue runes on her legs when she turned with her beer. She hiked her skirt up around her waist with one hand and cocked her leg forward. A hound was chasing a rabbit down her belly toward her crotch. She said: When you get your eyes full, open your mouth.

Whoops from the drinkers. Hoghead leaning to see. Wait a minute, he said.

But she had flipped her skirt down with an air of contempt and swaggered past with her beer.

I told you about that Suttree, called Cabbage. He's a hole findin fool.

Let's see that rabbit hole Ethel.

Let's see one of you loudmouthed fuckers buy a beer.

Buy her a beer Worm.

Fuck her. She's got a beer.

Give us a fishbowl Mr Hatmaker.

Ever who's playin get your dime up.

What are we playin for?

Make it light on yourself.

Who got my beer. Hey, Red?

Late summer darkness fell and lights came on within the tavern, the beerlamps and plastic clocks with country scenes. Suttree fell in among the winners from the bowling game and they set forth in a huge old Buick.

Idling in an alleyway under a yellow lightbulb by a clapboard wall where a man naked to the waist palmed to them a pint bottle in a paper bag. On to other taverns where in the smoke and the din and the music the night grew heady. At the B & J Suttree became enamored of a ripe young thing with black hair who wrought on the dancefloor an obscene poem, her full pale thighs shining in the dim light where she whirled.

He stood to dance, took two steps sideways and sat again.

He began to grow queasy.

He was looking down into a tin trough filled with wet and colorful gobbets of sick. Scalloped moss wept from a copper pipe. A man sat sleeping on the toilet, his hands hanging between his knees. There was no seat to the toilet and the sleeper was half swallowed up in its stained porcelain maw.

Hey, said Suttree. He shook the man by the shoulder.

The man shook his head in annoyance. A foul odor seeped up between his lardcolored thighs.

Hey there.

The man opened one wet red eye and looked out.

Sick, Suttree said.

They glared at each other.

Yeah, said the man. Sick.

Suttree stood spraddlelegged before him, swaying slightly, one hand on the man's shoulder. The man squinted at him. Do I know you?

Suttree turned away. Two other men come in were standing at the trough. He tottered into the corner and vomited. The men at the trough watched him.

They rolled through the dim shires of McAnally singing rude songs and passing a bottle about in the musty old car.

Wake up, Sut, and take ye a drink.

What's wrong with old Suttree.

Suttree's all right, said J-Bone.

He waved them away, his wheeling skull pressed for coolness against the glass of the quarterwindow.

I believe he's been taken drunk.

Get ye a drink here to sober up on. Hey Bud.

Suttree groaned and fended away with one hand.

At the door of the West Inn they were halted by a shaking head. Suttree hung between friends.

Dont bring him in here.

Callahan pushed past them through the door.

I didnt know that was you, Red. Just bring him on in and set him in the booth yonder.

A group of musicians played with fiddle and guitar a rustic reel and a drunk had taken the floor and begun to waltz like a mummer's bear. One shoesole was pared from its welt and gave to his shuffle a little offbeat slap. In a daring pirouette, vacanteyed and face agrin, he overlisted and careered sideways and crashed among a table of drinkers. They flushed like quail from under the spilled bottles and mugs, wiping at their laps. One had the drunk up by the collar but he saw Callahan smiling at him and grew uncertain and let him go.

Suttree, roused by the commotion, looked up. His friends were drinking at the bar. He reared from the booth and staggered into the center of the floor, looking about wildly.

Where you goin Sut?

He turned. To see who'd spoke. The seeping roachstained walls spun past in a wretched carousel. Two thieves at a table watched him like cats.

J-Bone had him under one arm. Where you goin, Bud?

Sick. Sicky sick.

They staggered toward the washrooms, a shed at the rear of the building and barren save for a toilet bowl. An opaque smoketarred lightbulb that looked like an eggplant screwed into the ceiling. A maze of corroding pipes and conduits.

The walls were papered in old cigarette signs and castoff cardboard up which piss rose wicklike from the floor in dark and flameshaped stains. Suttree stood looking down into the bowl. A beard of dried black shit hung from the porcelain and a clot of stained papers rose and fell with a kind of obscene breathing. J-Bone was holding him by waist and forehead. Hot clotted bile flooded his nostrils.

Walk him around.

Come on Sut.

He looked. They were going toward a dimlit shack. Somewhere beneath him his feet were wandering about.

Fuck it, he said.

Old Sut's all right.

I'm an asshole, he told a wall. He turned, seeking a face. I'm an asshole, J-Bone. A photograph of a family of blacks in some sort of ceremonial robes went past. He raised a hand and fondled the wallpaper's yellowed sleavings.

He was entering a room. Most stately. Nothing to be alarmed. Dark faces watched him through the smoke. Must nods to each. Appear plausible.

He heard voices rising louder. Hoghead's high cackling laugh. Here Sut.

He looked down. He was holding a jellyjar of white whiskey. He raised it and sipped.

I like the hell out of old Suttree, John Clancy said.

He was sitting on the lumpy arm of a stuffed chair. Something was under discussion. A slatshaped negress bent to look at him. He too drunk, she said.

Suttree lifted his glass in mute agreement but she had gone.

Someone rose from the chair. He must have been leaning against them because now he fell into the depths they had vacated, spilling the whiskey on himself. His face lay wedged in a rank corner of the upholstery.

He muttered into the musty springs.

Someone was helping him. He rose from a dream, a ragestrangled face screaming at him. He reeled toward the door. In the corridor he turned and made his way along to the rear of the house, caroming from wall to wall. A black woman stepped from out of the woodwork and came toward him. They feinted. She passed. He clattered into a bureau and fell back and went on. At the rear of the hallway he floundered through a curtain and stood in a small room. Somewhere before him in the dark people were breeding with rhythmic grunts. He backed out. He pulled at a doorknob. His gorge gave way and the foul liquors in his stomach welled and spewed. He tried to catch it in his hands.

God, he said. He was wiping himself on a curtain. He found a door and entered and collapsed in the cool dark. There was a bed there and he tried to crawl under it. It was important that he not be found until he'd had time to rest.

In his stupor he dreamed riots. A window full of glass somewhere collapsed in a crash. He thought he'd heard pistolshots. He struggled to wake but could not. He let his cheek go to a fresh spot on the floor where it was cooler and he slept again.

A dream of shriving came to him. He knelt on the cold stone flags at a chancel gate where the winey light of votive candles cast his querulous shadow behind him. He bent in tears until his forehead touched the stone.

When he woke his head was encoiled by some rank stench. A dull plaque of vomit furred his tongue. Dark faces bent between himself and the dusty bulb burning in the ceiling. Hey boy, hey boy, a voice was saying. He felt himself being jostled from side to side. He closed his eyes. Must ride out this hard weather.

I caint have it. Get him out of here.

He was hauled abruptly erect by his armpits. He looked down. Black hands cupped his chest. Ab? he said. Ab?

She bent to see into his face. Dull moteblown eyeballs webbed with blood. Wheah you buddies at? Hah?

You caint get no sense out of him.

He watched his heels dragging over the linoleum's faded garden.

I see that little white pointedheaded motherfucker he come in with I goin to salivate his ass with a motherfuckin shotgun.

Where are we going?

What he say?

Can you walk? Hey boy.

He caint shit. Get him on out of here.

White motherfucker done puked everwhere.

His feet went banging down some stairs. He closed his eyes. They went through cinders and dirt, his heels gathering small windrows of trash. A dim world receded above his upturned toes, shapes of skewed shacks erupted bluely in the niggard lamplight. The rusting carcass of an automobile passed slowly on his right. Dim scenes pooling in the summer night, wan inkwash of junks tilting against a paper sky, rorschach boatmen poling mutely over a mooncobbled sea. He lay with his head on the moldy upholstery of an old car seat among packingcrates and broken shoes and suncrazed rubber toys in the dark. Something warm was running on his chest. He put up a hand. I am bleeding. Unto my death.

A warm splatter broke across his face, his chest. He twisted his head away, waving one hand. He was wet and he stank. He opened his eyes. A black hand was putting away a limber hosepipe, buttoning, turning. An enormous figure toppled away down the sky toward the mauve and glaucous dawn of the streetlamps.

Sot's skull subsiding, sweet nothingness betide me.

I'd like these shoes soled I dreamt I dreamt. An old bent cobbler looked up from his lasts and lapstone with eyes dim and windowed. Not these, my boy, they are far too far gone, these soles. But I've no others. The old man shook his head. You must forget these and find others now.

Suttree groaned. A switchengine shunted cars in a distant yard, telescoping them in crescendo coupling by coupling to an iron thunder that rattled sashwork all down McAnally Flats. By this clangorous fanfare dull shapes with sidling eyes and pale green teeth congealed with menace out of the dark of the hemisphere. A curtain fell, unspooling in a shock of dust and beetlehusks and dried mousedirt. Amorphous clots of fear that took the forms of nightshades, hags or dwarfs or seatrolls green and steaming that skulked down out of the coils of his poisoned brain with black candles and slow chant. He smiled to see these familiars. Not dread but only homologues of dread. They bore a dead child in a glass bier. Sinister abscission, did I see with my seed eyes his thin blue shape lifeless in the world before me? Who comes in dreams, mansized at times and how so? Do shades nurture? As I have seen my image twinned and blown in the smoked glass of a blind man's spectacles I am, I am.

Trades commenced in the hot summer dawn. He rolled his swollen head, drew up his knees. A breeze stirred a child's sedge house nearby.

I am a mouse in a grassbole crouching. But I can hear come whicket and swish the clocklike blade of the cradle.

He woke with the undersides of his eyelids inflamed by the high sun's hammering, looked up to a bland and chinablue sky traversed by lightwires. A big lemoncolored cat watched him from the top of a woodstove. He turned his head to see it better and it elongated itself like hot taffy down the side of the stove and vanished headfirst in the earth without a sound. Suttree lay with his hands palm up at his sides in an attitude of frailty beheld and the stink that fouled the air was he himself. He closed his eyes and moaned. A hot breeze was coming across the barren waste of burnt weeds and rubble like a whiff of battlesmoke. Some starlings had alighted on a wire overhead in perfect progression like a piece of knotted string fallen slantwise. Crooning, hooked wings. Foul yellow mutes came squeezing from under their fanned tails. He sat up slowly, putting a hand over his eyes. The birds flew. His clothes cracked with a thin dry sound and shreds of baked vomit fell from him.

He struggled to his knees, staring down at the packed black earth between his palms with its bedded cinders and bits of crockery. Sweat rolled down his skull and dripped from his jaw. Oh God, he said. He lifted his swollen eyes to the desolation in which he knelt, the ironcolored nettles and sedge in the reeking fields like mock weeds made from wire, a raw landscape where half familiar shapes reared from the slagheaps of trash. Where backlots choked with weeds and glass and the old chalky turds of passing dogs tended away toward a dim shore of stonegray shacks and gutted auto hulks. He looked down at himself, caked in filth, his pockets turned out. He tried to swallow but his throat constricted in agony. Tottering to his feet he stood reeling in that apocalyptic waste like some biblical relict in a world no one would have.

Two bulletskulled black boys watched him come along the path toward the street, lurching out of the jungle with his head in his hands. Through splayed fingers a wild eye fell upon them.

Hey boys.

They regarded each other.

Which way is town?

They fled on bare soundless feet, spinning a lilac dust. He wiped his eyes and looked after them. In that shimmering heat their figures dissolved crazily until all he saw of them were two small twisted gymnasts hung by wires in a quaking haze. Suttree stood there. He turned slowly. To select a landmark. Some known in this garden of sorrow. He wheeled away down the narrow sandy street like the veriest derelict.

These quarters he soon found to be peopled with the blind and deaf. Dark figures in yard chairs. Propped and rocking in the shade of porches. Old black ladies in flowered gowns who watched impassively the farther shapes of the firmament as he went by. Only a few waifs wide eyed and ebonfaced studied at all the passage of this pale victim of turpitude among them.

At the end of the street the earth fell away into a long gut clogged with a maze of shacks and coops, nameless constructions of tarpaper and tin, dwellings composed of actual cardboard and wapsy tilted batboard jakes that reeled with flies. Whole blocks of hovels cut through by no street but goatpaths and little narrow ways paved with black sand where children and graylooking dogs wandered. He turned and started back, staggering under the heat, his stomach curdling. He wandered into a narrow alleyway and fell to his hands and knees and began to vomit. Nothing would come but a thin green bile and then nothing at all, his stomach contracting in dry and vicious spasms that racked him and left him sweaty and shivering and weak when they ceased. He looked up. Tears warped his sight. A small black child with brightly ribboned wool watched him from a bower in a hedge. With the snuffling of her breath she teased in and out of one nostril a creamy gout of yellow snot. Suttree nodded to her and rose and lurched into the street again.

He chanced a slotted eye through his fingers at the boiling sun. It hung directly overhead. He started across the open lots, going carefully with his thin shoes among jagged rings of jarglass and nailstudded slats. From time to time he would pause to rest, leaning forward with his hands on his knees or squatting on one heel and holding his head. He had sweated through his shirt and it stank horrendously. After a while he came out on another street and he went along until he saw in the distance a cutbank that might be a railroad right of way. He set off across the lots again and down alleys and over fences, trying to keep a fix on his destination. He crossed through a row of back yards by battered cans of swill where clouds of fruitflies droned and swung on the wind and dogs slouched away. A fat negress stepped from an outhouse door hauling up her bloomers. He looked away. She bawled out some name. He went on. A man called out behind him but he didnt look back.

He cut down an alley and went past a row of warehouses and at the end he could see the Dale Avenue market sheds and beyond them the gang tracks of the L&N merging toward the yards. He crossed the tracks and climbed the bank on the far side to Grand Avenue. Two boys were throwing rocks at a row of bottles down in the railway cut. Smoke on the water, one called.

Fuck you, said Suttree.

A wave of nausea washed through him and he paused to rest on an old retaining wall. Looking under his hand he saw dimly the prints of trilobites, lime cameos of vanished bivalves and delicate seaferns. In these serried clefts stone armatures on which once hung the flesh of living fish. He lurched on.

He stopped in the middle of the street before the tall frame house on Grand. Paintless boards smoked a bluish color. He called to a woman sitting on the porch. She leaned forward peering.

Is Jimmy there?

No. He's not come in from last night. Who is that?

Cornelius Suttree.

Lord have mercy I didnt know who that was. No, he's not here, Cornelius. I dont know where he's at.

Well. Thank you mam.

You come see us.

I will. He waved a hand. A police car was turning the corner.

They drove past. Before he got to the end of the street they had circled and pulled up alongside him from behind.

Where you goin, boy?

Home, he said.

Where you live?

Down off Front Avenue.

Beefy face, small eyes looking him over. The face turned away. They said something between them. The one turned back. What's happened to you?

Nothing, he said. I'm all right.

I believe you a little drunk aint ye?

No sir.

Where you been?

He looked at his crusted shoes and took a breath. I was visiting some people over here. I'm just on my way home.

What you got all over the front of you there?

He looked down. When he raised his head again he fixed his eyes across the cruiser's roof upon the bleak row of old houses with their cloven hanging clapboards and their cardboard windowpanes. A few blackened trees stood withering in the heat and in this obscure purgatory a thrush was singing. Mavis. Turdus Musicus. The lyrical shitbird.

I spilled something on me, he said.

You smell like you been dipped in shit.

Two boys were coming along the broken walk. When they saw the cruiser they turned and went back.

The door opened and beefy got out.

Maybe you better get in here, he said.

Dont put that stinkin son of a bitch in here. Call the wagon.

Well. You just stand right there.

I'm not going anywhere.

I'll tell you that, you aint.

He listened dreamily to the crackling of the intercom.

The paddywagon came down off Western and Forest avenues and pulled up in front of the cruiser and two policemen got out. They opened the door and Suttree walked toward it.

Boy if he aint a sweet blossom, one said.

There was a drunk inside sitting on the bench that ran the length of the wagon. Suttree sat opposite. The door banged shut. The drunk leaned forward. Hey old buddy, he said. You got a cigarette? Suttree shut his eyes and rested his head against the side of the van.

At the jail he stood before a little window and was asked to empty his pockets. He managed a faint smile.

The officer at his side nudged him with a nightstick. Empty them pockets, boy.

Suttree lifted his caked shirt. His pockets hung like socks.

You got any identification on you.

No sir.

How come you aint.

I've been robbed.

What's your name.

Jerome Johnson.

The officer was writing. We've had trouble with you before aint we Johnson?

No sir.

He looked up. I bet we aint. Get his belt and his shoelaces there.

They took him along the corridor toward the cells.

They opened the door to a large cage and he went in and they shut the door behind him. Someone slept in one corner, his head in a pool of clabbered void. There were no benches, no place to sit. A concrete scupper ran the perimeter of the cage. Suttree shuddered in a seizure of skullpangs. He sat on the floor. It was cool. After a while he knelt and pressed his head against it.

He must have slept. He heard the turnkey rapping along the bars, calling a name. When he came past Suttree spoke to him.

Can you call me a bondsman back here?

What's your name?

Johnson.

How long you been in?

I dont know. I was asleep.

You got to stay in six hours anyway.

I know. I was wondering if you'd check for me.

The turnkey didnt say he would or wouldnt.

After a while Suttree stretched out on the floor and slept again. He woke from time to time to shift a bone where it wore against the concrete. It was evening before the bondsman came.

A small dapper man in mesh shoes. He looked up at the foul enigma caged before him. You Johnson? he said.

Yes.

You want to make bail?

Yes. I dont have any money. You'll have to call.

Okay. Who do I call? He had out a pad and pencil.

Suttree gave him the number.

All right, he said. Wait here.

Sure, said Suttree. Listen.

What?

Tell them Suttree. But to ask for Johnson.

You can get in a lot of trouble that way.

I can get in a lot the other way.

Okay. What was it again?

Suttree.

The bondsman was shaking his head, writing the new name. You people are really something, he said.

He was back in a few minutes. He aint home, he said.

Did she say when he might be in?

Nope.

What time is it?

Around seven. He flicked his cuff back. Ten after.

Goddamn.

Dont you know nobody else?

No. Look, try it again in an hour, will you? You sure you got the right number?

21505. Right?

That's it.

What's the guy's name anyways?

Jim.

I know that. What's his full name.

Jim Long.

The bondsman gave him a funny little look. Jim Long? he said.

Yes.

Got a brother named Junior?

That's him.

The bondsman looked at him sideways.

What is it? said Suttree.

Shit.

What's the matter?

Why hell fire, the bondsman said. Both of em are right behind you in number eight. They been here since this mornin and cant raise bond neither.

He was looking at Suttree more curiously yet. Suttree's face began to wrinkle and go peculiar. A horse snigger leapt from his lips and his eyes wandered.

You're crazy as shit, said the bondsman.

Suttree sat down on the concrete floor and held his stomach. He sat there shaking and holding himself. You're a real nutwagon, aint ye? said the bondsman.

Later he called through the bars to his friends but they didnt answer. A voice somewhere asked why he didnt shut the fuck up. Later still the lights in the corridor ceiling came on. The man in the corner had not moved and Suttree didnt want to look at him if he were dead. He lay on the floor again and drifted in and out of a poor sleep. He dreamt whole rivers of icewater down his parched throatpipe.

At some hour unknown he woke to sounds of commotion. He had half his hand in his mouth. Looking up he saw a man stoop and swing a bucket of water through the bars over him. Sputtering, he got to his knees.

The bucket clanged to the floor. The man studied him there in his cage. Suttree turned away. In the corner his cellmate was standing. When Suttree looked at him the cellmate said: You dont shut up that hollerin I'm goin to knock your dick in your watchpocket.

He closed his eyes. The gray water that dripped from him was rank with caustic. By the side of a dark dream road he'd seen a hawk nailed to a barn door. But what loomed was a flayed man with his brisket tacked open like a cooling beef and his skull peeled, blue and bulbous and palely luminescent, black grots his eyeholes and bloody mouth gaped tongueless. The traveler had seized his fingers in his jaws, but it was not alone this horror that he cried. Beyond the flayed man dimly adumbrate another figure paled, for his surgeons move about the world even as you and I.

He scouted in the weeds until he found a suitable tin before going out to the road. The kerosene had rendered soft a patch of tar in the roadsurface and he knelt and began to dig it up with an old kitchen knife, stringy viscous gobs of pitch, until he had as much as he needed.

When Daddy Watson came by he had the skiff upturned on the bank and was patiently caulking the seams.

Well, you still alive, the old man said.

Suttree looked up, squinting in the sun. He wiped his nose against his forearm, sitting there holding the tarpot in one hand and the knife in the other. Hello Daddy, he said.

I allowed ye'd gone under.

Not yet. Why?

Didnt see ye. Where ye been?

Suttree daubed the rank black mastic along a seam and pressed it home. Jail, he said.

Hey?

I said I've been in jail.

Have? What for?

I fell in with a bad crowd. What brings you over here?

The old man pushed back his striped engineer's cap and readjusted it. Just on my way to town. Thought long as I was this close I'd check on ye. I allowed ye must of gone under.

I'm still in business. How's everything on the railroad?

Just by god awful.

Suttree waited for an enlargement upon this but none seemed coming. He looked up. The old man was rocking on his heels, watching.

What's the problem, Daddy?

Just railroadin is the problem, son. It's the nature of it, I'm convinced. He hauled forth an enormous railroader's timepiece and checked it and put it back.

How's old number seventy-eight?

Lord love her she's old and wore out about like me but she's faithful as a dog. Ort to give her a gold watch and chain.

He was leaning forward watching over Suttree's shoulder as he caulked.

You know, he said. I wish I could get you to come over to my yard with that stuff. I got a leak in my caboose roof needs somethin done about it.

Suttree bent forward and averted his face. Got a what? he shouted, eyes half closed with mirth.

Say I got leaky roof. Caboose roof.

Suttree shook his head. He looked up at the old man. Well, he said. If I've got any left I'll bring it over.

The old man straightened up. That's neighborly of ye and I'd take it as a favor, he said. He was hauling out the watch again.

I'd best get on to town if I'm to get to the store fore it closes.

What time is it, Daddy?

Four nineteen.

Well. Stop again when you can stay longer.

I'll do it, said the railroader. And dont forget to save me some of that there pitch if you've got it to spare.

Okay.

I allowed ye'd gone under when I didnt see ye on the river.

No.

Well.

He watched the old man go across the steaming fields, tottering stiffly in his overalls. When he reached the tracks he turned and lifted one hand farewell. Suttree lifted his chin and turned back to his work.

When he had the underside of the skiff daubed up he set the tar by and turned the skiff over and eased it along the mud into the river. He took the rope and walked out along the gallery of the houseboat and tethered it to the railing. He took the oars from where they stood against the side of the house and lowered them into the skiff. Slouched on the railing he watched the dried silt in the bottom of the skiff darken along the joints where the boards would swell shut in the water. As he stood there the five oclock freight ran out on the trestle downriver. Crossing the high span of black wickered steel like an enormous millipede, balls of smoke coughing from the blowhole in the engine's head and the sootcolored cars clattering after and leaving the air curiously serene behind the racket of their passage.

He pulled a bottle of orange soda from the river by a long cord and uncapped it and sat with his feet propped on the rail taking cool sips. A black woman appeared on the deck of the houseboat upriver and slung two rattling bags of trash overboard and went in again. Suttree leaned his head against the hot boards and watched the river go past.

The shadow of the bridge had begun to lie long oblique and sprawling upstream and pigeons ascending into its concrete understructure evoked upon the water before him shapes of skates rising batwinged from the river floor to feed in the creeping dusk. He closed his eyes and opened them again. Plovers along the shore jerking like wired birds in a shooting gallery. Down there a pipe piping gouts of soap-curd and blue sewage. Dusk deepened. Swifts vanished back over the pewter face of the river toward the city. On thin falcon wings night-hawks dipped and wheeled and a bat fluttered past, circled, returned.

Inside Suttree lit a lamp and adjusted the wick. With the same match he lit the burners of the little kerosene stove, two rosettes of pale blue teeth in the gloom. He set a saucepan of beans to warm and got down his skillet and sliced onions into it. He un-wrapped a packet of hamburger. Small moths kept crossing the mouth of the lampchimney and spinning burntwinged into the hot grease. He picked them out on the tines of the brass fork with which he tended the cookery and flipped them against the wall. When all was ready he scraped the food from the pans onto a plate and took it together with the lamp to the small table by the window and laid everything out on the oilcloth and sat and ate leisurely. A barge passed upriver and he watched through the cracked glass the dip and flicker of her spotlight negotiating the narrows beneath the bridge, the long white taper shifting in quick sidelong sweeps, the shape of the beam breaking upriver over the trees with incredible speed and crossing the water like a comet. A white glare flooded the cabin and passed on. Suttree blinked. The dim shape of the barge came hoving. He watched the red lights slide in the dark. The houseboat rocked easy in the wake, the drums mumbling under the floor and the skiff sidling and bump-ing outside in the night. Suttree wiped his plate with a piece of bread and sat back. He fell to studying the variety of moths pressed to the glass, resting his elbows on the sill and his chin on the back of his hand. Supplicants of light. Here one tinted easter pink along the edges of his white fur belly and wings. Eyes black, triangular, a robber's mask. Furred and wizened face not unlike a monkey's and wearing a windswept ermine shako. Suttree bent to see him better. What do you want?

When the River Queen passed he was in bed, drifting toward sleep. He heard the labored sludging sound of her wheel beyond his window. As if she bore through liquid mud. A party on deck in song. The voices carrying the water's acoustic calm, the old sternwheeler plying upriver with hard liquor and ladies of quality, soft lights above the green baize blackjack tables and the barman polishing the glasses and the danceband musicians leaning on the rail between sets, until the voices waned with distance and the last echoes honed away to a faint murmur of wind.

Right along here anywheres is okay, said Harrogate, pointing languidly out the open truck window.

The driver glanced sidelong and bored. You got to have a address, peckerhead.

What about the Smoky Mountain Market?

That aint a address. It's got to be where people lives.

He looked about, sitting up in the front of the cab like a child. What about the church yonder? he said.

Church?

Yeah.

Well, I dont know.

Do they not hold with goin to church?

The driver cut the wheel and swung left and pulled up in front of the church. All right, he said. Get your ass out.

He hopped down and reached and banged the door shut. Thanks, he called, waving one hand up to the driver. The driver didnt look. He pulled away and the truck disappeared down the street in the noon traffic.

Harrogate came batting his way through the jungle of kudzu that overhung the bluffs above the river until he found a red clay gully of a path going down the slope. He followed along through lush growths of poison ivy and past enormous mummy shapes of vinestrangled trees, banks of honeysuckle dusted in ocher, into a brief cindery wood where grew black sumacs, pokeweeds gorged with sooty drainage whose clustered fruit gleamed small baubles of a poisonous ebon blue.

The path switchbacked and ran out on a cutbank above an abandoned railsiding. He descended into the roadbed and went on. The old right of way lay dim among the weeds, the rails rusted, curving away over rotted ties and dark slag. He trudged along happily in his outland garb, his thin shoes cupping the rails. The river ran below him surly and opaque and shaping itself on the curious forms of limestone that jutted from the bank. By and by he came upon two fishbutchers slick with blood by an old retaining wall, holding a goodsized carp between them. He greeted them with a smile, a curiously attired person emerging from the shrubbery. They stayed their gorestained hands a moment to study him while the fish bowed and shuddered.

Hidy, he said.

These two regarded each other a moment and then looked down

at him. Blood dripped from the fish. Blood lay among the leaves in little jagged grails of bright vermilion. One beckoned with a dripping claw. Hey boy. Come here.

What do you want?

Come here a minute.

I got to get on. He was going along sideways over the ties.

Just come here a minute.

He sidled away and broke into a run. They watched him without expression until he had gone from sight in the weeds and then turned back to their fish.

A half mile down the track he came upon rolling stock on a siding, an old black iron locomotive with inscriptions of faded gilt and wooden cars quietly rotting in the sun. Creepers threaded the wrecked windows of the coaches, ancient and chalky brown with their riveted seams and welted coamings like something proofed for descents into the sea. He walked the aisle between the dusty green and gnawn brocaded seats. A bird flew. He came down the iron steps to the ground. A voice said: All right, young feller, off of them there cars.

Harrogate turned and beheld an overalled railroader coming down the tracks toward him, an oldtimer in a striped cap with a heavy brass watchchain hanging from him.

The country mouse turned to see which way to run but the man had paused to stoop above a rusted truck with his longspouted oilcan. He was shaking his head and muttering. Old black engine oil dripped from a seized journal. He raised himself erect and checked the time by the clocksized watch he wore in his bibpocket. Where's your buddies at today? he said.

Harrogate looked about to see if it was he that was addressed. A cat regarded him dreamily from the domed roof of the coach, belly weighed with pigeon eggs against the warm tar.

It's just me, said Harrogate.

The old man squinted at him. Your daddy aint a railroad man is he?

No.

I allowed maybe I knowed ye.

I'm new around here.

I dont know ye then.

My name's Gene Harrogate, said Harrogate coming forward. But the old man shook his head and waved him away and climbed laboriously over the couplings between the cars. I know all the people I want to know, he said.

You dont know old Suttree do ye? Harrogate called after him, but the old man didnt answer.

Harrogate went on down the line, under the old steel bridge and out from the shadow of the bluff past a lumberyard and a slaughterhouse. Rich odors of pinepitch and manure. The siding switched off among the yards and he crossed a field with a ragged camp of shacks sketched into the distance and a weedy sea of auto wrecks washed up on the flank of a hill. He came out upon a narrow road and after a while he came to a gate construed from an old iron bedframe all overgrown with dusty morninglories and hung about with hummingbirds like windtoys on strings. In the yard lay a man in greasy overalls with his head resting on a tire.

Hey, said Harrogate

The man reared up wildly and looked about.

I'm a huntin Suttree.

We're closed, said the man. He rose and crossed the yard toward a tarpaper shack covered with hanging hubcaps, no two alike. Bumpers were stacked against the wall and water dripped from a tap into a gastank halved open with a torch. Beyond in the rank and steamy foliage wrecked cars crouched and everywhere in this lush waste were blooming flowers and shrubs.

Look around if you want, the man called. Dont bother me. Dont steal nothin. He disappeared into the shack and Harrogate pushed open the gate and entered. The gate was weighted with a chainload of gears and closed gently behind him. The air was rich with humus and he could smell the flowers. Wild datura with pale strange trumpets and harebells among the debris. Great gangly rosebushes covered with dying blooms that collapsed at a touch. Phlox lavender and pink along a leaning wall of cinderblock and loosestrife and columbine among the iron inner works of autos scattered in the grass. He crossed to the shed and peered through the open door. The man was lying stretched out on a car seat.

Hey, Harrogate said.

The man lifted his arm from his face. What in the name of God do you want anyway? he said.

Harrogate was peering about in the gloom of this small hut crammed with the salvage of highway disasters. Faint country music came from a car radio in the floor. Tires rose in black serried pillars and batteries lay everywhere suppurating a dry white foam.

I'm a huntin old Suttree, he said.

He aint here.

Where might I find him at do ye reckon?

Web City.

Where's that at?

Up a spider's ass.

The junkman put his arm back across his eyes. Harrogate watched him. It was incredibly hot in the shack and it reeked of tar. He studied the outlandish collection of autoparts. You a junkman? he said.

What did you need?

Nothin.

What are ye sellin?

I aint sellin nothin.

Well let's buy or sell one.

I thought you was closed.

Now I'm open. I guess you've got a bunch of hubcaps you've stole.

No I aint.

Where are they?

I aint got none. I'm just out of the workhouse now for stealin watermelons.

I aint buyin no watermelons.

Harrogate shifted to the other foot. His clothes did not move. You live here? he said.

Mmm.

It's neat. I bet a feller could fix hisself a place like this for next to little or nothin, couldnt he?

The man's toes were pointed toward the ceiling and they spread and closed again in a gesture of noncommitment.

Boy I wisht I had me a place.

The man lay there.

Hey, Harrogate said.

The man groaned and rolled over and reached under the car seat and pulled out a quart jar of white whiskey and sat erect enough to funnel a drink down his gullet. Harrogate watched. The man deftly reapplied the twopiece lid and laying the half filled jar against his ribs he subsided into rest and silence once again.

Hey, said Harrogate.

He opened one eye. Boy, he said, what's wrong with you?

94

Nothin. I'm all right.

You want a job?

Doin what?

Doin what, doin what, the man said to the ceiling.

What kind of a job?

The man sat and swung his feet to the clay floor, the jar cradled in his arm. He shook his sweaty head. After a minute he looked up at Harrogate. I aint got time to mess with people too sorry to work, he said.

I'll work.

Okay. You see that frontended forty-eight Ford out there? That ragtop?

I dont know. They's a bunch out there.

This one is like new. I need the upholstery out of it fore it ruins. Seats, carpets, doorpanels. And I need em cleaned.

What are you payin?

What'll you take?

Harrogate looked at the ground. A black swarf packed with small parts in a greasy mosaic. I'll take two dollars, he said.

I'll give ye a dollar.

Dollar and a half.

You're on. They's wrenches in that box yonder and a screwdriver. The seats unbolts from underneath. Them door and winderhandle scutches are spring loaded you push in on em and knock the pins out with a nail. Armrests unscrews. When you get em all out I got some soap and they's a watertap at the side of the house.

Okay.

The man set down the jar and rose and went to the door. He pointed out the car. It was accordioned to half its length. Bring them sunvisors too, he said.

What happened to it?

Run head on into a semi. Froze the speedometer on the peg. You'll see it.

Harrogate looked at the car in some wonder. How many was in it?

Four or five. Bunch of boys. They found one in a field about two days later.

Did it kill em?

The junkman looked down at Harrogate. Did it what? he said.

Did it kill em.

Why no. I think one of em got a skint knee is all.

Boy I dont see how it kept from killin em.

The junkman shook his head wearily and went back in.

Harrogate got the toolbox and went out to the car. He pulled on one crumpled door and pried at it. He went around to the other one but it had no handle.

Hey, he said, standing in the door of the shack again.

What now?

I caint get in. The doors is jammed.

You may have to jack em open. Go in through the top and take one of them jacks yonder and some blocks. And quit botherin me.

He went back out, small apprentice, clambering up on the decklid and climbing down through the bows and stays and rags of canvas into the interior of the car. It smelled richly of leather and mildew and something else. The windshields were broken out and along the jagged jaws of glass in the channels hung cured shreds of matter and small bits of cloth. The upholstery was red and the blood that had dried in spattered shapes over it was a deep burgundy black. He propped his feet against one door and gave it a good kick and it fell open. Some kind of globular material hung down over the steering column. He climbed out of the car and bent down to find the heads of the bolts beneath the seats. The carpeting had been rained on and was lightly furred with pale blue mold. Something small and fat and wet with an umbilical looking tail lying there. A sort of slug. He picked it up. A human eye looked up at him from between his thumb and forefinger.

He set it carefully back where he'd gotten it and looked around. It was hot and very quiet in the little yard. He reached and picked it up again and studied it a minute and set it back and rose from his knees and went toward the gate, holding his hand before him, down the road toward the river.

After he'd washed his hand for a while and squatted and thought about things he started back toward the bridge. There was a lower path that kept to the very brim of the river, winding over roots and along blackened shelves of stone. Fragile mats of trampled growth hanging over the water. Harrogate studied the shape of the city cross-river as he went.

Under the shadow of the bridge the bare red earth lay in a strip of sunless blight. Rusty baitcans, tangled strands of nylon fishline among the rocks. He came out of the weeds and up past the ragpicker's firepit with its stale odor of smoked stones and stopped to study the darkness under the concrete arch. When that ragged troll appeared from behind his painted rock Harrogate nodded affably. Hidy, he said.

The ragpicker scowled.

I guess it's done took in under here, aint it?

The old hermit made no answer but Harrogate seemed not to mind. He came closer, looking things over. Boy, he said. You got it fixed up slick in under here, aint ye?

The ragpicker raised slightly up like a nesting bird disturbed.

I'll bet that there old bed sleeps good, said Harrogate pointing.

You better look out, spoke a voice from the high arches. That old man is mean as a snake.

Harrogate craned his neck to see who'd said it. Fat birds the color of slate crooned among the concrete trusses overhead. Who's that? he called, his voice returning all hollow and strange.

You better run. He's known to carry a pistol.

Harrogate looked at the ragpicker. The ragpicker flapped about and bared his teeth. He looked up again. Hey, he called.

There was no answer. Where's he at? said Harrogate. But the ragpicker just mumbled and withdrew from sight.

Harrogate approached closer and peered into the gloom. The old man was seated in a burst chair at the rear of his quarters. There were odds and ends of furniture standing all around on the rank dirt floor and there was a vaguely eastern carpet with a raw cord warp that was eating away the serried minarets and there were oil lamps and stolen roadlanterns and cracked plaster statuary that stood like ghosts in the semidark and earthen crocks and crates of bottles and bricabrac and mounded troves of shoddy and great tottering sheaves of newsprint and heaps of rags. The bed was old and ornate with crown and finial in cast brass.

Caint you read, boy? the old man's voice piped sepulchral from his lair.

Not real good.

That there sign says to keep out.

They lord, I wouldnt come in without bein asked. You got it fixed up slick in here, I'll say that.

The ragpicker grunted. He had his feet up in the chair with him and his thin polished shins shone like naked bones crossed there.

Dont they nobody bother ye down here?

I get a loose fool or two come by ever now and then, said the ragman.

How long ye been here?

97

About that long, the old man said, spacing a random measure between his palms.

Harrogate grinned and rose to the challenge. You know the difference tween a grocery store fly and a hardware store fly?

The ragman's eyes grew even colder.

Well, the grocery store fly lights on the beans and peas, and the hardware store fly lights on the nails and screws. Harrogate folded suddenly and slapped his thigh and cackled like a stricken fowl.

Boy why dont you get on down the road wherever you come from or was goin to one and leave me the son of a bitching hell alone?

Hell, I just stopped to say Hidy. I didnt mean nothin by it.

The old man closed his eyes.

Say listen. Is they anyone under the far end yonder?

The ragman looked. Across the river down the long aisle of arches lay the distant facing image of his own shelter. Why dont you go see? he said.

Danged if I wont, said Harrogate. If it aint spoke for we'll be neighbors. He waved and started up around the side of the bridge. We'll get along, he called back. I can get along with anybody.

It was midafternoon when he crossed into the city and descended the steep path at the end of the bridge, swinging down through a jungle of small locust trees filled with long spikes and blackened starlings that flew shrieking out over the river and circled and came back. He emerged onto the barren apron of clay beneath the bridge. Small black children playing there in the cool. Below them a black and narrow street. One of the children saw him and then they all looked up, three soft dark faces watching.

Hidy, he said.

They squatted immobile. Small wooden trucks and autos stalled in streets graded out with a broken shingle. Beyond them a brown clapboard house, foreyard a moonscape in clay and coaldust, a few sorry chickens crouched in the shade. A black man swung reposed and prone on a bench hung by chains from the porch ceiling and a line of faded wash steamed in the windless heat.

What are you all doin?

The oldest spoke. We aint done nothin.

You all live over yonder?

They admitted it with solemn nods.

Harrogate looked about. He reckoned he'd not be put to living next door to niggers leastways. He climbed down the bank and came out on the road and went on downriver past rows of shacks. The road was pocked and buckled and after a while it went to sand and dried mud and then nothing. A thin path wandered on through weeds hung with wastepaper. Harrogate followed after.

The path cut through heatstricken lots and fallow land and passed under a high trestle that crossed the river. A tramp's midden among the old stone footings where gray bones lay by rusted tins and a talus of jarshards. A ring of blackened bricks and the remains of a fire. Harrogate wandered about, poking at things with a stick. Pieces of burnt foil sunburst in blue and yellow. Dredging charred relics from the ashy sleech. Melted glass that had reseized in the helical bowl of a bedspring like some vitreous chrysalis or chambered whelk from southern seas. He dusted it on his sleeve and carried it with him. Across a smoking alluvial strewn with refuse to the faint rise of the railtracks and the river beyond.

A row of black fishermen sat along the ties where the tracks crossed the creek, their legs dangling above the oozing sewage. They watched their corks tilt below them in the creek mouth and did not turn to see him teeter past along the rail, his head averted above the sulphurous fart reek that seeped up between the ties.

You all doin any good? he sang out.

A baleful face looked up and looked away again. He stood watching for a while and then went on, tottering in the heat. The sun like a bunghole to a greater hell beyond. On the hill above him he could see the brickwork of the university and a few fine homes among the trees. He came out at length onto a small riverside street. His sneakers lifting from the hot tar with smacking sounds. A sidelong dog receded at a half trot before him down the street toward the shade of some lilac bushes by one of the combustible looking shacks there. Harrogate studied the landscape beyond. A patch of gray corn by the riverside, rigid and brittle. A vision of bleak pastoral that at length turned him back toward the city again.

He wandered Knoxville's sadder regions for the better part of the afternoon, poking in alleys, probing old cellars, the dusty lees or nether dank of public works. Him wide eyed in his juryrigged apparel not unlike some small apostate to the race itself, pausing here at a wall to read what he could of inscriptions in cloudy chalk, the agenda of anonymous societies, assignation dates, personal intelligence on the habits of local females. A row of bottles gone to the wall for stoning lay in brown and green and crystal ruin down a sunlit corridor and one upright severed cone of yellow glass rose from the paving like a flame. Past these gnarled ashcans at the alley's mouth with their crusted rims and tilted gaping maws in and out of which soiled dogs go night and day. An iron stairwell railing shapeless with birdlime like something brought from the sea and small flowers along a wall reared from the fissured stone.

He paused at some trash in a corner where a warfarined rat writhed. Small beast so occupied with the bad news in his belly. It must have been something you ate. Harrogate crouched on his heels and watched with interest. He prodded it gently with a curtainrod he'd found. From a doorway a girl watched him motionless and thin and unkempt. A crude doll dressed in rags with huge eyes darkly dished and guttering in her bird's skull. Harrogate looked up and caught her watching him and she went all squirmy with her hands pulling at the raveled hem of her dress for a moment before her head snapped back and he could see a ropeveined claw clutched in her hair and the girl jerked backward and disappeared through an open door. He looked down at the rat again. It was moving one rear leg in slow circles as if to music. It must have felt some cold pneuma pass for it suddenly shivered and then it let out its feet slowly until they came to rest. Harrogate poked it with the curtainrod but the rat only rolled loosely in its skin. Fleas were running out at the lean gray face.

He rose and nudged the rat with his toe and then went on down the alley. He crossed a tarred street bedded with bottlecaps and bits of metal, scattered patterns in niello and one improbable serpent, the ribbed spine polished by traffic and partly coiled in a pale bone omen he could not read. Overhead the bowls of stoned out polelamps. A lank black slattern stood hipshot in a doorframe. Hey boydove, you gettin any gravel for yo goose? Whoopla laughter scuttling after him and a gold tooth winksome, bawdy dogstar in the ordurous jaws of fellatio major.

He went where torpid blacks crouched or drowsed in doorways, stoops, on corners almost in the traffic. Old men like effigies with fingers laced and capped upon the heads of canes between their knees. In suits thought long extinct, perforated two-tone shoes, socks rolled in obscene tubes about their thin black ankles. A hawkfaced ebon freak importuned him, sussurous, long underlip leaking a clear drool. Flies clove the air like comets. He passed on. Eyes averted. Dark matrons at the upper windows in hot and airless dishabille, chocolate breasts leaning. Dusklovers. Ancillary disciples to the rise of night.

He'd come from the dwellingstreets of whites to those of blacks and no gray middle folk did he see.

Summer dusk had crept long and blue and shadows risen high upon the western building faces when he came up Gay Street. He went along the shopfronts like a misplaced poacher, his eyes squirreling about and his broken clown's sneakers flapping. At Lockett's he paused to admire dusty charlatan's props in the window, small boxes of sneeze powder, cigars laced with cordite, a stamped tin inkstain. Stapled to display cards from which the sun had bleached all message. A china dog bowbacked and grunting. Harrogate filled with admiration at such things. He stepped slightly back to note the merchant's name and then went on. Passing under the Comer's Sport Center sign, a steep stairwell and the muted clack of balls overhead. There it is, he said. Bigger'n life.

He turned up Union Avenue, past the Roxie Theatre, Webfoot Watts and Skinny Green on the bill with all-girl revue. Harrogate stepping around to see the tariffs. The girl looked down from her glass cage like a cat. He smiled and drew back. He went down Walnut Street past hardware stores and beer taverns and ramshackle poultry shops. He swung up Wall Avenue and into Market Square. His small face peering through the windows of the Gold Sun Cafe where supper plates were being sopped clean and rawlooking girls went up and back in their soiled white uniforms.

Down Market Street countrymen sat beneath canopies in canebottomed chairs or on upended peachcrates or perched on the leadcolored fenders of old Fords fitted out with crude truckbeds nailed up out of boards. Folks putting up their stuffs for this day, shops being closed. A few sunfaded awnings winched shut. Two roustabouts collected a beggar from the walkway and set him in a truck. Harrogate went on. An old man seated before a basket of turnips hissed him and gestured with his chin, seeking a buyer, Harrogate to his worn eyes no worse a prospect than others coming along. Harrogate watching the gutters for anything edible fallen from the trucks. By the time he reached the end of the street he had a small bouquet of frazzled greenstuffs and a bruised tomato. He went into the markethouse and washed these things at the drinking fountain marked White and ate them while he wandered down the vast hall with its rich reek of meat and produce and woodchaff. A few vendors squatted yet in their stalls, old women with tawed faces and farmers with their quilted napes. A honeyseller sitting quietly in immaculate blue chambray, his jars on the low table before him arranged faultlessly, the labels marshaled aislewise. Harrogate went by, chewing his lettuce. Past a long glass coffin where a few lean fish leered up with cold and golden eyes from their beds of salted ice. Windchimes tinkled overhead in the slow fanwash. He pushed open the heavy doors at the end of the hall with their hundred years' accretion of navalgray paint and stepped out into the summer night. Standing there wiping his hands on the front of him, his eyes drawn by the cryptic piping of hot neon across the night and by the chittering of goatsuckers aloft in the upflung penumbra of the city's lights. A streetsweeper puttered past with his cart. Harrogate crossed the street and went up the alley. A family of trashpickers were packing flat cartons onto a child's wagon, the children scurrying among the rancid cans like rats and as graylooking. None spoke. They had tied the folded boxes down with twine, a parlous and tottering load that the man steadied with one hand while the woman drew the cart along and the children made forays into trashbins and cellar doors, watching Harrogate the while.

He made his way by alleys and small dark streets to the lights at Henley Street where he'd earlier spied a church lawn. Here he found himself a nest among the curried clumps of phlox and boxwood and curled up like a dog. He had a few things he'd collected in his pocket and he took these out and set them alongside in the edging of mulch and lay back again in the grass. He could feel under his back the rumble of trucks passing in the street. He shifted his hips. He folded his hands behind his head. He must prop his upturned toes together to ease the weight of the enormous shoes from his bird's ankles. After a while he slipped them off and lay back again. Yellow lamplight clung in his lashes. He watched insects rise and wheel there. A hunting bat cut through the cone of light and sucked them scattering. They re-formed slowly. Soon two bats. Veering and rending the placid life that homed to ash in the columnar light. Harrogate awonder at how they did not collide.

He was sitting up in the shrubbery long before good daylight, waiting for the day to come for him to set forth in, watching the glozy headlights come out of the fog on the bridge and draw past him into the town. Shapes evolved out of the gray dawn. What he'd thought to be another indigent hosteled on the grass below him was a newspaper winded up against a bush. He rose and stretched and crossed the lawn to the street and went toward Market where all sorts of country commerce had begun.

Harrogate eased his way among the rotting trucks and carts at the curbside until he had the lay of things and then his scrawny hand darted out and seized a peach from a basket and tucked it down the windsock of a pocket that hung inside his trousers. The next thing he knew an old lady had him by the collar and was beating him over the head with a mealscoop. She was yelling in his face and spraying him with snuffjuice. Shit, said Harrogate, trying to pull away. A long ripping sound ensued.

Quit it. You're tearin my goddamned shirt.

Bong bong bong went the mealscoop on his bony head.

Give it back, she squalled.

Hell fire. Here. He thrust the peach at her and she immediately turned loose of him and took the peach and wobbled back to her truck and restored it to the basket.

He felt his head. It was all knotty. Shit a brick, he said. I didnt want the goddamned thing that bad. A legless beggar mounted on a board like a piece of ghastly taxidermy had come awake to laugh at him. Fuck you, said Harrogate. The beggar shot forward on ballbearing wheels and seized Harrogate's leg and bit it.

Shit! screamed Harrogate. He tried to pull away but the beggar had his teeth locked in the flesh of his calf. They danced and circled, Harrogate holding to the top of the beggar's head. The beggar gave a shake of his head and a tug in a last effort to remove the flesh from Harrogate's legbone and then turned loose and receded smoothly to his place against the wall and took up his pencils again. Harrogate went limping down the street holding his leg. Crazy sons of bitches, he said, hobbling among the shoppers. He was almost in tears.

He crossed through the markethouse and went up the other side of the square. Something was pulling at his shoe. He bent to see. Chewing gum. He sat in the gutter with a stick and scraped at it. Turning a pink blob of it on the end of the stick . . .

Harrogate coasted by the blind man in front of Bower's, watching the crowd. No one watched back. He returned, bent lightly, jabbed with his stick at the cigarbox in the blind man's lap. The blind man raised his head and put one hand over the box and looked about. Harrogate going up the street tilted the stick. A dime clung to the end of it. He swung about and came back. The blind man sat warily. Paleblue and moldgrown grapes caved and wrinkled in his eyesockets. Harrogate executed a fencer's thrust and came up with a nickel.

Hey you cocksucker, called the blind man.

Fuck you, said Harrogate, skipping nimbly on.

He went into the Gold Sun and ordered coffee and doughnuts, sitting at the counter among the morning smells of fried sausage and eggs. He rolled back the folds of his trouserlegs and examined his wound. The beggar's illspaced teeth had printed two little sickle shapes, the flesh blue, small pinlets of blood. Harrogate wet a paper napkin in his water glass and laved it over his queer stigmata. Son of a bitch, he muttered. He drank the coffee and slid his cup forward for more.

In the streets again he rubbed his little belly and set out for Comer's. Climbing the stairs. A small bent person at the landing watched. Who knew every cop in town in or out of uniform. Harrogate pushed open the green door with its wiremesh covered glass and entered. To his surprise the place was nearly empty. A blond youth was practising three rail banks at the second table. The rack was brushing the tables in the rear. A whimsical man with a paunch hanging over his changeapron and jaws knobby with tobacco. At Harrogate's elbow tickertape hung from a glass bell and several old men sat along the benches to the front of the hall and watched the day start in the street below.

Harrogate went to the counter where a man in an eyeshade was counting money. You know Suttree? he said.

What? said the man.

Suttree.

Ask Jake. He tilted his head toward the rear of the hall and went on counting. Harrogate went wobbling down the aisle past the tables, the cues racked up on the walls like weapons in some ancient armory. Hey, said the blond youth.

What?

You want to play some nine ball?

I dont know how to play.

Rotation?

I aint never shot no pool.

The blond youth studied him a moment, chalking his cue with a little rotary motion. He bent to shoot.

You know Suttree?

He stroked. The one ball went down the table, circled the racked balls from rail to rail and returned to drop in the upper corner pocket. Harrogate waited for the shooter to answer but the shooter took the ball from the pocket and set it up and bent again with his cue and did not look up. Harrogate went on to the rear.

You Jake? he said.

Yep.

You know Suttree?

He turned and looked down at Harrogate. He spat into a steel cuspidor on the floor and wiped his mouth with the back of his hand. Yeah, he said. I know him.

You know where he's at?

What'll you take for them britches?

Harrogate looked down. Them's all the ones I got, he said.

Well. He aint here.

I was wonderin if you might know where he's at.

Home I reckon.

Well where's he live?

He lives down on the river. I believe in one of them houseboats.

Houseboat?

Yep. Jake bent, the change in his apronpocket swinging. He began to brush the dust toward the corner pocket. Harrogate had turned to go.

What about that shirt?

What about it?

How would you trade?

Hell fire, said Harrogate. Yourn'd do me for a overcoat.

Jake grinned. Come back, little buddy, he said.

At the bottom of Gay Street he stood leaning on the bridge rail looking down at the waterfront. There's the goddamned houseboats, he said.

Coming down the steep and angled path behind the tall frame houses he thought he heard a voice. He tilted back his head to see. Half out from a housewindow high up the laddered face of soot-caulked clapboards hung some creature. Sprawled against the hot and sunpeeled siding with arms outstretched like a broken puppet. Hah, he called down. Spawn of Cerberus, the devil's close kin.

Harrogate clutched his lower teeth.

A long finger pointed down. Child of darkness, of Clooty's brood, mind me.

Shit, said Harrogate.

The window figure had raised itself to address some other audience.

See him! Does he not offend thee? Does such iniquity not rise stinking to the very heavens?

This viperous evangelist reared up, his elbows cocked and goat's eyes smoking, and thrust a bony finger down. Die! he screamed. Perish a terrible death with thy bowels blown open and black blood boiling from thy nether eye, God save your soul amen.

Shit fire, said Harrogate, scurrying down the path with one hand over his head. When he reached the street he looked back. The figure had wheeled to a new window the better to see the boy past his house and he leaned now with his face pressed to the glass, his dead jaundiced flesh splayed against the pane and one eye walled up in his head, a goggling visage misshapen with hatred. Harrogate went on. Great godamighty, he said.

He went down Front Street past a rickety store where blacks lolled and eyed his advent doubtfully and he took a dogpath across the gray fields toward the shantyboats, emerging onto the railway with his curious trousers striped with sootprints of the weeds he'd forded, the air hot and breathless with the smell of cinders and creosote and the fainter reaches of oil and fish standing off in a sort of haze along the river itself.

He climbed the mudstained cleated plank of the first houseboat and tapped at the door. A small eddy of garbage and empty bottles circled slowly in the water beneath him. When the door opened he was looking into the face of a coalcolored woman who wore an agate taw in one eyesocket. What you wants? she said.

I thought maybe old Suttree lived here but I dont reckon he does.

She didnt answer.

You dont know where he lives do ye?

Who you huntin?

Suttree.

What you wants with him.

He's a old buddy of mine.

She looked him up and down. He aint goin to mess with you, she said.

Shit, said Harrogate. We go way back, me and Suttree do.

Suttree was up at first light to run his lines. The gray shape of the city gathering out of the fog, upriver a gull, pale and alien bird in these midlands. On the bridge the lights of the cars crossed like candles in the mist.

Maggeson was already on the river when he set forth, standing like some latterday Charon skulling through the fog. With a long pole he hooked condoms aboard and into a pail of soapy water. Suttree paused to watch him but the old man drifted past without looking up, standing with prurient vigilance, in the cropped shore currents watchful and silent.

Suttree rowed in a sunless underregion of swirling mists, through bowls of cold and seething smoke. The bridgepier loomed and faded. Downriver a dredger. Two men at the rail smoking, stitched out of the fog and gone again, their voices faint above the puckered chug of the engine. The red of the wheelhouse light went watery pale and faded out. He oared slowly, waiting for the fog to lift.

When he ran his lines some of the fish were dead. He cut the droppers and watched them slide and sink. The rising sun dried and warmed him.

He was back by midmorning and sat on the rail and cleaned his catch. Ab's cat came and perched like an owl and watched him. He handed it a fish head and it bared a razorous yawn of teeth and took the head delicately and went back along the rail. Suttree skinned two catfish and wrapped them in newsprint and washed his knife and his hands in the river and rose.

Going up the river path he passed two boys fishing.

Hey boys, he said.

They turned huge eyes up at him.

Doin any good?

Naw.

Their bobbers lay quietly in the scum. Ringent pools of gas kept erupting in oily eyes on the surface. Mauves and yellows from the spectrum guttered and slewed in the dead current.

You boys like to fish?

We dont gots to.

Good for you, said Suttree.

At Ab's place he handed her the fish at the door and she motioned him past into the room. A thick funk of stale beer and smoke. She folded back the paper, old news repeated mirrorwise on the pale ribbed flesh. She poked a black finger in the meat.

Where's the old man? said Suttree.

He's in there. Go on.

In the far corner sat an enormous figure obscured in the gloom. Come in Youngblood.

Hey.

Set down. Bring the man a beer old woman.

I dont want anything.

Bring him a Redtop.

She shuffled past in her ruptured mules through a curtain to the rear. A squalid sunlight fell briefly. Everywhere from cracks or knotholes small hieroglyphs of light lay about in the cabin, on table and floor and across the cardboard beer signs.

When she came back she leaned across Suttree and clicked a wet bottle down on the little stone table. He nodded to her and raised it and drank. The black man now coalesced out of the semidark seemed to fill half the room. Where you from in the world, Youngblood, he said.

Right here. Knoxville.

Knoxville, he said. Old Knoxville town.

She was clattering about in the back room. After a while she came from behind the curtain again and sat in her chair with her feet up. She was instantly asleep, the blind eye half open like a drowsing cat's, her mouth agape. Toes peered from the mules like little clusters of dark mice. On her broad face two intersecting circles, fairy ring or hagstrack, the crescent welts of flesh like a sacerdotal brand on some stone age matriarch. Annular treponema. Read here why he falls in the streets. Another Jena, another time.

Suttree sat in the hot little room with the tombstone tables and sipped his beer. Water dripped constantly from the bottle. In the corner the poker table had been swept and the lamp filled. Flies walked about everywhere.

Get you another beer, Youngblood.

Suttree tilted the bottle and drained it. I got to go, he said.

The black wiped his eyes with one huge hand. Stories of the days and nights writ there, the scars, the teeth, the ear betruncheoned in some old fray that clung in a toadlike node to the side of his shaven head. You come back, he said.

Early afternoon in the city with his fish sold he ate the beef stew at Granny and Hazel's. He walked in the streets, a lonely figure. On Jackson Avenue he saw Maggeson in a dingy white suit and straw boater. The rubber baron, small eyes distorted behind the dished glass lenses.

Someone called to him, he turned. Hoghead Henry's small and jaunty shape was coming from an alleyway heralded by pigeons flapping upward into the sad air with right alarm, immune to Hoghead's huckleberry insouciance. He swept his rumpled linen beneath the band of his trousers with a slice of his flattened hand and gave Suttree a crooked grin. When did you get out?

Tuesday. Brother and Junior got out with me.

Hoghead grinned. They started up the street. Old Junior, the cops brought him in one night and turned him over to Mrs Long, he was about three fourths drunk and been in some kind of trouble, I forget, and Mrs Long told the cops, said: I dont know what's wrong with him. My oldest boy Jimmy never causes me the least trouble. Next night here they come with Jim.

Suttree smiled. I hear that old woman shot at you the other night.

Old crazy nigger woman. She shot about four holes in the wall. Shot a picture down. I ducked behind the sofa and she shot a hole in that and John Clancy said they was a rat the size of a housecat come out from under it just a shittin and a gettin it. He was layin in the floor and he said it run right over the top of him.

What did you do down there anyway?

Aw, you dont have to do nothin to stir up a bunch of old crazy niggers.

You know what she called you?

What'd she call me?

Called you a white pointedheaded motherfucker.

Hoghead grinned. They had me in the paper one time, they're always callin anybody towheaded that's got lightcolored hair, they had me in there and I'd said somethin smart to this juvenile judge and they put: said the twoheaded youth.

Suttree grinned. Where you going?

Just up here with some punchboards. Come go with me.

I pass.

Well, I got to get on. Stay out of the jailhouse, you hear?

I hear, said Suttree.

When he crossed the porch of Howard Clevenger's store on Front Street there was an old woman rummaging through a basket of kale there as if she had lost something in it. Oceanfrog Frazer was standing at the screendoor. He patted Suttree on the ribs. What's shakin, baby.

Hey, said Suttree.

They pushed through the door together. Atop the drink cooler squatted a black and ageless androgyne in fool's silks. A purple shirt with bloused sleeves, striped fuchsia trousers and matching homedyed tennis shoes. A gold leather motorcycle belt about a vespine waist. A hat from the hand of a coked milliner. Hi sweetie, he said.

Hello John.

Trippin Through The Dew, said Oceanfrog.

Hey baby.

Hey Frog, called a black from the rear of the store.

What you want?

Come here baby. I got to talk to you.

I aint got time to mess with you.

Suttree poked among the loaves of bread.

Oceanfrog lifted a carton of milk from the cooler and opened it and drank.

Hey Gatemouth.

Yeah baby.

You hear about B L's old lady catchin him?

No man, what happened?

She come in over there Sunday caught him in bed with this old gal and started warpin him in the head with a shoe. This old gal raised straight up in the bed buck naked and hollered at her, said: Lay it to him honey, said: I was married to a son of a bitch just like him.

A high whinny escaped the painted gaud perched at Oceanfrog's elbow. The mascaraed eyes sidled, the black and languid hands made draping motions about the elbows. Oceanfrog you is a mess, she said.

Old B L's crazy, said Gatemouth.

Suttree smiled among the rusting canisters of food at the back wall. He passed behind the hoglike bulk of Gatemouth in his chair. Hey baby, said Gatemouth. What's the haps?

Hey, said Suttree, moving toward the meatcase.

A discussion on the mating habits of possums ensued. A young black named Jabbo entered the store.

Hey baby, called Gatemouth.

Gate City, said Jabbo. Aint no town and it aint no city. He glared at Trippin Through The Dew. How about gettin your nelly ass off the dopebox.

Ooh, said the invert, sliding to the floor like a neon eel.

Gatemouth says a possum dont have a forked peter, Oceanfrog told the store.

I never, said Gatemouth. I said he dont screw her in the nose.

What's his peter forked for then?

Cause he's a marsuperal, motherfucker.

Oceanfrog laughed deep in the back of his throat. Shiny tombstone teeth, gums coral pink. Shit man, he said. You completely eat up with the dumb-ass.

Ask Suttree.

I dont know, said Suttree.

He dont want the whole river to know what a fuckin dumb-ass you is, said Oceanfrog. He tipped the carton of milk and rifled a long drink down his dark throat.

Who is that crazy motherfucker up in that house hollers at everbody? said Jabbo.

Where at honey? The queen of Front Street was solicitous. Jabbo ignored her. Up here, he said, pointing. Crazy motherfucker hollers the craziest shit I ever heard.

That's just the old crazy reverend up there, said Gatemouth. Hollers all the time: Are you warshed in the blood.

He can talk some shit.

I goin to slap his head sideways he dont get off of me.

He hollers at everbody.

I aint everbody.

He's a cripple.

He'll be crippled.

They has to carry out his slops and everthing.

He trimmed hisself, said Trippin Through The Dew.

Done what?

Trimmed hisself. With a razor. Just sliced em on off honey, what they tell me.

That wouldnt cripple you.

It would smart some, said Oceanfrog.

He was done crippled fore he done it.

I goin to trim his fuckin wig he dont quit that hollerin at me, said Jabbo.

Suttree ducked the yardlong coil of dead flies that hung from the ceiling and came to the counter with his purchases.

What else? said Howard.

That's it.

He totted with pencil on a scrap of paper.

Forty-two cents.

Suttree dredged up coins from his jeans.

Where you goin, Sut?

Home.

Sure you is. Tell me. Slip off up here somewheres and dip your wick in somethin.

Suttree grinned.

Old Suttree, said Oceanfrog. He caint fade nothin.

Why dont you put me on something?

Shit. You got it all locked now.

He aint interested in them nigger gals. Is you Suttree?

Suttree looked at Jabbo but he didnt answer.

Howard dropped the last of the groceries into the sack and slid it toward Suttree. He took it under his arm and nodded toward the dark idlers. See you, he said.

Hang loose, said Oceanfrog.

The screendoor clapped shut.

Ooh that's a pretty thing, said Trippin Through The Dew.

After he'd eaten his supper he snuffed the lamp and sat in the dark and watched the lights on the far shore standing long and wandlike in the trembling river. Down from Ab Jones's sounds of laughter carried over the black water like ghost voices, old dead revelers reminiscing in the night. After a while he rose and went out and up the river path to the door.

He sat in the corner and sipped a beer. Oceanfrog was sitting in for the house in a light poker game and Ab lay sleeping in the back room. Suttree heard him breathing in the dark when he went past his bedroom, going on to the cubicle behind the torn and stained plastic showercurtain, standing there half holding his breath, the boards in the reeking gloom splotched with a greenish phosphorescence, a sinister mold that glowed faintly. A section of galvanized gutterpipe sluiced the urine down to a rathole in the corner and out into the passing river. There was a small lizard of some kind wet and pale that clung to a naked stud and Suttree pissed on it and it wriggled out through a crack in the wall. He buttoned his trousers and spat into the trough. Reassessing the agility of germs in a sequence of them climbing falling water like salmon he wiped his mouth and selected a clean place on the wall and spat again.

He sat with the back of his head against the board wall and his mind drifted. Moths crossed the mouth of the lamp in its scroll iron sconce above his head, the shape of the flame steadfast in the pietin reflector. On the ceiling black curds. Where insect shadows war. The reflection of the lamp's glass chimney like a quaking egg, the zygote dividing. Giant spores addorsed and severing. Yawing toward separate destinies in their blind molecular schism. If a cell can be lefthanded may it not have a will? And a gauche will?

In another part of the room Fred Cash was reciting poetry. Suttree heard the last of the Signifyin Monkey and then the ballad of Jack-Off Jake the poolroom snake who fucked his way north to Duluth. He rose and got another beer. Doll in her slippers collected bottles and shuffled off mutely through the smoke and the gloom. Suttree traced with one hand dim names beneath the table stone. Salvaged from the weathers. Whole families evicted from their graves downriver by the damming of the waters. Hegiras to high ground, carts piled with battered cookware, mattresses, small children. The father drives the cart, the dog runs after. Strapped to the tailboard the rotting boxes stained with earth that hold the bones of the elders. Their names and dates in chalk on the wormscored wood. A dry dust sifts from the seams in the boards as they jostle up the road . . .

The cards whispered along the table, the bottles clinked. Under the floor the muffled bong of a barrel shifting. Doll rocked and snored in her chair with the cat in her lap and beyond the little window the houseboat shadowed by the city lights ran darkly in the river among the tarnished stars.

His subtle obsession with uniqueness troubled all his dreams. He saw his brother in swaddling, hands outheld, a scent of myrrh and lilies. But it was the voice of Gene Harrogate that called to him where he tossed on his bunk in the murmurous noon. Harrogate's hand in supplication from the tailgate of a truck, face waffled in the wire mesh, calling.

Suttree sat up groggily. His hair lay matted on his skull and beads of sweat trickled on his face.

Hey Sut.

Just a minute.

He pulled on his trousers and lurched toward the door and flung it open. Harrogate stood there amuck in his clothes, bright thin face, a frail apparition trembling and conceivably unreal in the heat of the day.

How you doin, Sut?

He leaned against the jamb, one hand over his eyes. God, he said. Was you asleep?

Suttree retreated a step into shadow. He did not take his hand from his face. When did you get out?

Harrogate entered with his country deference, looking about. I been out, he said.

How did you find me?

I ast around. I went to that yan'n first. They's niggers lives there. She told me where you was at. He looked about the little cabin. They was in bed up yonder too, he said. Boy.

Wait a minute, said Suttree.

What?

He turned him about in the light from the window. What are you wearing? he said.

Harrogate shuffled and flapped his arms. Aw, he said. Just some old clothes.

Did they rig you out in these at the workhouse?

Yeah. They lost my clothes what they give me at the hospital. I dont look funny do I?

No. You look crazy. He pulled at Harrogate. What is this?

Harrogate held his arms aloft. I dont know, he said.

Suttree was turning him around. Good God, he said.

The shirt was fashioned from an enormous pair of striped drawers, his neck stuck through the ripped seam of the crotch, his arms hanging from the capacious legholes like sticks.

What size do you wear?

What size what?

Anything. Shirt to start with.

I take a small.

A small.

Yeah.

Take that damn thing off.

He peeled out of the shirt and stood in a pair of outsize pastrycook's trousers with cuffs that reverted back nearly to his knees.

Why the hell didnt you cut the legs off those?

He spread his feet and looked down. I might not be done growin, he said.

Take them off.

He dropped them to the floor and stood naked save for his shoes. Suttree collected the trousers and hacked a foot or more from the legs with his fishknife and rummaged through his bureau until he found a shirt.

The shoes is mine, Harrogate said.

Suttree looked down at the enormous sneakers. I guess your feet might grow another four or five inches, he said.

I caint stand a tight shoe, said Harrogate.

Here, try this shirt. And turn these trousers up on the inside where it wont show.

Okay.

When he had dressed again he looked less like a clown and more like a refugee. Suttree shook his head.

I got shot in the bottom of my shoe, Harrogate said. He held up one foot.

Gene, said Suttree, what are your plans?

I dont know. Find me a place here in town I reckon.

Why dont you go back home?

I aint goin back out there. I like it uptown.

You could still come in when you took a notion.

Naw. Hell Sut, I'm a city rat now.

Where are you going to live?

Well. I thought you might know a place.

You did.

That old codger up under the bridge has got him a slick place. Nobody never would find ye up in under there.

Why dont you move in at the other end up here?

I looked at it but it's open to the road where you aint got no privacy. Besides they's niggers lives next door.

Oh well, said Suttree. Niggers.

Do you not know of anyplace?

How about the viaduct? Have you looked under there?

Where's it at?

You can see it right here. See?

Harrogate followed his pointing finger, looking out the open door toward the city where a smaller replica of the river bridge stood astraddle of First Creek.

You reckon it's not taken?

I dont know. It may be just crammed with folks. Why dont you go see?

Harrogate rose from the cot where he'd been sitting. He was eager to be off. Hell fire, he said. It'd really be slick if it wasnt took wouldnt it? I mean, bein uptown like it is and all.

You bet, said Suttree

The viaduct spanned a jungly gut filled with rubble and wreckage and a few packingcrate shacks inhabited by transient blacks and down through this puling waste the dark and leprous waters of First Creek threaded the sumac and poison ivy. Highwater marks of oil and sewage and condoms dangling in the branches like stranded leeches. Harrogate made his way through this derelict fairyland toward the final concrete arches of the viaduct where they ran to earth. He entered delicately, his eyes skittering about. There was no one in. The earth was cool and naked and dry. Here some bones. Broken glass. A few stray dogturds. Two bent and mangled parking meters with clots of concrete about their roots.

Boy, whispered Harrogate.

There was a little concrete pillbox filled with pipes and conduits where you could store things and with the weeds grown about outside there was never a retreat so secluded. Harrogate sat on his heels and hugged his knees and looked out. He watched the pigeons come and go up under the high arches and he studied the warren of shacks on the farther bank of the cut where they hung yoked by insubstantial brigades of torn gray wash. Dark and near vertical gardens visible among the tin or tarred rooftops and vast nets of kudzu across the blighted trees.

Come evening he had accumulated some crates and aligned them in a sort of storage wall and he had made a firepit of old bricks and he had his eye on other goods which required but fall of dark to come by. By then he was uptown salvaging tins from trashcans for cookware. Appropriating the mattress from a lounge on a houseporch. All the redglobed lanterns from a ditchside where watermains were under repair.

He sat by the fire a long time after he had boiled and eaten the vegetables pilfered from gardens across the creek. His little grotto glowed with a hellish red from the lanterns and he reclined on the mattress and scratched himself and picked his teeth with a long yellow fingernail.

When Suttree came by next noon on his way to the market the city rat had just returned. He ushered in his guest expansively. How you like it, Sut?

Suttree looked around, shaking his head.

What I like about it is they's plenty of room. Dont you?

You better get rid of those parking meters, Suttree said.

Yeah. I'll haul em off to the creek this evenin.

What's in here? He was peering into the little concrete vault.

I dont know. It's a slick place to keep your stuff though, aint it?

Overhead in the arches there was a dull snap and a violent flapping of wings.

Hot damn, said Harrogate, slapping his thigh.

A pigeon fluttered down brokenly and landed in the dust and wobbled and flopped. It had a rat trap about its neck.

That makes three, said Harrogate, scurrying to secure the bird.

Suttree stared after him. Harrogate removed the trap and climbed up into the vaulted undercarriage of the viaduct and reset it, scooping the scattered grain over it with one hand. Boy, he called down, his voice sepulchral, them sons of bitches is really dumb.

What are you going to do with them?

I got two in the pot yonder stewin up with some taters and stuff but if this keeps up I'm goin to sell em.

Who to?

Harrogate hopped down, the dust pluming from under his sneakers. He gave his trousers a swipe with his hands. Niggers, he said. Shit, they'll buy anything.

Well, said Suttree. I was going to ask you if you wanted some fish but I guess you've got enough to eat for a while.

Hell, come take supper with me this evenin. They's enough for two.

Suttree looked at the limp and downy bird, its pink feet. Thanks, he said, but I guess not. He nodded toward Harrogate's mattress. You need to get your bed up off the ground there, he said.

I wanted to talk to you about that. I got my eye on some springs down here by the creek but I caint get em by myself.

Suttree tucked his fish beneath his arm. I'll stop by later, he said. I've got to get on to town.

I got to figure some way to keep these dogs out of here too.

Well.

I'll have her fixed up slick next time you see it.

Okay.

Livin uptown like this you can find pret near anything you need.

Dont forget about the parking meters.

Yeah. Okay.

Suttree took a final look around and shook his head and went out through the weeds to the world.

Sunday he set forth downriver in the warm midmorning, rowing and drifting by turns. He did not run his trotlines. He crossed below the bridge and swung close under the shadow of the bluffs, the dripping of the oars in the dark of the river like stones in a well. He passed under the last of the bridges and around the bend in the river, through peaceful farmland, high fields tilted on the slopes and rich turned earth in patches of black corrugation among the greening purlieus and small cultivated orchards like scenes of plenitude from picturebooks suddenly pasted over the waste he was a familiar of, the river like a giant trematode curling down out of the city, welling heavy and septic past these fine homes on the north shore. Suttree rested from time to time on the oars, studying from this late vantage old childhood scenes, gardens he knew or had known.

He took the inside of the island, narrow water that once had served as race to the old dutchman's light mill and beneath which now lay its mossgrown ruins, concrete piers and pillowblocks and rusting axletrees. Suttree held to the shallows. Silt ebbed and fell among the reeds and small shoals of harried and brasscolored shad flared away in the murk. He leaned upon the dripping oars, surveying the shore bracken. Little painted turtles tilted from a log one by one like counted coins into the water.

The child buried within him walked here one summer with an old turtlehunter who went catlike among the grasses, gesturing with his left hand for secrecy. He has pointed, first a finger, then the long rifle of iron and applewood. It honked over the river and the echo drifted back in a gray smoke of sulphur and coke ash. The ball flattened on the water and rose and carried the whole of the turtle's skull away in a cloud of brainpulp and bonemeal.

The wrinkled empty skin hung from the neck like a torn sock. He hefted it by the tail and laid it up on the mud of the bank. Green fungus hung from the serried hinder shell. This dull and craggy dreamcreature, dark blood draining.

Do they ever sink?

The turtlehunter charged his rifle from a yellowed horn and slid a fresh ball down the bore. He recapped the lock, cradling the piece in his armcrook.

Some does, some dont. Quiet now, they be anothern directly.

What do you do with them?

Sell em for soup. Or whatever. The boy was watching the dead surface of the river. Turkles and dumplins if ye've a mind to. They's seven kinds of meat in one.

What do turtles eat?

Folks' toes if they dont be watchful wadin. See yan'n?

Where?

Towards them willers yander.

Down there?

Dont pint ye fanger ye'll scare him.

You pointed.

Thatn's eyes was shut. Hush now.

He opened his eyes. Redwings rose from a bower in the sedge with thin cries. He bent to the oars again and came down the narrows and into the main channel, the skiff laying a viscid wake on the river and the bite of the oars sucking away in sluggish coils. He tacked toward the south bank in order to bias the bend in the river, coming through the shadowline into a cooler wind. Sheer limestone cliffs rose cannellate and palewise and laced with caves where small forktailed birds set forth against a sky reaching blue and moteless to the sun itself.

Below here the river began to broaden into backwater. Mudflats spiracled and bored like great slabs of flukey liver and a colony of treestumps like beached squid drying grayly in the sun. A dead selvedge traversed by crows who go sedately stiff and blinking and bright as black glass birds from ort to ort of stranded carrion. Suttree shipped the oars and drifted to the bank and stood rocking and recovering as the prow of the skiff grated up against the mud, stepping ashore easily with the rope and mooring the skiff to a root with a halfhitch. He crossed through the high grass and went up the slope, climbing with handholds in the new turf until he gained the crest and turned to look down on the river and the city beyond, casting a gray glance along that varied world, the pieced plowland, the houses, the odd grady of the small metropolis against the green and blooming hills and the flat bow of the river like a serpentine trench poured with some dull slag save where the wind engrailed its face and it shimmered lightly in the sun. He went along the crest of the bluffs through the windy sedge walking up small birds that flared and hung above the void on locked wings. A toy tractor was going on a field in a plume of dust. Down there the island ringed in mud. Suttree scaled a slate out over the river. Turning, winking, lost. He descended through a heavy swale of grass and went on, fording a thorny wicker patch of blackberries, crossing the face of a hill past the promontory kept by the old mansion, a great empire relic that sat shelled and stripped and rotting in its copse of trees above the river and brooded on the passing world with stark and stoned out window lights.

Suttree went along the high rolling country above the river. Two seagulls tracked their pale shapes in the shadowed calm under the bluff and far downstream he saw an osprey turn very high and hang above the distant thunderheads with the sun parried pure white from underwing and panel. He has seen them fold and fall like stones and he stayed to watch it out of sight.

The path he followed wound along the hills through grass and bramble and cut crosscountry toward the lower reaches of the river. It angled down a long bank of shale, it went through a wood. When he came upon the river again it was upon a dead and swollen backwater of coves and sloughs where slime and froth obscured the shapes of floating jars and bottles and where lightbulbs peered from the slowly heaving jetsam like great barren eyes. He went along the narrow path past fishermen, old women, men and boys. Galvanized minnowpails were tied to stumps at the water's edge and picnic hampers stood in the shade. A little girl squatted with her skirt hiked and watched between spattered shins her water trickle along the packed clay. Old men nodded solemnly to Suttree as he passed. Howdy. Howdy. Doin any good?

He went down a strand of mud and crusted stone strewn with spiderskeins of slender nylon fishline, tangled hooks, dried baitfish and small bones crushed among the rocks. Toeing tins from their molds in the loam where slugs recoiled and flexed mutely under the agony of the sun. The path climbed along a wall of purple sandstone above an embayment and in the sunlit shallows below him he could see the long cataphracted forms of gars lying in a kind of electric repose among the reeds. Bird shadows scuttled past but did not move them. Suttree leaned against the face of crumbling stone and watched them. One of the gars came about slowly, the water stirring and going among the willows. His dull side gave back the light like burnt brass. The other three lay like dogs, heavy shapes of primitive rapacity basking in the sun. Suttree moved on. At the head of the cove a hogsnake snubnosed and bloated lay coiled and sleeping in the dry ruins of a skiff.

The path ran on to a landing and there was a biblecamp bus parked there and people in their clothes were floundering around in the water.

He descended the grassy bank among the watchers and took a seat. A preacher in shirtsleeves stood waistdeep in the water holding a young girl by the nose. He finished intoning his chant and tilted her over backwards into the river and held her there a moment and brought her up again all streaming and embarrassed and wiping the water from her eyes. The preacher was grinning. Suttree moved closer to watch. An old man nodded to him.

Howdy.

Howdy.

The girl had nothing on beneath her thin dress and it clung wet and lascivious across her cold nipples and across her belly and thighs.

You saved? said the old man.

Suttree looked at the old man and the old man looked back with eyes smoky and opaque.

No, he said.

The old man unscrewed a jar of dark brown liquid he held in his lap and spat into it and put the lid back again and wiped his mouth. Say you aint? he said.

No, Suttree said. He was watching the girl clamber out of the river.

The old man nudged another near him. Here's one aint saved. Says it hisself.

This old man looked past the first one's shoulder toward Suttree. Him?

Aye.

Been baptized?

You been baptized?

Just on the head.

Just on the head, he says.

That aint no good. It wont take if you dont get total nursin. That old sprinklin business wont get it, buddy boy.

The first one nudged Suttree. He'll tell ye right, he said. He's a lay preacher hisself.

Sprinklers, said the lay preacher in disgust. I'd rather to just go on and be infidel as that. He turned away. He was dressed in soft blue overalls and he was very clean. The other one eyed Suttree again. Suttree was watching the preacher in the river.

Tell him to get down yonder in the water if he wants to be saved, the second old man said. He put one hand to his mouth, his jaw muscles working.

It aint salvation just to get in the water, the first said. You got to be saved as well.

Suttree turned and looked at him. Can you take your shoes off? he said.

The second old man leaned to see him. Jesus never had no shoes, he said.

The first was motioning for quiet with one flapping hand. He turned to Suttree. Aint no need to damp your shoes, he said. A feller can repent shod or barefoot either one. Jesus dont care.

What do you think about the pope and all that mess over there? Suttree said.

I try my bestest not to think about it atall, the old man said. He suddenly flung one arm upward in a gesture of such violent salutation that people drew back from around him.

That's my grandniece Rosy yonder. Just turned fourteen and saved right as rain. Makes a feller wonder at the ways of the Lord, dont it? How old are you, son?

Pretty old, said Suttree.

Well dont fret. I was seventy-six fore I seen the Lord's light and found the way.

How old are you now?

Seventy-six. I was awful bad about drinkin.

I've done it myself.

The old man glanced again at Suttree. Suttree looked about, then leaned to his ear. You dont have a little drink hid do you?

The old man's eyes careened about in their seamed sockets. Oh lord no, he said. I've plumb quit. Lord I wouldnt have nothin like that.

Well, said Suttree.

He'd scooted away a bit and he turned to watch the ceremonies. The grandniece smiled at those on the bank. Some waved.

The other old man leaned across and jabbed at Suttree with a thick finger. Go on, he said. Get down in that water.

There she goes, said Suttree, pointing.

That's my grandniece, the old man said, waving to the waters beneath which she had subsided.

Two women on the grass in front of them were turning and giving them dark looks. Suttree smiled at them. On down the bank groups were unwrapping sandwiches and opening cold drinks. There was a fat woman spread on the ground with an enormous teat hanging out and a small child fastened to it.

Tell him to come to the meetin tonight, said the second man.

Come to meetin tonight, the first one said.

Where at?

Gospel tent just up off the highway yonder. Did you not see it?

No.

Lord it's big enough. You come to meetin. They havin the reverend Billy Byington and the Sunrise Singers is supposed to be there too.

They are?

Dadjim right. Same as you hear on WNOX.

The women were turning and scowling.

The old man unscrewed and spat into his jar again and leaned forward. You come tonight, he said. I hear tell they might be goin to have May Maude. That does the oldtimey note singin.

There was a man now going into the water like a sleepwalker. He had his hands before him and his eyes were half closed and he was singing some incoherence over and over. The preacher took a step toward him, so unsteady he looked, the preacher smiling with a kind of grave benignity. Friends on the bank seemed to sway with him. This new candidate flailed once, eyes widening in alarm. The preacher lunged toward him with hands out. The man came aright and surged forth, his coattails dipping, reaching for the preacher and then going suddenly sideways with a long moan. The watchers on the bank stiffened. His hands wheeled wildly in the air and this supplicant went from sight like a drunken music conductor.

Suttree shook his head. The old man gave him a little crooked grin, his jawseams grouted with black spittle.

The preacher was blessing the subsiding roil with one hand and with the other was groping about in the water.

Suttree chuckled. The two women rose together and moved away over the grass. A man who was with them but was enjoying himself anyway turned and grinned. Boys, he said, that ought to take if it dont drownd him.

The preacher had the man up by the collar. He was sputtering and reeling about and he looked half crazy. The preacher steadied him by the forehead, intoning the baptismal service.

Suttree rose and dusted the grass from his trousers.

You aint fixin to leave are ye? the old man asked.

I sure as hell am, said Suttree.

You better get in that river is where you better get to, said the one in overalls. But Suttree knew the river well already and he turned his back to these malingerers and went on.

He went up the river path, swinging along in the sunshine, crossing a slough by a driftwood bridge and following the backwater of the smaller river that flowed in on the left. An upcountry river that grew more green as he went until it was a clouded jade. He sat to rest on a dusty log and watched it pass. A bittern stood in singlefooted siege among the cattails and small waterserpents swam. A dog came upstream on the far side tongue lolled with the heat and at a listless trot that told a weary way to go. He whistled at it and it looked at him and went on. Passing upstream it set the halms of marshweed quivering where nesting fish moved out unseen.

Suttree rose. The bittern flew. He went on until he came to a country road. It was hot walking and he didnt hurry. By and by he came to a small house.

He crossed to the front porch and tapped at the door. There were freshly painted boxes on the porch with new flowers cracking the loam of their beds and wasps were hanging about the eaves. The door opened and a small old woman peeped out. Yes, she said.

Hello Aunt Martha.

She pushed open the screendoor. Lord have mercy, she said. Buddy? Why Buddy.

How are you?

Oh lord, she said. She was tiny and frail and the hand that tucked at him trembled like a bird. Come in, she said.

Where's Clayton?

He's asleep. He eat a big dinner and he's asleep. Oh my lord he'll just be so tickled.

They entered the cool semidark of the front room with her taking his elbow like one might a blind man or like a blind man might. He could smell the rich cookery of their Sunday noon meal. She did not take her eyes from him. Have you eat? she said.

I had breakfast late.

They went into the kitchen where dishes still sat at table. Beyond was a sunporch rife with plantlife and the sun fell warmly through the glass and across the floor and table.

Set down, Buddy, she said, her doll's hands fussing at him. Let me just warm you up some dinner.

Dont bother with that, Aunt Martha. I just stopped by for a minute.

It's not any bother. You just set there. You want a glass of cold sweetmilk?

Yes mam, I'd love one.

I'll have some ice tea in just a minute. Lord I was thinkin about you all this mornin.

Suttree stretched his feet beneath the table. She brought a jar of milk from the refrigerator and a tall glass, pouring as she went, talking.

I was sortin out some old things and got to lookin through them old albums and pictures and I thought about you.

He set the halfdrained glass of milk on the table and blew and wiped his forehead with the back of his hand. She poured it full again. I wish you'd come see us more, Buddy. What do you want to be so mean for?

Where are the pictures?

They're right here. Did you want to look at them?

If they're handy. If you dont care.

Why they're just right here.

He drank the rest of the milk and looked out at the flowers and the sun. She came in with two old leather photo albums and a blue shoebox. She laid these on the table and pushing the box to one side to make room she opened the first album. Just go ahead and look while I warm this dinner up.

He took her hand. It was thin and finely boned and cool. I couldnt eat anything, he said.

I wish you would.

He looked around. Just let me have a piece of that cake, he said.

You better eat somethin.

No.

She lifted a cracked cakebell and sliced away a heavy wedge of the chocolate cake it contained and laid it on a plate and set it by him.

He was bent over the album, confronting figures out of his genealogy. Who's this? he said.

She rested her hand on his shoulder and peered with him. Lord, she said, let me get my glasses, I caint make it out.

An ancient woman spreadeagled in a bed, dried hands at her sides, a cured looking face. She is bald save for sheaves of hair on either side her head and they lie opposed and extended upon the pillow like pale horns.

She came back with her spectacles and bent over the photo. That's

Aunt Liz just afore she died. She was bald pret near. This here's Roy's baby picture.

A tintype picked from the wedge of the pages. Sailorsuited poppet a fiend's caricature of old childhoods, a gross cartoon.

The old woman's slow hands sorted a loose packet of brown faded photographs, glasses riding down the bridge of her nose as she nods in recognition. She must set them back again with her finger, shuffling these imaged bits of cardboard, paper, tin. They have a burnt look to them, as if dried in a flue. Dark and haggard eyes peer out. In the photographs the children appear sinister, like the fruit of forbidden liaisons.

Who's that?

That's Uncle Carter. He was a goodlookin somethin, wasnt he?

Who's this little boy here?

That's John.

He leaned closer to see was there anything left of that face in the face he knew.

This must be about nineteen ten.

Lord, I guess. I dont know. Here's Helen.

How long has Uncle Carter been dead?

She looked high on the far wall of the kitchen as if perhaps it were written there. He died in nineteen twenty-six. Guess who that is, she said, pointing.

He looked at the darkeyed girl. It was a very old picture. Aunt Martha when he looked at her had one hand to her mouth and was regarding the photograph with a shy and wistful look. Suttree said: That's you, Aunt Martha.

She pushed at his shoulder. Shoo, she said. How did you know that was me?

Why it looks just like you.

Go on, she said. She shook her head slowly. I just loved that dress. Look here. Here's E C.

He looks good in a hat, Suttree said.

Lord, she said, laughing, you remember that?

Sure, he said.

This is Grandma Cameron. She was ninety-two when she died.

This is Uncle Milo.

He was a merchant seaman you know.

Suttree nodded. I remember you Uncle Milo. Lost under Capricorn all hands aboard a bargeload of birdshit one foggy night off the limeslaked coast of Chile. Souls commended to the sea's salt clemency.

He'd not been home for thirteen year.

Foreign stars in the nights down there. A whole new astronomy. Mensa, Musca, the Chameleon. Austral constellations nigh unknown to northern folk. Wrinkling, fading, through the cold black waters. As he rocks in his rusty pannier to the sea's floor in a drifting stain of guano. What family has no mariner in its tree? No fool, no felon. No fisherman.

Who is this, Aunt Martha?

Do you not know who that is?

He seized the faded picture and scrutinized the girl. She looked out at the void with one cast eye and a slack uncertain smile.

It's not Mama is it?

Why sure.

He turned the page. It doesnt look like her, he said.

The old lady turned back the leaf and regarded the picture. Well, she said, it's not a good likeness. She was a whole lot prettier than that. Here's Carol Beth.

How old was she when she died?

Nineteen. Lord that was a sad time.

This is a dog. He is dead too.

This is the house where the dead lived. It is gone, lost and gone.

What was the dog's name?

She bent to see. I disremember, she said. They had one one time named John L Sullivan cause it was the fightinest little thing you ever seen.

We had one named Jose Iturbi. Because it was the peeinest dog.

Oh Buddy, she said, slapping his arm. I'd be ashamed.

Suttree turned the page, grinning. Bits of ribbon, hairlocks fell slowly down over the photos. She reached past him to adjust these from obstruction. An old man came to light holding a baby in his arms. Proposing it stiffly before him like an offering, old lace and swaddled windings that hung from a small bald and squinting face.

That's you, she said, after a silence.

This is me, he said.

Cold eyes bored at him out of the cowled coverlet. The congenitally disaffected.

Lord you were such a angel your mother wished she had all boys.

Suttree's spine convulsed in a long cold shunting of vertebrae. He looked up at the old woman. She gazed at the photograph through her delicately wired eyeglasses with that constrained serenity of the aged remembering and nothing more. Let me fix some tea, she said.

He lifted the slice of cake and bit into it and turned the page. The old musty album with its foxed and crumbling paper seemed to breathe a reek of the vault, turning up one by one these dead faces with their wan and loveless gaze out toward the spinning world, masks of incertitude before the cold glass eye of the camera or recoiling before this celluloid immortality or faces simply staggered into gaga by the sheer velocity of time. Old distaff kin coughed up out of the vortex, thin and cracked and macled and a bit redundant. The landscapes, old backdrops, redundant too, recurring unchanged as if they inhabited another medium than the dry pilgrims shored up on them. Blind moil in the earth's nap cast up in an eyeblink between becoming and done. I am, I am. An artifact of prior races.

Some curious person in the past with a penchant for deathbed studies has remembered to us this old man upreared among his stained coverlets, stale smell of death, wild arms and acrimony, addressing as he did kin long parted in a fevered apostrophe of invective. The nurse swore they spoke back. He listened, no ranting fool. Commend him gently, whom the wrath he suckled at his heart has wasted more than years. Suttree remembered the blue pools of his dead eyes. He and his sisters filing past the tall old bed. Lifted up to see. Waxen flesh obscenely wrinkled. In the picture this old grandfather sat up in his yellowed bedding like a storybook rat, spectacles and nightcap and eyes blind behind the glass. And pictures. The old picnics, family groups, the women bonneted and with flowers, men booted and pistoled. The patriot in his sam browne belt and puttees, one of the all but nameless who arrived home in wooden boxes on wintry railway platforms. Tender him down alongside the smoking trucks. Lading bills fluttering in the bitter wind. Here. And here. We could not believe he was inside. Cold and dry it was, our shoes cried in the snow all the way home. The least of us tricked out in black like small monks mourning, a clutch of vultures hobbling in stiff black shoes with musty hymnals in our hands and eyes to the ground. Someone to be thanked for digging in such frozen ground. Weary chant told from an old psalter. The leaves clap shut dully. Pulley squeak, the mounded flowers sucked slowly into the earth. A soldier held the folded flag to Mamaw but she could not look. She pushed gently at it with one hand, a gorgon's mask of grief behind her black glove. Scoop of dirt rattling, this sobbing, these wails in the quiet winter twilight. Blue streetlights came up beyond the wall as we turned to go.

She came with the tea, a tall vase full, chocked with ice, a curl of lemon. He ladled sugar in.

That's Elizabeth again, said the old lady. That's as old a picture as there is, I reckon.

Between the mad hag's face and this young girl a vague stellar drift, the wheeling of planets on their ether trunnions. Likenesses of lost souls haunt us from old chromos and tintypes brown with age. Bloodless skull and dry white hair, matriarchal meat drawn lean and dry on frail bone, a bitter refund ashen among silk and lilies by candlelight in a cold hall, black lacquered bier on sawhorses wound with crepe. I would not cry. My sisters cried.

This here's Uncle Will. You might not remember him. He was like me, he couldnt turn his head to do no good. She turned her head stiffly to show.

Yes.

He was a blacksmith. They all had trades.

He was a drunk, he a grifter.

Suttree turned up a tinted photograph of a satin lined wickerbound casket with flower surrounds. In the casket a fat dead baby, garishly painted, bright fuchsia cheeks. Never ask whose. He closed the cover on this picturebook of the afflicted. A soft yellow dust bloomed. Put away these frozenjawed primates and their annals of ways beset and ultimate dark. What deity in the realms of dementia, what rabid god decocted out of the smoking lobes of hydrophobia could have devised a keeping place for souls so poor as is this flesh. This mawky wormbent tabernacle.

What say boy?

Suttree turned. Clayton was standing in the door scratching his stomach and grinning.

Hey, Suttree said.

They shook hands and Clayton patted him on the back.

Mama you know better than to let this fool in the kitchen. He'll eat us out of house and home.

Now you hush, Clayton.

What are you boring him with them old pictures for? You want a drink, Buddy?

Why I'll bet Buddy dont even drink, do you Buddy?

Oh no, Clayton said. Buddy wouldnt take a drink.

Suttree grinned.

Lord I raised some that will, said the old lady. I dont know where they get it at.

At Ab Franklin's, said Clayton, grinning and pouring at the sink.

I mean where they take after it from.

Clayton pointed with the bottle toward the albums. Take a look at a few of them old hard assed sons of bitches in there and tell me if you think any of em ever took a drink.

Why Clayton, said the old lady.

You sure you dont want a drink, Bud?

No thanks.

Put them old moldy pictures up and come out in the back here.

Suttree slid back his chair and rose and followed him out through the sunporch and into the yard, holding for a moment the cold glass of tea against his forehead. Clayton grinned at him.

You better have a little hair of the dog, Bud.

No, I'm all right.

Clayton lowered himself into a lawnchair and stretched his naked feet in the grass. Damn if I didnt tie one on last night, he said. The last thing I remember was somebody sayin did he have a hat.

Suttree held a folded bill toward him.

What's that?

Here. That twenty I owe you.

Hell, that's all right.

No. Here.

Hell, I dont need it.

Go on. He pushed it toward him.

You sure you cant use it?

No. Thanks a lot.

Clayton took the bill and tucked it into his shirtpocket. Well, he said. That old crossbar hotel has got some pretty high rates, aint it?

Suttree took a long drink of iced tea. It had mint in it. He liked the rough leaves against his lip and their rich smell. It does, he said.

Are you still fishin?

Yep.

You want a job?

Nope.

Clayton shook the ice in his glass. You're a funny son of a bitch, he said.

Suttree stood looking out across the fields behind the house toward the mountains. He raised his glass and drained it.

Set down, said Clayton, patting the arm of the other chair.

Suttree propped one foot in the seat of the chair and rested his elbow on his knee. A cool breeze swung the kettled creepers hung from the porchjoists.

I believe it's fixin to cloud up and rain, Clayton said.

Paper said it was supposed to.

How'd you come out?

I just walked.

Where from? You didnt walk out from town did you?

Well, I cut across from the river. I didnt have anything else to do.

I'll give you a ride back this evenin anytime you get ready.

That's all right, Suttree said.

Aunt Martha came from the kitchen with a fresh pitcher of tea.

You'll stay and take supper with us wont you?

I better get on back.

The old lady filled his empty glass. Why Buddy, she said, you stay and eat with us.

Thank you, but I better not.

Hell, just stay with us. You dont have anything to do.

The old lady bent and poured Clayton's half filled glass full. He sat looking down at it. Goddamn, he said. He pitched it out across the grass.

Why Clayton.

Clayton rose and went into the house muttering to himself.

Buddy, I do wish you'd eat with us.

I appreciate it, Aunt Martha, but I need to get back.

Let me bring you another piece of cake.

No thank you. Really.

She came no higher than his shoulder. He almost reached down to touch her.

Clayton called to him from the door: You sure you couldnt use a drink?

Suttree shook his head.

Clayton came out with his drink, one hand in his hippocket. They stood there in the shade, the three of them. Suttree drained his glass and handed it to the woman. I've got to go, he said.

They followed him into the kitchen and through the house. The aunt would have taken his elbow save that her hands were full. She set the glass and pitcher hastily on the table and caught him up. Suttree turned and was surprised to hear her talking of the weather. You let Clayton take you, she said. They will come a storm this evenin long fore you get back to town.

I wont melt, he said.

He got out the door. Clayton was looking past the top of her head. Take care Bud.

Buddy you come see us, you hear?

He went on down the path into the road. He turned and raised one hand. The old lady waved timidly with just her fingers and Clayton saluted with his glass. It was much cooler and the wind was rising. Coils of dust rose in the road and spun off like smoke and the sky to the west lay banked in a discolored mass of thunderheads.

When he reached the highway large drops of rain were falling. They made hot slapping sounds on the macadam. He could see the rain coming across the fields where the darkly overtaken blooms buckled and dipped. He pocketed his hands and slumped and countrylooking he went down the edge of the black highway in the advancing downpour.

Before he had gone far an old Hudson pulled alongside him and sat there rocking and smoking and chattering while a man leaned across and lowered the glass just enough to let his voice out.

Hop in, old buddy.

I hate to get in your car wet as I am.

Caint hurt this old car.

Suttree climbed in and they pulled away. He watched the steamy green landscape fade beyond the dance of water on the hood.

Boy it's come a clodbuster aint it, the man said.

It is that.

The man was leaning over the wheel to see. He nodded toward the dashboard where the radio was glowing. Listen at that there, he said.

Suttree inclined one ear. A dim voice in the dashboard had a story to tell.

Well he come down from there and he said: See ary raincloud up there? and he said: Nary one. And he said: Better go on up there and look again, and he went on up there neighbors and he come back down again and he ast him again, said did he see ary sign of a raincloud and he told em no, said he'd not saw sign one, and he said: Well, better go on up there one more time, and he done it, went up there, and directly he come down again and he ast him, said: Is they ary raincloud up there now? and he said yes, said: They's one up there about the size of ye hat, and he said: Well boy you better get off the mountain cause it's a fixin to rain.

The driver smiled. He can lay it down, caint he.

Suttree nodded.

I like to hear old J Basil. He's all the time sayin: Aint that right Mrs Mull. Old deep voice. And she'll say: That's right Mr Mull. You like to hear him?

He's all right, Suttree said.

Small birds were crossing the road in the windy sheets of rain. Going up a grade the wipers died and the glass peened over with rainwater. Suttree could not see out. Beyond radio and exhaust and valvechatter he could hear thunder rumbling away over the bewept hills.

They topped the hill and the glass cleared in a slow arc. Around a curve and Suttree pointed. I get out here, he said.

The man looked. Where? he said.

Here. Anywhere along here.

You not goin to town?

No. Just right here.

The driver looked about and he looked at Suttree. They aint nothin here, he said.

Just anywhere along here, Suttree said. This is where I get out.

The driver pulled up along the graveled shoulder and stopped. He watched Suttree. Suttree climbed out into the downpour.

I sure thank you, Suttree said.

You welcome, the man said.

Suttree banged the door shut and stood back. The car moved out onto the highway. Through the runneled glass he could see the man's face turn again, as if to fix him there.

Suttree crossed the road in the rain and blue motor smoke and descended an embankment into the fields. He went crosscountry among easy hills and sometime pastureland, through a copse of dark cedars where the ground was almost dry, down a long and narrow limestone draw where small flat cactus clung to the south walls and the rain swept grayly across the ledges and swirled away before him.

He came out on the bluff and went on up the hill toward the house. Came through the weeds upon a walkway of herringboned brick all but overgrown. Past cracked urns bedight with concrete flora, broad steps, tall fluted columns with their shattered paint. The immense and stark facade seemed to recoil before his footfalls.

As he entered the foyer three young boys dropped like stricken bats from a balcony above the main reception room to his right and lit soundless on the dusty floor and passed out through a window in the opposite wall.

A chandelier lay burst in the floor. He stepped around it and ascended the lefthand stairway, slowly curving into the dusky upper chambers, keeping to the wall because save random jagged spindles the balustrade was gone. At the top of the stairs stood newel and finial intact and solitary like a rococo hitchingpost.

He wandered dripping through the high rooms with their ruined plaster, the buckled wainscot, the wallpaper hanging in great deciduous fronds. Small mounds of human stool with stained shreds of newsprint. From an upper window he watched the three boys go along the brow of the hill in the rain. Wedges of dry cracked glazing lay among the broken panes of glass in the floor. Below the window a mossy courtyard where old concrete dolphins rusted in a dry fountain and the dark handkilned bricks of the walkways lay grown with moss and lichens. Black ivy crept the garden walls and small mute birds peeped out. Across the river, the rainy hodden landscape, he could see traffic going along the boulevard, locked in another age of which some dread vision had afforded him this lonely cognizance.

He emerged from the narrow back stairwell and came up the hall with slow tread over the weathersprung parquetry, past great doors of solid cherry split open in long fibrous cracks and plundered of their knobs and hardware. Into this drawing room with high plaster frieze and foliate scrollwork. Prolapsed and waterstained ceiling, the sagging coffers. He turned, a vain figure in the ruins. Blind parget cherubs watched from the high corners.

Hello, he called. A voice that went from room to room and back again.

Gods and fathers what has happened here, good friends where is there clemency?

One spring morning timing the lean near-liquid progress of a horse on a track, the dust exploding, the rapid hasping of his hocks, coming up the straight foreshortened and awobble and passing elongate and birdlike with harsh breath and slatted brisket heaving and the muscles sliding and bunching in clocklike flexion under the wet black hide and a gout of foam hung from the long jaw and then gone in a muted hoofclatter, the aging magistrate snapped his thumb from the keep of the stopwatch he held and palmed it into his waistcoat pocket and looking at nothing, nor child nor horse, said anent that simple comparison of rotary motions and in the oratory to which he was prone that they had witnessed a thing against which time would not prevail.

He meant a thing to be remembered, but the young apostate by the rail at his elbow had already begun to sicken at the slow seeping of life. He could see the shape of the skull through the old man's flesh. Hear sand in the glass. Lives running out like something foul, night-soil from a cesspipe, a measured dripping in the dark. The clock has run, the horse has run, and which has measured which?

He moved along the hall toward the dining room. Paint on these old paneled doors crazed and yellowed like old porcelain. Something more than time has passed here. In this banquet hall. Scene of old heraldic feasts. Suttree in silent recognition of the somewhat illustrious dead. Large companies seated. A fat marcassin to adorn the board. The male bonecoupling rearing white and steaming up from the broken meat. Eyes watch. A malediction for those belated on the road and now commence. Mad trenchermen in armed sortees above the platters, the clang of steel, the stained and dripping chops, the eyes sidling. Yard dogs and starving palliards contest the scraps among the straw. There is nothing laid to table save meat and water. There is no sound of human speech. Beyond the muted clamor at the board there is a faint echo of another chase. Far hue and cry and distant horns and hounds in pain with eagerness. The master of the table has looked up. Down murrey fields another hunt has cried the stag. A shield crashes to the floor and three white birds ascend to the rafters and roost uncertainly. The master wipes his fingers in his hair and his rising says that the feast is done. Outside darkness has begun and the hounds' voices are chimes in the distance that toll seven and cease. They wait for the waterbearer to come but he does not come, and does not come.

Suttree went out through the kitchen and through the ruined garden to the old road. Reprobate scion of doomed Saxon clans, out of a rainy day dream surmised. Old paint on an old sign said dimly to keep out. Someone must have turned it around because it posted the outer world. He went on anyway. He said that he was only passing through.

At night he could hear the sewage gurgling and shuttling along through the pipes hung from the bridge's underbelly overhead. The hum of tires. Faint streetlight fell beyond the dark palings of sumac and blackberry. He rubbed his stomach and belched in his crepuscular solitude, the lamp at his elbow turned down so that the small flame burned in the glass bell ruby black. He has eaten for his supper an entire chicken boiled in a lardpail he, and he himself is the batfowler who crossed like smoke the dark garden patches above First Creek, something out of the night that drifted bedraped with dead hens down toward the moonlit miasma whitening the cleft of the glen, the ragged trees that seemed to be breathing cold, crossing this small and wretched estuary by a fallen truckdoor and climbing rapidly the far side toward the arches of the viaduct.

Suttree came, each day new marvels. They sat in purloined lawnchairs and watched a pigeon ringing down, standing off with backing wings and neck hooked while his pink pettysingles reached to grasp the pole and then like the Dove itself descending the bird limned in blue flame and a hot crackle of burnt feathers and the thing pitching backward to fall blackened to the ground in a plume of acrid smoke.

Gene, Suttree said.

Slick aint it?

Gene.

Yeah.

What have you got that pole wired to?

Harrogate pointed. Them lightwires yonder. What I done, I got me some copper wire and wired it and tied one end to a rock and thowed it . . .

Gene.

Yeah.

What the hell do you reckon is going to happen when somebody touches that pole?

Harrogate had not even risen to secure the bird. He sat there squatting in the lawnchair with his arms wrapped around his knees, smoked odor of his ragged clothes, looking up at the pole and then at Suttree. Well, he said. I'd say it would knock em on their ass.

It would kill them.

Harrogate looked mildly speculative. You reckon it would? he said.

Another day pigs. A whole covey of red shoats loose from some hillside hogpen that crossed a clearing in the blackened vines and went on downcreek toward the river. Harrogate watched them and then suddenly sat very erect, looking around.

If them niggers catches you eatin one of their hogs they will have your ass, he said.

But they got to catch me.

He rose and started down the hill toward the road and toward the creekside jungle where the pigs had gone. As he went he studied the pens scattered among the trees on the hillside above him, eclectic shelters hammered up out of snuff signs and boards and odds of fencing all hung in plumbless suspension down the bald and raingutted slope. He could see no one hunting hogs. When he struck the path along the creek he could see the tracks of the pigs here and there in the patches of black mire like the delicately pointed prints of small deer. Coming past a collection of old waterheaters he started them and they flushed into the wall of ivy with high raspy snorts. He picked one out and dove after it. It went through a mass of vines and over a mound of broken fruitjars and disappeared with an agonized squall. Harrogate fetched up in a small clearing. He had tilted himself into a locust tree and was bleeding in several places. He could hear the pigs diminishing in the distance.

When they came out on the riverbank at the point they paused to test the air. They started downstream at about the time that Harrogate emerged from the brush and they checked and swung back along the creek, their noses dishing and their eyes white. They defiled down a gully to the water and bunched and jerked their noses at it and came back. Harrogate was closing on them like a gangly tiptoe spider. They veered with new alarm and snuffled and went on down the point.

Looky here at these pigs daddy.

A man rose up from the tall grass where he'd been sitting and put his hand on top of his hat and turned around. The pigs flared like quail. They passed Harrogate some to the left and some to the right all screaming and he looked about and threw himself finally in the general direction of the pigs and landed full length with a grunt.

When he came upon them next they were feeding in a bower of honeysuckle, turning up the black earth and devouring worms and grubs and roots with subdued hoggish joy. Harrogate watched them through the vines, admiring them for plumpness, salivating slightly. He had resolved upon a rush, the pigs being too wary for stealth. He came headlong through the honeysuckle, his eye on one pig and one pig only. They squealed and went rocketing away through the under-brush, his the fleetest of the pack. In no time they were gone. He stood leaning against a tree, his hand on his chest, panting. He turned around. There was a sustained muffled screeching coming from be-hind him. He retraced his steps and crossed the chopped ground of the clearing. Following the sound he came upon a pig with its head in a bucket. As he approached it went running. It crashed into a tree and fell back and lay there squealing. He ran to it and seized it by a hindleg. It kicked and peeled back a long flap of hide from his fore-arm. He dropped it again and tried to push the skin back over the wound. Goddamn, he said. The pig went on through the bushes.

He could hear it caroming about, the bucket banging and the pig screeching. He plunged after it. It ran head on into the creek and floundered there in the filthy water with gurgling screams. Harrogate launched out birdlike and fell upon the shoat with an enormous splash.

He came bedraggled and wet and filthy up through the woods dragging the pig by the hindlegs. Casting about for something to knock it in the head with. He finally selected a stick and laid the pig down, pinning the rear feet to the ground with one hand. He began to beat the back of the pig's head what of it showed above the bucket rim, knocking the bail off, denting in the bucket, raising bloody weals along the pig's neck and the pig shrieking until finally the stick broke and he flung it away. The pig gave a great jerk and he fell upon it to hold it down. Shit amighty, he said.

He came up with the pig holding it about the waist, the bucket against the side of his face and blood running all down the front of him, hugging it while it kicked and shat. Coming up the creek walking spraddlelegged and half staggering until finally he must stop to rest. He and the pig sitting in a copse of kudzu quietly getting their strength back like a pair of spent degenerates. Every time the pig squirmed Harrogate would call down into the bucket for it to quit. His arms were getting tired and the one that had been peeled was hurting. He struggled up again with the pig and got as far as the garden of waterheaters when his eye fell on a piece of pipe lying naked and unattached upon the ground. He picked it up and hefted it, the pig sagging in his arm, its forefeet sticking out. He laid the pig down, kneeling on it until he could get both hindfeet in a good grip, and then he raised the pipe and swung with all his strength. Blood spewed from under the edge of the bucket. The pig screamed and gave a mighty surge and began to run sideways in a circle, dragging through the black leaves and rubbish. Harrogate swung again. The bucket went skittering off and the pig's fearcrazed eye looked up at him. A whitish matter was seeping from its head and one ear hung down half off. He brought the pipe down again over its skull, starting the eye from its socket. The pig had not stopped screaming. Die goddamn you, panted Harrogate, swinging the pipe. The pig humped and stiffened. He bashed it again, spattering brains over the ground. It stretched out, trembled and quit.

Harrogate stood over his victim with a heaving chest and cursed it. He pitched the pipe away and hefted the pig by its hindlegs and got it over his shoulder, its bloody head flopping, the brains bulging soft and wet from one side of its broken skull. He labored up to the edge of the road and laid the pig in the dusty bushes and rested. Before starting across the road he checked to see that no one was about. Strange urchin dragging a dead pig. A trail of blood. Twigs, small stones clung to the clot of brains. He dragged it up the path and under the viaduct and laid it out on the cool earth and sat looking at it.

He honed his shoplifted pocketknife on a small stone and knelt down by the dead pig and took it by one leg and held it so for a minute and then let the leg go. He squatted on his heels and flipped the knife into the dirt two or three times, his forehead wrinkled. Finally he raised the pig's leg and stuck the blade into the pig's stomach. Then he had another thought and seized one ear and wrested the head up and hacked open the throat. Blood poured out and ran over the dirt.

Now he sliced the pig open and hauled forth the guts, great armloads of them, he'd never seen so many. What to do with them. He lugged them down the path and flung them into the bushes and came back. As he had no way of scalding the pig he had decided upon skinning it.

When the owner of the pig arrived he found a scrawny and blood-covered white boychild standing on what was left of his property sawing at it with a knife and hauling on the skin and cursing. The dirty half flayed pig looked like something recovered from a shallow grave.

He was a black of a contemplative nature and he was just slightly drunk and he stood leaning there against the abutment of the viaduct and took a sip from a halfpint bottle and slipped it back into his hip pocket and wiped his mouth and watched this spectacle of frenzied mayhem with a troubled gaze.

Ahhg, said Harrogate when he glimpsed him leaning there.

The owner nodded his head. Mmm-hmm, he said.

Hidy.

He turned his head and spat and regarded Harrogate with one eye slightly veiled. You aint seed a stray shoat abouts have ye?

A what?

Little old hog. A young, young hog.

Harrogate tittered nervously. Hog? he said in a high voice.

Hog.

Well. I got this one here. He pointed at it with the knife. The black craned his head to peer. Oh, he said. I thought that was somebody.

Somebody?

Yes. You say that's a hog?

Yes, said Harrogate. It's a hog.

You wouldnt care for me to look at it would ye?

No. No no. He gestured at it. Go ahead.

The black man came forward and bent and studied the pig's ruined head. He took hold of the tip of the ear and turned it slightly. This hog's dead, he said.

Yessir.

I swear if it dont look almost exactly like one I had up at my place.

It was just sort of runnin around.

What was your plans for this here hog if you dont care for my askin?

Well. I'd sort of figured on eatin it.

Unh hunh.

Did you mean to say it was yourn?

If I'm not mistook.

Well foot fire, if it's yourn why then just go on and take it.

The owner was looking about the little camp for the first time. You live here? he said.

Yessir.

I see lights over here of the night.

I generally keep a lantern goin.

I guess it's cold in under here. In the winter.

Well, I aint been here in the winter yet.

I see.

You say you live up on the hill yonder?

Yes. You can see my place from just out here.

Boy I like it down here dont you? I mean you're close to town and all. And they dont nobody bother ye.

The owner looked at Harrogate and he looked at the pig. Boy, he said, what do you reckon I'm goin to do with that there mess?

I dont know, said Harrogate in a quick nervous voice.

Well you better think of somethin.

I'd take it if you didnt want it.

Take it?

Yessir.

Is you prepared to compensate me for that there hog?

Do what?

Pay me.

Pay ye.

Now you got it right.

Harrogate was still standing astraddle the deceased animal and now he unstood himself from over it and wiped his bloody hands down the side of his trouserlegs and looked up at the owner. How much? he said.

Ten dollar.

Ten dollar?

It'd of brung ever cent of it.

I aint got no ten dollars.

Then I reckon you'll have to work it out.

Work it out?

Work. It's how most folks gets they livin. Them what aint prowlin other folks' hogpens.

What if I dont?

I'll law ye.

Oh.

You can start in the mornin.

What you want me to do with this?

The owner had already started out through the weeds. He turned and looked back at Harrogate and at the hog. You can do whatever you want with it, he said. It's yourn.

How do I find you up yonder?

You ast for Rufus Wiley. You'll find me.

How much a hour do I get? To work it out at? Harrogate was fairly shouting across the space between them there under the viaduct although Rufus was not yet thirty feet away.

Fifty cents a hour.

I'll take seventy-five, called Harrogate.

But Rufus didnt even answer this.

All that night cats moaned in the dark like cats in rut and circled and spat. Lean dogs came from the weeds highhackled and tailtucked with their lips crimpt and teeth bright red in the light of the roadlanterns. Beyond in the dark where the guts lay they circled and snapped and glided in like sharks.

He lay by a dying fire in the creeping damp and listened to the snarling and rending out there until some hour toward dawn when these windfall innards had been divided and consumed and even the most brazen cur had decided not to risk the red hell of lanterns surrounding Harrogate's hog where it hung. The spoilers all slunk away to silence one by one and only a thin cat squall came back, far, now farther, from the hill beyond the creek.

When Harrogate went down the little path toward the hoglot lugging the pail of slops before him in two hands all the small pigs had been returned to the pen and they greeted him with squeals and snorts, jostling along the fence, their pale hammershaped snouts working in the mesh. He looked back over his shoulder toward the house and then fetched the nearest a good kick in the head.

He poured the curdled stinking mess down a rough board chute and stepped back. The pigs grunted and shoved and slurped at the swill and Harrogate shook his head. In the adjoining pen the sow lay sleeping in mud. He moved along the fence and bent to study her. Striped lice the size of lizards traversed the pink nigh hairless swine's hide. He picked up a piece of coal and threw it and it made a dull thump against the fat barrel of her bulk. Her ears twitched and she raised up and snuffed about. The chunk of coal lay just behind her foreleg and she found it and set to eating it, grinding it up with great crunching sounds, a black drool swinging from her jowls. When it was gone she looked up at Harrogate to see if there were more. Harrogate pursed his lips and spat between her eyes but she seemed not to notice. You're crazier'n shit, he said. The hog tested the air with her snout and Harrogate turned and went back to the house.

Dont set that bucket in here, she said. This aint no hogpen.

Harrogate gave her a malignant look and went back out again.

When's dinner? he said, his face at the screendoor.

When it's done.

Shit, he said.

What you say?

Nothin.

I hear him say for you to cut some wood?

Harrogate spat and made his way across the small scrabbled lot to the woodpile. Pullets trotted off before him, a patchy band of birds in moult, small leprous fowl that scudded across the mud with bald pinshaft rumps. He picked up a handaxe used for splitting kindling and set about chopping ants in two as they crossed a pine log. Niggers, he said. Shit.

On the other hand he was eating pretty good. Long after he'd worked out the price of the shoat he was still around to fetch and carry or lie these last warm days in a den in the honeysuckle and read comicbooks he'd stolen, risible picturetales of walking green cadavers and drooling ghouls.

Next door but one lived a pair of nubile young black girls and he used to hang from a treelimb outside their window at night in hopes of seeing them undress. Mostly they just stepped out of their cotton dresses and went to bed in their undershifts. He tried to lure the younger one to his bower in the honeysuckle with promises of comicbooks. She said: Me and Marfa come down there directly she gets in.

They came sidling and giggling after supper and carried off his whole supply. Visions of plump young midnight tits, long dusky legs. It was September now, a season of rains. The gray sky above the city washed with darker scud like ink curling in a squid's wake. The blacks can see the boy's fire at night and glimpses of his veering silhouette slotted in the high nave, outsized among the arches. All night a ruby glow suffuses the underbridge from his garish chancel lamps. The city's bridges all betrolled now what with old ventriloquists and young melonfanciers. The smoke from their fires issues up unseen among the soot and dust of the city's right commerce.

Sometimes in the evening Suttree would bring beers and they'd sit there under the viaduct and drink them. Harrogate with questions of city life.

You ever get so drunk you kissed a nigger?

Suttree looked at him. Harrogate with one eye narrowed on him to tell the truth. I've been a whole lot drunker than that, he said.

Worst thing I ever done was to burn down old lady Arwood's house.

You burned down an old lady's house?

Like to of burnt her down in it. I was put up to it. I wasnt but ten year old.

Not old enough to know what you were doing.

Yeah.—Hell no that's a lie. I knowed it and done it anyways.

Did it burn completely down?

Plumb to the ground. Left the chimbley standin was all. It burnt for a long time fore she come out.

Did you not know she was in there?

I disremember. I dont know what I was thinkin. She come out and run to the well and drawed a bucket of water and thowed it at the side of the house and then just walked on off towards the road. I never got such a whippin in my life. The old man like to of killed me.

Your daddy?

Yeah. He was alive then. My sister told them deputies when they come out to the house, they come out there to tell her I was in the hospital over them watermelons, she told em I didnt have no daddy was how come I got in trouble. But shit fire I was mean when I did have one. It didnt make no difference.

Were you sorry about it? The old lady's house I mean.

Sorry I got caught.

Suttree nodded and tilted his beer. It occurred to him that other than the melon caper he'd never heard the city rat tell anything but naked truth.

In the long windy days of fall Harrogate joined the blacks to fish for carp at the point, smiling and incompetent. A pale arm among darker waving from the shore to Suttree as he set forth in the cool mornings.

Suttree busy caulking up the batboards of his shanty with old newsprint. The cooler days have brought a wistful mood upon him. The smell of coalsmoke in the air at night. Old times, dead years. For him such memories are bitter ones.

Trippin Through The Dew has a muskrat coat bought in a junk-shop on Central Avenue which he has dyed purple.

Mother She has come from upcountry with sacks and jars of the season's herbs. Her little yard lies deep with sere brown locust pods. In the trees small victims struggle, toad or shrewlet among the thorns where they have been impaled and the shrike who put them there trills from a nearby lightwire and it has begun to rain again.

And from his fleerglass window the shut-in watches for idle travelers on the path below, gripping the worn oak arms of his wheelchair, wishing all on to a worse hell yet.

The ragman hurried home with dark hard at his heels. When he reached the end of the bridge the lights went up behind him and he turned to look back for a moment before he ducked past the railing and down the red clay path to his home. Crouched before his fire he could see the stars come out in the darkening river. He kneaded his bony hands and watched the shapes flame took among the sticks of wood as if some portent might be read there. He smacked his gums and spat and gestured with his hands. He'd stood off a family of trashpickers in the alley that morning. There under the deepwalled shadows where the windows were barred and iron firestairs hung in chains overhead. Setting the dark brick corridor full of voices, aged but spoken with authority. Run them off like rats. And out of there you. And dont come back. Suttree rose from the rock where he'd been sitting and shook the stiffness from one knee. The old man looked up at him. From under the whites of his eyeballs peeked a rim of the red flame that raged in his head. You come back and find me dead, he began. Find me layin here dead, you just thow some coaloil on me and set me alight. You hear?

Suttree looked off toward the river and the lights and then he looked at the ragman again. You'll outlive me, he said.

No I wont neither. Will ye do it?

Suttree wiped his mouth.

I'll pay ye.

Pay me?

What will ye take? I'll give ye a dollar.

Good God, I dont want a dollar.

What would you have to have?

You wouldnt burn. He gestured with his hands. You wouldnt burn up with just coaloil thrown on you. It'd just make a big stink.

I'll get some by god gasoline then. I'll get five gallon and have it settin here at all times.

They'd send out the firetrucks when they saw that.

I dont give a good shit what they send. Will ye?

All right.

You wont take no dollar?

No.

I hold ye to your word now.

146

Whatever's right, said Suttree.

I aint no infidel. Dont pay no mind to what they say.

No.

I always figured they was a God.

Yes.

I just never did like him.

As he was going up Gay Street J-Bone stepped from a door and took his arm. Hey Bud, he said.

How you doin?

I was just started down to see you. Come in and have a cup of coffee.

They sat at the counter at Helm's. J-Bone kept tapping his spoon. When the coffee was set before them he turned to Suttree. Your old man called me, he said. He wanted you to call home.

People in hell want ice water.

Hell Bud, it might be something important.

Suttree tested the cup rim against his lower lip and blew. Like what? he said.

Well. Something in the family. You know. I think you ought to call.

He put the cup down. All right, he said. What was it?

Why dont you call him.

Why dont you tell me.

Will you not call?

No.

J-Bone was looking at the spoon in his hand. He blew on it and shook his head, the distort image of him upside down in the spoon's bowl misting away and returning. Well, he said.

Who's dead, Jim?

He didnt look up. Your little boy, he said.

Suttree set his cup down and looked out the window. There was a small pool of spilled cream on the marble countertop at his elbow and flies were crouched about it lapping like cats. He got up and went out.

It was dark when the train left the station. He tried to sleep, his head rolling about on the musty headrest. There was no longer a club car or dining car. No service anymore. An old black came through with his zinc sandwichtray and drink cooler. He passed down the corridor of the semidarkened car crying his wares softly and disappeared through the door at the far end. A racket of wheels from the roadway and a slip of cool air. The sleepers slept. The sad and dimly lit back side of a town went down the windows. Fencerails, weedlots, barren autumn fields sliding blackly off under the stars. They went across the flatland toward the Cumberlands, the old car rocking down the rails and the polewires sewing tirelessly the night beyond the cold windowglass.

He woke in various small mountain towns through the early hours of the morning, old people with baskets laboring up the aisle, black families with sleepy children clumping past, whispering, the rusty coaches wheezing and steaming and then the slow accumulate creaking and grating of iron as they pulled out again. It had grown cold in the night but he was numb with other weathers. An equinox in the heart, ill change, unluck. Suttree held his face in his hands. Child of darkness and familiar of small dooms. He himself used to wake in terror to find whole congregations of the uninvited attending his bed, protean figures slouched among the room's dark corners in all multiplicity of shapes, gibbons and gargoyles, arachnoids of outrageous size, a batshaped creature hung by some cunning in a high corner from whence clicked and winked like bone chimes its incandescent teeth.

In the cold autumn dawn that crept the fields he woke and watched the passing countryside through the glass. Light rain or mist, small beads of water racing on the pane. They crossed a creek by an old trestle, black creosoted timbers flicking past. On the gray water two boys in a skiff, motionless, watching the faces pass like a filmstrip above them. One raised a hand, a solemn gesture. In the distance smoking millstacks arranged upon a gray and barren plain. Somewhere beyond them the cold rain falling in a new dug grave.

The train lurched and rumbled. Went pounding down a long levee with marsh and swampland smoking in the bluish light, a white egret onelegged and livid in the water quartered to a darker antipode and rigid as a plaster lawnbird. Stark woods beyond, a few leaves falling. Suttree wiped his eyes with his shoulders and rose and went down the aisle past the stale and empty seats.

He stood between cars, the upper half of the door latched back and the cool morning wind blowing in. Leaning with his elbows propped, the car rocking and swaying as they came into the yards. Staccato lights tracking in the gray frieze out there. In an upper window a man in his undershirt with his braces hanging. Across the narrow space he and Suttree looked at each other for just a moment before he was snapped away. The gray steel trusses of a bridge went past, went past, went past. In the sidelong morning light he saw the shadowed halfshapes of auto shells crouched in dying ivy down a long and barren gut.

In the station Suttree stood bending to deal with a small man in a cage. Polished blue suit, a lapel badge. Ten oclock, the man said.

He nodded. There's no other transportation out there I dont guess.

The little man was stamping long rolls of ticket. He pouched his lower lip and shook his head.

Thanks.

Less you wanted to take a cab. Costs right smart.

Thanks, Suttree said.

He found a Krystal near the bus station and had scrambled eggs and toast and he looked through the newspaper but could see no news for him. At ten oclock he boarded the bus and leaned back and closed his eyes. Remorse lodged in his gorge like a great salt cinder.

What will she say?

What will her mother say?

Her father.

Suttree got up and swung down toward the door but the bus had already started. He hung by one hand swaying. All night he'd tried to see the child's face in his mind but he could not. All he could remember was the tiny hand in his as they went to the carnival fair and a fleeting image of elf's eyes wonderstruck at the wide world in its wheeling. Where a ferriswheel swung in the night and painted girls were dancing and skyrockets went aloft and broke to shed a harlequin light above the fairgrounds and the upturned faces.

They watched him from the porch, gathered there like a sitting for some old sepia tintype, the mother's hand on the seated patriarch's shoulder. Watched him coming up the walk with his empty hands and burntlooking eyes. Suttree's abandoned wife.

She came down the steps slowly, madonna bereaved, so grief-stunned and wooden pieta of perpetual dawn, the birds were hushed in the presence of this gravity and the derelict that she had taken for the son of light himself was consumed in shame like a torch. She touched him as a blind person might. Deep in the floor of her welling eyes dead leaves scudding. Please go away, she said.

When is the funeral?

Three oclock. Please Buddy.

I wont . . .

Dont say anything please I cant bear it.

By now the mother had come from the porch. She was dressed in black and closed upon them soundless as a plague, her bitter twisted face looming, axemark for a mouth and eyes crazed with hatred. She tried to speak but only a half strangled scream came out. The girl was thrown aside and this demented harridan was at him clawing, kicking, gurgling with rage.

The girl tried to pull her away. Mother, she wailed, Mother . . .

The old lady had gotten Suttree's finger in her mouth and was gnawing on it like a famished ghoul. He seized her by the throat. The three of them went to the ground. Suttree could feel something thudding at the base of his skull. The old man had come from the porch and was hitting him with his shoe. He tried to get to his feet. The girl was screaming. Stop it you all! Oh God, stop it!

Get the police, Leon, screamed the old lady. I'll hold him.

Suttree staggered erect in the midst of this sorry spectacle groaning like a bear. The old man had fallen back. The girl was pulling at the old lady but she was hanging onto his leg with a maniac's strength and gibbering the while. You ghastly bitch, he said, and fetched her a kick in the side of the head which stretched her out. With this the girl fell upon him in much the same manner. He flung her back and tottered away a few steps to get his breath. The old man was coming from the house loading a shotgun as he ran. Suttree vaulted through the hedge. He crossed a lawn and went through another hedge and down a small lane past some chickens in a foulsmelling pen, the birds flaring and squawking, Suttree crossing through another yard and coming out alongside a house where a man in a lawnchair looked up from the nothing he was contemplating and smiled curiously. Suttree nodded to him and went on down the drive into the road. He looked back but no one was coming. He walked on out to the highway and squatted by the side of the road to rest and when a car came down the pike he rose to flag it with his thumb.

In a few minutes another car came along and this one stopped. Suttree climbed in and said hello. The man looked at him once or twice with alarm. Suttree looked down at himself. The front of his shirt was ripped open and his left hand was covered with blood. He zipped up his jacket and they rode on in silence.

A small town in the flatlands. He had been here once but remembered it little. A fresh breeze was herding leaves along the walkways and little shopsigns swung and creaked in the smoky air. He pointed toward the curb and the man pulled over to let him out. Much obliged. The man nodding. Suttree could see him looking over the seat for bloodstains as he pulled away.

He went to the poolhall and washed up and looked at his hand. Four bright slashes on his jaw. He plucked small bits of harrowed flesh from the edges of the wounds and daubed at them with a wet paper towel. The face in the mirror that watched was gray and the eyes sunken. He put on his jacket and went to the front counter and asked to use the telephone. The man nodded toward it. There was a directory hanging from a chain. He opened to the back and found two listings under Funeral Parlors, dialed the first and spoke with a soft-voiced girl.

Are you people in charge of the Suttree funeral?

Yessir. That's at three oclock this afternoon.

Suttree didnt hear. The words *Suttree funeral* had caused him to let the receiver fall away from his ear.

Hello, said the girl.

Yes, said Suttree. Where is the burial to be?

At McAmon Cemetery.

Where is that?

The girl didnt answer for a moment. Then she said: The cortege will be going directly to the cemetery after the services. If you cared to join, or if you . . .

Thank you, Suttree said, but if you could just give me directions.

He walked about in the town. Peaceful and sunny in the mid Americas on an autumn day. The dread in his heart was a thing he'd not felt since he feared his father in the aftermath of some child's transgression.

He ate a sandwich in the drugstore and in the afternoon he started out toward the cemetery. Along a little country road where leaves lay in yellow windrows through the woods or tumbled over the dark macadam. It was an hour's walk and few cars passed.

Two stonework columns marked the entrance, the chain down and heaped in the grass. He went down the little gravel road among the stones until he saw on a hill a green canopy. Two men were sitting in the grass eating their lunch. Suttree nodded to them as he passed. Beneath the canopy were folding chairs in rows, a green canvas mound with flowers arranged.

He could not bring himself to ask if this were the place where his dead son was going and he walked on. If there were other burials in preparation he would see them.

In an older part of the cemetery he saw some people strolling. Elderly gent with a cane, his wife on his arm. They did not see him.

They went on among the tilted stones and rough grass, the wind coming from the woods cold in the sunlight. A stone angel in her weathered marble robes, the downcast eyes. The old people's voices drift across the lonely space, murmurous above these places of the dead. The lichens on the crumbling stones like a strange green light. The voices fade. Beyond the gentle clash of weeds. He sees them stoop to read some quaint inscription and he pauses by an old vault that a tree has half dismantled with its growing. Inside there is nothing. No bones, no dust. How surely are the dead beyond death. Death is what the living carry with them. A state of dread, like some uncanny foretaste of a bitter memory. But the dead do not remember and nothingness is not a curse. Far from it.

He sat in the dappled light among the stones. A bird sang. Some leaves were falling. He sat with his hands palm up on the grass beside him like a stricken puppet and he thought no thoughts at all.

In midafternoon an old Packard hearse came wending through the woods leading a few cars and circled the canopy on the hill and parked on the far side. The cars came quietly to rest and people in black emerged. Steel doors dropped shut softly one by one. The mourners moved graveward. Four pallbearers lifted the small coffin from the funeral car and carried it to the tent. Suttree came up over the hill in time to see it go. Some flowers fell. He walked up the hill above the gravesite and stood numbly. The little bier with its floral offerings had come to rest on a pair of straps across the mouth of the grave. A preacher stood at the ready. The light in this little glade where they stood seemed suffused with immense clarity and the figures appeared to burn. Suttree stood by a tree but no one noticed him. The preacher had begun. Suttree heard no word of what he said until his own name was spoken. Then everything became quite clear. He turned and laid his head against the tree, choked with a sorrow he had never known.

When all the words were done a few stepped forth and placed a flower and the straps began to lower, the casket and child sinking into the grave. A group of strangers commending Suttree's son to earth. The mother cried out and sank to the ground and was lifted up and helped away wailing. Stabat Mater Dolorosa. Remember her hair in the morning before it was pinned, black, rampant, savage with loveliness. As if she slept in perpetual storm. Suttree went to his knees in the grass, his hands cupped over his ears.

Someone touched his shoulder. When he looked up there was no one there. The last of the motorcade was moving down the little drive toward the gate and save the two sextons crouched in the hillside grass like jackals he was alone. He rose and went down to the grave.

There among flowers and the perfume of the departed ladies and the faint iron smell of the earth to stand looking down into a full size six foot grave with this small box resting in the bottom of it. Pale manchild were there last agonies? Were you in terror, did you know? Could you feel the claw that claimed you? And who is this fool kneeling over your bones, choked with bitterness? And what could a child know of the darkness of God's plan? Or how flesh is so frail it is hardly more than a dream.

When he looked up the gravediggers were watching him from the side of the hill. He called to them but they did not answer. Thinking him mad with grief perhaps. Perhaps he addressed his God.

You two. Hey.

They looked at each other and after a time rose slowly and came shambling down across the green like ordinaries in a teutonic drama. Suttree was sitting in one of the folding chairs. He gestured loosely at the grave. Can you fill this in now?

They looked at each other and then one of them folded his arms and looked down. Orville's comin with the tractor, he said.

We was just supposed to fold these here chairs and stack em, the other said. They got to come out and take the tent down.

Suttree stared at them. The one with his arms crossed began to rock up and down on his heels and look about.

Orville and them be here directly, the other one said.

Suttree rose from the chair and pulled back the canvas drop where it was thrown over the mound of earth. A few racks of flowers toppled. A pick and two spades lay there and he took up one of the spades and sank it into the loose dirt and hefted it and sent a load of clods rattling over the little coffin.

The two men looked at each other.

We got to get them straps, the one said.

You better get em then, said Suttree, swinging a spadeload of clay.

Well hold up a minute.

The smaller man stepped down into the grave to free the straps and the other one hauled them up.

You want this here wreath? said the man in the grave, raising up, just his head sticking out. He shook it. It's got dirty, he said.

Get out of there, said Suttree.

He climbed out and stood back. Orville and them'll be here in a minute, he said.

Suttree didnt answer. He labored on, shoveling the dirt, the two men watching. After a while they began to stir about, folding shut the chairs and stacking them against the corner pole of the canopy. Suttree stopped and took off his jacket and then bent to work again.

Before the grave was half filled a truck entered the cemetery gates towing a lowboy with a tractor chained to the bed. The tractor was rigged with a frontloader. They came up the hill and swung down alongside the tent. The driver of the truck looked down at Suttree, his chin on his arm. He spat and looked out over the cemetery grounds and opened the door and climbed down. I allowed you'd have this thing down, he called out.

Suttree looked. The other two men were smoking and grinning and shuffling their feet. The three of them looked over at him. He shoveled on. The driver in the lowboy climbed out and the four of them stood around talking and smoking. I dont know, one of them said. He just jumped up and went to shovelin.

I reckon he was. I dont know. No, he was settin up here on the side of the hill.

Hey, called one of the new men.

Suttree looked up.

We got a tractor here to do that with if you want to wait a minute.

Suttree wiped his brow with the back of his sleeve and kept on shoveling. The men trod out their cigarettes in the grass and set about uncleating ropes, gouging stakes from the ground. They hauled down the canopy and folded it out on the ground and Suttree worked on in the open air. They disjointed the pipework frame and loaded poles and ropes and canvas in the truck and passed the folded chairs in after.

We might as well leave the tractor on the float, one of the men said.

We goin to do them sods in the mornin?

We'll have to. It's done past quittin time now.

They sat in the grass watching him. Already it was evening and overcast and before he was done a small rain came cold and slowly falling out of the south autumn sky. Suttree pitched a final shovelful of clods over the little mound and dropped the spade and picked up his jacket and turned to go.

You can ride in with us if you want, one of the men said.

He looked up. They were squatting in the rear of the truck watching the rain. He went on.

Before he reached the cemetery gates a gray car with a gold escutcheon on the door came down the little gravel road and stopped alongside him. A paunchy man in tan gabardines looked up at him.

Your name Suttree?

Suttree said it was.

The man climbed out of the car. He wore a tooled belt and holster and his clothes were neatly pressed. He opened the rear door of the car. Get in, he said.

Suttree climbed into the back of the car and the door shut after him. There was a heavy screen mesh separating him from the front seat. As if the car were used for hauling mad dogs about. There were no door handles or window cranks. The driver looked at him in the mirror and the man in the gabardines looked straight ahead. Suttree leaned back and passed his hand over his eyes. As they came into town people watched him from the street.

Pull over here, Pinky, the man said.

They came to a stop at the curb.

Go get yourself a Coke.

I'm all right.

Go get yourself a Coke.

The driver looked back at Suttree and climbed out and shut the door. The sheriff leaned one arm across the back of the seat and regarded Suttree through the wire. Then he climbed out and opened the back door.

Get up here, he said.

Suttree climbed out and got into the front of the car. The sheriff walked around and climbed into the driver's seat. He studied Suttree for a minute and then he said: Let me tell you something.

All right, said Suttree.

He reached down and tapped Suttree's knee with his forefinger. You, my good buddy, are a fourteen carat gold plated son of a bitch. That's what your problem is. And that being your problem, there's not a whole lot of people in sympathy with you. Or with your problem. Now I'm goin to do you a favor. Against my better judgment. And it's not goin to make me no friends. I'm goin to drive your stinkin ass to the bus station and give you an opportunity to get out of here.

I dont have any money.

I never reckoned that you did. I intend to put up five dollars cash money out of my own pocket to get you started. I aint interested in where you go, but I aim to see to it that you go five dollars' worth in some direction and you and me both are goin to hope that you dont never come back. Now do you want to know why?

Why what?

Why I'm puttin up the five dollars.

No.

I thought maybe the economics of it might interest you. I hear tell you're supposed to be real smart.

I dont care.

The reason I'm investin five dollars in your absence is because the man whose daughter's life you ruined happens to be a friend of mine and a man I not only like but respect. And I'd like to see him have some peace of mind. I know he aint goin to thank me for this. What he'd like is to see you hung. But I know him for a fairminded man and a peacelovin man and I know that he'll be happier in his mind if he just gets you out of his sight. He might even come to forget there ever was a lowlife like you although I doubt it.

What do you get out of it?

Not a thing, good buddy.

You said I ought to be interested in the economics of it.

I said it but I dont believe it. It's not much economics anyway. About the only thing to be said for gettin fucked out of five dollars this way is that you wont catch the clap. I never expected you to understand.

No one cares. It's not important.

That's where you're wrong my friend. Everything's important. A man lives his life, he has to make that important. Whether he's a small town county sheriff or the president. Or a busted out bum. You might even understand that some day. I dont say you will. You might.

The sheriff turned in the seat and reached for the key and turned it. But the motor was already running and the starter made a sudden wild screeching sound. He muttered to himself and shifted the gears and they went on down the street.

The bus station was in the back of a cafe and when they pulled up in front there were two buses idling in the alley. The sheriff shifted and took out his billfold and lifted a five dollar bill from it and handed it across.

I suppose I have to take it, Suttree said.

You suppose correctly.

Suttree took the bill and looked at it.

Now, the sheriff said, I want you to take whichever bus out of here best pleases you and I want you to ride five dollars in that direction and I dont want you back. You got that?

I've got it.

Suttree was holding the money in his hand. The sheriff looked at him. You all right? he said.

Yeah. I'm all right.

I'm puzzled that you'd have the face to come here.

Well. You're puzzled.

I will say one thing: you've opened my eyes. I've got two daughters, oldest fourteen, and I'd see them both in hell fore I'd send them up to that university. I'm damned if I wouldnt.

How many sons have you got?

Not any. Look Suttree, I'm sorry as far as that goes. These people did want me to put you in jail.

I know.

Well. You get your ticket right in there. Dont let me see you on the street. You stay in there till your bus runs. You hear?

Suttree opened the door and climbed out. He looked down at the sheriff and then he shut the door.

You take care, the sheriff said.

Okay.

The sheriff had bent forward to see his face. Suttree turned and walked into the cafe.

He left the bus in Stanton Tennessee with three dollars still in his pocket. It was ten oclock at night. He walked down to a cabstand and bought a pint of whiskey from a driver and put it in his shirt and hiked out to the edge of town and stood in the road holding his thumb up at the lights that passed. None stopped. After an hour he walked on. It had turned cool. He could see lights far up the highway, a roadhouse or cafe.

The sign said it was a truck stop and there was a diesel rig pulled over on the gravel with the motor running. Suttree peered in through the plateglass window. A cold hall of a place. Plastic tables. Two boys playing a pinball machine. The driver sat at the counter drinking coffee. Suttree searched his pockets for a dime but he had none. He went in anyway.

An ancient waitress was cleaning out the coffee urn with a short-handled mop. When she saw Suttree she climbed down off the chair she was standing on and came shuffling up the aisle behind the counter. Suttree leaned on the counter next to the driver. The driver looked at him.

Is that your rig? said Suttree.

The driver set his cup down. Yeah, he said. That's my rig.

You reckon I could get a ride with you?

Where you goin?

To Knoxville.

I aint goin to Knoxville.

Well where are you going?

I aint goin to Knoxville.

The driver bent and sipped his coffee and Suttree stood looking down at him and then turned and left the cafe. He started back down the highway toward the town. The lights had dimmed, the town seemed farther at this midnight hour. Partway down the road he stopped and opened the bottle and drank.

The first building he came to was a church. There was a small illuminated glass case standing in the yard, white letters on a black plastic board within. Insects were swarming over the dimly lit church news. Suttree turned across the lawn and went to the back of the church and sat in the grass and drank the whiskey. After he had drunk a little of it he began to cry. He began to cry harder and harder until he was sitting there in the grass with the bottle upright between his knees, wailing aloud.

He must have slept. When he woke he was lying in the grass looking up at the heavens. A cloudless night strewn with stars. Salt taste of sorrow in his throat. He saw a star spill across the sky, a light trail of fire and then nothing. Hot spalls of matter rifling through the icy ether. Misshapen globs of iron slag.

The night had grown much colder. He lay in the grass shivering and he tried to sleep but he could not. After a while he rose and took the whiskey and went to the rear door of the church and tried it and it opened.

He was in a cellar. There were stacks of old newspapers and magazines along one wall and he stretched out on these and lay there. Then he sat up and took some to spread over him and lay down again. Then he started to cry again, lying there in the dark of the church cellar under the old newspapers.

It was midmorning when he woke. A truck gone out the pike had rattled the cellar door. He sat up in a flurry of newsprint and looked about. Light fell from a high window. Some kind of small bird was pecking in the grass there. Suttree rose and ran his hand through his hair. His throat was dry and his head hurt. The rest of the whiskey stood in the bottle on the floor and he fetched it up and held it to the light. It was about a third full and he unscrewed the cap and took a drink and shuddered and shook himself and then took another drink. Then he went out.

It took him all day to cross the state. He was unshaven and he looked bad. Toward evening he was in a nameless crossroads high in the Cumberland Mountains. A quarter mile down the road in the dusk stood a figure like his own, a wanderer longmirrored in the black asphalt, one arm aloft. Suttree walked on. It was a husky young boy and he had stationed himself in front of a small country store to try for a ride. Suttree walked on past. The store was closed and the windows boarded up and some twisted pipes grew from the concrete apron in front where a gaspump had been ripped up.

Hey, the boy said.

Hey, said Suttree.

You live around here?

No.

You aint got a cigarette on you have you?

The boy was walking down toward him, studying him with a kind of sly intensity that drifters seem to come by. No, Suttree said.

I saw you thumbin down there. Where you headed?

Knoxville.

I'm goin to Florida. I got a sister in Fort Lauderdale. He turned and spat. He had on a shortsleeved shirt and Suttree in his jacket was already cold. Dark as it was he could see him but poorly. Tattoos along one arm.

I'll go on down, said Suttree.

The boy changed his tone. Listen, he said. Why dont we hitch together. We might have a better chance.

Suttree looked at him. He was dressed in jeans and his hair was wild and he wore a general look of dangerous filth. A big meanlooking kid. I'll go on down, said Suttree. Let you have first shot.

You reckon anybody might stop along here after dark?

I dont know. Your guess is as good as mine.

Yeah?

Where did you come from?

The kid's eyes shifted. St Louis, he said.

St Louis, said Suttree. I've been through there.

Aint this a hell of a place to get stuck?

Yeah. Good luck.

Listen. How far is it to the next town?

I dont know.

Suttree had started off. Listen, the kid called again.

What?

You got a quarter you could let me have?

Suttree shook his head no.

The kid was walking down toward him. Come on, man, he said. I aint eat in two goddamned days. Hell, fifteen cents. Somethin.

I aint got a dime, Suttree said.

Let's see.

Suttree watched him. He was standing on the balls of his feet and he looked hungry. What? he said.

I said let's see. Let's see you turn your pockets out.

I told you I'm not holding anything.

The kid moved slightly to his left. That's what you say, he said. I'd like to see.

That's your problem, Suttree said. He stepped back and turned to go. As he did so the kid jumped him. Suttree ducked. They went to the ground together. Suttree could smell the stale sweat of him. The kid was trying to hit him, short chops with his big fists. Suttree pushed his face against his chest. Fear and nausea. The kid quit punching and tried to get him by the throat. Suttree rolled. They came up. The kid had hold of his jacket. Suttree swung at him. They closed, feet scrabbling in the gravel there in the near dark in front of the abandoned store. The kid turned loose of Suttree to hit him and Suttree dropped to one knee and seized the kid behind the calves and pulled him down hard on his rump. Then he was running down the highway. The kid's shoes slapping after him. Taste of blood in his mouth. But the footsteps faded and when Suttree looked back he could see in the deeper dusk by the roadside the kid crouched to get his breath.

You yellow cocksucker, the voice came drifting up the highway.

Suttree put his hand to his heart where it boomed in the otherwise silence of the wilderness. He went on up the road in the dark.

It is little more than dawn when the general comes down Front Street slumped on the box of his coalwagon, the horse named Golgotha hung between the trees and stumbling along in the cold with his doublejointed knees and his feet clopping and the bright worn quoits winking feebly among the clattering spokes. In the whipsocket rides a bent cane. There is a gap in the iron of one tire and above the meaningless grumbling of the wagon it clicks, clicks, with a clocklike persistence that tolls progress, purpose, the passage of time. When they stop it is in a violent shudder, as if something has given way. The general climbs and climbs down from his seat and goes to the rear and takes up his blackened basket and sets it in the street. He levers up the lantern glass and blows out the tiny flame. He hands down coal lump by lump until the basket is filled and with pain he hefts and carries it toward the dim house, through the chill fog bent and muttering, returning lightened but with no better speed or humor to where the horse stands sleeping in the traces.

They come trundling and slowly aclatter up the empty street, pass under the bridge and take the bitter and frozen fields toward the river. In the hoarcolored dawn they seem to be drifting, closed away in the cold smoke until just the general's shoulders and the slouched back of him with his hat perched on the shoulders of his clothes and the hat the horse wore float over the cold gray void like transient artifacts from a polar dream.

> Ooh coal, kindlin wood
> Would if I could
> Hep me get sold
> Coal now.

It was six degrees above zero. Suttree crawled from his bed, pulled on his coat and got his trousers and climbed up onto the bed to don them so cold the floor was. He squatted and fished his socks out from beneath the cot and shook out the dust and pulled them on and stepped into his shoes and went to the door. Mist swirled about him. The old black coalpedlar sat his cart, the horse sidled and stamped.

Couldnt you just leave a basket and go on?

I see you aint froze, said the general, climbing down.

Suttree got the basket from beside the door and came down the walk. The river was frozen between the houseboat and the bank, a thin skim of wrinkled ice through which fell chunks of frozen mud from the underside of the flexing plank. He threw the empty basket up on the wagon and took the full one from the old man.

I gots to have me some money today, the general said.

How much?

You owes me eighty-five cents.

How do you know?

The old man patted his gloved hands together. His head was wrapped in rags. I keeps it all in my counts, he said. You keep you own if'n you dont like mine.

Where do you keep them?

That's all right where I keeps em.

How much will you take?

What all I can get, I reckon.

Suttree set the basket on the frozen ground and reached in his trouser pocket. He had thirty-five cents. He gave it to the old man and the old man looked at it a minute and nodded and pulled a cord that went down into his clothing. A long gray sock appeared. The top of it had been fitted with an old brass pursecatch and he unsnapped it and dropped in the coins and lowered it back where it had come from and climbed up onto the wagon box.

Hump sleepyhead, he said.

The horse lurched forward. Suttree watched them cross the field, fording the pale vapors, the dead lamp hung by its bail from the tailboard, the cart tilting up at the tracks and tilting back again and descending from sight. Upriver he could see a hazy swatch of cold blue light where the sun was rising through the river fog but it was no light much and no warmth at all. He took the basket of coal and toted it back up the plank and went in. He didnt even bother to shut the door. He put the basket by the stove and took up the coalscuttle and shook it. Jacking open the cold stove door with his foot he tipped the scuttle, the coal clunking in, dry ash stirring upward. Suttree peered down the iron gullet, prying at the slag in the stove's belly with the poker. He crumpled a newspaper and dropped it down alight and held his hands to the fleeting warmth. The newspaper curled up in a tortured ash that rose in the stove's mouth, a charred gravure whereon lay gray news, gray faces. Suttree hugged himself and swore. An icy wind was singing in the cracks. He fetched the lamp from the table, removed the chimney and unscrewed the brass wickpiece and emptied the lamp oil into the stove. A white smoke rose. He struck a match and dropped it in but nothing occurred. He snatched up a piece of newspaper and lit it and poked it in. A ball of flame belched up. He did a few stiff dancesteps and went out to relieve himself.

Ice lay along the shore, frangible plates skewed up and broken on the mud and small icegardens whitely all down the drained and frozen flats where delicate crystal columns sprouted from the mire. He hauled forth his shriveled giblet and pissed a long and smoking piss into the river and spat and buttoned and went in again. He kicked the door shut and stood before the stove in a gesture of enormous exhortation. A frozen hermit. His lower jaw in a seizure. He cast about and got his cup and looked into it. He turned it up and tapped it and an amber lens of frozen coffee slid forth and went rocking and clattering around the basin. He took down the frying pan and set it on the stove and spooned the stiff gray grease. From his packingcrate pantry he selected two eggs and tapped one smartly on the rim of the pan. It rang like stone. He threw it against the wall and it dropped to the floor and rolled oblong and woodenly beneath the bunk. He hung the pan back on the wall and stared out the window. Frost ferns arched from the sashcorners over the glass and the river slouched past like some drear drainage from the earth's bowels. Suttree buttoned his coat and went out.

All the weeds were frozen up in little ice pipettes, dry husks of seedpods, burdock hulls, all sheathed in glass and vanes and shells of ice that webbed old leaves and held in frozen colloid specks of grit or soot or blacking. Wonky sheets of ice spanned the ditches and the ironcolored trees along the wintry desolate and bitter littoral were seized with gray hoarfrost. Suttree crossed the brittle fields to the road and went up Front Street. A parcel of black children came by from the store towing a child's wagonload of coal, chips and dust scavenged from a railsiding, going along quietly and barely clothed and seemingly dumb to the elements. Suttree's underjaw chattered till he had thought for his teethfillings. He crossed the street and crossing the store porch read the tin thermometer on the wall at zero or near it. He entered and went directly to the back without answering Howard Clevinger's courtly matin greeting. An old black widow was crouched by the grocer's stove on an upturned basket watching the fire through a jagged crack in the hot iron. She seemed to be in tears, so thick dripped the rheum from the red underlips of her eyeholes. She had a club foot and wore boots sewn up from an old carpet, blue balding pile with mongrel flowers, an eastern look about her, mute and shawled. She kneaded her hands each in each in their cropfingered army gloves and mumbled a ceaseless monologue. Suttree standing there inclined his head to hear, wondering what the aged dispossessed discuss, but she spoke some other tongue and the only word he knew was Lord.

Jabbo and Bungalow came in out of the weather in a bathless reek of cold wool and splo whiskey. They stood by the stove and nodded and spread their hands.

Cold enough for ye?

I'm frozen.

You needs you a good drink, Suttree.

Go on and give him one then, big time.

Bungalow looking at Jabbo with question.

Go on. Suttree aint too proud to drink after a nigger. Is you, Suttree?

The old woman vacated her basket and moved away to the wall.

I pass.

Where's the bottle.

Bungalow, lifting the front of his jersey, drew a pint bottle partly filled with a clear liquid from his waistband. The blacks looked warily toward the storekeeper. Jabbo took the bottle and unscrewed the cap and handed it toward Suttree.

Here go, man.

I cant use it.

Go ahead.

No.

I thought you said old Suttree didnt care to drink after a black man.

Why dont you come off that shit.

Jabbo was weaving very slightly like a krait just faintly disturbed. His sullen lip hung loose. He shook the bottle slowly. It's good whiskey man. Good enough for me and Bungalow.

I said I didnt want one.

Jabbo pressed the bottle against his chest.

Suttree raised his hand and gently put the bottle from him. The only sound in the store was the rusty creak of the damper swinging in the tin flue with the wind's suck.

It's Thanksgiving man. Have a little drink.

The bottle was at his chest again.

You better get that bottle out of my face, Suttree said.

You askin or tellin.

I said get it out of my face.

This aint Gay Street, motherfucker.

I know what street I'm on. Maybe you better get off those red devils. Why dont you offer Howard a drink?

He dont drink, said Bungalow.

Shut up, Bungalow. Come on, Mr Suttree, please suh, take a little drink with us poor old niggers.

Oceanfrog Frazer had entered the store. The members by the stove felt his presence, or perhaps it was the cold draft of air from outside or the way the damper fluttered. The old lady had moved off to a corner where she mumbled among the canned goods. Oceanfrog came from the cold to the stove, palms gesturing benison, an easy smile. He looked at the blacks and he looked at Suttree. Jabbo held the bottle uncertainly.

Friends and neighbors, said Oceanfrog.

Old Suttree wont take a drink, said Bungalow.

Shut up, Bungalow.

Oceanfrog'll take a drink, said Oceanfrog.

Jabbo looked at the bottle. Oceanfrog took it gently and held it to the light in spite of Howard Clevinger who was now looking toward the rear. The bottle was about two thirds dry. Oceanfrog tilted it. Bubbles shot upward through the liquid and a great boiling and churning occurred within the glass, the liquor scuttling down the neck of the bottle. Frazer's black cheeks ballooned. He leaned and spewed a long clear pisslike stream through the standing door of the stove and a ball of bluish flame leaped. Bungalow stepped back. Oceanfrog eyed the bottle sadly, his brows scorched up in little owlish tufts over the cold eyes.

That's awful whiskey, Jabbo, he said.

Are you all drinkin whiskey back there?

Aint nobody got any whiskey, Howard.

I better not hear of no whiskey drinkin in my store.

You all didnt ought to drink that old shit, Jabbo. Here.

What I want with that, motherfucker?

Oceanfrog, shrugging, dropped the bottle in the stove, Bungalow stepped back again. A whooshing disturbance occurred in the stove's bowels. What say, Suttree, said Oceanfrog.

Not much. How you?

Just tiptoein.

Feylovin motherfucker, said Jabbo.

I guess I goin to have to slap a black pumpknot on somebody's old bony head, said Oceanfrog. He didnt even look at Jabbo.

Shit, said Jabbo. He jerked his jacket up on his shoulders and reeled toward the door. Bungalow looked after him. To go or stay? He spread his feet and held his hands to the warmth while he thought about it.

What's wrong with him? said Suttree.

He thinks he's bad. Gets on them reds. Old Bungalow here, he dont do that shit. Do you, Bunghole?

Bungalow looked shyly at the floor. Naw, he said.

You look like you been hit with a blivet, Bunghole.

Bungalow didnt answer. He stepped back to make room for the old lady who had come to the stove again and was pulling at the basket and adjusting her skirts to sit. Suttree looked down at her as she refolded the shawl, at the thinly grizzled crown of her small skull. A few graybacks retreated in the rancid wool.

You aint got a turkey staked out somewheres today have you Bungalow?

I wisht I did.

I bet old Suttree does.

Not yet I dont.

Shit, said Bungalow. You know he is.

I guess in a bind we can eat at Bungalow's, said Suttree.

Shit. Aint nothin to eat at my house.

Oceanfrog had turned around to warm his backside. Suttree heard a little choking sob and looking down he saw that the old woman was crying to herself, dabbing at her nose with a bony knuckle.

That old Suttree, said Oceanfrog. You got to watch him. He's a rathole artist. Tell him open his coat there Bungalow, see if he aint got a turkey under it. He looked at Suttree, then he looked down at the dollshaped pile of sticks at his feet. He stooped. Hey, he said. What's wrong with you, little mama?

She was muttering and talking and sobbing to herself and she didnt seem to notice she'd been spoken to.

Hey Howard, said Oceanfrog. Who is this old woman?

How would I know.

How would Howard know? said Oceanfrog. He went to the box and lifted the lid and poked around and came back with a half pint of milk and opened it and bent and put it in the old woman's hands. When

Suttree left she was still holding it and she was still talking but she wasnt crying anymore.

He went on up the street. Two small boys were coming along. Hey boys, he said.

What's your name? said one.

Suttree. What's yours?

No answer. The other one said: His name's Randy. He's my brother.

Suttree looked at them. They were wreathed in steam and small sacs of mucus hung from their nostrils. Who's the oldest?

Randy's brother looked at the ground a minute. Allen is, he said.

Suttree grinned. How many of you are there?

I dont know.

You better come on, said Randy.

We'll see you, Suttree said.

He watched them. Skipping down the street, one look back. Ashcolored children hobbling down the gloom. This winter come, gray season here in the welter of sootstained fog hanging over the city like a biblical curse, cheerless medium in which the landscape blears like Atlantis on her lightless seafloor dimly through eel's eyes. Bell toll in the courthouse tower like a fogwarning on some shrouded coast. A burnt smell in the air compounded of coalsoot and roast coffee. Small birds move through the glazed atmosphere with effort.

He crossed the street at the top of the hill and went through the rimey grass toward the post office. Down the long marble corridor and out the far side. Up this alley. Sheer brick walls the color of frozen iodine. Slow commence of traffic, pitch and clang of trolleys. Newsmen stamping at their corners, fingers stirring the coinage in their soiled changeaprons. On Market Street beggars being set out like little misshapen vending machines. Whole legions of the maimed and mute and crooked deployed over the streets in a limboid vapor of smoke and fog. The carlights seemed to tunnel through gauze. Pigeons gurgled and gaped from their ledges on the markethouse, winged shapes flapped forth through the gray haze. Shivering, he made his way toward the dewy neon windowlight that bears the painted ham.

Suttree studied the breakfast through the glass, stroking the lavender lunule on the side of his jaw. None there he knew save one, Blind Richard at coffee. He shrugged up his coat about his shoulders and entered.

A few heads turned. Old codgers bent above their gruel. A clack of china teeth. In a shroud of cold he stood within the door, then made his way down the counter.

Richard, he said.

Gray head goggling fowlwise on a scarious neck, turning. The soapfilled eyesockets.

Hey Suttree. How you doin?

Okay. How are you.

Other'n bein froze I caint complain. The blind man cracked a squaloid smile all full of toothblack and breakfast scraps.

Are you holding anything?

Smile draining. Aye, gape those barren lightshorn eyeballs.

What did you need, Sut?

Let me have a dime.

Richard sought about in a gray pocket. Here you go.

Thanks Richard. He moved down the counter to an empty stool and ordered coffee. Steaming cup of morning purgative. Ponderous white chipped cup with the sandy rim. Spectra winking, pinlets of oil atop impotable tarleachings. He brimmed the cup with cream. Beyond the steambleared windowpanes warped figures shrouded up in overcoats went wobbling past. He sipped the coffee. Ulysses entered. He hung his hat carefully and eased himself down on the stool by Suttree and laid his paper by and took up the menu. You still glutting the labor market, I see, he said.

Morning Ulyss.

Been anyone in here this morning hiring?

Not yet. Let's see a piece of the paper.

Ulysses separated the sheets and passed him a section. He folded the menu and replaced it in the rack and looked up. Two scrambled with ham and coffee, he said. The Greek nodded. Suttree thumbed forward his cup for a refill.

Turned off a bit chill hasnt it? said Ulysses.

They spread their papers. Two cups of coffee clattered to. They were at passing cream and sugar, stirring idly.

Jo Jo says it went down to six above, said Suttree.

Mmm, said Ulysses.

The ham and eggs arrived on an oblong platter of gray crockery.

Suttree folded the paper and laid it on the counter at Ulysses' elbow.

You want to see this piece? said Ulysses.

No thanks. I've got to go.

Dont rush off.

Suttree drained his cup and rose. The Greek looked up from turning rashers of brains at the grill. Suttree pitched the dime on the counter and buttoned his coat.

How's J-Bone these days, said Ulysses.

About the same.

He doesnt come around much anymore.

He's working now.

Ulysses smiled. Another victim fallen to employment, eh?

All these good men, said Suttree.

He went by Gay Street to the lower end of the town, down Hill Avenue past the Andrew Johnson and Blount Mansion to the viaduct. A little stone stairway descended from the street. No sign of life in the cold clay warren below.

Gene.

Voice croupy in the cavern. He looked about. After a while he called again. From the little concrete vault that housed sheathed pipes and strange gray vats of electricity came a muffled answer.

It's me, said Suttree.

Pinched face at the door. Harrogate crawled out and squatted on the ground. He wrapped his arms about the folded bones within his denim trouser legs and looked up at Suttree. He was a pale blue color.

Well, said Suttree.

Shit, said Harrogate.

What happened to your bed?

Harrogate gestured over his shoulder. I pulled the mattress in yonder. I've never knowed such cold as this.

Well get off your ass and let's go uptown.

I went up to the hotel a while back. This nigger come over ast me what it was I wanted and I had to leave again.

You got any money?

Not a cryin dime.

Well come on let's go. You'll freeze down here.

I done already am. Shit.

Harrogate rose and spat and heisted up his shoulders in a shuddering gesture of despair and crossed the frozen ground toward the stairs. You could see the shape of his shoulderblades through the army jacket he wore. They climbed to the street above, hands in pockets.

Have you eaten anything?

Harrogate shook his head. Shit no. I'm a mere shadder.

Well, let's see about getting some groceries in your skinny gut.

You got any money?

Not yet.

Shit, said Harrogate.

They hiked up the cold and desolate street. A bitter wind had risen and little balls of soot hobbled along the walks. Old papers rose and rattled in an alleyway and a paper cup went scuttling. These lone figures going through the naked streets swore at the cold and something like the sun struggled at ten oclock sleazy and heatless beyond the frozen pestilential miasma that cloaked the town.

At Lane's Drugs they peered in.

They're closed.

It's Thanksgiving.

Harrogate looked about. Well hell, he said.

We'll go down to Walgreen's. They always have a turkey dinner.

Large posters hung within the glass facade. A steaming plate of turkey meat with dressing and potatoes and peas and cranberry sauce. The price was fifty-nine cents.

How does that look? said Suttree.

Harrogate just shook his head.

They filed through the door and Suttree went to the cash register. A blond girl in glasses raised up from below the counter with cartons of cigarettes to fill the little shelves. Hey good-lookin, she said.

Hi Mary Lou.

What are you doin?

I came to eat.

She looked past him and around. Okay, she said.

I brought a friend.

Okay, she said.

He smiled and pursed his lips in a kiss and he and Harrogate made their way down along the counter and climbed onto stools.

Two turkey dinners, Suttree said.

She wrote on the green ticket. You all want coffee?

You want coffee, Gene?

Hell yes.

Two coffees.

They sipped water from little paper cones in openwork holders.

Quit looking so nervous, Gene.

Yeah yeah, sure sure, said Harrogate. He was staring at the gaudy cardboard placards above the fountain with their icecream sundaes and model sandwiches. He looked about and he leaned toward Suttree. I thought you said you didnt have no money, he whispered.

I thought you said you had some.

I'm gettin the fuck out of here.

Suttree took hold of his sleeve. I was just kidding, he said.

You sure?

Sure.

Harrogate unbuttoned his jacket and began to look about more easily. Coffee arrived.

How did you sleep last night?

He spooned great lavings of sugar. Not worth a shit, he said. You?

Suttree just shook his head. The stripling on the stool beside him with his heron's legs dangling smelled like a smoked jockstrap. Even the waitress's eyes went a little funny when she passed and she herself no rosegarden.

Looky here, said Harrogate.

She set before them each a white platter. Sliced turkey and dressing pooled over in thick gravy and steaming creamed potatoes and peas and a claretcolored dollop of cranberry sauce and hot rolls with pats of creamery butter. Harrogate's eyes were enormous.

You all want some more coffee?

Yes mam.

Harrogate had his mouth so crammed with food his eyes bulged. Take it easy, Gene. There's no prize at the bottom of the plate.

Harrogate nodded, slumped over the plate and encircling it with one arm while he scooped falling forkfuls toward his underjaw. There was no conversation. Down the counter a man sat reading the newspaper. The waitresses lollygagged about, dragging foul dishclouts across the stainless steel equipment. Suttree took in this scene of stone eyed boredom while he ate. He'd have ordered second plates around had it not been for attracting attention.

With his belly full Harrogate's countenance grew cute and his eyes began to sidle. They drank more coffee. He leaned toward Suttree.

Listen Sut. Let me have the checks and we'll slip on around to the other side and look at the magazines till we see the coast is clear and then we'll ease on out.

It's all right.

Hell, save your money. We may need it. Listen, they're easy here.

Suttree shook his head. They're watching you, he said.

What all do you mean, watching me?

You look suspicious.

I look like it? What about you?

They can tell I'm all right just by looking.

Why you shit-ass.

Suttree was laughing with his mouth full of coffee.

Come on Suttree. Hell, you can go out first if you want and I'll foller ye.

Suttree wiped his chin and looked down at the sharp and strangely wizened childsface rapt with larceny. Gene?

Yeah?

You waste me.

Yeah. Well.

In the street they stood facing downwind, picking their teeth.

What are you going to do?

I dont know. Freeze.

Dont you know anybody over on the hill you could sort of visit?

I dont know. I could go up to Rufus's maybe.

Well get somewhere. I'm going over to see how the old man is. We'll figure something out.

I believe it's the end of the world.

What?

Harrogate was looking at the pavement. He said it again.

Look at me, Suttree said.

He looked up. Sad pinched face, streaked with grime.

Are you serious?

Well what do you think about it?

Suttree laughed.

It aint funny, said Harrogate.

You're funny, you squirrely son of a bitch. Do you think the world will end just because you're cold?

It aint just me. It's cold all over.

It's not cold by Rufus's stove. Now get your ass up there. I'll see you later.

A colder wind was coming upriver across the bridge. Suttree scurried along like a hunchback. When he got to the other side he scrambled down the frozen mudbank and ducked under the bridge. There was no fire.

Ho, he called.

Oh, said a voice from the arches.

He entered and looked about. The old man's bed and the old man's cart and the mounds of junk and rags and furniture. Frozen seepage hung from the bell joints of cesspipes overhead. Suttree turned and went back up the bank to the street and crossed the bridge again.

He went up Market and up the hill to Vine Avenue and the halfdollar dosshouse there, old darkened brick and gabley mansard roof shingled up in slates the shape of fishscales. He looked for a bell but there were just the wires hanging from a hole so he tapped on the glass of the sidelights. They gave soft and soundless in their lead muntins. He tapped on the door. After a while he tried the knob. The door was unlocked and he entered. Into a cold and narrow hallway. He shut the door and went down in the semidark calling out hello. No one was about. He paused at the coiled banister finial and gazed up the cold black stairwell. He listened. A sound of snuffling. Someone spat. He came back along the hall and opened a door. Upon a drawing room full of derelicts. It looked like the hatching of some geriatric uprising, this congregation of the ravaged on their rickety chairs all gathered about a patent iron stove, old graylooking men crouched by the warmth in the barren room, nodding and muttering and hawking gobbets of spit clogged with dust and blood against the hot iron to sizzle and stink. The ragpicker was crouched in the corner on the old hearth almost behind the stove. Suttree saw him look up, eyes that could not see far. The ragpicker didnt know who had come in until Suttree said his name.

Who's that? he said, craning his neck and looking up.

Suttree.

Ah, said the ragpicker.

Suttree smiled. A warm odor of filth hung in the room cut through with a reek of urine.

What are you doing?

Mildewing. You?

I'm freezing.

This is just the commence of it. I look for the river to freeze over. You better draw your lines. The ice'll cut em. You never will find em. I've seen it to happen. Bet me.

Suttree squatted and held his hands to the fire. A man with a mauve face like the faces of the dead was looking down at him.

How long have you been up here? said Suttree.

Since two days ago.

Suttree looked around. Mauve man was looking at a hole in the floor. A quivering string of drool hung from his lower lip halfway to his shoe.

How long do you plan on staying?

The ragpicker shrugged up his buzzard's shoulders. For however long it stays cold. I dont care. I just wisht I could die and I'd be better off.

Suttree ignored this. He'd heard it all before. How many do they have staying here? he said.

The ragpicker waved his hand. I dont know. What all's here, I reckon. Aint no other place in the house warm that I know of.

Where are the rooms, upstairs?

Yeah, upstairs. The beds is all took.

Mauve man had been listening. Cecil's aint took, he said.

Well. Cecil's aint took.

Who's Cecil?

Just old Cecil. He died.

Oh.

He never died in the bed though.

Where'd he die?

Uptown. He got too drunk to come in and I reckon he passed out. He was froze, they said. I dont know.

He froze, said Mauve man. Old Cecil did.

Cecil froze.

Old Cecil froze from head to toes

And stiffer than a tortoise

In spite of drinking strained canned heat

And dilute Aqua Fortis

Suttree waved away these things from his ears. Cecil was being discussed by the company. All agreed that the day of his death was a cold one. Today even colder. It's colder than a welldigger's ass said one, another said A witch's tit. A nun's cunt said a third. On Good Friday.

Suttree leaned and touched the old man's arm. His coat with the eaten elbows. The ragpicker jerked awake and turned a baleful red eye on him.

Who do you see about a room here?

He aint here.

It's fifty cents isnt it?

By the night it is. You can rent by the week and beat them rates. Two fifty. If you've got it. What's wrong with your place? You've not got thowed out have ye?

It's for somebody else.

Well you better tell him to come on. With this weather. You caint look for somebody to die just ever day.

When is whatsit due back?

I caint say.

Can I look upstairs?

You can look anyplace you take a notion because he aint here.

Do you need anything?

I need everthing.

Suttree rose.

Bring something for the pot, said the ragman, and you can sit in. He gestured upward with a gray hand webbed in part of a sock. A lardpail simmered on the one eye of the iron stove and a pieplate with a rock in it lifted along one edge like a thin frogjaw and belched forth a gout of steam and clapped shut again.

I'll see what I can do, said Suttree. He eased his way around the edge of these half addled aged and rumsoaked dotards and ascended the stairs.

Muted light fell through a window at the end of the hall. The doors had all been unpinned from their hinges and taken away. Suttree peered into an old boudoir with mattresses along the walls. Tattered gray army blankets. A thin little man was squatting by the window masturbating. He did not take his eyes from Suttree nor did he cease pulling at his limp and wattled cock. It was deadly cold in the room. Suttree turned and went back and down the stairs.

Mrs Rufus opened the door.

Cold enough for you? said Suttree.

She motioned him in.

Harrogate was sitting by the stove with a parcel of blacks all of whom were drunk or working at it. When Harrogate turned and raised his head Suttree saw that the city rat himself was reeling.

How the hell did you manage to get drunk this quick? he said.

Drinkin whiskey is how. Have a goddamn drink Sut. Give him a drink Cleo.

An angular black with splayed teeth held forth a quart picklejar half full of splo. Suttree waved it away.

Where's Rufus?

He aint here.

I can see that.

I told that fool not to give him none of that whiskey, said Mrs Rufus from behind him in a muted shriek.

I never poured it down his thoat, said a dark dwarf by the stovedoor.

Suttree looked around. Well fuck it, he said.

Who is this cat? said a tawny freckled halfbreed. Small skull covered with snips of copper wire.

He's cool man, he's cool, said Harrogate, having fallen easily into the way of things.

Suttree turned and went out. He pulled the door to behind him and went on along the little cinder path past the hoglot, a pair of snouts working in the fence mesh to get the wind of him. Long ears tilting, pale eyes watching from their purlieu of frozen mire. He went out to the road and across the viaduct toward town. The lightest rain of soot was falling and a handful of small birds flared suddenly about him, moving through the bitter air with a faint rasping sound. Suttree looked down at the blackwater creek swirling below, the gray panes of scalloped ice. He went on toward the town, a colorless world this winter afternoon where all things bear that grainy look of old films and the buildings rise into an obscurity prophetic and profound.

He went up Central, slumped and hands deeply pocketed. An eyeless beggar addled with the cold sat in the empty feastday street singing a canticle to his eternal night and holding out a simple frozen claw for whatever might fall almswise. Suttree hawked up and thooked forth a clot of phlegm against a boarded storewindow and started across the street. As he did so his eye fell on a cartoken in the gutter. He bent to claim it. Small brass coin stamped through with a K. He crossed the street and swung up through the open door of a standing trolley and dropped the coin in the glass cage and went down the aisle. The driver watched him in the mirror. Suttree eased himself into the cold leather seat and looked out.

Lights came on above the shops, a neon sign here, sudden paltry spanglements against the bluegray dusk. A fabled miscellany in this pawnshop window. The door clattered and hushed shut and the trolley lurched forward. The pale domes of light in the clerestory waxed more yellow. The seats to the front of the streetcar were vacant yet two blacks hung by one arm each like gibbons from the chrome rail overhead and swayed with the gathering speed. With the heel of his hand Suttree cleared a small window in the frosted glass and peered out at the few figures receding along the walks. Fellow citizens in this bewintered city. A passing rack of hot neon washed his own sad countenance from the glass. He leaned his head against the cold pane, watching pedestrians toil from pool to pool of lamplight, trailing wisps of vapor, bent figures, homebound. He could smell the old varnished wood of the sash and the brass of the catches. The trolley slowed, surged forth again. Cars passed below, a rumpling sound of tires over the bricks. The buildings dropped away. They were going by a frozen mudflat, lunar, naked, spoored with fossil dogtracks. Under the billboard lights small sprawling mica constellations.

The lightwires slung past in shallow convections pole to pole and the loneliness rode in his stomach like an egg.

Bell ching. This archaic craft grinding to a halt. People shuffling out through the folding door. A wet pneumatic hiss, clanking into motion once again. Your face among the brown bags old lady. Waiting to cross. Blinking at the transit of these half empty frames slapping past. Beyond in a yellowlit housewindow two faces fixed aspectant and forever in some domestic vagary. Rapid his progress who petrifies these innocents into stony history.

They swung past the deserted park, the midway, the ferriswheel like a burntout armature standing black and cold against the farther streetlamps. The trolley heeled hard by a brick wall and went rattling down an alleyway where scrawled fucks in rainwashed chalk flashed past the window under the crackling blue stroboscope of the antenna. They wheeled through a long carbarn and pulled to a stop with dimming lights.

End of the line, buddy, the driver called back.

I'll just ride on back to town with you, Suttree said.

Well you'll have to come up here and put a token in the box.

I thought you could ride as far as you wanted on one token.

Not on this streetcar.

Suttree rose and made his way down the aisle, his eye studying the floor for a chance of coin or token among the matchstems and gumwrappers. Listen, he said, cant I just ride on back?

Fares is one way, said the driver.

I dont have another token.

They're five for thirty cents. Or you can put in a dime.

I dont have any money.

Oh well, said the driver. He reached and got his little leather bag and rose. This would be a pleasant world if everybody could just ride and ride.

He descended the steps with his satchel and crossed through the dim electric gloom of the terminal toward the dispatch office. Suttree went out to the street.

A few carlights came owllike from the murk and receded. He stood beneath a streetlamp with his thumb out. In his thin coat he was cold to the bone in moments. The streetcar hove from the carbarn and sucked by the soft yellow bore of the headlamp went trundling past. Blacks nodding in their windowstrips. A trolley of dolls or frozen dead.

Suttree with one foot in the gutter glared numbly after the helmless driver and the springworn trucks moaned and lolled on their shackles and a blue tailstar clicked along the wires and the trolley drew away into the night. He gripped his thighs through his threadbare pockets and set off along the weedy walkway. The lights of Knoxville quaked in a faint penumbra to the west as must the ruins of many an older city seen by herders in the hills, by barbaric tribesmen shuffling along the roads. Suttree with his miles to go kept his eyes to the ground, maudlin and muttersome in the bitter chill, under the lonely lamplight.

The old railroader had a fire going in the little iron stove and he'd pulled his bed crosswise before it for warmth. Suttree slid the door shut. Back down the tracks the gray ruins of summer weeds looked wrinkled and very old.

Come set by the fire, the old man said. I didnt know it was so cold.

I've brought it all inside with me. How have you been?

Mean as ever. How you makin it?

I'm about froze out. Thought I'd better check on you to see were you still living.

The old man chuckled to himself. Well lord, he said. A little cold wont kill me I dont reckon. Set down.

He raised himself up slightly and rocked to one side as if he would make room and then subsided in the same place. Suttree sat on the edge of the bunk. Strangely like his own. The rough army blanket. The old man had been reading a coverless book and he laid it down and removed his glasses and pinched the bridge of his nose. A small desk stood against the wall and in the pigeonholes were yellowed time-tables, waybills and tare sheets. In the far corner a great stack of old newsprint and magazines. The old man's eyes must have followed his. I give up on the newspapers, he said.

Why's that?

I never read one but what somebody aint been murdered or shot or somethin such as that. I never knowed such a place for meanness.

Was it ever any different?

How's that?

I said was it ever any different.

No. I reckon not.

Well it's always been in the papers hasnt it?

Yes. I just give up on it is all. I get older I dont want to hear about it. People are funny. They dont want to hear about how nice everthing is. No no. They aint somebody murdered in the papers their day is a waste of time. I give it up myself. Seen it all. It's all the same. Train wrecks of course. Natural catastrophe. A train wreck'll make ye think about things.

Did you ever see a train wreck?

Oh yes.

What's the worst one you ever saw?

Seen or heard tell of?

Either one.

I dont know. I seen a boiler cut loose in Letohatchie Alabama blowed the whole locomotive cab and all up onto a overpass and just left the trucks settin on the track. They'd stopped to take on water but fore they could fill her the crown sheet went. I seen that. But they was one blew up in the roundhouse in San Antonio Texas in the year nineteen and twelve that blowed the whole roundhouse down and a lot of other buildins besides. They found one chunk of the boiler that weighed eight ton a quarter mile from the wreck. Another piece weighed almost a thousand pound tore a man's house down a half mile away. I was just a young man at the time but I remember readin it like it was yesterday. Had all the pitchers in the paper. I think they was twenty-eight killed and I dont know how many maimed for life.

Suttree looked at the old man. A thousand pound piece of iron went a half mile? he said.

Oh yes. Hadnt hit this feller's house it might still be goin.

Would you have liked to have seen it, Daddy?

The old man looked at Suttree in alarm. Seen it? he said. Where from?

I see, said Suttree.

Course they's been a lot worse wrecks than them. They was a Pennsy engine left the track in Philadelphia about ten year ago, hotbox caused the axle to break, thowed some cars into a bridge and killed eighty people all told. Your worst wrecks was the telescopes. One car would run inside another and just gather everbody up out of their seats and make a big mud pie out of em at the end. Then of course they was bridges and trestles. I remember two trains run out on a doubletrack trestle up in Kentucky goin in opposite directions, about the time they got abreast of one another the whole thing just folded up and dropped into the river. Trestle, locomotives, tenders, cars, folks. All of it. Kaploosh. Back then most of ye trestles was just wood. The coaches was wood too and they had stoves in em about like thisn here and when they'd wreck they'd tip over and set the coaches afire and burn up everbody inside. I tell ye, ridin a train back in them days was a thing you give some thought to.

The old man rose heavily from the bed and opened the stove door and dumped in coal from the scuttle and sat back down again. He dabbed with the back of one knuckle at his nose. Outside it had grown almost dark and a cat appeared at the clerestory window and whined.

You caint get in that way, idjit, the old man called. You come to the door like everybody else.

When I was young I didnt care for nothin, he continued. I was always easy in the world. Saw a right smart of it. Never cared to go just wherever.

How did you happen to end up here?

I aint ended yet. Used to hobo a right smart. Back in the thirties. They wasnt no work I dont care what you could do. I was ridin through the mountains one night, state of Colorado. Dead of winter it was and bitter cold. I had just a smidgin of tobacco, bout enough for one or two smokes. I was in one of them old slatsided cars and I'd been up and down in it like a dog tryin to find some place where the wind wouldnt blow. Directly I scrunched up in a corner and rolled me a smoke and lit it and thowed the match down. Well, they was some sort of stuff in the floor about like tinder and it caught fire. I jumped up and stomped on it and it aint done nothin but burn faster. Wasnt two minutes the whole car was afire. I run to the door and got it open and we was goin up this grade through the mountains in the snow with the moon on it and it was just blue lookin and dead quiet out there and them big old black pine trees goin by. I jumped for it and lit in a snowbank and what I'm goin to tell you you'll think peculiar but it's the god's truth. That was in nineteen and thirty-one and if I live to be a hunnerd year old I dont think I'll ever see anything as pretty as that train on fire goin up that mountain and around the bend and them flames lightin up the snow and the trees and the night.

They nodded and shivered in the fogged car while the gray dawn hovered without. They groaned and stirred and slept. Sometime in the night Sharpe had come awake freezing, coatless, and climbed out to stir about in the alleyway, gathering pieces of cratewood and paper. J-Bone reared up in the front seat. What's that? he said.

What time is it Jim?

I dont have a watch. Where's that smoke coming from?

This fire here.

J-Bone raised himself and looked over the back of the seat. Sharpe had a small fire going in the floor of the car and he was holding his hands over it. J-Bone leaned over the seat and held his own hands out for warmth. Watch Cabbage's leg there, he said.

Sharpe jostled the bony knee.

Hey Cabbage, get your leg out of the fire.

Cabbage reared up wildly and subsided.

Better crack that window hadnt we? said J-Bone.

They grinned at each other across the smoke and the flames.

I'm about to freeze my ass off. What time do you reckon it is?

I dont know. What time's it get light?

Shit if I know. You sure they open at five?

Yeah. Have for years.

Sharpe was peering out across the blueblack night, the buildings stark and tall, the few streetlamps encoiled in fog.

It's gettin smoky in here, said J-Bone.

Does Suttree have a watch?

No. I dont think so. He bent to see. Suttree lay slumped under the wheel with his folded hands between his knees.

Sharpe cranked down the rear window. Smoke was rolling blackly through the car.

Cabbage raised up and looked at Sharpe with drunken sleepshot eyes. What's happening? he said.

We're waiting on that five oclock beer.

The fucking car's on fire.

We're tryin to get warm, Cabbage, said J-Bone.

Cabbage looked from one to the other of them. You sons of bitches are crazy, he said. He opened the door and lurched out into the alley.

J-Bone got out on the other side. Come on Sharpe. Let's walk around some fore we freeze.

See if you can see some more wood out there.

Suttree woke and looked out the window. A garbage truck had gone down the alley. He sat up. He was alone in the car. He opened the glovebox and reached around inside and shut it again. He felt under the seat and he looked in the back. The remains of the fire lay in a blackened crust of burnt rubber on the floor. He looked out down the alley. He was shaking with the cold.

He climbed stiffly from the car and shut the door. Traffic was commencing in the murk, headlamps boring past in pale shrouds. A dog crossed in the hobbled lights. Suttree stove his hands deep in his pockets and hunched his shoulders and went toward the street.

They were seated in a row on stools within the watered windows of the Signal Cafe and they were drinking beer. An old newspedlar sat at the front of the counter humped over his coffee. Suttree swung through the door blowing on his hands and took a stool.

This goddamn Suttree is a five oclock alarm clock, said Sharpe.

Wasnt no danger of sleepin over with Sut along.

Let me have a Redtop, said Suttree to the counterman.

You rest well Sut?

You sons of bitches would let a man lay out there and freeze to death.

I was goin to come out there and get you, Bud.

We run out of firewood.

How long you all been in here?

This is our first one. Hell, he just opened this minute.

Suttree seized the bottle before him and drank and hiked his shoulders up and drank again. Across the street a neon sign that once said Earle Hotel said le Ho. Two workers with their lunchboxes in their armpits stamped and smoked on the corner. Suttree looked at his companions. Their bottles rose and fell like counterweights. I thought five oclock never would get here, said J-Bone.

By nine oclock that night they were twelve or more, all good hearts from McAnally. An hour later they were at a roadhouse called the Indian Rock.

They threaded their way among the tables, Billy Ray Callahan stopping where girls had gone to dance and left purses among the drinks. Callahan draining the glasses and taking the money from the purses and moving on, smiling and nodding to friends and strangers, past a table where a big boy was sitting, Callahan smiling at him invitingly.

What say, big boy.

Big boy looked away.

They pulled tables together and ordered Cokes and set out pints of whiskey. Under the tilting smoke the dancers whirled and the music with its upbeat country tempo scored like an overture the gatherings of violence just beneath the surface, the subtle exchanges in the heated air. Suttree and J-Bone made their way toward the men's room. Cabbage on the floor already dancing mightily, the girl laughing. Kenneth Tipton at a nearby table holding out his hand.

We've got to get these cunts, said J-Bone.

Let's not get too drunk.

When they got back their table was gone. The drinks lay in a pile of glass and icecubes on the wet concrete floor and the table lay caved in a corner. Suttree saw one of the legs in someone's hand. The area was clearing fast, people moving along the walls. Suttree saw Hoghead move with stealth along the rear of a phalanx of battlers and draw back and hit a boy behind the ear and move on. Earl Solomon came pedaling backwards out of the line and slammed up against the wall. Paul McCulley was trading punches with three boys all by himself down by the ladies' room door and the door kept opening and closing and girls looking out by turns.

We better get some of them off of Hulley Babe, said J-Bone.

They started down the room but before they'd gone far someone fell into J-Bone. J-Bone shoved him and he turned around and took a swing and at it they went. Suttree made his way on to where Paul was and grabbed a boy by the wrist and whipsawed and flung him into a table full of half empty drinks. He screamed something at Suttree but it was lost in the melee. Paul hit one of the other boys and he went down and got up and walked off. The third one hit Suttree in the side of the head. Suttree squared off and ducked and the boy looked and saw McCulley coming for him and said: I aint fightin the two of ye.

Why you crawfishin son of a bitch, McCulley said. You didnt mind it the other way around. He shoved the boy back against the wall but the boy turned and ran.

Get that little fucker, Red, called McCulley.

Callahan was standing bloodyheaded in the middle of a pile of fallen bodies looking about. He reached and took the boy by the shoulder almost gently. Pow, he said. Suttree turned his head. McCulley had his arm around him hugging him and laughing and taking him directly into the thick of it.

Who the fuck are we fighting? said Suttree.

Who the fuck cares? If he aint from McAnally bust him.

And they are whelmed in dark riot, the smoking hall a no man's land filled with lethal looking drunks reeling about with bleeding eyes and reeking of homemade whiskey. A scuffling of feet, fists thudding. Long endless crash of glass and chairs and overhead the intermittent whoosh of whiskey bottles crossing the room like mortar shells to explode on the block walls. A wave of bodies swept over Suttree. He struggled up. In the midst of it all he found Kenneth Tipton seemingly encased in a nimbus of peace, holding his wrist and working his hand open and shut. I've fucked up my hand, he said. Then he was swept away.

The floor was slick with blood and whiskey. Someone hit him under the eye. He tried to see J-Bone but he could not. He saw Callahan go by, one eye blue shiny, smiling, his teeth in a grout of blood. His busy freckled fists ferrying folks to sleep. He saw a bottle in a fist rise above the melee, saw it powdered on an unknown skull.

The fight washed up against the ladies' room wall and the structure groaned and slewed. Suttree saw a head snap back and cave a cracked dish shape in the wallboard. Somebody had an old boy in the corner with handkerchiefs trying to stop his ear from bleeding and the old boy was ready to whip his nurse to get back into it. Slapping away the hand attending him, his ear hanging half off. The bouncer was working his way like a reaper through the crowd by the wall, flattening people with a slapstick. When he came upon McCulley, McCulley hit him solidly in the jaw. The bouncer reeled back and shook his head and came on again and swung with the slapstick. It made an ugly sound on the side of McCulley's head. McCulley swung again and caught the bouncer in the face. Blood flew. The bouncer fell back and recovered. Both were preparing to swing together when McCulley's knees gave way and he knelt in the glass and the blood. The bouncer moved on, making his way toward Callahan. Behind him came a man lugging a floorbuffer.

A heavy machine, he could just by main strength raise it. When he hit the bouncer with it the bouncer disappeared.

Suttree tried to work his way toward the wall but a heavy arm came athwart his eyes. He spun. Surrounded now by strangers. The man with the floorbuffer washed up nearby. The buffer rose trembling above the crowd. It came down on no head but Suttree's.

He felt the vertebrae in his neck crack. The room and all in it turned white as noon. His eyes rolled up in his head and his bowels gave way. He distinctly heard his mother say his name.

He was standing with his knees locked and his hands dangling and the blood pouring down into his eyes. He could not see. He said: Do not go down.

He swayed. He took a small step, stiffly fending. What waited was not the black of nothing but a foul hag with naked gums smiling and there was no madonna of desire or mother of eternal attendance beyond the dark rain with lamps against the night, the softly cloven powdered breasts and the fragile claviclebones alabastrine above the rich velvet of her gown. The old crone swayed as if to mock him. What man is such a coward he would not rather fall once than remain forever tottering?

He dropped like a zombie among the din and the flailing, his face drained, his eyes platelike with the enormity of the pain behind them. Someone stepped on his hand as he was crawling across the floor. He tried to rise again but the room had composed itself into a tunnel down which he kept falling. He did not know what had happened to him and his eyes kept filling up with blood. He thought he'd been shot and he kept telling himself that the damage could be repaired if nothing else befell him dear God to be out of this place forever.

He pulled himself up a swaying wall and tried to see. All that frantic bedlam before him seemed to have slowed and each whirling face swam off in perfect parallax like warriors and their mentors twinned, a roomful of hostile and manic siamese. Ahhh, said Suttree. Making his way toward the door he realized with a faint surge of that fairyland feeling from childhood wonders that the face he passed wide eyed by the side of an upturned table was a dead man. Someone going with him saw him see. That's fucking awful, he said. Suttree was bleeding from the ears and couldnt hear well but he thought so too. They stumbled on like the damned in off the plains of Gomorrah. Before they reached the door someone hit him in the head with a bottle.

He must have fallen foul of yet other hands afterwards because when he woke in the hospital he had a broken finger, three broken ribs, a mouthful of loose teeth and one missing. He tried to move but the jagged ends of bone in his chest were like scissors. His head was pounding and his vision skewed in some way and he was vaguely amazed at being alive and not sure that it was worth it. He raised his eyes and felt the dried blood crack across his forehead. Lights kept rising one by one and after a while he realized that they were bulbs in a corridor ceiling and that the periodic squeaking sound was a caster on the cart that was wheeling him. The emergency room was filled with people bleeding. Grumous battlers with misshapen heads. All watched over by hordes of police. They wheeled Suttree on. Bearing his pained bones in their boat of flesh. To where the deadcarriage waits in the dark. Perhaps the wrath of God after all.

Friends row by row watched his passing and waved at him with their fingers and whispered among themselves. Who'd spoke of disorders of the soul and news of night. When you asked for the shop of the heart's apothecary we thought you mad. We saw you took down to the brainsurgeon's keep, deep in the cellar, under the street. Where saws sang in stoven skulls and wet bonemeal blew from an airshaft in the alleyway. Out there in the blue moonlight a gray shecorpse being loaded into a truck. It pulled away into the night. Horned minstrels, small dancing dogs in harlequin garb hobbled after.

The night is cold and colder, a fog moves with menace in the streets. Malefic stirrings underfoot, a foul breath rising visibly from the pierced sewerlids. The watertruck goes by like a nightbeast, its drumshaped brush clanking. Water wells inkblack in the streets repeating the polelamps in glozy rosettes that dish and slide in the wash like radiolarians pale with phosphorous on a midnight sea. The sweepers broom the trash along the flooded gutters, their yellow slickers bright with wet. They leap to the truck and ride with brooms aloft like figures done in lacquered wax, like hortatory gnomes. The hotel nightlights shine behind the drawn venetian blinds and the slatted patterns on the curbside cars give them the look of anchored smallcraft with lapstrake hulls. Out there in the winter streets a few ashen anthroparians scuttling yet through the falling soot. Above them the shape of the city a colossal horde of retorts and alembics ranged against a starless sky. Uneasy sleeper you will live to see the city of your birth pulled down to the last stone.

Suttree heard people discussing his skull. Could he but see himself. His head half shaved and gray and numb with novocaine. An old doctor with a mosquitoclamp and a needle stitched his scalp. Suttree still in his street clothes, one sleeve cut away, stained and stinking with blood and beer and shit. A nurse sat with his elbow in her lap, picking out pieces of glass with a pair of forceps and placing them in a steel tray.

He woke in a small white room. Late evening. Bird shadows oblique upon the wall. He raised his head and looked about. Two pigeons on the windowsill ruffled their feathers. A westerly view, cold winter sunlight. Constant beyond the sounds of traffic in the streets there boomed a slow roll of surf. His head was swathed in bandages and his hand hurt. He held it up. One finger wrapped and resting in an aluminum holder. His hand separated into two hands side by side both injured. He blinked his eyes and they rejoined. Callahan, you bastard, he said. He lay back and slept.

When he woke again he saw that he was not in a room but in a ward. The screen had been pushed away from his bed and he could see down a long hall many men in beds like his. Night time, yellow bulbs burning in the ceiling. A nurse was going down the ward with a cart collecting the dinner trays. He had to keep blinking his eyes to keep things ordered and discrete. He seemed to be in an old folks' home. Iron beds filled with gray octogenarians propped upright in nightshirts, humped and hawking and leering beadily at one another like paranoids.

Suttree tried to raise himself onto one elbow but his chest hurt. He was wrapped in tape to his armpits and he had an image of burial windings here in this room among the dying. He tried to focus his eyes. To see one person in the ward who looked as if he might have more than days to live. A cold sweat broke out upon him. He felt his head. Terminal brain damage under the towels? He tried to recite the multiplication tables and this filled him with sexual memories and caused him to lie back smiling. He slept and in his sleep he saw his friends again and they were coming downriver on muddy floodwaters, Hoghead and the City Mouse and J-Bone and Bearhunter and Bucket and Boneyard and J D Davis and Earl Solomon, all watching him where he stood on the shore. They turned gently in their rubber bullboat, bobbing slightly on the broad and ropy waters, their feet impinging in the floor of the thing with membraneous yellow tracks.

They glided past somberly. Out of a lightless dawn receding, past the pale daystar. A fog more obscure closed away their figures gone a sadder way by psychic seas across the Tarn of Acheron. From a rock in the river he waved them farewell but they did not wave back.

In the morning the old men were upright and drooling with the first light. Two nurses came down the ward with breakfast trays. The one named Miss Aldrich bent above him smiling and went away again. An enameled namepin. Her white starched frock crackled like sheetiron and her crepesoled shoes went silently as mice.

Suttree had been taken from his bloodied clothes and bathed and laid out in clean coarse linen. Miss Aldrich helped him down the long corridor, the old men watching furiously from their rows of beds on either side. Her soft breast against his elbow, crossing from band to latticed band of morning sunlight where it fell through the barred windows. He stood in a concrete room painted white and pissed painfully a few drops into an oldfashioned urinal and came out again. She was waiting for him. Did you do your business? she said, smiling.

Just a little.

Number one or number two?

Suttree couldnt remember what the numbers corresponded to. Wee wee, he said. He felt completely stupid.

She took his elbow to help him back to his bed.

I can make it all right, he said.

I know.

Oh.

Arent you ashamed?

Of what?

Getting into such a terrible fight. You havent seen yourself in a mirror, have you?

Suttree didnt answer. What's wrong with my head? he said.

You broke it.

Broke it?

Yes.

Is it bad?

No. Well, it's not good. It is fractured.

I keep seeing double.

It'll go away. Here.

Suttree tried to get into the bed painlessly. Shit, he said. He sat with care. How many ribs?

Three.

Who else is here?

You mean your little friends?

Yes.

None. Most of them were treated and taken to jail. A few escaped I think. Are you ready for some breakfast?

I guess so. Am I?

Why not.

She brought him a tray with a bowl of oatmeal and milk and a cup of watered coffee.

Is that it? he said.

That's it.

She fluffed his pillows, helped him to sit. Soap scent of her hair and her breast brushing across his eye.

I suppose this is Knoxville General? he said, sniffing the porridge.

She smiled. So you dont even know where you are.

Isnt it?

What makes you think you're in Knoxville?

Come on.

Yes. At St Mary's you get poached eggs. But you have to say your prayers first.

She put her hand to her mouth. Oh, she said. You're not a Catholic are you?

I've been defrocked. This tastes like wet mattress stuffing.

But do you like it?

Just so so. Listen, what is this ward? It looks like where they lock up dangerous incurables.

It's just a ward. Most of our patients are older people.

Older? There's no one in here under ninety. What do they do, unload them here to die?

Yes.

I see.

They're all indigents. Some of them they bring down here from the nursing home when they get too sick. It's an experience.

I'll bet.

You created quite a sensation.

What, among the inmates?

No, silly. Among the nurses.

She brought him the morning paper but he couldnt focus on the print. She cranked up the old metal bed, moving about, flirting with him and smelling good. She told him of her life in the nurses' home, her wide face full of humor. She roomed in the old morgue along with the other nurses in training. Their beds all leveled under two legs with bricks where the concrete floor sloped toward the drain. At supper she brought her girlfriend, a short heavyset nurse, with instructions to take care of him.

Just remember I saw him first, she said. She winked at Suttree. I'll see you tomorrow.

But he was afoot and gone with fall of dark. Hobbling down the corridor in his nightshirt past the snoring elders and through the door at the end. A little vestibule. Through the wired glass he could see out into the lobby where the night nurse sat at her desk. Suttree turned and went back through the ward to the doors at the other end. A further corridor, dimly lit. He came upon a washroom and a closet where white orderly coats and jackets hung from pegs above the mopbuckets and jugs of chemicals. He dressed quickly in the first clothes to hand and he looked at himself in the glass. A wounded peon.

He found a door that opened onto the main hall of the hospital and he walked toward the light at the entrance and out into the night. He went down the street toward Central Avenue and crossed to the Corner Grill. His toes were so folded in the old black shoes he'd found that he could hardly walk.

Strange apparition to enter the dim of the little tavern on a quiet Saturday night. Big Frig rose to help him to a booth with elaborate solicitousness and he and the brothers Clancy reckoned him sole survivor of a madhouse rising, an icecream rebellion, before leaning to hear of his trials.

He got a quart of milk from the store and with the bottle under his arm crossed through the winter twilight the littered benchland to the river and home. He had not been asleep long before someone tapped at his door.

What is it?

Aint dead in there are ye?

No.

Aint seen ye about. Allowed ye was dead.

I'm all right.

He lay in the dark listening to the crazed railroader breathing beyond the door. The old man muttered something but Suttree could not make it out.

What? he called.

He was blowing his nose.

Suttree got up and scratched about on the table for a match and lit the lamp and came to the door in the shorts and sweater he'd worn to bed.

Hidy, said the old man.

Come on in.

Was you in bed?

It's all right. Come on in.

The old man entered stiffly in his striped overalls, his shadow bobbing and looming anxiously behind him. Cold in here, he said.

Suttree set the lamp on the table and went to the stove to poke the fire up.

What happent to your head?

I got hit with a floorbuffer.

Say you did?

What time is it?

Could you not hear it comin?

No. What time is it?

He was hauling at the chain, looking about the dim little cabin.

What are you up to?

I was just on my way in. Thought I better check on ye, aint seen ye and all. I thought ye'd died on me.

You and old Hooper are just alike. All you either one talk about is dying. What do you do, sit around and cheer one another up?

Oh no. I see him seldomer and seldomer. A man gets to my age he thinks about dyin some. It's only natural.

What, dying or thinking about it?

Do what?

I thought you were going to tell me what time it was.

The old man tilted the watch in his hand toward the lamp. I caint see good in here, he said.

You want a glass of milk?

I dont use it thank ye.

Suttree poured his tumbler full and drank and regarded the old man. I make it eight forty-six, the old man said.

Suttree rubbed his eyes.

We all got to go sometime.

He looked at the old man.

I said we all got to go sometime. You get older you think about it. Young feller like you.

The old man gestured in the air with his hand, you couldnt tell what it meant. He sat in the chair by the table, still holding the watch in the palm of his hand.

You want a cup of coffee?

No, no. I'm just on my way in.

Suttree leaned back against the wall and sipped the milk. He could feel the air in the cracks like cold wires. The old man sat there, seemed transfixed by the lampflame like a ponderous cat. After a while he heaved up his shoulders and sighed and put away his watch. He rose and adjusted his cap. Well, he said. If I'm goin to cross that river tonight I'd as well start now.

You take care.

He looked about the little cabin. Well, he said. I'm satisfied you aint dead anyways. I'll look for ye on the river.

Okay.

Suttree didnt get up from the bed and the old man raised his hand and went out into the night. A few minutes later Suttree heard the dogs start up along Front Street and later still when he wiped the water from the glass and peered out he could see the old man on the bridge, or rather he could see the faintest figure disturb the globes of light one by one slowly until the farther dark had taken him.

In the morning he went down the river again to run his lines. Two boys from the riverfront down off the foot of Fifteenth Street had just come in. When Suttree passed they were handing up a string of carp wet and yellow with rubber mouths sucking. One of them chained the boat with an old bicycle lock and they moved up the bank in their cheap black shoes, stopping now and again to pluck the winter nettles from their trouserlegs. Suttree raised his hand and they nodded, tossing their heads like small vicious horses and going on across the tracks.

His own lines came up heavy with dead fish. He cut the droppers one by one and watched the pale shapes flare and rock and sink from sight. He tied on new baited snells and recovered the current with the oars. He looked at the gray sky but it did not change and the river was always the same.

In just spring the goatman came over the bridge, a stout old man in overalls, long gray hair and beard. Sunday morning before anyone was about. A clicking of little cleft hooves on the concrete and the goats in their homemade harness drawing tandem carts cobbled up out of old signs and kindlingwood and topped with tattered canvas, horned goatskulls, biblical messages, the whole thing rattling along on elliptical wheels like a whimsical pulltoy for children. Loose goats flowed around the man and the wagon. A lantern swung from the hinder axletree and a small goat face peered from the tailboard, a young goat who is wearied and must ride. The goatman strode in his heavy shoes and raised his nose to test the air, the cart rumbled and clanked on its iron wheels and they entered the town.

Goats fanned over the post office lawn on Main Street and began to graze, the goatman watching them paternally, hiking along at the head of his curious circus. An officer of the law spoke to him:

Get them damned goats off the grass.

The goatman located the voice with narrowed eyes.

Let's go, oldtimer.

Them's mulish goats at times, said the goatman.

Off, said the lawman, pointing.

You Suzy. Get off that there grass now. It aint for you. All of you now.

The goats grazed on with soft goat bells, with goat's ears tilting.

Them goats needs to be on a lead or somethin you want to bring em thew here.

You caint do nothin with em.

This aint no place for a bunch of damned goats.

We just passin thew, said the goatman.

One of the goats defecated copiously on the paving. Dry round turds that rolled like buckshot. She moved on to the green with grace, the ambling tolerance of goathood, fat teats winking from between her legs. The policeman looked at the goatman.

I want them goats out of here.

They goin.

This aint Sevierville or some damned place where you can bring a bunch of goats through the middle of town any time you've a notion and let em shit all over the place.

I came thew there but I never stayed over.

Well let's be for goin thew here and not stayin over.

Come on honey, the goatman said to the nanny that stood sleeping in the traces. She opened one eye, a cracked agate filled with sly goat sapience. The goatman patted her rump where bones reared up beneath the hide that you could hang a hat on. A puff of dust. She moved. They passed the policeman in a sedate trundling. Little goat peering from the wagon. The goatman calling. Hoo now. The tiny clatter of goathooves in the silent Sunday morning and the goats and the cart and the goatman going on in a penumbra of sunlight, a cartwheel trapped and squealing in the trolleytrack till he stoops to lift it out, stout goatman, strange hat in one hand, the company swinging out and down Market Street toward the river, a bunched and sidling halfcircle of goats starting and checking and wheeling past the goatman down the steep hill and the goatman himself with his back to the cart to check its descent.

Suttree woke in late morning with the cabin filled with sunlight, light lapping on the farther wall where it played off the water, a faint bleating of goats. He rose and went out to the deck in his shorts, stretching in the sabbath noon, a dreamy tranquillity. The river lay empty of traffic and the sawmill's small skylights winked in the sun crossriver with their crooked glass. He propped himself on the rail and looked about. The field between the railroad and the river was filled with grazing goats and there was a small strange hooded wagon there and a rigid windless spire of smoke standing in the bright air.

Goats, he said, scratching his chin.

He looked upriver, Jones's tavernboat, the marble company, the curve of the river toward Island Home. The stand of canes tilting at the point and the dark folk fishing there in overalls and faded floral wear. He looked toward the field again.

He counted as many as two dozen. A small one tethered to the wagonwheel stood on buckling legs. A bearded man in overalls came to the rear of the wagon and got something from within and disappeared again. Suttree went in and dressed.

The goatman looked up at his approach. He was wearing little wire eyeglasses and he was reading from the bible. He went back to his reading and Suttree squatted by the fire and watched him, the old man's finger moving on the page, his lips forming the words. After a few minutes he laid the book aside and took off the spectacles and folded them and placed them in the bib pocket of his overalls. He looked up at Suttree, one eye lightly squinted.

Morning, said Suttree.

And a good day to you, said the goatman. Aint the law I dont reckon are you?

No. I live in that houseboat yonder.

The goatman nodded.

Suttree looked up at the wagon. A large blue sign atop it read

JESUS WEPT

Pretty day, aint it? said the goatman.

It is. How many goats have you got?

Thirty-four.

Thirty-four.

Sally died.

Oh.

She never was real stout.

I guess you like goats pretty well.

Well, I've got used to em. We been on the road fourteen year now.

How come you to have so many?

Had nothin to do with it. Goats will be goats. I used to have more'n what I got now. Didnt have but one kid this spring. I think old Billy yonder's gettin too old to cut the mustard.

Suttree looked out over the field at the goats grazing. Three small black boys had come across from the road and stood now uncertainly just outside the goatman's camp and regarded him with wide eyes.

Come up boys, he said.

They made their way to the head of the wagon where a huge old billy goat was tethered. They stood around looking at him.

Can you touch him? one said.

Why sure. Just go on and rub his head.

He wont bite?

Naw. Scratch his old head there. He likes that.

One reached out tentatively and began to rub the goat's nose. The goat sniffed at the boy's sleeve and began to nibble at it.

He's eatin your sweater Loftis.

I dont care.

He stroked the huge whelked horns.

Where you goin with these here goats?

Down the road, said the goatman.

What you wants with these goats anyway?

Little or nothin. Good fresh milk. God's best cheese.

You have any other animals? said Suttree. Dog or anything?

No. Just goats. I think a feller gets started with goats he just more or less sticks to goats.

I guess so, said Suttree. He had squatted in the grass. The goatman's fire puttered gently among the stones. By the river goat bells clanked thinly in the soft forenoon.

Say you live right yonder? said the goatman.

Yes.

What, live by yourself do ye?

Yes.

Well, it's got a lot to recommend it. Aint never been married?

Once, said Suttree.

I had three and it was three too many. He squinted his eyes and pinched the bridge of his nose. The good book says that there'll be seven women for every man. Well somebody else can have my other four what about you?

Suttree smiled and shook his head noncommittally. He was making a little noose from a weedstem. One of the black boys had come to the rear of the wagon where the young goat was tied and the young goat reared and tugged at his rope.

He aint used to folks yet, said the goatman.

When will he be?

I dont know. Talk to him some there. He'll come around.

Here goat, said the black boy.

The other two had come to the edge of the fire and stood looking at the men squatting there. The goatman eyed them critically. What's your name? he said.

Lonnie.

Lonnie you need you some goat's milk to chink up the slats in them ribs what do you think?

I aint never had none.

Be watchful of them elbows you dont knife somebody. Who's your buddy there?

He aint my buddy, he's my brother.

He dont talk much I guess.

He wont say nothin lessen he knows ye.

You know this feller here? He nodded toward Suttree.

He's a fisherman, said Lonnie's brother.

Thought you said he didnt talk.

Lonnie looked at his brother and his brother looked at the ground.

Is that right? said the goatman, turning to Suttree. You a fisherman?

Suttree nodded.

Make a livin at it do you?

A poor one.

It's a honorable trade. What do you fish for?

Carp, catfish.

What do you catch?

Suttree smiled. Carp and catfish, he said. Might catch a drum now and then. Or a gar.

Man dont always catch what he fishes for.

No.

You aint got any catfish today have you?

I might. You want some?

I wouldnt care to have just a mess for myself.

I'll see what I can do. It'll be this evening. I usually run my lines late on Sundays.

The goatman turned to him. On the sabbath?

The fish dont know the difference.

The goatman shook his head. Cant say as I hold with that.

They sat silently for a moment. The old man smelled of goats and woodsmoke. The boys were going from goat to goat down the field by the river.

Why did Jesus weep? said Suttree.

Eh?

He pointed up at the sign. Why did Jesus weep?

Dont know scriptures?

Some.

He wept over folks workin on Sundays.

Suttree smiled.

Jesus wept over Lazarus, said the goatman. It dont say it, but I reckon Lazarus might of wept back when he seen himself back in this vale of tears after he'd done been safe and dead four days. He must of been in heaven. Jesus wouldnt of brought one back from hell would he? I'd hate to get to heaven and then get recalled what about you?

I guess so.

You can bet I intend to ask him when I see him.

Ask who?

Jesus.

You're going to ask Jesus about Lazarus?

Sure. Wouldnt you? Oh I intend to have some questions for him. I'm goin to be talkin to him some day just like I'm talkin to you. I'd better have somethin to say.

Suttree rose and swiped at the seat of his trousers and looked off down the river. Well, he said. I'll bring you a catfish if I get one.

I dont require a big one.

No. It's okay if it's caught on Sunday?

Just dont tell me about it.

All right.

I wouldnt want to aid and abet.

No. Here come some more fans.

A group of people were picking their way across the pitted lot toward the goatman's camp.

I preach at four, said the goatman. Ought to be a good crowd here by then.

Preach?

I preach ever Sunday at four oclock rain or shine. Just straight preachin. No cures, no predictions. Folks ask me about the second comin. Most aint heard of the first one yet. You be here?

Suttree looked down at the goatman. Well, he said. If I'm not, just go ahead and start without me.

He went up the river path toward Ab Jones's. The three black boys had one of the goats by the horns and were going around in circles with it while one of them attempted to climb on its back.

A white derelict named Smokehouse opened the door. He recalled Suttree dimly through drinkgalled eyes and stood aside for him to enter.

How's Tom, said Suttree.

Tom's okay, said the derelict.

Suttree entered the dim room with its odor of stale beer and the urinous smell of chitlins cooking in the back. The derelict shut the door and hobbled on his twisted legs to the wall where he'd left his broom leaning.

Where's Ab? said Suttree.

Aint seen him.

Where's Doll?

She's back in the back.

What happened to your head?

What happened to yours?

Suttree smiled and rubbed the patch of stubble hair at the back of his head. The derelict had a massive bandage taped across the left side of his forehead.

I got hit with a floorbuffer, Suttree said.

I got hit by a bus.

Again?

Smokehouse nodded, looking down at the floor, sweeping futilely at the trash.

Doesnt it hurt? said Suttree.

Some.

Some?

I got drunk first.

Oh.

I wouldnt do it without I got drunk first. I got more sense than that.

Well how do you manage to keep from getting killed if you're drunk?

It aint easy. That's how come that bus run over my legs that time is cause I got too drunk. You got to keep your head about you.

How much will you get this time?

I dont know. They dont want to settle. I may have to get me another lawyer.

What will you do with the money if you get it?

Smokehouse looked up from the floor. He seemed surprised by the question. Well, he said. Get drunk, I reckon. Least I wont have to sweep the floor for no niggers.

For a while.

The derelict pushed at the trash. The sun dont shine up the same dog's ass ever day, he said.

I hope not, said Suttree.

Things is come to a sorry pass when a white man has to look to a nigger for work.

Hard times on the land. Suttree agreed.

You dont have a little drink on ye anywheres do ye?

Suttree had not. Smokehouse had started a new tack when the curtain flipped back and Doll in her disheveled housecoat held out a halfdollar coin.

Run get me two packs of Luckies, she said.

He stood his broom carefully against the wall and took the coin and got his hat from the back of a chair where he'd hung it and shuffled out the door, his racked body like something disjointed and put back by drunken surgeons, the elbows hiked out, the feet bent wrong. Doll watched him with her one watery eye. Mornin, she said.

Morning, said Suttree. How's the old man?

I dont know. He laid up in the bed. Go on back.

I dont want to bother him.

He aint asleep. Go on. She held the curtain back for him.

Suttree entered a room darker yet, some sort of heavy material curtaining the window on the river, a rich funk of nameless odors. There was a radio playing so softly that he just could hear it.

The footrail of the bed came right to the door and Jones lay in the bed like a tree. Who that? he said.

Suttree.

Youngblood. Come in.

You not asleep?

No. I just restin. Come on in.

He raised himself up slightly in the bed and Suttree heard him catch his breath.

I just stopped by.

Set down. Where your beer?

I didnt want one.

Hey old woman. He was groping around in the near dark for something and finally came up with a bottle and unscrewed the cap and drank and put it back. He wiped his mouth with the heel of his hand. Hey, he called out.

She appeared at the curtain.

Bring this man a beer. Set down Youngblood.

Suttree could see him better. He shifted his huge frame and so clearly was he in pain that the fisherman sat at the foot of the bed and asked him what was wrong.

Dont say nothin to her.

What happened?

Same old shit. Your little blue friends. Hush.

She came to the curtain and handed a bottle of beer into the room. Suttree took it and thanked her and she went out again, no word.

Did they put you in jail?

Yeah. I got out about eight oclock this mornin. Made bond. She think I been out whorin I reckon.

Suttree smiled. Werent you? he said.

The scarred black face looked grieved. No man. I too old for that shit. Dont let her know it of course.

Are you all right?

202

Aint nothin. I got to keep my shirt on she dont see the tape.

Who taped you?

Me.

You know how to do that?

I done it a few times fore this.

I guess you have.

Bein a nigger is a interestin life.

You make it that way.

Maybe.

Suttree sipped the beer. It was very quiet in the cabin.

They dont like no nigger walkin around like a man, Jones said. He had drawn his bottle forth and unscrewed the cap and was taking a drink.

Can you get up and around.

Yeah. I aint down, just restin.

If you need anything I can get it for you. If you need some whiskey.

I know you would. I'm okay.

Well.

You got a good heart, Youngblood. Look out for you own.

I dont have any own.

Yes you do.

Where are they?

Jones wiped his mouth. Let me tell you about some people, he said. Some people aint worth a shit rich or poor and that's all you can say about em. But I never knowed a man that had it all but what he didnt forget where he come from. I dont know what it does. I had a friend in this town I stood up for him when he got married. I'd give him money when he was comin up. Used to take him to the wrestlin matches, he was just a kid. He's a big man now. Drives a Cadillac. He dont know me. I got no use for a man piss backwards on his friends.

Suttree was sitting at the foot of the bed. He took a sip of the beer and held the bottle between his hands.

You see a man, he scratchin to make it. Think once he got it made everthing be all right. But you dont never have it made. Dont care who you are. Look up one mornin and you a old man. You aint got nothin to say to your brother. Dont know no more'n when you started.

Suttree could see the huge veined hands in the gloom, black mannequin's hands, an ebon last for a glovemaker's outsize advertisement.

They were moving as if to shape the dark to some purpose.

I used to work on the river. The Cherokee. Then I was on the Hugh Martin. The H C Murry. It had a better store than them uptown. After the first war they wasnt no more packetboat trade. I was born in nineteen and hundred. Of a night you could hear them boats howlin on the river like souls. The old Martin had a steamhorn could and used to did bring the glass out of folks' sashes. I went on the river when I was twelve. I weighed a hunnerd and eighty pound then. This white man shot me cause I whipped him. I didnt know no better. I was older then, must of been fourteen. Dumb as shit. I went home and got better and fore I could see him to kill him somebody had done done it. Cut his head off. Wasnt no friend of mine. Thowed my black ass in the jailhouse. Went up the side of my head with they old clubs and shit. I laid there in the dark, they aint give me nothin to eat yet. That was my first acquaintance of the wrath of the path. That's goin on forty year now and it dont signify a goddamn thing. These bloods down here think it's somethin to whip up on some police. They think that's really somethin. Shit. You aint got nothin for it but a busted head. You caint do nothin with them motherfuckers. I wouldnt fight em at all if I could keep from it.

Suttree bent to see his face. Jones blinked, eyeballs like eggs in the mammoth black skull. He must have read his pale friend's look because he said almost to himself: That's the truth.

How did you get out?

They found his head. Man had it in a shoebox.

He was unscrewing the bottlecap, taking a drink. His eyes closed and opened slowly in the gloom. This man was a gambler and a whoremaster. He never drunk nor smoked. Run a whorehouse on Front Street that was well known in them days. Boats come in, the hands would all turn out for his place. Streets full of whores, queers any color. Thieves. They come out like roaches whenever you had a dockin. Then this feller cut his head off and carried it around in a shoebox with him. He got drunk one night down on Central Avenue and started showin the old head around. Folks runnin screamin into the streets. Next day I's out.

Was he crazy?

Who?

The murderer.

I dont know. He didnt kill him to rob him. I guess he was a little bit crazy.

Would you have killed him?

I dont know. I reckon I would if that was how he'd of wanted it.

Suttree took a sip of his beer. He could hear Smokehouse in the outer room again, puttering about, glass clinking. He looked at Jones. Have you ever killed anyone? he said.

Not on purpose, said Jones.

It was dark when he came in from running his lines. The nose of the skiff broaching rafts of drifted trash and skeins of shorelight in the black river. Radio music from a shack on Front Street carrying clearly over the night waters. The slamming of a door. He could see the lights at Ab Jones's and downriver he could see the fire at the goatman's camp with the goatman's cart in silhouette and dark goat shadows shifting in the forward reach of light. He boated the oars and stalled against the tirecasings alongside his houseboat and stood up in the skiff and made fast.

He had a livebox made from angleiron and chickenwire hanging in the river by a rope and he hauled this up and opened the top and transferred the fish from the boat to the box and lowered it into the river again. Then he hefted a small catfish up from the floor of the skiff, holding it by the gills, and climbed over the rail and went down the walk to the river path and down to the goatman's camp.

A few people were gathered at the fire. When Suttree came up the goatman turned as if he'd sensed him there and he smiled and nodded.

I thought you'd forgot me.

I brought your fish.

I see you did.

You've not eaten supper have you?

No no. You?

Suttree shrugged.

You welcome to share with me if you like.

I dont much like fish.

That there is a nice one.

Suttree handed down the fish and the goatman took it and held it to the fire to see.

What do I owe you?

I dont know, said Suttree. We can trade it out if you like.

Trade it out, said the goatman. I dont know what I'd trade. Aint got nothin but some picture postcards I sell.

That'll be okay.

Postcards?

Sure. Why not?

The goatman looked at Suttree, then rose and turned toward the wagon. The eyes of the visitors at his fire followed him. He rummaged through his duffel and called out to Suttree. How many you want?

I dont know. What do you get for them?

Ten cents.

Well, what about a half dozen?

He came from the wagon with the cards. The fish bowed and shivered in the firelight.

Take these, he said.

Suttree took the cards. The cards were old but the goatman by the fire was not changed from him that posed upon them.

Okay, said Suttree.

Aint no need to rush off.

What makes you think I was rushing off?

I dont know. But you welcome to stay.

I'd better get on.

The goatman watched him. He was trudging out across the field with his chin down so that withdrawing in the firelight he looked like a headless revenant turned away from the warmth of men's gatherings.

Say, called the goatman.

Suttree turned.

You know if you had you a goat or two down here they'd be good company. You never would be lonely.

What makes you think I'm lonely? said Suttree.

The goatman smiled. I dont know, he said. I aint wrong.

It is told first by Oceanfrog Frazer to idlers at the store. How a madman came down from the town and through the steep and vacant lots above the river. Frazer saw him plunging past in a drunken run, fording a briarbush with no regard and on across the stony yard until he was capsized by a clotheswire.

He's murdered someone, Oceanfrog said.

The fallen man mauled at the earth like a child, not even putting a hand to his throat where the wire had all but garroted him. He scrabbled off on hands and knees across the dirt and soon he was running again. He ran fulltilt into the barbedwire fence at the lower end of the lot.

He's crazy, said Oceanfrog. He stepped to the door and called to him.

The man turned. His clothing was ripped and the shreds of his shirtfront lifted about him like confetti in the breeze and he was covered with blood.

What are you doing? called Oceanfrog.

The man screamed. A high parched gurgle like a rutting cat. Then he turned and ran again, following the fence, out of the lot, crashing through the crude pole gate and crossing the road and disappearing in the fields by the river.

A few dead bats or dying appeared in the streets. Roving bands of unclaimed dogs were herded off to the gas chamber. Harrogate kept himself attuned, somehow fearing that he might be next. One day by Suttree's he said he'd seen a bat.

A dead one?

Just up yander.

You'd better go get it, said Suttree. It's worth a dollar.

It's worth what?

A dollar. You have to take it to the Board of Health. It was in the paper.

You're shittin me.

No, it's worth a dollar.

Why would anybody want to give a dollar for a old dead bat?

They think they've got rabies. It says not to touch them, just scoop them up and put them in a bag.

Harrogate had already started out the door.

Hey Gene.

Yeah.

Do you know where to take it?

No, where do I go?

General Hospital. Out Central.

Yeah. I know where it's at. That's where they took me.

It was true. Legal tender for all debts public and private. He had the bill changed at Comer's, dropping it with a careless flourish onto the glass countertop. He took the change downstairs to Helm's and got a dollar for it and changed the dollar at the Sanitary Lunch but no one seemed to notice. Already schemes were clambering through his head. He bought a chocolate milk and sat wedged in the row of theatre seats at Comer's before a twodollar check game and pondered and sipped the milk.

Fucking rat poison, he said, suddenly looking up through the smoke and the din toward a far wall with wide eyes.

People turned to look at him. Cocky paused in midstroke at the table, the cue quivering in his old palsied hands. Harrogate rose and drained the carton of milk and dropped it in a spittoon and went out.

Ratlike himself, quietly in the dimestore aisles. A small box of pellets slid between the lowermost shirtbuttons to lay against his skin. Things to be done. The Ford hood that he portaged on his shoulders up the river path had sheltered chickens. He stopped often to rest. It had rained in the night and his clothes were soaked from the bushes.

Scarlet trumpets of cowitch overhung the little house and wildflowers bloomed up through the twisted shapes of steel by whatever miracle renders grease and cinders arable and the junkman's lot was a garden more lovely for the phantasm from which it sprang. Harrogate paused at the fence and leaned his hood there. He pushed open the weighted gate, starting a hummingbird from the flowers in the dooryard. Rainwater still dripped from the tarpaper eaves and it lay in bright pools and slashes on the gray and steaming backs of the autos where they reared above the grass and fronds like feeding bovines. He rapped at the open door. The cane at the corner of the shack rattled gently in the wind. Everything lay quiet and sundabbled in this quaint garden by the river.

What can I do for ye? said the junkman.

Harrogate stepped back and looked. The junkman was hanging half drunk from the one small window.

You remember me dont ye? said Harrogate.

No.

Well, listen. I need a car hood.

Just a minute.

He appeared at the door. With splayed fingers attacking the matter that webbed his eyes.

What kind? he said.

It's a Ford.

Any particular year?

I dont know. I got it out here if you could match it up.

The junkman spat and looked at him and started down the stoop past him.

Where's it at? He was standing in the yard with his palms in the small of his back, squinting about.

Right yonder leanin against the fence.

The junkman followed his pointing finger. I hope it dont lean too hard, he said. He sauntered over to the fence and looked down. He gave the hood a shove and it fell over in the dust with a sad bong. The junkman looked it over and he looked at Harrogate. Hell son, he said. What's the matter with thisn?

I hope they aint nothin the matter with it. I just need me one more.

The junkman looked at him for several minutes and then he went back across the little yard and entered the shack again.

When Harrogate peered in he was lying on the cot with one arm across his eyes.

Hey, said Harrogate.

I aint got time to mess with you, the junkman mumbled.

Listen, said Harrogate. I need two alike to make a boat out of.

The junkman removed his arm from his face and looked at the ceiling.

I wanted to get em welded together and tar up the holes so I could have me a boat.

A boat?

Yessir.

How do you sons of bitches find me?

It aint but just me.

All you crazy sons of bitches. I wish I could catch whoever it is keeps sendin em down here.

I just come by myself.

Yeah. Yeah.

Have you not got a hood to match thatn?

I got a forty-six, it's the same cept for the chrome, you can have it for six dollars if you want it.

Well I wanted to talk to you about that.

He looked like an enormous turtle going to the river, staggering under the weight of the welded car hoods, the aft one dragging a trail in the summer dust. He hadn't found any way to take the pot of tar so he'd tied it to one ankle and it scuttled along after him.

He put in above the packing company, sliding his boat through the grass and down the mud of the bank. The water that trickled in looked like ink beading over the tarred floor. He bent and untied the tarpot and set it in the boat and then stepped in cautiously. The steel flexed with a little dead buckling sound somewhere. He gripped the sides, going along on his knees. The back end lifted from the mud and he was adrift in the river.

Shit a brick, said Harrogate with cautious enthusiasm. He pulled off his shirt and sponged up the water to better see where the leaks were. Drifting past the packing company, the lumberyard.

What is that? called a watcher from the shore.

Boat, called Harrogate back.

By the time he reached the bridge he was sitting in the center with his feet spread before him, taking the sun and enjoying the river breeze. He came in at Goose Creek, paddling with his fingers. Up the small estuary, under the low bridge of the railway, lying on his back, muddobber nests overhead and lizards in little suctioncup shoes sliding past his face, easing himself along the wall with one hand. And under Scottish Pike and up the creek, standing in the stern of his new boat and poling with a stick he'd found, the rounded prow browsing through the rippled sludge that lay thick on the backwater.

He spent the night under the boat, it upturned like a canoe and propped with sticks, a small fire before him. Vestal boys came down to visit and to envy. One among the younger was sent for a chicken from his mother's yard and they plucked it and roasted it on a wire and passed about a warm RC Cola and told lies.

He came out of the creek into the river the next morning rowing with a board and a split paddle in oarlocks made from a dogchain. An eerie rattling apparition stroking through the fog. He'd not gone far before he was near run down by the dredger from the gravel company just set out downriver. A face passed high up the bank of fog, not even looking down from the floating wheelhouse. Harrogate had stood in his boat and raised a fist but the first bowwave almost tilted him out into the river and he sat quickly in the floor again and called a few round oaths.

He rowed upriver with his back to the rising sun, envisioning a penthouse among the arches and spans of the bridge he passed beneath, a retractable ropeladder, his boat at anchor by a stanchion, the consternation of a marveling citizenry. At Suttree's he pulled in and rapped on the floor of the deck with his knuckles. Hey Sut, he called.

Suttree raised up in his bunk and looked out. He saw a hand from the river holding onto the houseboat deck. He rolled out and went to the door and around and stood there in his shorts looking down at the city rat.

Slick aint it? said Harrogate.

Can you swim?

This time tomorrow you will be talkin to a wealthy man.

Or a drowned one. Where the hell did you get that thing?

Made it. Me and old drunk Harvey.

Good God, said Suttree.

What do you think of it?

I think you're fucking crazy.

You want to go for a ride?

No.

Come on, I'll ride ye.

Gene, I wouldnt get in that thing and it on dry land.

Well, I got to get on.

Harrogate pushed off and took up his trailing oars. I got a lot to do, he said.

Suttree watched him go on up the river, the little keelless contraption skittering and jerking along. It went pretty good.

Harrogate turned up First Creek and rowed beneath the railway trestle and continued on until he came to a narrows composed of abandoned machinery and high tiered tailings of garbage. He wired his boat to a small tree and went backwards up the bank admiring it.

He tried to nap but lying there in the heat beneath the viaduct with the traffic overhead he had such fantasies of plenitude that his feet made little involuntary trotting motions. By late afternoon he was up and about, flexing his sling with its new red rubbers and firing a few flat stones through the lightwires where they caromed and sang enormous lyrenotes in the budding tranquillity of evening. An addled cock crowed from the black hillside. He looked to his appurtenances and set forth.

He emerged from the creek mouth past the curious dark fishermen, oaring slowly and studying the sky. He stroked his way upstream, past the last of the shacks and as far as the marble company. Coming about on the placid evening calm and easing back the oars alongside and taking up his sling. Pinching up the leather in his fingers. Pouring the pellets. One flew. And there. A goatsucker wheeled and croaked. He hove back on the sling bands nearly to the floor and let go. And again. Random among the summer trees houselights came on along the southern shore. The neon nightshapes of the city bloomed, their replicas in the water like discolored sores. Across the watered sky the bats crossed and checked and flared. Dark fell but that was all. He was drifting beneath the bridge. He laid down the sling and took up the oars and came back.

It was a hot night for heavy thinking. He lay with his hands composed upon his chest. Beyond the bridge's arching brow drifting fireflies guttered against the night and the wind bore a heady scent of honeysuckle.

It was a grayhaired and avuncular apothecary who leaned not unkindly down from his high pulpit. Enormous fans stirred overhead, shifting the reek of nostrums and purgatives. Beyond the counter ranged carboys and galleypots and stainedglass jars of chemic and cottonmouthed bottles cold and replete with their particolored pills. Harrogate's chin rested just at the cool stone trestle and his eyes took in this alchemical scene with a twinge of old familiarity for which he could not account.

May I help you? said the scientist, his hands holding each other.

I need me some strychnine, said Harrogate.

You need some what?

Strychnine. You know what it is dont ye?

Yes, said the chemist.

I need me about a good cupful I reckon.

Are you going to drink it here or take it with you?

Shit fire I aint goin to drink it. It's poisoner'n hell.

It's for your grandmother.

No, said Harrogate, craning his neck suspectly. She's done dead.

The chemist tore off a piece of paper from a pad and poised with his pen. Just let me have the name of the person or persons you intend to poison, he said. We're required to keep records.

Suspecting japery, Harrogate grinned an uneasy grin. Listen, he said. You know about these here bats?

Oh yes indeed.

Well, that's what it's for. I dont care to tell you because they aint nobody else but me could figure out the rest of it.

I'm sure that's true, the chemist said.

I didnt bring nothin to fetch it in. You got a jar of some kind?

How old are you? said the chemist.

I'm twenty-one.

No you're not.

What'd you ast me for then?

The chemist removed his glasses and closed his eyes and pinched the bridge of his nose between his thumb and forefinger. He donned the spectacles again and looked down at Harrogate. He was still there. I can't sell strychnine to minors, he said. Nor to folk of other than right mind. It's against the law.

Well, said Harrogate. That's up to you.

Yes, said the chemist.

Harrogate backed sidling down the pale medicinal corridor, past ordered rows of canisters and jars. The rotors overhead sliced through the antiseptic air slow and constant. He pushed back the door with one hand. Bell ching. A slender rod came sucking out of a little piston. The chemist had not moved.

You're just a old fart, called Harrogate, and ran.

Suttree just shook his head. He was sitting with his trousers rolled and his bare feet hanging in the river.

Come on, Sut.

Gene.

Yeah.

I am not going in no goddamned drugstore and buy strychnine. Not for you. Not for anybody.

Hell Sut, they'd sell it to you. If I tell you what I want with it will you?

No.

They sat there watching Suttree's toes resting on the river.

Listen, Sut . . .

Suttree put his forefingers in his ears.

Harrogate leaned more closely. Listen, he said.

He waited down on Stinky Point, one eye for measuring the sun's decline, the other weathered out for his friend's coming. He had a pieplate with a piece of high and wormy hog's liver in it and he was cutting this up in small gobbets with his pocketknife. Suttree came through the weeds hot and perspiring and squatted on the bank and drew a small package from the hippocket of his jeans. Here, you crazy son of a bitch, he said.

Harrogate's black rat's eyes glazed over with joy. He untied the string and lifted a glass vial from the paper and examined it. A pale label with a green skull and bones. Shithouse mouse, he said. Thanks Sut. I sure as shit appreciate it.

You owe me two dollars.

Old buddy, that kind of money aint nothin now. You'll have it in the mornin.

Suttree watched him go on through the weeds to the river where his boat rode tethered to a cinderblock by a length of wire. He turned and smiled back and stepped neatly into the boat, holding the bottle in one hand, the tin of liver in the other. He sat carefully and laid his things out before him and leaned slightly forward and unpocketed the small catapult he'd fashioned from a treefork. Unwiring himself from the land he took up his makeshift oars and feathered gently into the current and away.

From the deck of his houseboat Suttree watched the antics of this half daft adolescent with a mild disgust. Standing amidships in his cocklecraft Harrogate tacked here and there. In the quiet evening the face of the river grew glassy. Suttree muttered to himself. He'd not muttered long before a bat came boring crazily askew out of the sky and fell with a plop onto the surface of the river and fluttered briefly and was still. Suttree sat up in his folding chair. Bats had begun to drop everywhere from the heavens. Little leatherwinged creatures struggling in the river. Harrogate oaring among them. One dropped with a mild and vesperal bong on the tin of Suttree's roof. Another close by in the water. Lying there on the dark current it seemed surprised and pitiful.

Harrogate in his tin coracle was hefting them aboard with a dipnet of his own devising. A bullbat fell bandywinged. A swift, a swallow. Along the dimming shore of broken fence and rubble and over the sparse colonies of jakelike dwellings a new curse falling, a plague of bats, small basilisks pugnosed with epicanthic eyes and upreared dogs' ears filled with hair and bellies filled with agony. In the smoke and burgundy dusk they dimpled the face of the river like lemmings. Two small black boys had packed a halfgallon picklejar with ones they found and screwed down the lid to keep them until needed. In the floor of Harrogate's boat the brown and hairy mound grew, strange cargo, such small replicas of the diabolic with their razorous teeth bared in fiends' grins. By dark he had a half a boatload and by the warehouse lights he struck a landfall just below the creek and tied up. He sat on the bank and drank in the evening calm and the winey honeysuckle air and waited for the last of the crawling pile of bats to die. When they had done so he loaded them in his sack and staggered up the bank and home.

In the morning he set out with them. A light heart and deep rejoicing for the fortune of it made the load less heavy yet he still must rest here and there by the streetside. By such stages he labored out Central Avenue small and bowed and wildlooking.

What you got in the sack son?

He peered from under the load at his inquisitor lounging in the open window of the halted cruiser. He shifted the weight a little higher on his shoulder. Bats, he said.

Bats.

Yessir.

What, ballbats?

No, them little'ns. Flittermouses.

The policeman's face bore a constant look of tolerant interest. Set the sack down son and let's see what all you got there.

Harrogate rolled the sack from his shoulder and lowered it to the paving and spread the drawstrung mouth with his thumbs. A musky smell rose. He tilted it slightly policeward. The officer thumbed his cap back on his head and bent to see. A prefiguration of the pit. Vouchsafed a crokersack vision of hell's floor deep with the hairy damned screaming mute and toothy toward the far and heedless city of God. He raised his head and looked at the waiting Harrogate and he looked at the bright sky above Knoxville and he turned to the driver.

You know what he's got in that sack?

What's he got?

Dead bats.

Dead bats.

Right.

Well.

What do you think?

I dont know. Ask him where he's goin with em.

Where you goin with em?

Up here to the hospital.

The officer had his chin resting on his shoulder. His face went blank. Rabies, he said. He turned to the driver and said something and they pulled away. Harrogate shouldered the bats and set forth again.

He climbed the marble stairs and went past the old columns of the portico and down the hall to a desk. Howdy, he said.

A nurse looked up.

I got some more.

What?

Some more. Bats.

I dont know what you're talking about.

Bats. I got a whole damn . . . I got a whole sackful.

She stared at him warily.

Looky here, he said, pointing.

She stood up and leaned over and looked down. Harrogate fumbled with the sack, trying to see her tits. She put her hand to her collarbone. He spread the sack open and she leaped back.

It's a mess of em, aint it?

Get those things out of here, she whispered.

Where do I take em?

But she had gone down the hall on her white crepe shoes. She came back with a man in a white tunic. Him? said the man.

Harrogate stood his ground.

Let me see what you've got there.

He held open the mouth of the sack.

The man turned pale. He gestured at the nurse. Call the clinic, he said. Tell them we've got about a bushel of dead bats up here.

She was dialing.

Where did you get them? said the man.

Just here and there, said Harrogate.

A woman was coming down the hall. The man went to her and ushered her back toward the door.

Dr Hauser says to bring them on, said the nurse, holding one hand over the mouthpiece of the telephone.

Tell him we're on our way.

I guess you aint used to gettin this many at a time, said Harrogate.

They sat him in a little white room and gave him a box of vanilla icecream. He watched the sunlight on the walls with dreamy content. After a while a nurse brought him a little metal tray with a hot lunch.

You can just take it out of what all you owe me, Harrogate told her.

The afternoon set in and he grew bored. He went to the door and looked out. An empty corridor. He sat some more. It grew warmer. He lay on the tile floor with his hands cradling his head. His mind roved over storewindows. He saw himself ascending the stairs at Comer's in pressed gabardines and zipper shoes, a slender cigar in his mouth, an italian switchblade knife silver bound with ebony handles in one pocket, a gold watchchain draped across the pleats of his slacks. Greeted by all. Pulling the roll of bills from his pocket. He went back down the stairs and came up again in different attire, a pullover shirt like Feezel's. Dark blue. With pale gray trousers and blue suede shoes. Belt to match. The door opened. He sat up.

Mr Harrogate.

Yes mam.

Dr Hauser would like to see you.

They went through three doors. The doctor was standing at a bench among bottles and jars. The nurse closed the door behind him. Harrogate stood there with his hands hanging down inside the pockets of his capacious trousers. The doctor turned and looked dourly across the upper rims of his glasses at him.

Mr Harrogate?

Yessir.

Yes. Would you just come with me a minute?

Harrogate followed him into a tiny office. A little white cubicle with glass bricks in the ceiling. Occasional pedestrians walked overhead, muted heels and sunlight. The pipes that hung from the ceiling were painted white. He looked everything over.

That was quite a collection of bats, said the doctor.

They's forty-two of em.

Yes. None rabid at all. We were curious. We couldn't find any marks on them.

Harrogate grinned. I figured you might reckon they'd been shot or somethin. Many of em as they was.

Yes. We examined one.

Mm-hmm.

Strychnine.

Harrogate's face gave a funny little twitch. What? he said.

How did you do it?

Do what?

How did you do it? Poison forty-two bats. They only feed on the wing.

I dont know nothin about it. They was dead. Listen. I brought one down here before and nobody never said nothin. They never said they was a limit on how many you could collect on.

Mr Harrogate, the city is offering a reward for any dead bats found in the streets. We have what could become a critical situation here with rabies. That's the purpose of the reward. We have not authorized the wholesale slaughter of bats.

Do I get the money or not?

You do not.

Shit.

I'm sorry.

Well.

I would like to know how you managed to poison them.

Harrogate sucked at his black foretooth. What will you give me? he said.

The doctor leaned back in his chair and studied him all over again. Well, he said, feeling the spirit of things, what will you take?

I'll take two dollars.

That's too high. I'll give a dollar.

Make it a dollar and a quarter.

All right.

That includes the dinner and the icecream.

Okay.

I done it with a flipper.

With a flipper?

Yessir.

The doctor looked at the ceiling. Ah, he said. I see. What? Did you poison scraps of meat and then shoot them in the air?

Yeah. Them sons of bitches like to never quit fallin.

Very ingenious. Damned ingenious.

218

I can figure out anything.

Well, I'm sorry your efforts were for nothing.

Maybe a dollar and a quarter aint nothin to you but it is to me.

When Suttree called on him he found a shrunken djinn hulked over an applebox tracing with a chewed pencil stub a route beneath the city on a map of it. A sanguine scene, there by the bloodcolored light of the construction lantern. At Suttree's approach a bright red cat rose from before the lamp and moved away into the dark. Harrogate looked up, feet tucked and bright smile, a diabolic figure across which the shadow of a moth passed and repassed like a portent.

How did you make out?

Set down Sut. Not worth a shit.

Wouldn't they pay?

Naw. I got to hand it to em. They're smart.

Well.

I'm glad you come. Looky here at this map.

Suttree glanced at it.

It shows where all the buildings is and you can measure it on here, see, on this here scale?

Yeah?

Well shit. I mean, what with them caves down there and it all holler and everthing?

So?

Lord, Sut, it's tailormade. They're just askin for it.

Suttree rose. Gene, he said, you're crazy.

Set down Sut. Looky here. The goddamned bank is only . . .

I dont want to look. I dont want to hear.

Harrogate watched him wane from the gory light toward darkness.

It's a dead lock, Sut, he called. I need you to help me.

Beyond in the dark of the town late traffic passed.

Sut?

A chained dog yapped from the shackstrewn hillside across the creek.

I need you to help me, he called.

In the early months of that summer a new fisherman appeared on the river. Suttree saw him humped over the oars in a skiff composed of actual driftwood, old boxes and stenciled crateslats and parts of furniture patched up with tin storesigns and rags of canvas and spattered over with daubs of tar. A crazyquilt boat sculled through the loose fog by a sullen oarsman who looked not right nor left.

Standing at Turner's stall Suttree stared down into the long glass bier. Little beads of water ran on the heavy slant panes in their nickel and porcelain mortises. Inside on a bed of crushed ice dimly lit and lightly garlanded with parsley sprigs lay a catfish with a nine inch dinnerplate in its mouth. Old men kept drifting by to peer in and comment. A little card rested against the broad yellow flank. It said: Caught in the Tennessee River June 9 1952. Wt. 87 lbs.

Mornin Suttree, said the fishmonger.

Where the hell did you get this?

Some Indian brought it in here this mornin. Aint that a fish?

It's the biggest catfish I ever saw.

Old Bert Vincent was by a little while ago, said it was the biggest he ever seen personally.

I dont guess you'll be needing any fish this morning.

Not this morning.

Suttree crossed through the markethouse and went on toward niggertown with his fish.

In the evening he watched the Indian set out again on his one line below the railway trestle. And back. He hove to in the blue shadow under the bluff and drifted from sight. Eighty-seven pounds, Suttree muttered.

On his run downriver in the morning he watched for the Indian's skiff. He saw it swinging loosely below the sheer rock of the south shore. Trash hung in the vines all down the face of the bluff and a thin faultline angled up and switched back until it gained the rim of a cave a hundred feet above the river. Up there watching was the fisherman. Suttree raised his hand. The figure on the cliff gestured back. Suttree eased the oars into the river and went on.

When he came back upriver the Indian was cleaning fish on a rock at the foot of the bluff. When he saw Suttree he stood up and looked up at the cave and wiped his hands on the sides of his jeans.

Suttree eased the skiff alongside the rock and shipped the inside oar.

There was a shallow pool among the rocks and from the bottom countless fish heads stared up through the silty water to the streaked sunlight of a world dead to them. Coiled viscera ebbed in the murk and a few tins gave back a baleful light. Howdy, he said.

Hey, said the Indian.

How's it going?

Okay.

I saw that blue cat down at Turner's. I dont see how you got it in the boat.

Yeah, said the Indian.

Suttree looked out over the water and he looked up at the Indian again. A tall and ocherskinned stranger in a pair of busted out brogans, the sorry clothes, the stove knees and elbows not patched but simply puckered shut with crude stitching. Pinned to his shirt and joined by their weighted wire he wore a pair of china eyes that had once swung in a doll's skull.

I live up the river yonder, said Suttree. Just above the bridge in that first houseboat.

The Indian nodded. I seen you, he said. In the sun his homecut hair looked blue and his eyes were black. Suttree couldnt tell if he was looking at him or just down at his shoes.

There's the size I catch. Suttree held up the smallest catfish in the boat.

You want some bait?

Bait?

Sure.

What kind you got?

Wait on me till I get you some.

Suttree watched him, sculling to recover the current. He went up the bluff like a goat.

When he came back he handed down a jar to Suttree. Suttree took it and looked at it and turned it against the sun and unscrewed the cap and sniffed at it. Goddamn, he said.

The Indian had squatted on the rock to watch him more closely and now he slapped his thigh and laughed.

Shit, said Suttree. He clapped the lid back over the mess.

Dont smell it, said the Indian, grinning.

Now you tell me. He tilted the jar at arm's length. Will it stay on the hook?

Sure.

Well. Thanks. Maybe I'll catch one of those big mammyjammers.

Sure, said the Indian.

Suttree set the jar on the seat and pushed off from the rocks. Thanks again, he said. Come see me.

The Indian stood and put his hands in his pockets and gave a little toss of his chin. Okay, he said.

The next week he didnt see him. The crazy boat was gone. Suttree tried the bait but the odor of it, the gagging vomit reek, was more than he could stand. He'd wash his hands again and again after molding it on the hooks. The third morning he caught two turtles and he let the jar descend down through the duncolored water behind the last flaring dropper and went back to his cutbait and doughballs.

Monday morning someone rapped at his door and he turned out in the dawn chill to find the Indian there. He wore the same clothes, the same shoes. The tandem eyeballs still pinned to his pocket. Hey, he said.

Come on in, said Suttree.

How you do with the bait?

Okay. Kept catching turtles.

Hey. Turtles. Snappers, hey?

Yeah. Watch your head.

The Indian stooped and entered and turned.

Sit down. Suttree motioned loosely toward the dim interior.

Them is good to eat, said the Indian. Best meat there is.

Yeah, well. They're a lot of trouble to fix.

You bring him to me. I show you how to fix him.

You want a cup of coffee?

Sure.

Have it in a minute. Go on, sit down.

The Indian sat on the bunk and crossed his legs.

I didnt see you for a couple of days.

No.

Suttree ladled water out of a lardpail into the coffeepot and lit the burner. He measured in the coffee. I used to know an old guy who shot turtles down on the river. I never see the meat for sale though.

Yeah, well. I sell em sometime.

Suttree set the pot on the burner and put the lid on and turned the flame up. He got down the spare cup. It had a dead spider curled in it and he pitched the spider into the trash and rinsed both cups. When the coffee perked he poured the cups full and turned and handed one to the Indian.

He took the cup gravely and blew on it. He gave off a rich acidic smell of woodsmoke and grease and fish. Sparse whiskers on his fine skin. His arms lean, longmuscled, blueveined.

I never ate one, Suttree said.

One what?

Turtle.

You come to my place sometime I fix him for you.

Okay, said Suttree.

The Indian sipped the coffee and regarded him above the cuprim with grave black eyes. I got thowed in jail, he said.

When?

Last week. I just got out.

What did they have you for?

Vag. You know. They got me once before.

How did you get out?

They let me sweep up. They let me clean up and then they let me out. I come down this mornin and my boat was gone.

Where did you leave it?

Just down here. I reckon some boys took it.

Have you looked for it?

Yeah.

Suttree watched him. Well, he said. Why dont we go in my boat and see if we can see it.

I'll pay you.

It's all right.

He got his shoes and socks. These river rats will steal anything that's not nailed down.

They might of sunk it.

Would it sink?

Put enough rocks in it.

Suttree shook his head.

They went downriver with Suttree rowing and the Indian bailing, bending toward each other at their tasks.

They had a hell of a nigger in there, the Indian said.

Where's that?

In the jail. They had this great big nigger. They fought all over the jailhouse. They'd go in there and bust his head with slapsticks. He'd come around after a while and start cussin em all over again.

Suttree stayed the oars.

He raised some knots on a few of them jailers, the Indian said.

Did he get out?

Yeah. Somebody come and got him yesterday.

Suttree rowed on.

They went past the last bridge and down the bend in the river. They watched the shore.

That's not it is it? said Suttree, pointing.

The Indian shaded his eyes. No, he said. It's just some trash.

Suttree dabbed his eye against his shoulder with a shrugging motion and went on.

You want me to row awhile?

No. It's okay.

They found the skiff awash in shallow water near the head of the island. Suttree eased alongside and laid back the oars. The Indian stood.

Is it stove? said Suttree.

No. I dont think so.

They must still be here on the island.

The Indian scanned the steaming reaches of reed and willow. A plover was crossing the siltbar like a gallery bird. Suttree stepped out with the rope and they pulled the skiff ashore.

There was a little path going up the island through the weeds. They went with caution. Redwings circled and cried.

They entered a clearing where charred sticks and blackened stones marked a fire. A few empty bean tins. They walked around the glade.

Looks like they skedaddled, Suttree said.

Yeah.

They cant be far.

Let em go, the Indian said.

Yeah?

Sure.

Okay.

They turned and defiled out of the glade, Suttree behind the Indian. Dragonflies kept lifting from the tops of the reeds like little chinese kites.

What's your name? said Suttree.

The Indian turned and looked back. Michael, he said.

Is that what they call you?

He turned again. No, he said. They call me Tonto or Wahoo or Chief. But my name is Michael.

My name's Suttree.

The Indian smiled. Suttree thought maybe he was going to stop and shake hands but he didnt.

They got the boat bailed and afloat and Suttree shoved it out onto the pale brown waters. The Indian took up the oars and brought it about headed upriver. What do I owe you? he said.

Not anything.

Well. Come see me and I'll fix you that turtle.

Suttree raised his hand. Okay, he said. Watch out for the cops.

The Indian dipped the oars into the river and pulled away.

Suttree stepped into his skiff and walked to the rear of it and shoved off from the flats with one oar. The Indian's patchwork boat was soon far upriver, light winking off the sweeps where they'd been broken and pieced back with tacked and flattened foodtins. He eased his own oars into the water and started up the inside of the island. He watched for sign of the thieves along the shore and he saw a muskrat nose among the willows and he saw a clutch of heronshaws gawping from their down nest in the reeds, spikelet bills and stringy gullets, pink flesh and pinfeathers and boneless legs spindled about. He tacked more shoreward to see. So curious narrow beasties. As he pulled abreast of them a rock sang past his ears. He ducked and looked toward the shore bracken but before he could collect himself another rock came whistling out of the willows and caught him in the forehead and he fell back in the boat. The sky was red and soaring and whorled like the ball of an enormous thumb and a numb gritty feeling came up against the back of his teeth. One oar slid from its lock and floated off.

The skiff drifted down past the landing and down past the end of the island. Suttree lay sprawled in the floor with blood running in his eyes. A tree branch turned against the sky. He pulled himself up, gripping the side of the skiff. He could taste a tincture of iron in his throat and he spat a bloody mucus into the water. He knelt over the side and palmed water at his face and his face was slippery with blood and blood lay in the water in coagulate strings. He touched gently an eggshaped swelling. His whole skull was throbbing and even his eyes hurt. He looked upriver toward the island and swore murderously. The other oar was floating a few yards downriver and he sculled after it. Light kept winking up on the riffles and blood was dripping from his forehead and he felt half nauseous. He recovered the drift oar and rowed back upriver in the main channel. He watched along the shoreline of the island but he saw nothing. After a while his head quit bleeding.

Doll came to the door at Ab's and looked him up and down. Hunh, she said. What happen to you?

Some son of a bitch hit me with a rock.

Mm-mmm, she said, shaking her head. Come in.

How's Ab?

She shut the door behind him.

Suttree turned in the stale and darkened room. Why didnt you tell me he was all screwed up?

I caint do nothin with him.

Where is he, in the back?

She gestured him on with one hand and he pushed back the curtain. At first he could not see him well but gradually the black's half closed and swollen eyes appeared, his glistening misshapen face. His broken mouth moved painfully. He said: Hey Youngblood.

Suttree heard his breath suck in the quiet. Hey Ab, he said. How are you.

I'm okay. I's just slippin me a nap. What you up to in the heat of the day? You catchin any fish?

Not to amount to anything. Have you had a doctor?

A throaty laugh shook the sagging bedsprings. He moved his head on the pillows as if he'd seek a darker place to rest it. What I needs with a doctor?

I think you need some help.

That may be. But I aint in need of bein patched up and prayed over.

What can I get you?

Ah Youngblood. I dont need nothin.

Somebody told me you tried to whip everybody at city jail.

You caint do nothin with them crackers. They needs they wigs tightened ever little bit.

I remember the last time they picked up Byrd and Sam Slusser you saw cops for weeks all over Knoxville with bandages and black eyes limping around.

Jones chuckled.

I guess far as that goes we might look for some this week.

Ah, said Jones. Aint but one of em I wants.

Who's that, Quinn?

226

Jones didnt answer. How's you little buddy? he said. He aint drownded hisself in that boat yet is he?

Not yet.

He come by here other day tryin to sell the old woman what he call scobs.

Scobs?

What he call em. Look like old pigeons to me. He had em all dressed and everthing. He some kind of a mess, aint he?

He's crazy as a mouse in a milkcan.

Jones chuckled.

I'm going uptown. You want me to bring you anything?

Naw.

You sure you okay?

He turned his battered face. Do somethin for me, Youngblood.

Name it.

Go see Miss Mother for me. Tell her I needs to see her.

Wouldnt Doll go for you?

Doll dont want me to have no truck with her. She wont run her off if she comes down here. You tell her.

What else?

That's all. I'd be much obliged.

Okay. Take care and I'll see you later.

Yeah, said the black.

He crossed the fields and went up Front Avenue and turned down a steep cinderpath past a run of chickens, a sleeping dog. The path went through a locust wood and the huge beanpods hung everywhere in a sunlight stained and made obscure by windblown papers staked out among the blackened upper branches, tents of newsprint and trash and the ruins of kites all tattered and rainleached and impaled upon the locust spikes. He crossed an iron sewer main half out of the ground and he descended into an old limestone sink that had been filled back as a city dump and graded over years ago. Now it was a small glade and there was a raw board shack in the center of it. Suttree came down the path and out from the last of the trees. The ninekiller flew. A few garish outland birds leaned from the limbs to watch him, gaudy longtailed fowl, he didnt know what kind. Their moult feathers lay about in the dust of the yard. He crossed to the door and tapped with his knuckles.

It opened on a female dwarf coalblack in widow's weeds who wore little goldwire spectacles on a chain about her neck. Scarce four feet tall she was, her hand on the doorknob at her ear like a child or a trained house ape. She looked up at Suttree and she said: Well, you aint come for yourself I dont reckon.

No mam, he said. She turned her head and cocked it slightly. He said: I came for Ab Jones. He wanted to know if you could come over to his place.

Come in here, she said, stepping back.

He entered with a peculiar feeling of deference. When she shut the door behind them they were in almost total dark. She led the way along a hall and through a curtained doorway. Black drapes were tacked to the window sashes. He could make out a table and some chairs and a small cot.

Set down, she said.

He sat at the table and looked about. She had left the room. Strange effects began to accrue out of the semidark like figures in a dream. On the table was an assortment of silver vases and candlesticks and porringers and bowls all covered over with sheets of yellow cellophane. There was a fireplace that held a broken coalgrate propped on bricks and there was a beveled lookinglass above the mantel. On the mantel a lamp, a vase, a marble clock. What appeared to be a stuffed bird. Smaller objects harbored in the gloom. An electric fan on the table kept turning from side to side and washing him with periodic gusts of fetid air. Flowered wallpaper had been glued over the shack's naked boards and the joints had laddered and split the paper. Everywhere hung portraits of blacks, strange family groups where the faces watched gravely from out of their paper past. Hanging in the dark like galleries of condemned. Their homemade clothes.

He heard the creak of a cellar door. On the hearth cut flowers in a blue coalscuttle stirred and trembled.

He could hear her coming from outside, doorlatch and the scuffle of her soft shoes. She entered and closed the door behind her. In the light of its closing he saw a coatrack hung with little fairground birds that swung or turned on their wires in the wind. She came to him and took his head in her hand and held up something small and oddly shaped and wrapped in an old socktoe. Suttree fended it off. Wait a minute, he said. What is that?

Hold still, she said.

He reared back. In his hand her forearm felt like a thin piece of kindling.

Aint a fool a wonderful thing? she said. It's ice, boy. Now set still.

He subsided into the chair and she laid the cold wet rag against the knot on his forehead and took his hand in her own, a thin little thing you'd remember from touching hands with a monkey through the bars or having a pet coon. She guided his hand to the ice and he held it there. A small rill of water ran down his nose. His head began to feel nicely numb.

You'd better bring some of this for Jones, he said.

What's got with him?

He got beat up pretty bad down at the jail last week. I guess that's why he wants to see you.

He dont care nothin about that. He want to kill his enemies is what he want.

Kill his enemies? Suttree had his head bent forward to let the water drip.

Mm-hmm.

Which enemies?

Standing there by the chair where he sat her eyes were level with his. She looked at him. A face wherein lay everything and nothing. A visage hacked from cold black wax. She gestured with one hand, extending her arm and suggesting the world that stood beyond the thin board walls and beyond the locust forest, a gesture both grave and gracious that acknowledged endless armies of the unbending pale. That was all. She put a finger in her mouth to adjust her teeth.

Suttree stood and said that he must go.

She held back the curtain and he went through and made his way to the door. He paused there with his hand on the knob. What should I tell Jones? he said.

I caint make no call down there.

He really wants you to come.

Mm-hmm.

He needs you to come.

I knows that.

Can I bring him up here?

He knows where I'm at.

Well.

He opened the door. White sunlight blinded him. Thank you for the ice, he said.

Mm-hmm, she said.

By the time he reached the street the ice was gone and he stopped in Howard Clevinger's to get another piece. Lifting the rusty lid of the drinkbox and sorting through the cold water for a rightsized chunk, the smooth shapes sliding about among the bottlenecks with bits of paper and flakes of fallen paint. Gatemouth was watching him from the rocker and when he raised up from behind the lid and clapped the piece of ice to his forehead he laughed and wheezed and rocked and shook his head.

Ho ho, said Suttree.

Who went up the side of yo head, baby?

Suttree leaned back. On the cardboard ceiling were tacked odd-shaped bits of paper.

Who you jump salty with, Sut?

I ran into a door.

Hee hee, chuckled Gatemouth.

Where's all your nutwagon friends today?

Out amongst em.

Good, said Suttree. He held the ice to his head and went out. Clevinger, slouched in his chair with his arms crossed, opened one eye when he passed the counter and closed it again. Suttree went up the hill toward town.

It was late afternoon when he returned. He sat on the porch and watched the river pass. Before dark fell he rose and went up the river to Ab Jones's.

Two white men were drinking beer in the corner and Doll was frying hamburgers on the little burner in the galley. He went through the room and pushed back the curtain. The bed was empty. He pushed back the plastic shower curtain on the other side. Jones was standing at the urinal, bracing himself up with one hand against the wall. He was wearing a pair of khaki undershorts and even in the dim light from the small window on the river Suttree saw such galaxies of scars and old rendings mended and slick and livid suture marks as made him gasp. He looked like some dusky movie monster patched up out of graveyard parts and stitched by an indifferent hand. Suttree let the curtain fall.

What did she say, Youngblood?

She said for you to come up there.

He was looking at the floor, waiting for an answer. Jones didnt answer.

I told her you needed her to come but she wouldnt have any part of it.

Well.

You want me to try again?

Naw. Go on out there and get you a beer.

Do you think you could make it up there?

I'll get up there one of these days.

Suttree went back to the front room.

You want a hamburger? Doll said.

Suttree said he would.

He got a beer from the cooler and crossed to the far corner and sat down. The two men watched him. Suttree took a long pull from the bottle and set it on the marble at his elbow. She came shuffling over in her houseshoes and set a thick plate before him with a hamburger and some pickles and went back.

Hey, said one of the men.

Suttree looked at them.

How come he gets his first? He come in after us.

She looked up from behind the plywood counter. Her one eye blinked. She looked enormously tired. He work here, she said.

They looked at Suttree. He raised the hamburger and took a good bite. It was heavily seasoned with pepper. Rich grease and mayonnaise dripped to the plate.

Hey buddy, you work here?

Suttree looked at them. They didnt look good.

How about bringin us a couple more beers, good buddy.

He pointed toward Doll. Tell her, he said.

Hell, she said you worked here. Do you not wait tables?

Shit boy, we might be heavy tippers and you not know it.

Suttree set the beer down and leaned forward in his chair. I'm going to tell you goofy pricks something, he said. If you cause that big son of a bitch to come out here as bad as he feels he is going to kill you where you sit.

They looked toward the rear where he'd pointed. One turned to the other. Is he back there? he said.

Shit if I know.

I thought he was in jail.

Suttree looked at Doll. She was turning the pats of meat, her sullen face shining with grease and steam.

We'll see you outside, motherfucker, said the man at the table.

Sure, said Suttree. He finished his hamburger and drained the beer bottle and rose. He set the plate and bottle on the counter and wiped his mouth with his sleeve.

What do I owe?

You dont owe nothin.

Thanks Doll.

Dont you bring that witch down here.

Suttree grinned. She wouldnt come, he said.

Mm-hmm. She came from behind the counter with the plates and Suttree went on to the door. He listened for the men to say something but they didnt.

He crawled into bed without lighting the lamp and he was up not much past daybreak and out to run his lines.

When he came back upriver with his catch the Indian's skiff was moored to the rocks under the bluff and the Indian hailed him from the top with a piercing whistle.

Suttree waved.

The Indian cupped his hands and called for him to pull in. Suttree feathered the left oar and came up under the shadow of the rocks. The Indian was working his way down the path. Suttree sat the oars and waited.

I got us a turtle, the Indian said. He bent to look at Suttree. What happened to you?

What?

He pointed at Suttree's head. Suttree put a finger gently to his wound. I got that yesterday. Your buddies.

My buddies?

When I was coming back up after I left you somebody cut loose at me with a flipper.

He was a hell of a shot.

Suttree looked up to see if he was smiling but he wasnt. He rose and went down the rocks. Come on, he said. I'll show you your supper.

Suttree climbed from his skiff with the rope and made fast. The Indian had taken up a cord from among the rocks and was hauling it in hand over hand. A hulking shape loomed and subsided. It entered the shadowline of the rock pool and scuttled slowly among the ebbing fish heads. Suttree shaded his eyes. It rose up, dragged by its head, a mosscolored shadow taking shape, a craggy leathercovered skull. The Indian braced his feet and swung it up dripping from the river and onto the rocks and it squatted there watching them, its baleful pig's eyes blinking. It was tied through the lower jaw with a section of wire and the Indian took hold of the wire and tugged at it. The turtle bated and hissed, its jaws gaped. The Indian had out his pocketknife and now he opened it and he pulled the turtle's obscene neck out taut and with a quick upward motion of the blade severed the head. Suttree involuntarily drew back. The turtle's craggy head swung from the wire and what lay between the braced forefeet was a black and wrinkled dog's cunt slowly pumping gouts of near black blood. The blood ran down over the stones and dripped in the water and the turtle shifted slowly on the rock and started toward the river.

The Indian undid the wire and flung the head into the river and reached up the turtle by its tail and swung it trailing blood toward Suttree for him to heft.

Suttree reached to take it by one hindfoot but when he touched the foot it withdrew beneath the scaly eaves of the shell.

Here, you can get him by the tail.

He reached past the Indian's grip and took the headless turtle. Blood dripped and spattered on the stones.

What do you think he'll weigh?

I dont know, said Suttree. He's a big son of a bitch. Thirty pounds maybe?

May be. Lay him down here and we'll dress him.

Suttree laid the turtle on the rock and the Indian scouted about until he came up with a goodsized stone.

Watch out, he said.

Suttree stepped back.

The Indian raised the stone and brought it down upon the turtle's back. The shell collapsed with a pulpy buckling sound.

I never saw a turtle dressed before, said Suttree. But the Indian had knelt and was cutting away the broken plates of shell with his pocketknife and pitching them into the river. He pulled the turtle's meat up off the plastron and gouged away the scant bowels with his thumb. He skinned out the feet. What hung headless in his grip as he raised it aloft was a wet gray foetal mass, a dim atavism limp and dripping.

Plenty of meat there, said the Indian. He laid it out on the rock and bent and swished the blade of his knife in the river.

How do you fix it, said Suttree.

Put him in a pot and cook him slow. Lots of vegetables. Lots of onions. I got my own things I put in. Come on I show you.

I've got to get on to town with these fish. How long does it take to cook.

Three, four hours.

Well why dont I come back this evening?

Okay.

Suttree looked at the saclike shape of the shucked turtle dripping from the Indian's hand.

You be sure and come, the Indian said.

I'll be here.

He pushed off in the skiff and took up the oars. The Indian raised the turtle and swung it before him like a censer.

As he left the markethouse it was beginning to rain. Merchants were out with poles winching down their awnings. The vendors scurried among their trucks, stowing their produce more inboard and a crazed prophet in biblical sandwichboards tottered past muttering darkly at the heavens. Suttree went up the alley and up the back stairs at Comer's.

A company of mutes were playing check at the rear table and some raised their hands in greeting. Suttree raised back, going to the washbasin for paper towels. One of the mutes gestured at him, carving words with a dexter hand in the smoky air. Suttree was drying his face. He thought he had the gist of it and nodded and formed words with his own fingers, puzzled, erased, began again. They nodded encouragement. He fashioned his phrase for them and they laughed their croaky mute's laughter and elbowed one another. Suttree grinned and went on to the lunchcounter.

Eddie Taylor was playing bank pool in the sideroom onehanded against a stranger and spotting him two balls. Suttree sat at the counter and turned his stool to watch. The balls rifled across the felt and whacked viciously into the pockets, Taylor laughing, joking, chalking his cue. Bending, stroking. The ball smoking back down from the end rail. Whop.

The Knoxville Bear, called out Harry the Horse on his way to the cashregister.

Stud was wiping the counter at Suttree's elbow. What for ye, Sut, he said.

Let me have a chocolate milk.

Buddy boy, said Jake.

Hey Jake.

Jake spat into the stainless steel spittoon and wiped his mouth. The bear can walk the balls to the pockets caint he.

Yes he can, said Suttree.

While he was drinking his milk small weird Leonard took a seat beside him and leaned to case the game at the table and leaned back. Hey Sut?

Hey Leonard.

What the fuck is a yegg?

A yegg?

Y E doubleG.

Suttree looked at Leonard. Who called you that?

What is one?

Well. I dont know. A yegg is a . . . I guess a hoodlum.

Hoodlum huh?

More or less.

Yeah. Okay.

I never heard the word except in this crazy newspaper.

Yeah, well. Leonard looked about nervously and rose. I'll see ye, Sut.

Suttree watched him go out toward the front and the stairs. Stud, he said. Hand me that paper.

He found the story on page two. Yeggs last night boarded the River Queen, popular Knoxville excursion boat, in what was apparently an unsuccessful robbery attempt. He smiled and finished the milk and laid his dime on the counter and pushed back the paper.

The Jellyroll Kid was in a check game at the front table and when Suttree sat in one of the lopsided theatre seats the kid sidled to him and turned down his cupped hand for Suttree to read his pills. He had the one and the twelve. Suttree noted them with a poker face. You shoot up here with the big dogs do you? he said.

It's just a dollar. The kid was watching the table. He'd broken the rack and the twelveball was hung in the corner pocket. Flop set his cue crutch up on the felt and laid the cue in it and stroked and sighted, sawing the cue smoothly, holding the crutch under his stump. He shot the eight in the side pocket and the cueball kissed its way along the balls on the rail and tore out the oneball and nudged a ball up against the twelve. The twelve dropped into the pocket.

Check, called Jellyroll, taking the pill from his pocket and wedging it under the rail at the head of the table. Flop looked up at him and chalked his cue and laid by the crutch and set the cue on the rail and began to stroke back and forth and sight. Jellyroll looked off down the hall. Jerome Jernigan turned his eyes up in disgust. Flop stroked the oneball into the corner.

Double, said Jellyroll, throwing his pill on the table.

Shit, said Jerome.

Rack, said Jelly.

The Jellyroll Kid, said Jake, shucking the balls up out of the pockets and rounding them up with the rack.

Jelly threw a quarter on the table and collected his dollars from the other players and funneled the pills back into the leather bottle and shook it and handed it to Suttree. Suttree tipped it and let two pills fall into his palm and passed the bottle to Flop.

That's the luckiest son of a bitch in the world, Flop said.

Jellyroll broke the balls on the table. Suttree turned up the pills and looked at them. He had the one and the fifteen.

Which way can I go, Sut?

Suttree looked at the table. The eightball was sewn up.

You can go any way you want.

I dont even want to know what I've got, said Jelly. He shot the fifteen into the corner and chalked his cue.

Check, said Suttree, rising and putting the fifteen pill under the rail.

How's that fourteen look, Sut?

That's too hard a shot, Jelly.

Jelly walked around the table and sighted on the oneball and banked it across the side.

Double, said Suttree.

No shit? said Jelly, raising up and grinning.

Rack, said Jerome.

Flop shook his head. The other man stood up and threw his pills on the table and took the pillbottle and emptied the pills out onto the felt. Let him draw his own fuckin pills, he said.

Yes, said Jelly. I aint had the eightball a time.

How sweet it is on the Jellyroll Kid, said Jake, racking up the balls.

The stranger was counting the pills back into the bottle. Jellyroll grinned and winked at Suttree. Kenneth Tipton told me he got in a check game up here last week with four highschool boys. He was the last to draw pills and when he went to draw them there wasnt but one left in the jug. He held it up and asked could he borrow one from somebody.

Suttree grinned. Jimmy Long got in a bank game up here with a hustler one time, they butted heads for about an hour, finally this hustler says: Let's play one game lefthanded for ten. Old J-Bone says okay and this hustler *was* lefthanded.

Jelly laughed and bent and broke the balls and reached for the pillbottle. Suttree rose.

Where you goin Sut?

I've got to go.

Shit, dont leave now. We'll go drink a beer here in a minute.

I'll see you later.

Jelly was looking at his pills. Drink some mash and talk some trash, he called out.

Suttree went past the counter. Hey Fred, he said.

Buddy boy, said Fred.

He pushed open the door and nodded to the sentry at the top of the stairs and went down the stairwell to the street.

In the evening he rowed back across the river with six bottles of cold beer under the seat. The shadow of the bluff lay deep and cool along the south shore of the river. He swung in alongside the Indian's patched skiff and tethered his rope and tucked the sack of beer under his arm and started up the bluff.

The path wound up by a steep and narrow way and near the top of the rise came out upon a natural terrace in the rock and a cave. The Indian did not seem to be about. A soapkettle was lodged on a rock hob and the gray flaky ashes when he toed them broke open to an orange heart of burning wood.

Hey Michael, he called.

A lizard crossed the stone floor and slithered into the weeds.

Suttree tipped up the rim of the kettle's lid with a stick. A wafted breath of fragrant steam slid out. The stew simmered gently. He let the lid drop and went to the mouth of the cave and looked in. A red clay floor that shaped itself among the rocks. On the right was a table made from a plank propped on stones. He ducked under the low limestone ledge and entered and set the beer down. Just within the last reaches of daylight he could make out the footrail of an old iron bed.

It was damp in the cave and it smelled of earth and woodsmoke. Suttree went back out. He called again but there was no answer. He walked to the edge of the bluff and looked out. The city lay quiet in the evening sun and innocent. Far downstream the river narrowed with distance where the pieced fields lay pale and hazy and the water placid much like those misty landscapes in which Audubon posed his birds. He sat in a tattered lawnchair and watched the traffic on the bridge below. There was no sound save for a bird that conjured up forbidden jungles with its medley of whoops and croaks. Suttree saw it put forth from the bluff and flutter in midair and go back. He leaned his head back. A mayfly, delicate and pale green, drifted past. Lost ephemera, wandered surely from some upland pastoral. The chat came from its bower on the bluffside and fluttered and snatched the mayfly and returned. After a while it sang again. It sang grok, wheet, erk. Suttree got up and went into the cave and got one of the beers. He returned to the chair and sat and wiped the mouth of the bottle with the web of his thumb and held it up and toasted mutely the city below and drank.

It was almost dark when the Indian returned. He came down the slope above the cave and dropped to the stone floor and crossed to where Suttree sat.

Hey, said Suttree.

How you doin?

Okay. Get yourself a beer there. I set them inside on that table. You want one?

Yeah.

The Indian crossed the little terrace and lifted the lid from the pot and sniffed. How's it doin?

Okay.

He stirred the mixture with a peeled stick and clapped the lid back over it and pushed more wood into the fire. He came from the cave with the beers and handed one to Suttree and squatted on his heels at the edge of the bluff. The John Agee was coming downriver, her stern paddles trudging the brown waters. They sipped their beers. The lights of the city were beginning to come up across the river. The lamps along the bridge winked on. Cryptic shapes of neon gas bloomed on the wall of the night and the city reached light by light across the plain, the evening land, the lights in their gaudy penumbra shoring up the dark of the heavens, the stars set back in their sockets. Bats came from flues and cellars to flutter over the water like rough shapes of ash tumbled on the wind and the air was clean and fresh after the rain.

You're not from Knoxville, Suttree said.

No.

How long you been here?

Just this summer.

Suttree looked out over the lights of the city. What will you do in the winter?

I dont know.

You'll freeze your ass off up here.

How cold does it get.

Got down to zero last winter.

The Indian turned his head and laid the flat of his chin on his shoulder and spat and turned back to watch the river.

I almost froze in that shantyboat. Stove and all.

The Indian nodded.

What do those signify?

The Indian looked down. He touched the doll's eyes. Them? I dont know. Good luck.

I guess they must work. Judging by that catfish.

Dont you have nothin?

A good luck piece?

Yeah.

No. I guess not.

The Indian rose. Wait a minute, he said. I'll get you something.

When he came back from the cave he handed Suttree a small lozenge of yellowed bone. Suttree held it up and looked at it. It had a hole bored in one end and he turned it in his hand to feel if there were not some carving on it but there wasnt. A few hairline cracks. A tooth? He rubbed its polished surface.

What is it?

The Indian shrugged.

Where did you get it?

I found it.

Do I have to wear it or can I just carry it in my pocket.

You can just carry it if you want to.

Okay.

Dont forget about it.

No. He held it up.

You cant just put it away and forget about it. said the Indian. He drained his bottle and rose and crossed the terrace to the fire. He ladled the stew up into heavy white china bowls and came and handed one to Suttree. Suttree took it in both hands and balanced it and stirred. He spooned up a piece of the meat and cradled it in his mouth to cool it. He chewed it. It was succulent and rich, a flavor like no other.

The Indian came from the cave with two more beers and a lighted lamp. He set the beers down and he set the lamp on the stone and crouched like an icon and began to ladle the stew into his jaws. Suttree watched him eat, his eyes dark and trancelike in the soft orange light, his jaws moving in a slow rotary motion and the veins in his temple pulsing. Solemn, mute, decorous. In his crude clothes crudely mended, wearing not only the outlandish eyes but small lead medallions that bore the names of whiskeys. Sitting solemn and unaccountable and bizarre. He reached and took up his beer and drank. He rocked the bottle and studied the foam within the brown glass. I found them in a fish, he said.

The eyes?

Yeah.

What about my piece?

It was in the cave yonder. How you like the turtle?

It's damned good.

The Indian set the bottle down and took up his spoon. How long you been on the river? he said.

This is my second year.

The Indian shook his head. You wont stay.

Maybe not.

What got you fishin?

I dont know. I sort of inherited my line from another man. Suttree reached down and got his beer and drank. Dry weeds at the edge of the rock rattled and hissed in the wind.

What happened to the other man?

I dont know, said Suttree. All he said was not to look for him back.

There was no one in the Huddle save a few whores and weird Leonard, pale and pimpled part-time catamite. They were sitting at the black table drinking beer and sharing ribald tales oft told and partly true of johns and tricks. When he saw Suttree at the bar he rose up and came over.

Hey Leonard, said Suttree.

Listen Sut. I got somethin to ast you.

I've got something to ask you.

He looked about. Come on back in the back, he said. Get ye a beer. Mr Hatmaker, give us a fishbowl over here.

Fat city, said Suttree. Where'd you score?

I got me a little walkabout off old crazy Larry this mornin. Here. Come on back in the back.

They eased into the booth and Suttree cocked his feet up and took a sip of the beer and leaned back. Leonard did the same. After a while Suttree said: Well?

Well.

Well go on.

You ask yourn first.

You know what mine is.

No I dont. What is it.

I'd like to hear the true story. The paper said you finally jumped overboard.

What the fuck, Sut. What are you talkin about?

The River Queen.

Leonard looked around. Hell fire, he whispered hoarsely. That wasnt me.

Then what are you whispering about?

I didnt do it. May God strike me . . .

Suttree seized his upraised hand. Not with me sitting this close.

Leonard grinned.

Did you really have to swim for it?

I dont know nothin about it Sut. I keep tellin ye.

Okay. What was it you wanted to ask me.

Well.

Go ahead.

Shit, I dont know where to start.

Start at the beginning.

Well you know the old man's been sick a long time.

Okay.

And you know the old lady draws that welfare.

All right.

Well she draws so much for everbody. I mean she wouldnt let Sue move out on account of it would cut it down and she gets medical for the old man and he draws unemployment on top of that so she draws good money.

All right.

Well if the old man was to die she wouldnt get but about half what all she's gettin.

Suttree sipped from his bowl again and nodded.

Well . . .

Go on.

Well he's done died.

Suttree looked up. I'm sorry to hear that, he said. When was it?

Leonard passed the top of his closed fist across his forehead and looked around uneasily. That was what I wanted to talk to you about.

Okay. Go ahead.

Well. Shit.

Hell Leonard, go on.

Well. He died see?

I do see.

And Mama stands to lose about half her check.

Well, she wont have the expense of him.

He aint been no expense. She's been savin to get her some things she needs. She done got a steamiron.

Well Leonard if he's dead he's dead. You cant keep him in the back room and make out like . . .

Leonard's finger traced along the top of the table through the water pooled off the frozen mug. He didnt look up.

I mean he wont keep with hot weather coming on. Suttree smiling, smile slowly fading. Leonard gave him a funny little look and went back to scribbling in the water.

Leonard.

Yeah.

When did he die?

Well. He sat erect and rolled his shoulders. Well, he died . . .

Yeah, you said. When?

Last December.

They sat in silence, looking at their mugs of beer. Suttree passed his hand over his face. After a while he said: Did you ever get her refrigerator back?

Naw. She got her anothern.

What did you do, run an ad in the paper?

You mean on her old one?

On her old one.

Naw. Hell fire Sut, I never meant to sell it. This old guy stopped me in the street ast me did I know anybody had one for sale. I told him no but I kept thinkin about it and I got to drinkin whiskey with Hoghead and them and we run out of whiskey and I knowed where the old guy lived and went on over there and then we went to the house on account of she was at work and he offered to give me fifteen dollars for the refrigerator and I said twenty and he said okay. Fore I knowed what happened he had it dollied up and out the door and loaded and gone. I wouldnt of done it had I not been drinkin.

Leonard?

Yeah?

What the fuck are you going to do about your old man?

I wanted to talk to you about it. If we could just get him out of there without anybody bein the wiser we could still draw on him.

You're crazy.

Listen Sut. We're painted into a corner anyways. I mean what if we was to just call up and say he died? I mean hell fire, you caint fool them guys. Them guys is doctors. They take one look at him and know for a fact he's been dead six months.

How does it smell in there?

It smells fuckin awful.

Leonard took Suttree's empty bowl to the bar and refilled it. When he came back they sat in silence, Leonard watching Suttree. Suttree shrugged his shoulders up. Well, he said. He couldnt think of anything to say about it.

Leonard leaned forward. Listen, he said. I just need somebody to help me with him. I can get a car . . .

Suttree leveled up a pair of cold gray eyes at him. No, he said.

If I could just get you to help me load him, Sut. Hell, it wouldnt be no risk to you.

Suttree looked across the table at that earnest little face, the blond hair, the pimples, the eyes too close together. Strange scenes of midnight stealth and mummied corpses by torchlight, old snips from horror movies, flickered through his head. Listen Leonard, he said.

I'm listening.

What does your mother think about all this? I mean, I cant see her going for this crazy hustle.

She aint got no choice. See, what it was, it got out of hand Sut. We left him in there just to finish out the week. You know. So we could draw on him for the full week? Well, the week ended and I said hell, wont hurt nothin to let it go a few more days. You know. And draw that. Well. It just went on from there.

Aint that the way though? Suttree said.

It wasnt nobody's fault Sut. It just got out of hand.

Suttree lifted his beer and sipped it and set it back and looked at Leonard. You're not shitting me are you? he said.

About what?

This whole thing. Are you telling me the truth?

Goddamn Sut. You think I'd kid about a thing like this? Hell, even Lorina dont know he's dead.

What does she think is going on in the back bedroom?

She just thinks he's sick and she caint see him. That's all.

How old is she?

I dont know. Six I guess. She starts school this year. Maybe seven. Look Sut, we can get him out while she's in bed of a night. The old lady'll help us. We'll just haul him out and put him in the trunk. I got some wheelrims and some chains we can use.

What the fuck are you talking about?

Some old rims and stuff. To weight him with.

Weight him with?

Yeah. We'll have that old fucker so loaded down he wont even show up for judgment day.

Where the hell are you going to put him?

Leonard straightened up and looked around. We got to hold it down, he whispered.

Okay.

We'll dump him in the fuckin river of course. You got a better idea?

I sure do.

Okay. Let's hear it.

Forget this goofy goddamned notion and just call the police or whatever and tell them to come and get his stinking ass.

Leonard looked at Suttree. He shook his head. You dont understand, he said.

I understand I'm not getting mixed up in it.

Listen . . .

Get Harrogate to help you. Loonies ought to stick together.

He aint got a boat. Listen Sut . . .

The hell he aint got a boat.

You got to be shittin me Sut. I wouldnt set foot in that fuckin thing.

Suttree drained his mug and stood. I've got to go, he said. You do what you want but count me out.

In the cool of the mornings he'd run his lines, out with the sun on the foggy river. Afternoons he'd walk in the city but he kept much to himself. He came upon Smokehouse uptown and the old derelict pawed him and begged for a coin. Suttree was holding his pocket with one hand while he reached in with the other but then he looked at Smokehouse and said no. He moved past the old cripple but found him fallen in at his elbow, hobbling along on his twisted legs like a broken disciple. Hey, called Smokehouse, though he wasnt a foot away.

Hey yourself, said Suttree.

Hell fire, let me have somethin. A dime. Goddamn, Bud, you got a dime aint ye?

Mine's the greater need, said Suttree.

This brought the old man up short. He watched Suttree go on up Market Street. He called out again but Suttree didnt turn. That's right, called the derelict. That's the way to treat a old cripple man never done nothin but favors for ye.

He made his way down Vine among blacker mendicants but he kept his silver to himself such as he had of it. An old negress in rags washed up on the paving beneath the Human Furniture Company like a piece of dark and horrid flora ran her wasted leg over the walkway before her and invited whomever to walk upon it. It lay there like a charred treelimb. Whomever smile wanly and look away and she calls down upon them the darker curses of a harried god. Her eyes are red with drink, her geography is immutable. Whereas the quick are subject to the weathers of a varied fate and know not where a newer day will find them she is fixed in perpetuity, steadfast, a paradigm of black anathema impaled upon the floor of the city like a medieval felon.

Suttree passed by, in these days moving through the streets like a dog at large. Such old things strangely new, the city seen through eyes unscaled. The repetition of its own images had washed out and leveled it and he saw upright and arrant on the dead alluvial grimmer shapes, the city of his remembrance a ghost like him and he himself a shape among the ruins, prodding dried artifacts like some dim paleontrope among the bones of fallen settlements where no soul's left to utter voice at what has passed. A garrulous jocko was miming buggery behind a young black girl passing on the walk and she turned on him with hot eyes and he fled laughing. The gallery of indolents draped among trashcans and curbstones pointed and croaked. Give it to you mammy, she told them, and the black mummer mimed masturbation at her, two hands holding an imagined phallus the size of a lightpole while the watchers hooted and slapped their knees. To Suttree they appeared more sinister and their acts a withershins allegory of anger and despair, clutches of the iniquitous and unshriven howling curses at the gates and calling aloud for redress of their right damnation to a god who need be interceded with bassackwards or obliquely. Some knew him to nod to and nodded but the hand he raised to greet them with seemed held in a gesture of dread. He moved on in the accomplished dusk. Night found him in the B&J with Bucket and J-Bone and he danced with a young girl who slewed against him shamelessly. Blackhaired, her grimestreaked legs fullthighed under the thin dress, she moved with a kind of lyrical obscenity. She had a tooth out in the front and when she smiled she'd poke the tip of her tongue in the gap. When the place closed they rode through the streets in the back of a cab and he cupped her breast in his palm and she put her tongue in his mouth. He clove her damp and naked thighs with his hand, the moist warm pouched everything tucked under his finger in the silk-crotched crevice there. He took her to Ab Jones's first. An after-hours place, he told her. He'd had them leap from the cab at the sight of his own dark houseboat there on the deserted riverfront. They drank in a corner and he took her down to his shack and lit the lamp and turned the wick low in the glass.

She sat there on the cot in her pale blue drawers while he ran his tongue in her ear. Her drinking her beer, quivering a little. Bitter taste of wax and the weight of her plump young tit naked in his hand. As she lay back he could see her dull hypoplastic doll's face and her full vapid look for a moment before her head went under the dark of the wall. He fell asleep sprawled against her.

He'd been sleeping he knew not how long when a light flared somewhere and the joints in the shanty wall were lit like a bead curtain. He thought it was the sweep of a barge's shorelight but he heard a motor running just beyond his door. He thought police. The motor ceased and the lights dimmed to nothing. He heard a car door slam. He sat up in the cot.

What is it? she said.

I dont know.

Steps on the catwalk, a knock at the door.

Who is it? said Suttree.

It's me.

Who?

Me. Leonard.

Mother of God, said Suttree.

Who is it? said the girl.

Suttree rose from the cot and scrabbled about for his breeches. He got them on and went to the table and turned up the wick in the lampchimney. The girl sat up in the bed with her arms folded across her breasts. Who is it? she said. She was pulling the sheet over herself.

Suttree opened the door. Leonard had not lied. It was himself. Eyes huge and earnest. He spoke in an excited whisper. I got him, he said.

You what?

I got him. He's in the trunk.

Suttree tried to shut the door.

You're breakin my goddamned foot, Sut.

Get it out of the fucking door then.

Listen Sut . . .

I said no, goddamnit.

It's too late Sut. I got him out here I'm tellin you.

You're crazy Leonard. You hear me?

I'll pay ye, Sut.

Get away. Go get one of your faggot friends to do it.

You caint get them motherfuckers to do nothin. Listen, the old lady told me to tell you she never would forget you for it. Listen . . .

You tell him to watch his mouth, the girl called out. There's ladies in here if he dont know it.

Who the fuck is that? said Leonard.

Suttree sagged against the jamb. The lamp on the table behind him was smoking and he stood away from the door and adjusted the wick. You son of a bitch, he said.

Leonard came in and shut the door behind him and leaned against it. He smelled peculiar. Whew, he said. I was afraid you might not be home.

Would to God I wasnt, said Suttree. He pushed back a chair and slumped wearily at the table.

Why didnt you tell me they was someone in here? said Leonard. He nodded affably toward the girl in the bed. Hidy, he said.

Why dont you just go away, said Suttree.

Listen. Come on outside where we can talk.

No.

He glanced impatiently at the girl. We caint talk in here, he whispered hoarsely.

I want to go home, the girl said.

Suttree laid his head on the table. Leonard tugged at his elbow. Sut? he said. Hey Sut.

He got up and got his shoes and put them on. He pulled on his shirt.

Where you goin? the girl wanted to know.

I'll be right back.

I want to go home.

Just wait a minute, will you?

They walked down the plank and out through the weeds and Suttree sat down. It was a warm night and the city behind them drawn upon the dark with its neon geometry seemed somehow truer than the shape it wore by day. The lights on the far side of the river stood recast in the water like torches shimmering inexplicably just beneath the surface.

Leonard.

Yeah Sut.

Sit down.

He sat. We better get started, he said.

Leonard do you really have your father in the trunk of that car there?

Hell Sut. You dont think I'd kid about a thing like that do you?

Suttree shook his head sadly. He groped about and plucked a handful of weeds and let them fall again. After a while he said: Whose car is it?

Whose car?

Yes.

I dont know. Hell Sut, it dont make no difference whose car it is.
The car is stolen.

Well, shit. I aint goin to sell it or nothin. I just borrowed it is all.
Hell Sut, they'll get their car back. There wont be no heat about the
fuckin car.

I see.

There aint nothin to worry about.

No. Of course not.

They sat in silence. Leonard stirred uneasily. After a while he said:
Are you ready?

Am I ready?

Yeah.

No. I'm not ready.

Well listen Sut . . .

I sure as fuck am not ready.

Well it aint gettin no earlier.

I will never be ready.

We caint just leave him in the goddamned car. You know that, Sut.

I know that?

Well what the hell.

You crazy bastard. Why me?

You got a . . .

A boat. I know. Mother of God.

Hell fire Sut, I've done done the worst of it. Gettin the car and the
chains and all. It wont take no time.

But Suttree had risen from the weeds. Just dont say another word,
he said. Just be quiet.

What about her?

You get in the car and go down to just above that tree there. There's
a landing. I'll get the boat.

When he went back in she was dressed. I want to go home, she said,
and I mean it.

Suttree took up the lamp from the table. You can wait or you walk,
he said. It's strictly up to you.

I dont know where I'm at, she said petulantly.

I'm sure of that, said Suttree. You're not alone, either.

You aint goin to leave me in the dark, she called. But Suttree was
gone.

He got the boat and rowed down to the landing and pulled in

sideways. When they raised the trunklid of the car a vile stench came flooding out. He stepped back half gagging. Great God, he said.

Bad aint it?

Bad? Suttree looked at the stars. That's the awfullest stink I ever smelled.

That's the biggest reason we had to get him out of the house.

God you're a sick bastard.

Well give me a hand with him.

Just a minute.

Suttree pulled off the cotton undershirt he wore and tied it around his lower face.

Okay, said Leonard.

Leonard's father was wrapped in the sheets he'd died in months before. Leonard was setting out wheelrims and a pile of chain. He got hold of the body and wrestled part of it over the car bumper. Suttree held the lamp.

Get his feet there, Sut, and I'll haul on his arms.

How did you get him in there?

What?

Suttree freed his mouth from the shirt. I said how did you get him in there?

Me and the old lady done it. He aint all that heavy.

Suttree took hold of the limbs beneath the sheet with sick loathing. They dragged the body out and it slumped to the ground with a nauseating limberness. Leonard's father lay like a dead klansman. By the light of the lamp on the bare ground they could see strange brown stains seeping through the sheets. Suttree turned away and went to sit on the bank for a while.

They dragged the remains down to the boat and Suttree stood in the transom and hauled the thing aboard, goggleheaded under the thin cotton, against his naked chest. Leonard bearing up behind with the lamp, chains clanking.

They rowed far downstream. Leonard saying Hell, Sut, any place is good and Suttree rowing on. They looked like old jacklight poachers, their faces yellow masks in the night. The corpse lay slumped in the floor of the skiff. The lamp standing on the stern seat with its thin spout of insects caught in its light the wet sweep of the oars, the beads of water running on the underblades like liquid glass and the dimples of the oarstrokes coiled out through the city lights where they lay fixed among the deeper shapes of stars and galaxies fast in the silent river.

Coming about below the railway bridge Suttree shipped the oars. Leonard was at wrapping his father in chains, fastening them with dimestore locks, chaining up the wheelrims through the center holes. One of the old man's legs lay twisted in the floor of the skiff and Suttree could see the stained flannel pajamas that he wore.

I think that'll get it, Sut, said Leonard.

Think it will?

Yeah. Shit, this'll take his ass to the bottom like a fucking rocket.

Are you going to say a few words?

Do what?

Say a few words.

Leonard gave a sort of nervous little grin. Say a few words?

Arent you? I mean you're not going to bury your father without anything at all.

I aint burying him.

The hell you're not.

I'm just puttin him in the river.

It's the same thing. It's the same as burial at sea.

Well goddamn, Suttree.

Well?

This old son of a bitch never went to church in his life.

All the more reason.

Well I dont know no goddamned service nor nothin. Shit. You say it.

The only words I know are the Catholic ones.

Catholic?

Catholic.

Leonard regarded his chained and hooded father in the floor of the skiff. Hell fire. He sure wasnt no Catholic. What about that part that goes through the shadow of the valley of death. You know any of that?

Suttree stood up in the skiff. The river about them was black and calm and the bridgelights rigid where they lay upstream in the water.

Give me a hand with him.

Leonard looked up, one side of him softly lit by the lamp at his elbow, his shadow in the night enormous. He leaned and took hold of the cadaver and together they raised him. They laid him across the seat, one leg already reaching over the side into the river as if the old man couldnt wait. Suttree put his foot against the thing and shoved it. It made a dull splash and the white sheets flared in the lamplight and it was gone. Leonard sat back down in the stern of the skiff. Whew, he said.

Suttree washed his hands in the river and dried them on his trousers and took up the oars again. Leonard tried him in conversation on several topics as they came back up the river but Suttree rowing said no word.

Suttree drunk negotiated with a drunk's meticulousness the wide stone steps of the Church of the Immaculate Conception. The virtues of a stainless birth were not lost on him, no not on him. The moon's horn rode in the dark hard by the steeple. An older sot wobbled in the street without, caroming along a wall like a mechanical duck in a carnival. Suttree entered the vestibule and paused by a concrete seashell filled with sacred waters. He stood in the open door. He entered.

Down the long linoleum aisle he went, and with care, tottered not once. A musty aftertaste of incense hung in the air. A thousand hours or more he's spent in this sad chapel he. Spurious acolyte, dreamer impenitent. Before this tabernacle where the wise high God himself lies sleeping in his golden cup.

He eased himself into the frontmost pew and sat. By his knee on the pewback a small brass clasp springloaded for the gripping of hatbrims. A little bracket containing literature. Long leatherpadded kneebenches underfoot. Where rows of hemorrhoidal dwarfs convene by night.

He looked about. Beyond the chancel gate three garish altars rose like gothic wedding cakes in carven marble. Crocketed and gargoyled, the steeples iced with rows of marble frogs ascending. Here a sallow plaster Christ. Agonized beneath his muricate crown. Spiked palms and riven belly, there beneath the stark ribs the cleanlipped spearwound. His caved haunches loosely girdled, feet crossed and fastened by a single nail. To the left his mother. Mater alchimia in skyblue robes, she treads a snake with her chipped and naked feet. Before her on the altar gutter two small licks of flame in burgundy lampions. In the sculptor's art there always remains something unsaid, something waiting. This statuary will pass. This kingdom of fear and ashes. Like the child that sat in these selfsame bones so many black Fridays in terror of his sins. Viceridden child, heart rotten with fear. Listening to the slide shoot back in the confessional, waiting his turn. Light pierced, light fell from the pieced and leaded glass of the windows in the western wall, light moteless and oblique, wine colors, rose magenta, leached cobalt, cinnabar and delicate citrine. The stainedglass saints lay broken in their panes of light among the pews and in the summer afternoon quietude a smell of old varnish and the distant cries of children in a playground. Memories of May processions, a priest in a black biretta rising from his carved oak faldstool to shuffle heavyfooted down the aisle attended by churlish and acnefaced striplings. The censer swings in chains, clinks back and forth, at the apex of each arc coughing up a quick gout of smoke. The priest dips the aspergillum in a gold bucket. He casts left and right, holy water upon the congregation. They pass out the door where two scullery nuns stand bowed in fouled habits. There follows a troop of small christians in little white fitted frocks. They bear candles. They are singing. Cornelius has set Danny Yike's hair on fire. An acrid stench. A flailing about the boy's head by a dracular nun. Patch of blackened stubble at the base of his skull. The boys laughing. The girls in white veils, white patentleather shoes with little straps. Snickering into the roses they hold in their prayerclasped hands. Small specters of fraudulent piety. At the foot of the steps a pale child collapses. Her rose lies dwindled on the stone. Some others taking cue drop about her. They lie on the pavement like patches of melting snow. Folk rush about these spent ones, fanning with folded copies of the *Sunday Messenger*.

Or cold mornings in the Market Lunch after serving early Mass with J-Bone. Coffee at the counter. Rich smell of brains and eggs frying. Old men in smoky coats and broken boots hunkered over plates. A dead roach beneath a plastic cakebell. Lives proscribed and doom in store, doom's adumbration in the smoky censer, the faint creak of the tabernacle door, the tasteless bread and draining the last of the wine from the cruet in a corner and counting the money in the box. This venture into the world of men rich with vitality, these unwilling churched ladling cream into their cups and watching the dawn in the city, enjoying the respite from their black clad keepers with their neat little boots, their spectacles, the deathreek of the dark and half scorched muslin that they wore. Grim and tireless in their orthopedic moralizing. Filled with tales of sin and unrepentant deaths and visions of hell and stories of levitation and possession and dogmas of semitic damnation for the tacking up of the paraclete. After eight years a few of their charges could read and write in primitive fashion and that was all.

Suttree looked up at the ceiling where a patriarchal deity in robes and beard lurched across the cracking plaster. Attended by thunder, by fat infants with dovewings grown from their shoulderbones. He lowered his head to his chest. He slept.

A priest shook him gently. He looked up into a bland scented face. Were you waiting for confession?

No.

The priest looked at him. Do I know you? he said.

Suttree placed one hand on the pew in front of him. An old woman was going along the altar rail with a dusting rag. He struggled to his feet. No, he said. You dont know me.

The priest stepped back, inspecting his clothes, his fishstained shoes.

I just fell asleep a minute. I was resting.

The priest gave a little smile, lightly touched with censure, remonstrance gentled. God's house is not exactly the place to take a nap, he said.

It's not God's house.

I beg your pardon?

It's not God's house.

Oh?

Suttree waved his hand vaguely and stepped past the priest and went down the aisle. The priest watched him. He smiled sadly, but a smile for that.

The ragman laboring up beneath the mound of ripe bedding in which he had entombed himself for sleep looked like a melted candle. He sat cowled and scowling out upon the new day. A draft of dank air went among his silken chinwhiskers and a faint miasma rose off of him like heat from a summer road.

Now he hobbled about in his ragged underwear with his withered and rickety shanks trembling, gathering his clothes in one hand and poking among the mounds of paper for dry ones with which to start his fire. The sound of morning traffic upon the bridge beat with the dull echo of a dream in his cavern and the ragman would have wanted a sager soul than his to read in their endless advent auguries of things to come, the specter of mechanical proliferation and universal blight. Two fishermen passed along the river path, misty figures going silently save for the fragile rattling of their canes, lifting hands toward him where he stood with his palms spread above a thin and heatless spire of smoke, the rank earthy smell of the barren mud beneath the bridge rife with the morning damp, the river passing smoky and silent and overhead in the arches of the bridge the inane and sporadic clapping of pigeons setting forth into the day.

He mumbled and massaged his hands above the fire. He took his kettle to the river and dipped it full of water and came back. The mist was running off the river in little tongues and lapping eddyplaces and there was hope of sunlight somewhere beyond the eastern murk.

He went with his despair through the warrens of the city towing his kindlingwood cart with a sound in those lightless corridors like guts rumbling.

In the belly of an iron trashbin big enough to hold a pokergame he sorted out mementos all the morning long. Indemnified bottles cast off by the idle rich. Redeemable at two cents per. Newsprint for baling. Useless bones. A dead rat, a broken broom, part of an inkpen. A side of gangrenous bacon filled with skippers. The wreck of a fruitcrate which his eyes saw as kindling, salvageable, saleable. A passing truck muted out the footsteps of the kitchen boy from the Sanitary Lunch. The old man felt the door above him darken and looked up with eyes terrible to see the round mouth of a swillcan tipping. He leaped back flailing and was upended by a turtling box. A lapful of lettuce and old bread, nothing worse. The can rattled and clanged. In the distance a trolley answered. The old man appeared in the door of the bin like some queer revenant rising in smokeless athanasia from the refuse to croak a slew of bitter curses out upon the world but the kitchen boy didnt even look back.

I went down this river in the fall of ought one with a carnival dont ast me why. I followed it two year. I seen street preachers come off the circuit in the early summer and bark and shill with the best of em and go back to preachin in the fall. We went to Tallahassee Florida. They was a bunch of loggers come off the river at Chattanooga with us went into town and got drunk we had to wait the train on em. They'd done chained the locomotive to the rails with logchains. We never left out of there till five in the mornin. Had two boxcars loaded with old carny gear. We seen a feller hung in Rome Georgia stood up there on the back of a springwagon and told em all to go to hell he never done it. They drove that wagon out from under him he turned black in the face as a nigger.

Suttree smiled. Is that where you learned ventriloquism?

Where's that?

In the carnival.

No.

I see, said Suttree.

I seen strange things in my time. I seen that cyclome come through here where it went down in the river it dipped it dry you could see the mud and stones in the bottom of it naked and fishes layin there. It picked up folks' houses and set em down again in places where they'd never meant to live. They was mail addressed to Knoxville fell in the streets of Ringgold Georgia. I've seen all I want to see and I know all I want to know. I just look forward to death.

He might hear you, Suttree said.

I wisht he would, said the ragpicker. He glared out across the river with his redrimmed eyes at the town where dusk was settling in. As if death might be hiding in that quarter.

No one wants to die.

Shit, said the ragpicker. Here's one that's sick of livin.

Would you give all you own?

The ragman eyed him suspiciously but he did not smile. It wont be long, he said. An old man's days are hours.

And what happens then?

When?

After you're dead.

Dont nothin happen. You're dead.

You told me once you believed in God.

The old man waved his hand. Maybe, he said. I got no reason to think he believes in me. Oh I'd like to see him for a minute if I could.

What would you say to him?

Well, I think I'd just tell him. I'd say: Wait a minute. Wait just one minute before you start in on me. Before you say anything, there's just one thing I'd like to know. And he'll say: What's that? And then I'm goin to ast him: What did you have me in that crapgame down there for anyway? I couldnt put any part of it together.

Suttree smiled. What do you think he'll say?

The ragpicker spat and wiped his mouth. I dont believe he can answer it, he said. I dont believe there is a answer.

In the summer of his second year in the city Harrogate began to tunnel toward the vaults underground where the city's wealth was kept. By day in the dark of dripping caverns, stone bowels whereon was founded the city itself, holding his lantern before him, a bloodcolored troglodyte stooped and muttering down foul corridors, assaying vectors by a stolen scout compass that spun inanely in this nether region so gravid with seam and lode. Coming from his day's labors slavered over with a gray paste that on contact with the outer air began to cure up and flake away leaving on his skin and on his clothing a dull cast of claydust so that he looked like something that had been smoked, his eyes collared up in cups of grime, the red rims raw as wounds.

Summer was full on and the nights hot. It was like lying in warm syrup there in the dark under the viaduct, in the steady whine of gnats and nightbugs. Coming up Henley Street one morning he was amazed to see a truck fallen through the paving. Settled on an enormous cracked asphalt plate some five feet below grade with a ring of spectators gathered about it and the driver climbing from the hole swearing and laughing.

I reckon once a feller got in under there he could go anywheres he took a notion right in under the ground there couldnt he?

I dont know, Gene. There's lots of cave under there. Suttree was pulling a wire minnowbucket from the bottom of the river by a long cord. He swung it dripping to the rail and opened the top and lifted out two beers and let the cage back down. He opened the beers and handed one to Harrogate and leaned back against the houseboat wall.

That goddamned truck like to of fell plumb out of sight.

I saw it.

What if a whole goddamned building was to just up and sink?

What about two or three buildings?

What about a whole block? Harrogate was waving his bottle about. Goddamn, he said. What if the whole fuckin city was to cave in?

That's the spirit, said Suttree.

He'd sit by night in the light of his red roadlanterns while honeysuckle bloomed in the creek gut. Poring over obsolete city maps, tracing out a course on paper scrawled with incomprehensible runes, strange symbols, squatting, a cherrycolored troll or demon cartographer in the hellish light charting the progress of souls in the darkness below. When Suttree came up the little path through the weeds the city mouse's cat rose and stretched and went out the other side. Harrogate looked up from his work.

How's it going? said Suttree.

Hey Sut. Come on in.

He approached, not without a certain wariness here where enormities proliferated. Harrogate was dragging an old chair over the clay and dusting it off for Suttree to sit in. Suttree bent over the charts laid out on the applebox.

How's it look? said Harrogate.

How's what look?

My deal there. He gestured with one hand at the maps.

Suttree looked down at the thin pink face, teeth pink and black in the red light. He shook his head and sat in the chair and crossed his legs. Harrogate had taken up one of the charts from the table and was looking at it. I aint got no way of knowin how deep I am, he said.

You've got no way of knowing how crazy you are.

I'm goin to have to have some help.

You sure are.

I need somebody to tap or somethin. Where they think I'm at.

Where they think you're at.

Yeah.

Suttree closed his eyes. He pinched the bridge of his nose and shook his head slowly. Harrogate had bent himself once more to the work. Wielding a plastic protractor, his tongue out at the corner of his mouth, reinventing plane geometry. Suttree soon enough found himself watching over the city mouse's shoulder. By the time the cat came back he was sitting at the little crate himself, describing angles, formulas, the small face of the apprentice felon nodding at his elbow.

In the damp and alveolar deeps beneath the city he probed with a torch he'd stolen, sighting courses from stone to stone to reckon by and charting with his crazed compass a fix of compounded errors.

Down old caverns where carboncolored water leaked from overhead or treacly sipes of sewage. Through a region of ruptured ducting and old clay drains and into a dark stone gullet skewered by a jointed cesspipe. Everywhere a liquid dripping, something gone awry in the earth's organs to which this measured bleeding clocked a constantly eluded doom.

One afternoon he entered a large vault in which stood from floor to dome and slightly tilted a slender flue of cold white light. Harrogate drew back. There was a scrabbling sound overhead, dirt sifted down. A shadow stained the little figure of light on the stone floor and was snatched away. He advanced cautiously. With the beam of his flashlight he severed the shaft and watched it knit back again. It was only light, a cool bore of it standing moteless in the dark like a phosphorescent rope taut in the black of the sea's deeps. He balanced it on his palm. Through a small hole in the roof he could see the sky.

Harrogate rose by faults and ledges, the torch in his teeth. He hung by his nails from a seam in the rock, he peered out with a cautious eye. A spray of pine needles stirred against the depthless blue. A lizard scuttled, a bird. He listened. Beyond the drone of insects and the sound of the wind he thought he heard distant traffic but he was not sure. He made his way back down to the floor of the vault and squatted there tapping his fingers against his knee, the shaft of light terminating in the top of his head without apparent pain or power of inspiration.

He unfolded from his pocket the damp and thumbblacked map of the city whereon he'd traced with grocer's crayon deadreckoned reaches, corrected tangents, notes on distance. He held the light above his head and fastened down a mark with his finger.

Shit if I know where I'm at, he said to the silence.

Am at, said a soft stone echo.

He folded his chart and rose. He studied the pale thin probe from the outer world and he finally climbed up and stopped the hole with his rolled map.

He never found it from the outside. After wandering about for days he came back and took the map down again. He'd brought some oily rags filched from a can at the gas station on Henley Street and he lit these in the chamber and went out. All day he looked along the edge of the city and down by the river and anywhere he could see or hope to see a pine tree. He began to suspect some dimensional displacement in these descents to the underworld, some disparity unaccountable between the above and the below. He destroyed his charts and began again.

That year there were locusts. They howled in the green trees like panthers, struggled in their fallen hundreds on the river's face.

He fell listless and enervated from histoplasmosis.

He feared in the lightless depths great rats, beveltoothed and bare of tail, spiders hairy or naked or lightly downed or partly bald, rope-shaped reptiles, their fangs, their tuningfork tongues. Their memberless economy of design. Bats hung in clusters like bunches of dark and furry fruit and the incessant drip of water echoed everywhere through the spelaean dark like dull chimes. In the pools lay salamanders cold and prone and motionless as terracotta figurines.

The matches that he struck periodically to test the air burned with an acetylene blue and he'd watch the flame draw down the matchstem and wink out and the darkness would hood him almost audibly. Sitting there with his thumb on the button of the flashlight and listening until the terror rose up in his throat and then pushing the button and creating again the filthy basilica in which he sat, the batclotted arches, the high amorphous convolutions of limestone from which scum dripped. Gray sewage percolating down through faults and bedding planes. Dark leachings from the city's undersides and speleothems accresced out of some grim slime quietly oozing in the dark.

Harrogate stepping from pool to pool of blue sludge in a tunnel where the light of his torch found trace of human work. A few old timbers black with rot, a bucket, a bone. He turned the bone in his hand, inspecting the minute chamfering of miceteeth, vermiculate scrimshaw, the brown and corallike fluting of the marrowed bore. Wherein lay a slick millipede. He dropped it clattering on the rock. The millipede ran like a train. He retrieved the bone and looked it over, holding it for size against various parts of his anatomy. Bet me, he said softly. They's somebody down here murdered.

He loaded it into a hindpocket and set forth again, his light in one hand and a clawhammer in the other, the channel narrowing, turning. A region of old timbers crossed with chalk, boards laid over the wet red clay of the cave's floor.

He was brought up by a wooden wall against which the corridor terminated neat and flush. Harrogate studied this barricade with his flashlight and he studied the wet stone ceiling and the walls. With the hammer he prized away a chunk of pulpy wood until he got the board levered up. He took it in both hands, dropping the hammer, the flashlight in his armpit illuminating odd points above his head. The board gave with a gradual springy feeling and fell at his feet. He trained the flashlight on the place. Behind the boards was a wall of solid concrete. Knotty grain and the marks of a circlesaw in the masonry. He set the claws of the hammer under the next board and pried it up and ripped it away. With the hammer he went tapping across the face of the barricade listening. The tapping went down the chamber and returned. He sat in a pile of slag and studied what to do. And were they walling in or walling out? He tapped at the empty rubber toecap of his outsize sneaker with the hammer. After a while he raised his head. Dynamite, he said.

The times that Suttree called on him now he found him deeper yet in his plottings, frowning over his charts, composing campaigns to entrap the phantoms with which he was beset.

How are you doin? he said.

Okay.

You breached the bank vaults yet?

Nope. But come here and look.

Harrogate rose from his table and went back toward the darker arches to the little concrete bunker. He beckoned with one finger.

What is it?

Come see.

Suttree approached and looked in.

Looky here, said the city mouse.

What is it?

Suttree was kneeling. He reached into the dark and felt a wooden box where cold waxed shapes like candles lay. He lifted one out and turned it to the light.

Gene, you're crazy.

That's the real shit there. Buddy boy that'll get it when Bruton Snuff wont.

You cant blow it. You dont have a detonator.

I can blow it with a shotgun shell.

I doubt it.

You keep your old ear to the ground.

Gene, you'll blow yourself up with this shit.

I thought you said I couldnt blow it?

Suttree shook his head sadly.

Hot summer nights along the river and drunkenness and tales of violence. Steps in the dead of night, hollow as the clop of hooves on the shantyporch boards where Suttree lay silent within, breathing in the dark. He heard his name said.

He lit the lamp and held it up to see the junkman at the window like a drunken burglar. He rose from the cot to let him in, steering him as he crossed the floor in his reeling step like a strange and midnight dance lesson there in the little shack.

The junkman sat, he looked up. Was you asleep?

No.

He nodded enormously, his head rising and falling a foot or more. Didnt allow ye was. I knowed ye for a night owl. You got a smoke? I'm give out.

I dont have any.

The junkman was patting his pockets.

You didnt walk all the way over here for a cigarette did you?

No.

Wasnt the Smoky Mountain open?

I dont know. You aint got a little drink laid back anywheres have ye?

I may have a beer about half warm. You want that?

Be better'n a poke in the eye with a stick.

Suttree rose and went out and took up the minnowbucket and got a beer out of it. He carried it back in the shanty and got the opener and uncapped the beer and handed it to the junkman. Harvey stalked the bottle with a veering hand and seized it and blinked and drank.

Where'd you get in the mud at?

He looked down. He appeared to be wearing puttees, slavered with mud as he was to his knees. I mired up, he said. Like to never found your place dark as it is. Like to of fell in the fuckin. He paused to belch. Fuckin river.

Do you want me to row you back over?

Harvey took a drink of the beer and eyed Suttree blearily. His face was very white and the wrinkled pouches of skin beneath his eyes looked translucent. Goin to see Dubyedee, he said. No good son of a bitch.

You dont need to see him at this hour of the night. Why dont you let me run you home.

The junkman shook his head testily. See my no good shitass brother.

If you start across that bridge the cops'll get you.

They never got me comin over.

You better wait till tomorrow.

Harvey was holding the bottle in his hands between his knees. I'll get me a goddamned pistol, he said, nodding his head.

Pistol?

Goddamn right.

You going to shoot your brother?

Fuck no. Shoot them goddamn thieves.

What, over at your lot?

Goddamned right.

Hell, they're just kids.

They're fuckin thieves. Steal anything they can get their hands on.

Why dont you just run them off?

Might as well shoot em now. Fore they get any bigger.

He took a drink of the beer and wiped his mouth with the palm of his hand. Just like girls, he said. They grow up and hit in along about thirteen or fourteen and they's a few of em start screwin everbody in town. That's ye whores. It aint that they're young. All whores is young sometime just like all thieves is. You dont wait till you're old to start peddlin your ass or stealin either one. Nip em. He paused. Nip em in the bud.

Why dont you get a watchdog?

I done had one of them.

What happened to it?

I dont know. I believe they stole it.

You better let me run you across the river.

You can run me up to Goose Creek if you want to. He was looking up and regarding Suttree in the dim lamplight with one eye squint.

You dont need to go up there.

Fuck I dont.

You can see him tomorrow.

You know what he ast me?

265

What?

Ast me how come it was that I was always sober enough to buy a wreck but too drunk to sell one.

Well?

Well what?

Well what's the answer?

The junkman glared at Suttree for a moment and then shook the empty bottle. You aint got another one of them have ye? he said.

I'm afraid that's it.

You reckon old Jones'd find a man a drink at this hour?

I reckon old Jones'd find a man a pumpknot on his bony head if he banged on that door after the lights were out.

Somebody'll kill that nigger one of these days.

Yes, they will.

Wonder what about Jimmy Smith?

Jimmy Smith will shoot you.

The junkman shook his head sadly at the utter truth of this. He rose unsteadily. He smiled. Well, he said. Maybe old Dubyedee will have a little drink.

You can stay here if you want.

The junkman waved a hand about. I thank ye, he said, but I best be huntin that drink. I believe a little drink'd do me more good right now than just about anything I can think of.

Suttree watched him totter down the planks in the band of yellow light. He veered, he stood with one foot, he went on. When he reached the shore he raised one hand.

Come back, called Suttree.

The junkman raised the hand again and kept going.

It was a full two miles out Blount Avenue to his brother's junklot and the junkman reeled along in the lamplight through a floating world of honeysuckle nectar and nightbird cries and distant dogs that yapped at their moorings.

He made his way across the little wooden bridge and past the dim shapes of the cars and stood before the housetrailer.

Dubyedee!

The waters of Goose Creek purled past the tirecasings and bodypanels in the farther dark of the yard.

Come out you old fart.

He stumbled among the articles of their common trade. Blood black and crusted in these broken carriages. A shoe.

Dubyedee! Come out, goddamnit.

He had ceased calling and was sat within a truck when a light came on in the trailer. The door opened and light fell across the yard among the cluttered shapes and Clifford stood looking out. What do you want? he said.

Want Dubyedee. Harvey spoke through the steeringwheel spokes in which his head lay cradled.

What? said Clifford.

He raised his head. Clifford hung in the white web of the broken windshield. I want Dubyedee, he said.

He aint here.

Where's he at?

He aint here. He dont live here now.

It's just old drunk Uncle Harvey aint it?

You said it, I never.

No, you never. You smug sack of shit.

What?

I said you're a smug sack of shit.

Clifford's head turned in silhouette in the doorframe as if he'd turned to spit. He aint here, Harvey. Go on home.

He aint here Harvey. Go home Harvey. Where's he live at now?

You caint get out there. It's too far.

I'll be the judge of that. Where's he live at?

Why dont you come up and I'll give ye a cup of coffee.

Harvey shook his head. Aint you somethin, he said.

What?

I said you sure are somethin. Clifford old buddy. You sure are. Get some coffee in him. Clifford you favor your old man more than a little, did you know that?

You want some coffee I'll fix ye some. Otherwise I'm goin to bed.

Lord God, Clifford, dont let me keep ye from your sleep. I'd not do it for the world.

The figure shored up in the doorway shifted. You can sleep in the shed if you want. I'll give you the key.

You aint got a drink in there have ye?

No.

Then you aint got nothin in there I want.

The light withdrew up the path. Then it vanished from the small-paned window in the door. Harvey smiled and leaned back in the truck.

Clifford!

Dogs hereto sleeping woke with howls all down the creek.

Clifford!

The light snapped on again. The door opened.

What now, goddamnit?

You wasnt asleep was ye?

I got to work tomorrow Harvey. Some of us is got to work for a livin yet.

Is he payin ye now Clifford? Or you still just gettin your keep.

He pays me.

Big boy like you.

If you dont want nothin I'm goin to bed.

I'll tell you what I'm makin if you'll tell me what you are.

You aint makin nothin is what you're makin. Cause you dont do nothin but lay drunk.

What you are, what you are, said Harvey aimlessly.

You dont need to know.

Dont need to know, dont need to know. You sure you aint got a little drink in yonder?

I told you I'd fix you some coffee if you want it.

Let me tell you about your coffee, Clifford. You want to hear about your coffee?

Clifford didnt want to hear. He shut the door again and the lights went out.

What about your daddy, called Harvey. Want to hear about that thievin son of a bitch? Want to hear how he robbed his own brother blind? Clifford?

Lying in his cot in the early hours Suttree half asleep heard a dull concussion somewhere in the city. He opened his eyes and looked out through his small window at the paling stars, the sparse electric jewelry of the bridgelights hung above the river. Perhaps an earthquake, seams shifting deep in the earth, sand sifting for miles down blind faults in eternal dark. It did not come again and after a while he slept.

Coming back upriver in the hot noon he kept to the south shore and passed under the bridge and passed the lumber company and the packinghouse and moored the skiff at the foot of the path that led to the junkman's lot and the road beyond. A brief spate of summer rain had fallen in the morning and the smell of it in the shoreland woods rose rank and steamy like the air in a hothouse. On the narrow path he met a cluster of deferential blacks who passed sidling, their eyes cutting to and back like horses. A light clank of baitbuckets and a bristling of canes. The cars in Harvey's lot lay humped and black in the sun with visible heat rising from them in the wrinkled air. Suttree passed through a reek of milkweed and oil and hot tin toward the little bedstead gate.

He found him senseless and hanging half off the ragged army cot. The little shack smelled of grease and tarpaper and filth. Suttree took the junkman up by arm and elbow and eased him back onto the bed, solicitous yet somewhat loath to touch him in his leprous rags. Harvey rolled a whited eye and muttered and fell back. Suttree looked around the little cabin. Floor strewn with gears, axleshafts, batteries. Tottering columns of tires. A cupboard of hubcaps like curious silver, mangled and banged, painted or stamped with loutish new world crests.

He stood in the door and looked out over the junkman's lot. Tall hollyhocks by the weighted gate and dockweed blooming and begonias down along the remnants of the fence. In the corner of the lot a stand of sunflowers like some floral enormity in a child's garden. Suttree sat on the cinderblock steps. The flowers moved in the wind. He could not see the river but there was a barge going upstream through the trees like a great train of wares ferrying soundlessly by means unknown up the valley floor. On the far shore a riprap of broken marble. Rough shapes of iron rusting in the sun. In the gloom of the shack the junkman groaned and turned. One among a mass of twisted shapes discarded here by the river. Suttree turned and saw him fend with his arm some phantom, a gesture of dread such as the mad favor, his anguish no less real. Suttree rose and went out through the gate and the gate clanged gently shut behind him.

When Harrogate pulled the string on his homemade detonator he had one finger in his ear. The explosion blew him twenty feet up the tunnel and slammed him against a wall where he sat in the darkness with chunks of stone clattering everywhere about him and his eyes enormous against the unbelievable noise in which he found himself. Then he was sucked back down the tunnel in a howling rush of air, his clothes scrubbing away and peelings of hide until he found himself lying on his face in the passage with a shrieking in his ears. Before he could rise it returned and snatched him up again and scuttled him back along the floor in a cloud of dust and ash and debris and left him bleeding and halfnaked and choked and groping for something to hold to. Dont come no more, he cried aloud in the ringing vault. I done had enough. Far back through the broken wall he could hear the echoes of the blast shunting row on row down the cavern to ultimate nothingness.

He lay very quietly. He was bruised and bleeding and numb all over and he began to cry. His head was ringing and he was half deaf yet he could hear in the horrid darkness shapes emerge from the reeks and crannies, features stained with boneblack, jaws adrip. He could hear the blood running in his body and he could hear the organs working, the lungs filling and collapsing. Little girls in flowered frocks went tripping out through stiles of sunlight and their destination was darkness as is each soul's. Coming toward him was a soft near soundless mass. Sucking over the stones. Seeking him out. He pulled himself up and listened. Coming down the tunnel. Something nearing in the night. A sluggish monster freed from what centuries of stony fastness under the city. Its breath washed over him in a putrid stench. He tried to crawl. He scrabbled blindly among the stones in the dark. He was engulfed feet first in a slowly moving wall of sewage, a lava neap of liquid shit and soapcurd and toiletpaper from a breached main.

When Suttree saw the piece in the paper that said: *Earthquake?* he read and knew. He folded the paper and rose and went out the door and down the steps.

At Harrogate's there was no one home, not even the cat. He stirred the cold ashes in the firepit, he poked among the city rat's belongings.

In the afternoon he went about where the rat was known but no one knew where he could be.

It was evening when he came upon Rufus down on Front Street. He was sat in a gutterful of lamplight before the store as if he were waiting for it to open. He raised up when he saw who it was. Hey Sut, he said. How you makin it?

Just slidin, said Suttree. What are you doing?

Aw just settin. He pushed back his cap with his thumb and rubbed his head and smiled.

Suttree sat beside him on the little stone curb.

You want a drink? He canted the bottle he held to one side for the light to follow the label. They looked at the bottle together in silence. Get ye a sup. Tastes pretty good.

Suttree took the bottle and twirled off the little fluted plastic cap and hooked a good shot of it back.

Smoke rose from his noseholes.

Agh gie gie, he said.

Oh yes, said Rufus, shaking his head profoundly. It'll talk to ye. Great God.

Rufus took the bottle from him gently and supped a good sup and stood it carefully in the road before them. Suttree wiped his eyes with the balls of his fingers. The vapors seemed to have risen to his brain. Even the smell of honeysuckle that had choked the air with its hot and winey perfume and memories of summer eve was burned away. He looked at Rufus with watery eyes. Have you seen Harrogate? he said.

Harrogate? Rufus turned and jerked his head back and frowned at Suttree across his shoulder. The city mouse? Naw. He aint been round. What you wants with him?

I think he's all fucked up somewhere.

Wherever he at he's fucked up. Aint no news in that.

Did you hear that earthquake last night?

I did. Rattled the glass in my windersashes. Woke my old lady up. You hear it?

Suttree nodded.

Get ye a little old drink there, Sut.

I dont believe I can stand it.

Why that there's a nice little whiskey.

The whiskey stood in the road.

I got a old dog stobbed up in my slopbarrel, said Rufus.

Suttree nodded. His lips moved as if he were repeating this to himself.

I caint get near him to fetch him out. He keeps wantin to bite me.

How did he get in there?

Fell in I reckon. Eatin my slops. I aint tippin out my slops for no fool ass dog.

No.

I remember from when I was a boy down in Loudon County and I had this uncle used to make whiskey all the time. We went up to his still one evenin and he had five barrel of mash settin around on the ground workin and we got up there and in ever barrel one they was a old hound. They was stobbed up in them mashbarrels to they neck and they was drunk and just a singing to beat the band. You never seen a more pleasant sight. We set on the ground and laughed and the more we laughed the louder they'd sing and the more they sung the louder we'd laugh.

How did you get them out?

We cut us a green hickory and run it through they collars and got one either end and snaked em out. They was some might too drunk to walk hardly.

Well why dont we get this one out of your mashbarrel like that?

He aint got no collar on.

I see. Well why dont we get a rope on him and haul him out?

We might could try it. I hate to go up there at all.

Why is that?

Old lady's put out with me.

Well you got to go sometime.

I know it. But sometimes I just purely hate it.

Come on. You cant sit down here all night.

Suttree stood up and Rufus rose and dusted the sag of his trouser-seat with two handswipes and stooped, tilted, recovered, seized the bottle and reared upright. Beat no drink atall, dont ye? he said to the bottle.

They labored up the switchback path through the kudzu and came out in a dark little lane. It was a clear night and they walked slowly and the black man would pause again before they reached the house to take another drink and restore the bottle to the pocket of his ample trousers. Suttree could smell above the honeysuckle a sour reek from the hoglot like the smell of vomit. Through the vines stood a window-light. Rufus held up one finger and they paused and consulted.

Let me get my lannern.

Okay.

Suttree crouched in the lane. He heard a door open and close and then in a moment he heard a high shrieking voice that seemed to speak in a tongue unknown to him. The door opened and Rufus came from the porch holding up the lantern and adjusting the wick.

They walked out past the shed and Rufus lifted a nail out of the hasp-staple on the smokehouse door and entered and reappeared with a hank of coarse rope. They went on along a fence patched up from scraps of board and tin. Something scuttled off among the weeds. A hog grunted in the dark. Rufus held the lantern up and in the light Suttree saw the dog's eyes.

Yonder he is.

Suttree took the lantern and approached the dog. A sodden hound with wet bread hanging from his head, stogged to the neck in a slopdrum. He had his forepaws on the rim of the drum and as Suttree approached he bared his teeth in the lamplight.

Cant he get out? said Suttree.

He dont appear able. I see him rear up a time or two but he caint get pulled loose enough from that slop to jump.

Well hand me that rope.

Watch you dont get too close. He'll growl and make at ye.

Hold the lantern.

You watch him now.

Suttree fetched an empty drum and stood it bottom up alongside the dog and stood on it. The dog turned to face him. He made a noose in the rope and dropped it over the dog's head and the dog's teeth closed on the air with a dull wet chop. When he felt the rope tighten about his neck he began to moan.

Suttree doubled the rope in his fist and began to haul on the dog. The dog's eyes rolled wildly and it began to scrabble at the drum.

Great God this son of a bitch is heavy.

It rose strangled and dripping from the barrel and slid over the side and collapsed in a foul wet mass on the ground.

They stood watching it, Suttree on the drum holding the lantern. It looked like some strange medieval beast lying there gasping and stinking. Suttree steered the rope off the hound's neck and after a while it rose and shook itself and staggered off heavily through the honeysuckles.

Suttree coiled the rope save for the fouled noose of it and dragging this behind they went back up the path and sat on the porch. Rufus snuffed the lantern and leaned back against the post and closed his eyes. Then he opened them and patted his pocket where the bottle lay and then he closed them again. You caint see his lights now, growed up like it is, he said.

Whose lights?

The city mouse. When it's growed up thisaway you caint see over yonder. I dont know if he been there or not.

I dont believe he was there last night.

He might of got off drunk with Cleo and them. They gives him whiskey all the time.

Suttree nodded. Across the gut the lights of the city lay staggered on the night. You know any caves around here? he said.

Rufus opened his eyes. Caves? he said.

Do you know any?

They's a big cave yon side of the river. Cherokee cave.

I mean on this side.

They's caves all in under Knoxville.

Do you know how to get into them?

You dont want to mess around in no caves. What you wants to mess around down in under the ground for?

If you dont tell me how to get in those caves I'm going to get that dog and put him back in your slopbarrel.

Rufus grinned. He straightened out one leg across the porch and reached in his pocket for the bottle. Sheeit, he said.

I may get two dogs.

Harrogate wounded and covered in shit found in his pocket a pennybox of matches and a candlestub and made a light. The slender flame leaned and fluttered. He groped in the sewage for his flashlight, up and down the passage. When he found it he fetched it up and shook it and worked the button back and forth but it would not light. He knelt there looking about at the stone walls surrounding. Hot wax ran on his hand and he scratched at it absently. He began to clamber back up the tunnel toward higher ground.

He bathed himself in a black pool while the candle grew squat. Checked his injuries. Dismantled and put back the flashlight and tried it. Unscrewed the bezel that held the lens, took out the bulb and held it to the candlelight but he could not see wires or no wires. He watched the candle. It wasnt dripping. It just looked as if it were being sucked down through the stone.

He left it burning there and went as far as the edge of the light, his small shadow swallowed up finally in the greater dark beyond. He turned and came back. He squatted and watched the flame totter. The dank stone room grew smaller, drew in about him. He crouched in the smallest cup of light with his hands joined at the back of the flame as if he would gather it to him. Hot oil ran on the stones. The wick toppled and dropped with a thin hiss and dark closed over him so absolute that he became without boundary to himself, as large as all the universe and small as anything that was.

Suttree went by a wellrope down a dry brick cistern. Odor of earth and moss, the old brick dark and crumblesome. The floor of the cistern had fallen in and he went down a tailing of rubble and broken brick into a hole in the earth. He turned on the flashlight he carried and stepped down into the darkness.

He followed a narrow passage where the floor was mud and strewn with old bottleglass. The walls inscribed with names and dates scratched in the soft wet stone. The corridor narrowed and gave onto a drafty blackness where his light went from wall to far wall, an enormous and slaggy tureen traversed by plumbing. Great jointed runs of sewerpipe and tubes of cable cold and wet. He entered warily. No sound but a distant timeless dripping. He listened for any faint sound of traffic in the streets above but that world seemed gone altogether. The grotto lay like a sea cave, smooth and curving, a thing shaped to hold the wind where no wind was. He turned, his light going along the walls, the muddy flowstone and the high domed roof where hung stone teeth and tongues of wet black slag. He crossed the room, patches of dark sludge in the floor like pools of tar. At the far side a round tunnel went on through the rock and Suttree stooping followed after.

He searched the underground until he thought it must be evening and when he emerged again at the foot of the cistern he was surprised to find the day hardly half spent. He looked back down the cistern but he had no heart for going there again.

That evening he visited Harrogate's diggings under the bridge but there was no sign he'd been there. He ran his trotlines before daybreak in the morning and went again to search for him.

He checked out narrow side passages and he watched the little mudspits in the cave's stone floors for footprints but there seemed to have been no travelers here for years. The names and dates on the stone grew old. Cimmerians passed on without progeny. Some lack of adventure in the souls of newer folk or want of the love of darkness. His light ran over the ceilings, the carinated domes, stone scallopings and random hanging spires. The ribbed palate of a stone monster comatose, a great uvula dripping rust. Blades of false cuspidine. Hematite deep burgundy and loded with iron, clotted in the shape of stone offal. Or malachite in green coprolitic stools like small stone turds becrept a brassy green.

He found pale newts with enormous eyes and held them cold and quailing in his palm and watched their tiny hearts hammer under the blue and visible bones of their thimblesized briskets. They gripped his finger childlike with their tiny spatulate palps.

At the end of the day he came upon pieces of light in an upper wall of the tunnel and he squatted and listened and he thought he heard very faint and far the cries of children. He switched off the light and sat in the dark. He sat there for some time. The children's voices went away. The three shapes of light on the floor of the cavern began to climb the farther wall. After a while he rose and went with his own light back the way he'd come.

On the fourth day he found footprints in a patch of gray loam. Tennis shoe tracks and big ones at that. He set his own shoe inside. A little further he found a fresh candybar wrapper. He passed through a large cavern where bats lined the roof, their leather elbows jostling in their sleep, a constant reedy murmuring of squeaks like those numberless cries that Bishop Hatto must have heard in his tower prior to being consumed by mice. Suttree pressed on, down the carious undersides of the city, through black and slaverous cavities where foul liquors seeped. He had not known how hollow the city was.

The air was becoming more tainted, a rising sulphur reek of sewage. Where this smell thickened worst he found the city mouse crouching. He was leaning against a wall and looking back down the tunnel toward the beam of light approaching. He looked like something that might leap up and scurry off down a hole. Suttree squatted in front of him and looked him over.

How about gettin that light out of my eyes, said Harrogate.

Suttree lowered the light. Their faces were blackened like miners or minstrels and the city mouse wore only shreds of clothing and he was covered with dried sewage. True news of man here below. He was looking down at the pool of light.

I thought I was dead. I thought I'd die in this place.

Are you all right?

There was people down here.

What?

There was people down here.

You were seeing things.

I talked to em.

Let's go.

I hate for anybody to see me like this.

Suttree shook his head.

I'd give ten dollars for a glass of icewater, said the city mouse. Cash
money.

Suttree would see her in the street, dawn hours before the world's about. A hookbacked crone going darkly and bent in a shapeless frock of sacking dyed dead black with logwood chips and fustic mordant. Her spider hands clutching up a shawl of morling lamb. Gimpen granddam hobbling through the gloom with your knobbly cane go by, go by. Over the bridge in the last hours of night to gather herbs from the bluff on the river's south shore.

He saw Jones all these summer evenings. Sat with friends under a caged windscrew the size of a plane's prop and in the howling wind drank dripping beers and watched the cardplayers in their wet shirts mutter and smoke and deal. Jones spoke no more of the witch. Then one evening he leaned toward Suttree where he sat at the small marble table. Say she wont come down here? He said.

Who.

He snuffled. His eyes shifted but he seemed to be watching the cardtable. That old nigger witch, he said.

Ah, said Suttree. That's what she says.

The black nodded.

Why dont you go up and see her?

He shrugged.

She said it wasnt yourself you wanted to see her about.

He looked at Suttree and looked back to the table again. Who she say I want to see her about.

Your enemies.

Ah, said Jones.

They went in the evening through the locust wood, insects so named screaming in the greenery, beneath great blooms of newsprint and into the steaming sink.

She was tending her garden, stooped with a hoe, a figure the size of a child. The homedyed black of her gown fugitive at back and shoulders from the sun. When she saw them she raised up and went into the house. They crossed the yard. Past the little rows of tomato plants and late runner beans. Suttree tapped at the door and they stood looking out at the little glade. After a while he tapped again.

When she came to the door she was bareheaded and she wore her spectacles. She stood aside for them to enter as if they'd been expected.

They followed her down the little hall in all but darkness toward an open door beyond which stood a table and a lamp burning. Jones stooped to enter, Suttree followed. They stood in the kitchen. Suttree looked about. The walls were hung with pictures, the pictureglass all dull with grease. He bent to study a clan of blacks, some thirty or more all formally aligned, old patriarchs and men and women and small children peering out and in the center seated and shawled what appeared to be a scorched rhesus monkey.

She was standing across the room and the light was poor and she could not have rightly known which photograph among the many he was looking at and yet she said: She was born in seventeen and eighty-seven.

Who is she?

My grandmama. She was a hunnerd and two when she died.

She looks almost that old in the picture.

She's dead in the picture.

Suttree looked at her. The goldwire frames catching the light, the little round panes of glass. He leaned to see the picture again. Someone in the photograph behind the grandmother was holding her head up and her eyes were glazed and sightless. Suttree could not stop looking at this cracked and lacquered scene from times so fabled. The hands at the neck of the creature seemed to be forcing her to look at something she had rather not see and was it Suttree himself these sixty-odd years hence?

Are you in the picture? he said.

I aint in it. That was in Fayette County Kentucky. They kep her in a rootcellar till they could fetch the man to come and take the picture. Her children set with her down there of a night with candles.

Was that before you were born?

No. I was there. I never come out in the picture. I was there when it was took but I never come out.

Where were you in the picture?

Right yonder in that dead place.

He bent to see. On the far right there was a grayed-out patch, a ghost in the photo among her pellagrous predecessors. Here? he said.

She nodded, the little spectacles winking in the lamplight. Set down, she said.

Suttree sat beneath the picture. Jones was still standing almost in the middle of the little room and he seemed suddenly mindless, a great tottering zombie that she must take by one elbow and steer to the table although he has been here before. She's sewn him up like a hound with carpetthread and the blood beading very fine and bright from the pursings of black flesh, stanching lesser holes with cataplasms of cobweb, binding him in bedlinen. With him drunk at the door two days later demanding to be undone and sewn looser because he could not bend. Eyes raddled with blood, reeking of splo whiskey.

He sat. The crowned tooth of flame shifted and reshaped within the glass. Her neckware winked, tin amulets, a toadstone, an ebon baal that hung from a necklace of braided hair. She spread her hands. Under the black and dusky skin you could see how the fingerhinges were fashioned, the lean and jointed bonepipes. She said: I dont know which of these two souls is the worst troubled. Let me see your hand.

Jones laid his hand on the table. Fingers like old bananas, that fat, that brown. She sat slowly and took the hand palm up in her dark little claws and shut her eyes. Then she looked down at it. She bent closer. What's that? she said.

Jones looked. That aint nothin. Just where I took a knife off of some fool.

She pressed his seamy palm with her fingertips. She leaned back. Suttree was studying a photograph above the table to his right. A black boy in uniform who has watched the camera with some suspicion of his own expendability. The old woman said: You wants him here?

The youngblood? The youngblood can stay.

She bent forward and her eyes opened and her mouth made a little popping noise like a turtle's. Gimme five dollah, she said.

Jones raised one hip and reached into his pocket. He brought out a large roll of bills fastened with a rubber band and he dealt a five onto the tabletop. She took it and folded it and it disappeared somewhere about her person and she took his hand again. She began to recount for him aspects of his past. Legends of violence, affrays with police, bleeding in concrete rooms and anonymous coughing and groans and delirium in the dark.

Jones looked up. I aint interested in all that, he said. I just dont want to leave Quinn here and me gone.

You caint buy that.

I caint buy it with five dollar.

A flickering look of impatience in her blueblack face. She told a tale of retribution, silver seals but cannot buy such powers.

She has bored a keep in a treebole and hid therein the dung of her enemy and plugged it shut with an oakwood bung. She leans to them in terrible confidence: His guts swoll like a blowed dog. He couldnt get no relief. His stool riz up in his neck till he choken on it and he turn black in the face and his guts bust open and he die a horrible death a screamin and floppin in his own mess.

Jones nodded. He said that that would suit him fine. Suttree smiled against the back of his hand but the ogress waggled a finger before them both. She rose and went to a cupboard above the cookstove, climbing with surprising agility from a chair to the top of the stove and reaching up and taking down a small and moldy leather poke. She brought it with her to the table and she spread over the naked boards a cloth of black damask, smoothing the creases with hands as black, more deeply creased. She sat with her hands folded so and she rolled her soapy old eyes at them. She took up the pouch and held it and closed her eyes. Her fingers undid the mouth of the little bag and when the strings hung loose she held it clenched by the neck as if what crouched inside might otherwise out. She began to sway lightly back and forth and she was holding her head up very stiffly and something was moving in the black folds of her throatskin as if she were swallowing repeatedly. Suddenly she opened her eyes and looked about and with a motion almost violent raised the leather bag and upended it over the table. Out clattered toad and bird bones, yellow teeth, frail shapes of ivory strange or nameless, a small black heart dried hard as stone. A joint from a snake's spine, the ribs curved like claws. A bat's skull with needleteeth agrin, the little pterodactyl wingbones. Tiny pestles of polished riverstone. These things lay shapen still and final upon the black damask and the dark gospeler of their constellation who would in moments now postulate the denial of the old lie that beholder and beheld are ever more than one, this dusky fugitive of the pyre with whom they trafficked studied the figures briefly and looked away. Looked away, let shut the seamy doors of her eyes. They sat in silence.

Jones spoke. He said: What do it say?

About you it dont.

About Quinn then.

It dont say. It aint you nor Quinn neither. It's him.

Suttree felt the skin on his scalp pucker.

Why aint it me? said Jones.

I caint make it be if it aint.

Do it again.

No.

Jones blinked heavily.

You should of come alone, she said. She still had her eyes shut and Suttree thought that she was talking to Jones but when she opened them she was looking at him.

He did not go back. He passed her in the street one evening toward the summer's end but she might have been any black crone at all, stooped and shawled and silent save for the shuffling of her feet in the gutter. She did not look up nor did she speak and he could smell her on the night wind, lank harridan, a stale musty odor, dust dry. She passed in a light creaking of bones, dried bulb ends grating in their cups. Stranger yet he saw her a final time that year in the streets uptown in the full light of noon and she did look at him. Suttree shunned those adder's eyes in which the sun lay split. She has borne her wares in a catskin bag through the brick alleyways and tarpaper lanes. Something moved her mouth very like a smile. The antique teeth like seedcorn. An odor of violated graves. Her small shadow fell against him like a bird and she passed on. He stood looking after. Five fingers to five pressing he constructed a tactile plate of glass between his fingertips. Then he turned and went on. Give over, Graymalkin, there are horsemen on the road with horns of fire, with withy roods. He ran among the crowds dodging and veering. The jar of his heels on the pavement kept stopping the fans that spun above the shopdoors.

In late October he pulled his lines. Leaves were falling in the river and the days of windy rain and woodsmoke took him back to other times more than he would have liked. He made himself up a pack from old sacking and rolled his blanket and with some rice and dried fruit and a fishline he took a bus to Gatlinburg.

He hiked up into the mountains. The season had gone before, some trees gone barren, none still green. He spent the night on a ledge above the river and all night he could hear the ghosts of lumber trains, a liquid clicking and long shunt and clatter and the jargon of old rusted trucks on rails long gone. The first few dawns half made him nauseous, he'd not seen one dead sober for so long. He sat in the cold gray light and watched, mummied up in his blanket. A small wind blew. A rack of clouds troweled across the east grew mauve and yellow and the sun came boring up. He was moved by the utter silence of it. He turned his back to the warmth. Yellow leaves were falling all through the forest and the river was filled with them, shuttling and winking, golden leaves that rushed like poured coins in the tailwater. A perishable currency, forever renewed. In an old grandfather time a ballad transpired here, some love gone wrong and a sabletressed girl drowned in an icegreen pool where she was found with her hair spreading like ink on the cold and cobbled river floor. Ebbing in her bindings, languorous as a sea dream. Looking up with eyes made huge by the water at the bellies of trout and the well of the rimpled world beyond.

Suttree lay on a warm rock above the river and watched the trout drift and quarter over the cold gray stones. He had baited his small hook with ricegrains. The trout stood or sidled or turned among the pouring leaves. Bulltrout with rutwarped snouts, pale trout with velvet fins. They would not bite.

First he left the roads, then the trails. Small creeks half dry in this late season now the rains have gone. Scrambling up a stone throat pool to pool he saw a mink go black and bowbacked limping over the rocks. Dark mucronate droppings steaming on a shalepane replete with bones, scales, shellshards. At night a high cold wind sucked the fire he squatted by in the eye of the dark. A thin wind, thin air, hard to breathe and bitter cold.

In the morning turning up the frostveined stones for bait he uncovered a snake. Soporific, sleek viper with flanged jawhinges. Fate rid-den snake, of all stones in the forest this one to sleep beneath. Suttree could not tell if it watched him or not, little brother death with his quartz goat's eyes. He lowered the stone with care.

That afternoon he crossed the watershed and started down through a dark spruce forest. Ravens flew over the vast high country, the slopes falling away all heather and gray weather wood into the clouds below. He made a fire beneath a shelf of rock and watched a storm close over the valley down there, ragged hot wires of lightning quaking in the dusk like voltage in some mad chemist's chambers. Rain fell, leaves fell, slantwise and wild, a silver storm blowing down the eaves of the world. He'd found a few wild chestnuts and he watched them blacken in the coals. He cracked and cooled them. All things contained of tree therein, leaf and root. He ate. He'd no food other and he thought his hunger would keep him awake but it didnt. He could hear the long wild sough of the wind in the high forest as he lay there in his blanket staring up at the heavens. The cold indifferent dark, the blind stars beaded on their tracks and mitered satellites and geared and pinioned planets all reeling through the black of space.

In the morning there was snow at the higher elevations, a fairyland dust on the peaks. He had bound up his feet with the crokersack and now he simply wrapped the blanket about his shoulders and went down along the ridge, a hermetic figure, already gaunted and sunken at the eyes, a week's beard. Going shrouded in his blanket through the forest beswirled about by cold gray mist, gray weather, cold day, moss the color of stone. The wind sharp in the dry bores of his nostrils. Down through the pale bare bones of a birch forest where the claw-shaped leaves he trod held little ferns of ice.

Below him ravens rode up like things of wire and crepe weightless on the updrafts. They rocked and wheeled and slid away over the high vast emptiness with lost windmuted croaks.

Suttree in the woods was surprised to find small flowers still. He fell into silent studies over the delicate loomwork in the moss. Annular forms of lichens fiery green that sprawled across the stones like tiny jade volcanoes. The scalloped fungus that ledged old rotted logs, flangeous mammary growths with a visceral consistency and pale indianpipes in pulpy clusters among the debris of humus and rich decay and mushrooms with serrate and membraneous soffits whereunder toads are reckoned to siesta. Or elves, he said. In breeks of kingscord, shirts paned up of silk tailings, no color like the rest. A curious light lay in the forest. He was squatting in the rich and murky earth, the blanket about his shoulders. He wondered could you eat the mushrooms, would you die, do you care. He broke one in his hands, frangible, mauvebrown and kidneycolored. He'd forgotten he was hungry.

He came down an old logging road past the ruins of a CCC camp and swung through the woods toward a stone bridge beyond the sere or barren trees. The road crossed above. The river path went through the low stone arch along a bar of silt where blackened turds lay by pale wet clots of tissuepaper.

When they were building the highway through the mountains a horseman came this way along the river, the gravel peppering the water behind the horse's heels and the horse lined out lean and flat and the rider wide-eyed with the reins clutched. Two boys fishing from the bridge watched him clatter down and pass beneath. They crossed to the other side of the bridge to see him go but the horse was downriver with the stirrups kicking out loose and it ran riderless out on the gravel bar and into the river in an explosion of steam. A pale breadth of buckskin flank turning in the cold green pool.

The rider did not appear. They found him dangling by his skull from a steel rod that jutted from the new masonry, swinging slightly, his hands at his sides and his eyes slightly crossed as if he would see what was the nature of this thing that had skewered his brains.

Suttree went up the narrow valley and deeper into the mountains. Over old dry riverbeds of watershapen stones that lay in the floor of the wood. His beard grew long and his clothes fell from him like the leaves. At these high altitudes the trees were stunted spruce and dark and twisted and nothing moved save he and the wind and the ravens. The spruce trees stood black and bereaved of dimension in the shadow of the high cloven draws, against the sky processional and nunlike ascending in the dusk.

He'd taken to sleeping more and the walking made him dizzy. He'd watch the fire for hours, the curious incandescent world of settling embers, small orange grottoes and the way the wood looked molten there or half translucent. He had begun to become accompanied.

First in dreams and then in states half wakeful. One day in the full light of autumn noon he saw an elvish apparition come from the woods and go down the trail before him half ajog and worried of aspect. Suttree sat in the moss and rested. The woods looked too green for the season. Before two days more had gone he hardly knew if he dreamt or not. Lying on a gravel bar with the tips of his fingers in the icy water he could see his face above the sandy creek floor, a shifting visage hard by its own dark shadow. He stretched himself and bowed his lips and sucked from the passing water. Taste of iron and moss and a silken weight on his tongue. A newt, small, olive, paintspattered, arrowed off downside a rock toward the bubbled green of the deeper pool. The water sang in his head like wine. He sat up. A green and reeling wall of laurel and the stark trees rising. Articulating in the slight lift of the forest wind some arboreal mute's alphabet. Pins of light near blue were coming off the stones. Suttree felt a deep and chilling lassitude go by nape and shoulderblades. He slumped and crossed his wrists in his lap. He looked at a world of incredible loveliness. Old distaff Celt's blood in some back chamber of his brain moved him to discourse with the birches, with the oaks. A cool green fire kept breaking in the woods and he could hear the footsteps of the dead. Everything had fallen from him. He scarce could tell where his being ended or the world began nor did he care. He lay on his back in the gravel, the earth's core sucking his bones, a moment's giddy vertigo with this illusion of falling outward through blue and windy space, over the offside of the planet, hurtling through the high thin cirrus. His fingers clutched up wet handfuls from the bar, polished lozenges of slate, small cold and mascled granite teardrops. He let them fall through his fingers in a smooth clatter. He could feel the oilless turning of the earth beneath him and the cup of water lay in his stomach as cold as when he drank it.

That evening he passed through a children's cemetery set in a bench of a hillside and forlorn save by weeds. The stone footings of a church nearby was all the church there was and leaves fell few and slowly, here and here, him reading the names, the naked headboards all but perished in the weathers of seasons past, these tablets tilted or fallen, titles to small plots of earth against all claiming. A storm had followed him for days. He turned in an ashen twilight, crossing this garden of the early dead by weeds the wind has sown. Brown jasmine among the nettles. He saw small figurines composed of dust and light turn in the broken end of a bottle, spidersized marionettes in some minute ballet there in the purple glass so lightly strung with strands of cobweb floss. A drop of rain sang on a stone. Bell loud in the wild silence. Harried mute and protestant over the darkening windy fields he saw go with no surprise mauve monks in cobwebbed cowls and sandals hacked from ruined boots clapping along in a rude shuffle down small cobbled ways into an old stone town. Storm birds rode up dark and chattering and burst away like ash and mice were going down their homeward furrows like tailed shot.

He crossed in the twilight a pitchgreen wood grown murk with ferns, with rank and steaming plants. An owl flew, bow winged and soundless. He came upon the bones of a horse, the polished ribcradle standing among the ferns pale and greenly phosphorescent and the wedgeshaped skull grinning in the grass. In these silent sunless galleries he'd come to feel that another went before him and each glade he entered seemed just quit by a figure who'd been sitting there and risen and gone on. Some doublegoer, some othersuttree eluded him in these woods and he feared that should that figure fail to rise and steal away and were he therefore to come to himself in this obscure wood he'd be neither mended nor made whole but rather set mindless to dodder drooling with his ghosty clone from sun to sun across a hostile hemisphere forever.

That night he did not even make a fire. He crouched like an ape in the dark under the eaves of a slate bluff and watched the lightning. Down there in the wood the birchtrunks shone palely and troops of ghost cavalry clashed in an outraged sky, old spectral revenants armed with rusted tools of war colliding parallactically upon each other like figures from a mass grave shorn up and girdled and cast with dread import across the clanging night and down remoter slopes between the dark and darkness yet to come. A vision in lightning and smoke more palpable than wortled bone or plate or pauldron shelled with rot.

The storm moved off to the north. Suttree heard laughter and sounds of carnival. He saw with a madman's clarity the perishability of his flesh. Illbedowered harlots were calling from small porches in the night, in their gaudy rags like dolls panoplied out of a dirty dream. And along the little ways in the rain and lightning came a troupe of squalid merrymakers bearing a caged wivern on shoulderpoles and other alchemical game, chimeras and cacodemons skewered up on boarspears and a pharmacopoeia of hellish condiments adorning a trestle and toted by trolls with an eldern gnome for guidon who shouted foul oaths from his mouthhole and a piper who piped a pipe of ploverbone and wore on his hip a glass flasket of some smoking fuel that yawed within viscid as quicksilver. A mesosaur followed above on a string like a fourlegged garfish heliumfilled. A tattered gonfalon embroidered with stars now extinct. Nemoral halfworld inhabitants, figures in buffoon's motley, a gross and blueblack foetus clopping along in brogues and toga. Attendants attend. Suttree watched these puckish revelers pass with a half grin of wry doubt. Dark closed about him. The lightning lapsed away and he could hear the grass kneeling in the wind. He raked leaves to him in his arms and struck a match with fingers stiff and fumblesome. They crackled along the edges and small hot sparks went singing down the wind. He tried again and gave it up. He curled into his blanket there on the high cold ground and he knew he should be cold but he had not been so for days.

In this condition the next morning he passed a deerstand where a small man in overalls crouched with a crossbow. Suttree paid him no more mind than any other apparition and would go on but that the man spoke to him. Hey, he said.

Hey, said Suttree.

The hunter had the crossbow pointed Suttree's way and he cocked his head. What are you? he said.

Suttree began to laugh. He let his blanket fall from his shoulders and he bent from the waist laughing.

The hunter looked anxious at this. Hush, he said. Quit that.

Okay.

The man spat. It dont make no difference noway, he said. You've done run everthing off.

Are you real? said Suttree.

I didnt mean to thow down on ye thataway, said the crossbowman vailing his piece. He looked the traveler over. Not that I aint proud to be heeled and such a crazy thing as you look run loose in these woods. How long ye been scoutin thisaway?

I dont know.

Are ye lost?

I think I know what state I'm in. I doubt you can direct me out of it.

You're lost or crazy or both.

Quite so.

You wouldnt tell on a feller for poachin him a little deermeat would ye?

I dont dine at the king's table, said Suttree.

The hunter spat to one side and shook his head at Suttree. You're loony as a didapper, he said.

At least I exist, said the wanderer. He wafted up the hem of his blanket and gestured at the hunter with it. Begone, he said.

The hunter recoiled and brought his crossbow up again.

Begone I say, said Suttree, shucking the tattered blanket at him.

Why you dipshit idjit if anybody begones anywhere it'll be you with a arrowbolt up your skinny ass.

Suttree batted his eyes. Are you real? he said.

Damned if you aint beyond the bend in a queer road. Where'd you up from anyways?

From over the mountain.

What are you, a yankee or somethin?

I'll tell you what I'm not.

What's that?

A figment. I'm not a figment.

A what?

A figment. A frigging figment. He crooned a weird laugh. The hunter stared at him.

What have you there? said Suttree.

A little sense for one thing.

Is that a crossbow?

I've heard it called that.

How many crosses have you killed with it?

It's killed more meat than you could bear.

Shoot it.

What for?

I want to see. You shoot it.

I think I'll just keep it strung and handy.

Suttree rose from where he'd squatted. Pale liver spots listed across his vision. The woods had grown dim.

It's snowing, he said.

A delicate host expired on his filthy cuff. He pulled the blanket closer. He looked down at himself, at the rags of crokersack, the spats of knitting that had been his socks, at the twill trousers black with woodash, the bulbed green knees of them hanging. He had a beard an inch long and his hair was wild and matted with leaves and the eyes the hunter watched were black and crazed and smoking.

How do I get out of here? he said.

Where is it you're headed?

Out of these mountains.

Well, you're about nine mile from Cherokee.

Which way?

Right yon way. You'll come to the road about two mile.

Thank you.

You run crazy in these woods regular do ye?

No, said Suttree. This is my first time.

He did not come to the road. Coming down a stony draw through green and well nigh lightless grottoes where lay stones and windfall trees alike anonymous beneath the mantled moss he saw cross through a bosky glen two equine phantoms pale with purpose: one, the next, and gone in the dark of the forest. Suttree stumbled out of the woods onto a bridlepath. Faint smell of stables. Broken green horseturds steamed in the cold of the humus earth. He followed the path until it began to veer back toward the mountains and then he entered the woods again.

Nor was he out of them that evening. The snow had not stopped falling and he sat in the feathered darkness and heard it sifting through the woods with just the faintest whisper. He drowsed and woke and nodded off again. He wondered would he freeze, sitting there under a balsam tree watching the snow encroach toward his toes. The rich smell of the branches and the needles in which he sat carried him back to old Christmases, those sad seasons. He dreamed sad dreams and woke bitter and rueful. The snow had stopped and the trees stood stark against a paler sky. With first light he rose and went on.

All day this halfmad outcast staggered through the snow and what a baleful heart he harbored and how dear to him. In midafternoon he came upon a freshet and he turned downstream, his breath pluming. He could smell the water. Going down through the snow where ice tines hung from boughs above their replicas in graygreen pools like jaws from fierce jurassic carnivores. Until late in the day he came out of the snow and crossed through a broad bottomland where the ground gave wet and spongy underneath. In his darker heart a nether self hulked above cruets of ratsbane, a crumbling old grimoire to hand, androleptic vengeances afoot for the wrongs of the world. Suttree muttering along half mindless, an aberrant journeyman to the trade of wonder.

He was wandering in a swampy wood, a landscape of cane and alder where gray reeks swirled. Cognate shapes among the vapors urged him on and in this sad glen under a pale sun he felt he'd grown improbable of succor and he began to run. Headlong through the bracken and briers in whose crushed wake he left small tattered stars of the rags he wore. Until at last he washed up in a little glade and fell to his knees gasping. Clouds lay remote and motionless across the evening sky like milt awash in some backwater of the planet's seas and a white woodcock rose from the ferns before him and dissolved in smoke.

A curling bit of down cradled in this green light for the sake of my sanity. Unreal and silent bird albified between the sun and my broken mind godspeed.

He woke in full daylight by the side of a road. A truck had passed. Leaves stirred about him. He struggled up. His blanket lay in the ditch. His head was curiously clear.

The town that he came to was Bryson City North Carolina. He passed a shabby tourist court and went down the sidewalk in his blanket peering about at the sudden tawdry garishness in which he found himself. At the maze of small town mercenary legend, the dusty shopwindows, the glass bulb of a gaspump. Cars slowed in passing him. He entered the first cafe he came to and sat slowly in a booth. Some stark and darker bearded visage peered him back from the shiny black formica of the tabletop. Some alien Suttree there among the carven names and rings and smears of other men's meals.

What for ye? said a leery matron.

The menu. I dont have a menu.

The old bird's eyes honed by past injustices to a glint just between suspicion and outrage swept over him and to the wall.

Yonder it is.

He looked. Chalk script on a slate. Country steak, he said. Mashed potatoes and beans. Cornbread. And bring me a cup of coffee.

You get three vegetables.

He looked again. Let me have the apples, he said.

She finished writing and padded off on her white wedgeheeled shoes to the rear of the place. In the cameral shutting of the kitchen door he saw a black hand picking at the seat of a pair of greasy jeans. A dark wood clock above the door told a time of two twenty. Suttree seized the water tumbler she'd left and drank. A long cold drink laced with chlorine. His head swam. A pall of fried grease hung in the room. He rose from the booth and went to the counter and got a newspaper and came back. He looked in the upper corner for the date but there was none.

Whoever heard of a newspaper with no date, he said aloud, tearing open the sheets. Here. December third. How long is that?

He stared blankly across the empty dining hall. A huge and blackened trout hung bowed on a board above the counter and knew not. Nor the naked leather squirrel with the vitreous eyebulbs. A dull wooden clicking he'd thought some long coiled component of his forelobe together with the fading colored pictures and the receding attendance of horribles segued into a shrunken indian passing across the glass of the cafe front and the dull tocking of applewood clockworks from above the door. He turned to the paper. A rash of incomprehensible events. He could put no part of it together.

The kitchen door swung out and she came bearing coffee. A thick rimmed cup of sepia crockery. Beads of grease veered on the dishing meniscus of inky fluid it held. He poured cream copiously from a tin pitcher and laced in sugar and stirred. The smell of it flooded his brain and when he sipped it it seemed like an odd thing to drink. He sipped again. The waitress reared above the rim of the cup. He leaned back. A plate of corn muffins fell before him. A small oblong platter with thick flour gravy wherein lay a slab of waffled beef and the vegetables. Suttree could hardly lift his fork. He buttered one of the muffins and bit into it. His mouth was filled with a soft dry sawdust. He tried to chew. His jaws worked the mass slowly. He tried to spit it out and could not. He reached in his mouth and fished it forth with his fingers in thick clogs of paste which he raked off on the side of the platter. He cut away a section of the steak with his fork and eased it past his teeth. His eyes closed. He could taste nothing. His throatpipe seemed grown shut.

He mouthed the piece of meat like an old gummy man, dry smacking sounds. The waitress moved about the room refilling saltcellars, her eyes on him. He caught her watching from the sideboard. He spat in the plate.

Is there something wrong with me? he demanded.

She looked away.

What is this crap?

Other people eat it, she said.

He stabbed at the potatoes with his fork. The imago does not eat, he told the plate mutteringly. Fuck it. He let the fork fall and looked up at the waitress.

Will you take this away and bring me some soup.

You'll have to pay for it.

Suttree watched her with his fevery eyes.

If you didnt want it you ought not to of ordered it, she said.

Will you please bring me some goddamned soup like I asked?

She turned and stalked off to the kitchen. He pushed the plate from him and laid his head on the table.

A hand jostled his elbow. Suttree jerked upright.

What's the matter here? said a man in cook's whites. The waitress hovered behind.

What do you mean what's the matter?

Did you cuss her?

No.

He's a damned liar. He did too do it.

I asked her to bring me some soup.

He cussed me and his dinner and everthing else.

We dont allow no cussin in here and we dont allow no trouble. Now let's go.

He had stood back for Suttree to rise, to pass. He did. He and his blanket. He was shaking with rage and frustration.

He aint paid, said the waitress.

Suttree glared at her.

Just get on out, the man said. I dont need your money.

He stood in the street. He could hear doors closing all back through his head like enormous dominoes toppling in a corridor. He shouldered the blanket and went on. A black man he passed looked him over and called back to him. Suttree turned.

They'll vag you here, said the black.

Suttree didnt answer.

I'm just tellin you. You do what you want.

He was gone. Somewhat jaunty, coatless in the cold. Suttree eyed the sun, cold worn and bonecolored above the chill overcast. He shuffled on. His knees kept grasshoppering out sideways and this way. He passed a storewindow and backed up. The glass was printed with the first three letters of the alphabet and in the hall beyond was a long counter and behind that were shelves ranked with bottles.

He wheeled in through the door, adjusting the blanket as he went. Two men at the counter watched him come. One turned and found something to do and the other rose up from his elbows and stood in charge.

I cant serve you, he said.

Suttree still had his mouth open. He closed it and opened it again. He looked at the bottles. He looked at the counterman.

You better go on, said the counterman.

Where's the bus station, said Suttree.

Where you left it, I reckon.

Suttree suddenly began to cry. He didn't know that he was going to and he was ashamed. The counterman looked away. Suttree turned and went out. In the street the cold wind on his wet face brought back such old winter griefs that he began to cry still harder. Walking along the mean little streets in his rags convulsed with sobs, half blind with a sorrow for which there was neither name nor help.

At the bus station he bought his ticket, smoothing out the crumpled bill on the counter, the grave face of the emancipator looking back from the currency. With the change he bought a candy bar and he sat alone on a bench in the empty waiting room in his blanket eating the candy in micesized bites and reading from a black leatherette copy of the Book of Mormon he found in a pamphlet rack. The candy he managed to get down but the words of the book swam off the page eerily and he thought he'd never read a stranger tale.

The hands on the bald white clockface above the ticket office went by fits and starts. At ten till four he rose and went out, the book in his hand and his hand at his breast and the blanket about him like an itinerant simonist. The baggageman watched warily the shuffling exit of this latterday crazyman.

A driver in a shiny blue suit looked him up and down.

Is this the bus to Knoxville? Suttree said.

He said that it was. Suttree offered his ticket and the driver drew a punch from its holster and punched the ticket and handed it back and Suttree mounted the steps into the bus.

All the faces that he passed were watching out the windows but as he went by they turned and followed him with their eyes. A parcel of old ladies. A young man in pressed twill. At the rear of the bus Suttree swung around and the faces all turned back. He lay down on the rear seat.

When he woke they were swinging through the mountains and he was being shifted up and back on the seat as the rear of the bus followed. He sat up. His blanket had fallen to the floor and he got it and tucked it around him. The coach was filled with stale cigarette smoke and the windows were weeping. A few small domelights shone on magazines up the aisle. Beyond the windshield a pair of red taillights slid away and reappeared and swung back across the front of the bus again. Suttree slept, tottering upright on the seat.

It was after nine oclock when they reached Knoxville. He clambered down on queasy legs and climbed the steps to the terminal. In the men's room he studied himself. An unshorn ghost in a black beard peered back from the glass with eyes like old furnace flues. He pulled the blanket from his shoulders and rolled it and tucked it beneath his arm. His jacket hung in ribbons. He touched the sharpened bones of his face. He raked back his hair with his hands. When he glanced down at his shoes the tiles of the floor seemed to be undulating like the scales of some cold enormous fish. An eye watched from a partly open toilet door. He staggered out. His feet made no sound in the empty arcade and he seemed to go for miles toward the lights of the street.

At night in the bed high in the old frame house on Grand he listened to the engines switching in the yard, the long iron collision of couplings running out in the dark by the warehouse walls until the lamplit night echoed with their hammerings like some great forge where arms for a giants' tournament were being beaten out against the sun's rising and in the light of passing locomotives the shadows of trees and powerpoles raced within the cocked sash of the window across the peeling walls to blackness. He slept and slept. All day the house was empty. She'd come at noon and fix him soup and a sandwich until he felt like a child in some winter illness. Recurrences of dreams he'd had in the mountains came and went and the second night he woke from uneasy sleep and lay in the world alone. A dark hand had scooped the spirit from his breast and a cold wind circled in the hollow there. He sat up. Even the community of the dead had disbanded into ashes, those shapes wheeling in the earth's crust through a nameless ether no more men than were the ruins of any other thing once living. Suttree felt the terror coming through the walls. He was seized with a thing he'd never known, a sudden understanding of the mathematical certainty of death. He felt his heart pumping down there under the palm of his hand. Who tells it so? Could a whole man not author his own death with a thought? Shut down the ventricle like the closing of an eye?

He got up and went to the window and looked out. The houses stood above the railyard with a kind of doomed austerity, locked in a sad frieze against the gray midwinter sky. From each chimney like a tattered rag a tongue of coalsmoke swirled. Beyond the tracks lay the market warehouses and beyond these the shapeless warrens of

McAnally with its complement of pariahs and endless poverty.

He woke in the paler gray of noon to find Blind Richard groping toward him from the door.

Bud? he said, standing there on the boards in the barren room like a medicineshow clown, casting about in the dead air with his frozen grin.

Hello Richard.

The blind man sat on the bed and lit a cigarette and toyed at the ash with the tip of his little finger. Well, he said. I heard you was sick.

I'm all right.

What was it you had?

Suttree eased himself among the sooty sheets. I dont know, he said. Something or other.

Mrs Long look after ye good?

Oh yeah. She's good.

Good a woman as ever walked. Ast anybody. Dont take my word for it.

How are you getting along?

I wisht McAnally was full of em like her. Me? I aint braggin much. Well.

The blind man looked about. Dark sockets clogged with bluish jissom. Smoke drawing upward alongside his thin nose. He knit his yellowed fingers in a mime of anxiety and leaned toward Suttree. You dont have a little drink hid away do ye? he said.

No I dont.

Didnt much allow ye did.

Suttree watched him. How long have you been blind, Richard?

What?

I said how long have you been blind. Were you always blind?

The blind man grinned sheepishly and fingered his chin. Oh, he said. No. I dont remember. I've forgot.

Where did you get that lump?

He touched a faint yellow swelling above his eye. Red done that, he said.

Red did?

Yeah. He comes over you know. Comes over to the house. He sets all the doors about halfway shut. I got in a hurry or I never would of run into it. I know him.

How's everything down at the Huddle?

It's about like you left it.

They sat there in silence on the bed. Beyond the baywindow lay a deadly and leaden sky. Dimpled by the motewenned glass. A small gray rain had begun.

Well, said Richard. I better get on.

Dont rush off.

I've got to get on home.

Come back.

You get well now, said the blind man. You do what Mrs Long tells ye.

I will.

He went down the stairwell holding to the wall. Suttree heard the door close. A few sad birds along the wires watched the rain fall. One had a crooked leg. Gray water was leaking from a rotted length of gutterpipe. As he lay there the water grew more pale and the rain fell and the water grew quite clear and the water beaded on the lacquered leaves of the old magnolia tree in the yard looked bright and clean.

Late Saturday and all day Sunday drunks would come and sit on the bed and talk and sneak him whiskey. None asked if what he had were catching. Mrs Long on her duckshaped shoes came to the top of the landing to complain in her shrill voice and groggy sots clung halfway up the spindleshorn balustrade while ribald laughter rocked in the barren upper rooms of the rotting house.

He came down to dinner, good plain food served in the shambles of patched and tacked furniture destroyed in drunken rages over the years. Another week and he was on the streets again.

His first day uptown he weighed himself on the free scales in front of Woodruff's. He looked at the face in the glass.

He went to Miller's Annex and called on J-Bone.

Up and about eh? Did they run you off at the house?

No. I slipped off after your mama went back to work.

How do you feel?

I feel okay. I feel pretty good.

Where will you be later on?

I dont know. I'm going up to Comer's.

You think you feel well enough to drink a beer?

I might get well.

J-Bone grinned. Old Suttree, he said. He's hell when he's well.

What time you get off? Five thirty?

Yeah.

I'll see you then.

Okay Bud.

When he came through the door at Comer's Dick winked at him and raised his hand. Hey Buddy, he said. Got a letter for you.

Suttree leaned on the counter.

You've lost a little weight havent you?

Some.

Where you been?

I was over in North Carolina for a while.

Dick turned the letter in his hand and looked at it and handed it over. It's been here about two weeks, he said.

Suttree tapped the letter on the counter. Thanks Dick, he said.

He sat among the watchers by the wall and crossed his legs the way the old men do and opened the envelope. It was postmarked Knoxville and there was a letter from his mother and a check from his Uncle

Ben newly dead. He looked at the check. It was for three hundred dollars. He tapped it in his hand and got up and went to the water-cooler for a drink and came back. He wadded the letter and dropped it into the spittoon.

Where you been Buddy boy? called Harry the Horse.

Hey Harry, said Suttree.

Harry stood shapeless in his shirt and changeapron by the cashregister. Bill Tilson made a few slow judo feints and laid the edge of his hand athwart Harry's ear. Ah, said Harry. That was on the bone.

On the bone, called Tilson dementedly, passing on along the tables.

Suttree looked up from the check to the racked cues along the wall, the old photos of ballplayers. A quiet figure there in the bedlam of ballclack and calling and telephones, the tickertape unspooling the sportsnews. Fuck it, he said. He rose and went to the front counter.

Can you cash a check for me, Dick?

Sure Bud. He laid the check on the sill of the cashregister and rang open the drawer. He read the check. Fat city, he said. How do you want it?

A couple of hundreds and some twenties.

With the money folded in his front pocket he went down the stairs to the street again.

He went to Miller's and bought underwear and socks and went out through the Annex and crossed through the markethouse. Old Lippner akimbo in his abbatoir. By the side door blind Walter stood sleeping with his dobro and Suttree touched his sleeve. The blind eyes opened and rolled up. Suttree pressed a folded bill into his palm.

You the only man I ever saw could sleep standing up.

An enormous set of teeth appeared and a strong black hand gripped his forearm. Hey fish man. Naw you wrong. Black man taught it to the mule.

You think I could learn it?

You might if they wouldnt let you set down nowheres.

Suttree smiled. I'll see you later.

The blind man pocketed the bill. I hope you catches the river out, he said.

Suttree crossed the street to Watson's. There in the basement he found his size in a rack of sportcoats and selected a pale camelhair and tried it. Faint lines of dirt along the shoulder seams where it had hung. He looked at himself in the mirror. He took a comb from his pocket and combed his hair.

He found a pair of black mohair trousers that had a small tricor-nered tear at the rear pocket. Couldnt see it with the jacket on. The slacks and the jacket came to thirteen dollars and ninety cents and he paid and went upstairs and bought a yellow gabardine shirt with handstitched collar and pockets.

In a window above Market Street the old tailor stood peering out through the lettered glass, the dusty ells and bolts of cloth spooled out in the window easing the repose of dead flies and roaches. Suttree came up the dark and musty wooden stairwell and swung through the door with his package.

Nice trousers them, said the old man as he measured the inseam with a tattered yellow tape. He gripped the waistband and tugged at them. He put his arms around Suttree's waist and brought the tape together at his navel. The old man barely came to Suttree's shoulder.

You want some out of the seat too.

I think they'll be all right, Mr Brannam. I've lost some weight.

The tailor tugged at the seat of Suttree's new trousers and looked dubious. You going to carry your lunch here? he said.

Suttree smiled. They're really my size, he said. I'll fill back out.

How much you going to fill?

About twenty pounds.

The tailor pulled again at Suttree's waist and shook his head.

They're okay. Let's just do the cuffs.

When you dont get fat you bring em back, okay?

Okay. There's a little tear there in the back too.

I see him, said the tailor, marking with his chalk.

Suttree waited in a wooden folding chair while the trousers were cuffed and he paid the old man and thanked him and went down the stairs again.

He bought a pair of shoes at Thom McAn's that had zippers up the side and were the color of blood. With his packages he climbed the stairs to Comer's and at the rear of the premises he stripped and washed and put on his new clothes. His old ones he wrapped in the paper and he left them with Stud at the lunchcounter. Stud took the package and looked back again and whistled and Jake took hold of him by the shoulder and turned him around and looked him over and sniffed at his cheek and tried to kiss him.

Get away you ass, Suttree said.

Ulysees came over to view him with his quiet cynic's smile. Well, he said. Looking rather affluent there, Bud. He kneaded Suttree's sleeve between his thumb and forefinger. Oy, he said. Iss qvality.

Suttree crossed Gay Street to the Farragut and went downstairs to the barbershop. He passed Tarzan Quinn coming up, freshly powdered, swinging his billyclub by its thong to and fro into and out of his enormous hand.

An aged black took his new coat and he climbed into a chair.

Yessir, said the barber, flinging the apron ticking over him.

Shave, haircut, shine . . . You do manicures?

No, said the barber. We dont have a manicurist.

Okay. Shave, haircut, shine. And dont spare the smellgood.

The barber brought a steaming towel and wrapped his face and tilted him back in the chair. Suttree lay in deep euphoria, his legs crossed at the ankles, his new shoes easy on the nickleplated grating of the footrest. He listened dreamily to the pop of the razor on the strop.

He half dozed in the chair while the barber pulled his face about, the razor slicing off the hot lavendar foam. Peace seeped through to Suttree's bones. The barber raised him up and began to trim his hair with scissors. The black had settled at his feet with his wooden box of polishes and begun to work over the shoes. The second barber read the newspaper. No one spoke. Suttree's dark locks dropped soundlessly to the tiles. Gentle barber. He drifted.

The barber talced the back of his neck and whipped away the apron and stood back. Suttree opened his eyes. He raised the shoes up one and then the other and looked at them. He climbed down from the chair and looked at himself in the mirror.

The old black held his coat while he paid and then helped him on with it and dusted his shoulders with a little broom. Suttree dropped a half dollar into his palm and the old man made a sort of bow and said thank you sir and the barber said come back.

In the streets a colder wind on his shaven nape. Bobbyjohn stood on the corner with Bucket and Hoghead and two boys he did not know. They seized upon him with great joy. Bobbyjohn was offering him two dollars for the coat, waving the money about.

Where's your stick? said Hoghead. You caint go around lookin like that and no stick to beat the women off with.

Old Suttree's caught himself a hell of a fish somewheres.

He and J-Bone ate dinner at Regas. Bobby smiled when she brought them the menu.

What are you goin for, Bud?

I think I'll go for the large fillet steak.

Believe I'll go for the veal cutlet.

Hell, get the steak.

The cutlet's good, Bud.

Get the biggest fucking steak they own.

The steaks arrived on iron platters sizzling in their own juice and there were steaming baked potatoes with pithy cores to melt the butter over and there was sour cream with chives and hot rolls and coffee. Suttree popped a chunk of steak into his mouth and sat back in the chair and closed his eyes, chewing.

Good aint it Bud?

J-Bone dipped a roll into his platter and raised it dripping with dark gravy and loaded it into his jaw. Lordy, he said.

Where we going tonight?

Anywhere suits me. What about the Carnival Club?

Is this Thursday?

Sure is, said J-Bone. The place will be crawling with lovely young cuntlets.

I'm for that, said Suttree.

He woke in Woodlawn among the menhirs of the dead. He raised himself onto one elbow and looked out across the ordered landscape of polished stones, the pale winter's grass and black trees. He brushed the chaff from his sleeve. An oxblood stain was seeping up his white socks from the new shoes. He staggered to his feet, brushing at himself. His trousers were caked with great patches of mud at the knees and he was damp and cold. Suddenly he crammed both fists in his pocket. His eyes wandered in his head as he grappled with the murky history of the prior night. Dim memories. A maudlin madman stumbling among the stones in search of a friend long dead who lies here. He pulled from his watchpocket a small wet folded paper. It was one of the hundred dollar bills somehow put by. Suttree crossed the spiderfrosted grass of the cemetery toward the fence and the road.

The sun was not so high he could not take his bearings by it and he set off in what he figured to be the direction of the town. A bus passed in a blue stink of diesel smoke, the windows filled with faces.

He brushed his hair back and grimaced at the riders. He shaped a curse in the air after them with a leanboned hand.

A half mile down stood a roadside store. Suttree at the drinkbox lifted out an orange bottle and opened it and drank. The woman who kept the store watched him from under her wrinkled eyelids.

I'm not loose from the circus, he said.

What?

I said do you have any aspirins.

She turned and reached a small tin box of them from a shelf behind the counter. Suttree opened the box and emptied the contents into his hand and dropped them into his mouth like peanuts and washed them down with a swig of the drink.

What do I owe you?

Fifteen cents, she said. Old nervous eyes.

Gravegrass clung to his trousers. He pulled the hundred dollar bill from his pocket and spread it out on the counter. She looked at it and she looked at him. She said: I caint change that.

That's all I have.

Well I dont have change for nothin like that.

Well I'll have to owe you then.

He took the bill up and put it back in his pocket.

You'll have to pay, she said. I dont know ye.

I'll write you a check.

She just stood there.

Do you have a counter check?

I dont have no checks.

Do you have a paper bag?

Have what?

A poke.

How big of a one did you want? She was rummaging under the counter.

Any size, said Suttree.

She raised up with a bag. Thisn here's the biggest I got.

That's fine. Do you have a pen?

She had a pen.

Suttree wrote out an enormous I O U across the face of the bag and signed his name and turned the bag around so she could read it. She took small rimless eyeglasses from her apron and bent over the bag. Suttree laid the pen down and left.

He kept off the high roads, going by dogpaths through the hobo jungles down along the railroad tracks. A yardman watched him from the baywindow of a caboose, a bitten sandwich upheld in one hand, his jaws moving slowly. He came out by the L&N depot and went up a brickpaved street past the House Hasson warehouse and over a little concrete bridge with plumbingpipe handrails cold and gritty in his palms. Small waters coiling far below about the feet of the viaduct's diamondshaped stanchions. Along a wall of concrete grown with bright green fur. Suttree climbing toward a watered sun.

He crossed under the Western Avenue viaduct and went up Grand Avenue. A dog went before him at its cambered winking trot. He took off his coat and shook it and put it on again. Ionic order much in evidence in these old streets. Weathercracked columns, plaster capitals clogged shapeless with paint. A dead lot strewn with brickbats and blackened timbers. Walkways of weathered marble, of herringbone brick. The walkway at 1504 where each brick read Knoxville Brick Company, long defunct. Suttree passed under the gray magnolia tree and up the steps to the porch of the tall gray house and in.

At night he leaned in the octagonal windowbay and looked out over the switching yards and the warehouses like a child in a pulpit in the dark of an empty church. He could hear singing from the Grand Avenue Mission down the street where revelers caroled perhaps perverse and secret deities behind their plywood windowpanes.

Next evening he took the bus out Magnolia Avenue and stood before the old brick house where he'd gone to school, the untrue glass with black stars stoned through the panes and the wind cutting along in a razory whistle intermittent with the gnashing of weeds in the dark of the lot. He went in by the back door where the cafeteria once had been. The floorboards creaked underfoot, small life scrabbled away. He placed his hand on the newel post and went up the stairs.

Through old classrooms, the dusty clutter of desks. On the blackboards scrawled obscenities. A derelict school for lechers. Suttree had been sitting at his old desk for some time before he noticed the figure standing in the door.

This old bedroom in this old house where he'd been taught a sort of christian witchcraft had two doors and Suttree rose and went out the other one. He descended the front steps and went to the fireplace where he lifted back the iron mask and on one knee reached up the chimney throat and took down a small billikin carved from some soft wood and detailed with a child's crayon.

When he came past the stairway the priest was mounted on the first landing like a piece of statuary. A catatonic shaman who spoke no word at all. Suttree went out the way that he'd come in, crossing the grass toward the lights of the street. When he looked back he could see the shape of the priest in the baywindow watching like a paper priest in a pulpit or a prophet sealed in glass.

In the spring of his third year on the river there were heavy rains. It rained all through the latter part of March and into April and he had set but one line in the rising river and followed it each day with a cold loathing while the rain fell small and gray for miles upon him. It was cold and damp in the shanty and he kept a fire in the little stove through the bleak afternoons and sat at the table by the window with the lamp lit, gazing out at the swollen river coming down from the gutted upcountry and sliding past with a slaverous mutter and seethe.

Bearing along garbage and rafted trash, bottles of suncured glass wherein corollas of mauve and gold lie exploded, orangepeels ambered with age. A dead sow pink and bloated and jars and crates and shapes of wood washed into rigid homologues of viscera and empty oilcans locked in eyes of dishing slime where the spectra wink guiltily.

One day a dead baby. Bloated, pulpy rotted eyes in a bulbous skull and little rags of flesh trailing in the water like tissuepaper.

Oaring his way lightly through the rain among these curiosa he felt little more than yet another artifact leached out of the earth and washed along, draining down out of the city, that cold and grainy shape beyond the rain that no rain could make clean again. Suttree among the leavings like a mote in the floor of a beaker, come summer a bit of matter stunned and drying in the curing mud, the terra damnata of the city's dead alchemy. The fish he raised up from the flood in this season themselves looked stunned.

He stood hard into the oars to come back against the current. Past the bridge risers where small ugly rips broke on the concrete and the boatshaped upstream face rode in a bone of curling froth. Along this clay shoulder where the river gnawed and pulled with her leathery brown waters.

In the fluted gullies where the river backed or eddied spoondrift lay in a coffeecolored foam, a curd that draped the varied flotsam locked and turning there, the driftwood and bottles and floats and the white bellies of dead fish, all wheeling slowly in the river's suck and the river spooling past unpawled with a muted seething freighting seaward her silt and her chattel and her dead.

One morning while he stood on the gallery in the dim early light watching the river he saw an empty skiff go by. Next came looming out of the yellow mist a patchwork shack composed of old slats and tarpaper and tin snuff signs all mounted in wild haphazard upon a derelict barge and turning with the keelless rotations of a drunken bear, going downriver to founder cumbrously against a pier, list and halt, sidle and grope past with the next wall of the shack coming about and along it like plaster caryatids hung there in a stunned frieze above the licking river the figures of four women and two men, pale, rigid, deathless, wheeling slowly away below the bridge and gone in the mist.

Suttree watched the transit of this foggy apparition with no surprise. Two days later when he went downriver he saw the shantyboat pulled up under some willows on the south bank below the sand and gravel company. There was a line of wash hung out and a small skiff swung at tether below the mooring. Some coon hides were tacked flat to the wall, bleached a pale cream color. You'd have thought them to be wares but the hides were dry and all but hairless and seemed forgotten.

Suttree oared past while a group of wide faces watched from a window. When he came back in the afternoon there was a chair on the roof of the shanty and in it a man sleeping. The wash had been taken down and smoke was rising from a stovepipe elbowed through one wall. The skiff was gone.

As Suttree passed beneath the bridge he saw the skiff coming down. A thin young boy was rowing it. Suttree let one oar trail and lifted a hand in greeting. The boy nodded at him, one eye blueblack and swollen closed, and went on.

In the morning he went down early and as he passed the houseboat he saw a young girl come out along the little veranda and turn and squat, her skirts gathered in the crooks of her elbows. Through the fog Suttree was presented with a bony pointed rump. She pissed loudly into the river and rose and went in again.

He was back before noon with his catch. He came up close by the bank and swung around the houseboat. A woman was peering down at him, a stonejawed and apparently gravid slattern resting her belly on the rim of the washtub and regarding him through clotted rags of hair.

Howdy, he said.

She nodded.

I saw you all come down the other mornin. I live cross the river. He rested an oar under his elbow and pointed.

She said uh-hunh.

Suttree smiled. He said: I figured since we were kind of neighbors

I ought to stop and say hidy anyway.

She reached down into the tub and brought something up from the bottom of it. He's asleep, she said.

The mister is?

Yep.

He dipped the oars to stay against the current. You've got a good-sized family, dont you?

She watched down into the tub. How her face must look back from the dead well of blue washwater, rocking and licking in what shapes. We got four, she said. Three girls. She paused and pushed her nose against her arm and snuffled. And a boy, she said.

I believe I saw him the other day.

You aint the one hit him in the eye are ye?

No mam.

Somebody hit him in the eye, she said. With a beadle of soap-softened wood she subdued the grayish rags that stewed in the pot. She lifted something out and wrung it and laid it on a bench.

Where are you all from?

We was from up around Mascot.

I see, he said.

She glanced down at him and went back to her washing. After a minute she said: Looks like you got you some fish there.

Yes mam. You all like catfish?

We eat it some.

I've got plenty here, if you'd like one for your supper.

She looked down into the bottom of the skiff. What would you have to have for one? she said.

He began to sort among the fish. I'll just give you one, he told her.

Well. I'd rather just to pay ye.

Here. He stood in the skiff and handed up a sleek fourpounder.

She took it expertly behind the gills and looked it over. What do I owe ye? she said.

Not anything.

Well, let me pay ye.

I dont want nothin for it.

Well, she said.

I run a trotline on down a ways.

Well.

I got plenty.

Well, I better put him in here.

He sat down and leaned into the oars, watching her go in with the catfish. Before he had pulled more than a few yards upstream she was out again. He thought she had come back to her washing but she called to him across the water. Hey, she said.

Yes mam.

He's awake now if you wanted to see him.

Well, I dont want to bother him.

He said to thank ye for the catfish.

You welcome. Tell him I'll come by in a day or two.

Well, she said. Come back when you can.

The next day there was no one about but the day following the man was in his chair again reading a newspaper. Suttree hailed him as he came alongside and the man folded the paper and squinted down at him.

Hey, he said.

How you getting along?

Right tolerable. You the feller sent that catfish by the other day?

I just had more than I needed.

Well I wanted to thank ye. My old lady fried it up and we et it for supper and sure enjoyed it.

Good, said Suttree.

He turned his head and spoke down a ventilator pipe rising from the roof. Hey old woman, he said.

A muffled snarl came back.

You got any coffee fixed?

He started to turn back to Suttree and his face flickered a small annoyance. He leaned to speak into the pipe again. Fix some, he said. Then he looked down to where Suttree sat in his skiff. Come up, he said, and take some coffee with us.

I dont want to put you out.

Aint no bother. She's got some ready. Just tie up there. Watch them lines. I got me some thowlines out. Just pull in down there on the lower end. Here, thow the rope.

He had climbed down off the roof and was going along the walkway talking and waving the folded paper about. Suttree pulled the skiff in and tossed his rope.

Come on in, said the man as Suttree climbed aboard. He pushed aside a curtain of knotted twine and ushered him in with a grand expansiveness.

As Suttree entered three girls flew to the far wall of the room whinnying like goats and subsided in a simpering heap together on a bed there. Suttree nodded to the woman and she said him a quiet howdy and pointed out a chair. He looked around. There were beds all along the wall and a table in the center of the room with a faded piece of oilcloth and miscellaneous white crockery draped with breakfast remnants.

Set down, the man said. Get ye a chair. Boy wait till you hear what all happened to us.

Suttree could imagine. He glanced again toward the bed and glimpsed a flash of young thighs and dingy drawers. The three of them together were looking at a magazine and stealing crazed looks at him past the edges of it. He sat in one of the low cane chairs and tilted it backward against the bunk behind him and smiled at the man.

Do you know Doren Lockhart?

No.

Well, he's the one I beat out of forty dollars in this here tong game Sunday afternoon. He's supposed to be a big gambler up there. I knowed he was mad. I busted him plumb out. He tried to get up some money to get back in the game but time he done that me and Gene Edmonds had all the money and was gone. Old Gene was with us. Where's that coffee at, woman?

I caint perk it no faster than what it's perkin.

Anyway we'd drunk some whiskey and everthing and I went to bed. What time was it I went to bed?

He waited a minute and then went on.

About ten oclock. Course I always was a sound sleeper.

A flurry of girls' laughter rose and died.

And time I woke up it was getting on towards daylight and we was comin past Island Home. I looked out the winder and seen trees goin by and I said: Lord God, we're plumb adrift. Neighbor, we was. I come up from there and went on out and about that time they was a airplane took off over on the island and I looked downriver and seen Knoxville comin up and knowed where we was at. That son of a bitch had crep up in the night and sawed us loose.

He leaned forward with his hands on his knees and looked at Suttree with a hard eyed squint as if to see which way lay his sympathies. What about that? he said.

Well, said Suttree.

The woman set a cup of coffee in front of him. You use milk and sugar?

No mam, that's fine like it is.

Bring him some of them cakes.

Have you got any way to get back up there? Suttree asked.

Why hell no. It costes to get a tow if you can get somebody to do it even. What do you think about a son of a bitch would do that?

Suttree regarded him over the rim of the cup. He lowered the cup and cradled it in both hands. Well, he said. I guess I'd call him a poor loser at the least.

You daggone right he is, said the man, leaning back.

What do you aim to do?

Lord I dont know. I thought about huntin me a job down here. You dont know where there is one do ye?

I dont know. You might find something. If you go out Blount Avenue here there's a woolen mill and a fertilizer plant. Then there's the sand and gravel company right here. You could ask around.

Well much obliged. I just need to get set up back upriver so as to start in musselin come summer.

The woman set a plate of cookies on the table.

Start what? Suttree said.

The man looked at him. He looked behind him at the woman and toward the girls on the bed. Then he leaned toward Suttree again. Musselin, he said.

Musselin?

Yeah.

Suttree looked at him. What's that? he said.

The man leaned back and crossed his feet in a chair. Mussel brailin, he said. When the river gets down low towards middle and late summer we go up on the shoals of the French Broad and set us up a mussel camp. I've got everthing. I got a boat for it and everthing.

What do you do with them?

Sell they shells. The womenfolk clean em and me and the boy drags for em.

What do they do with them?

The shells?

Yes.

Different things. Make buttons out of em, the biggest part. Some I reckon they grind for chicken grit.

What are they worth?

They fetch round in about forty dollar a ton.

Forty dollars a ton?

That's right.

That doesnt seem like a whole lot.

The man smiled. Them little fellers is heavier than what you might think. Asides they's more money in it than just that.

The woman poured his cup full. The man didnt seem to notice, sitting there waiting for her elbow to move on out of the way. When she had done he leaned forward. They's more to it than just the shells, good buddy. He looked about craftily. More to it than that.

He stayed to dinner. By then the old man had told him about the pearls and even showed him some. Taking from some secret place on his person a small purse tailored from the scrotum of a treefox and setting out the pearls on the oilcloth. Suttree turned one in his hand and held it to the light.

If we had another hand we could run two boats, the old man said.

Can you make any money at it?

The old man turned away in mirthful derision. Money? Shit, boy. Whyyy . . .

Suttree stared at the pearls. The little cabin had filled with a rich steam of cookery. Plates were clattering and the woman and the oldest girl whispered together at the stove.

How would you go shares if you was interested? the old man said.

Suttree looked up. He looked around the cabin. Shares, he said?

They's six of us. Everbody works.

Let her set the table, Reese, the woman said.

Reese raised his elbows. He hadn't taken his eyes off Suttree. Would you go fifths? Not takin out nothin for ye board.

Suttree scooped the pearls into his palm and funneled them back into the purse. His voice sounded far away. I might go fourths, he said.

A soft young breast crossed his nape. The girl leaned and dealt from a tray of old and mismatched silver.

The man took the purse and hefted it in his hand and eyed Suttree. It's hard work, he said.

Suttree nodded.

The old man grinned. Make ye sleep good of a night.

Suttree had started with a question but the old man suddenly flung his hand across the table. Partner, he said. You're on.

When they sat for dinner it was a tight fit and Suttree looking around the table couldnt help smiling. The boy came in with his swollen eye as they were taking seats and he studied Suttree without much interest. The two younger girls didnt know where to look at all.

This had emboldened the oldest one who set her shoulders and flung her hair back and passed Suttree a platter of biscuits. She was extraordinarily well put together with great dark eyes and hair. The head of the house stood to better grapple with the joint of pork before him. The boy was ladling a great load of beans aboard his plate. Suttree buttered one of the buoyant looking soda biscuits and watched the pale slices of pork fall under the knife, the man turning the roast and finally seizing it in his hands, the white knob of bone coming from its socket with a sucking sound and breaking like a great pearl up through the steaming meat.

He forked the greasy slabs of meat onto what plates he could reach and told the woman at the end of the table to pass hers. Suttree ladled thick gravy onto his pork and biscuits and reached for the pepper. Beans were coming downtable and fat sweet potatoes and coffee was being poured around. He gripped his fork in his fist in the best country manner and fell to.

Dont be shy, called the old man. Eat a plenty.

Suttree nodded and waved his fork.

Harrogate saw them going along Blount Avenue Sunday morning. They wore outfits all cut from the same bolt of cloth and in the church pew standing six across they looked like a strip of gaudy wallpaper cut into those linked dolls madfolk pass their time in fashioning. People could not stop looking. The preacher forwent his station at the door when services were over and there was no one to shake the hands of these new and startling parishioners. Small boys had gathered outside to jeer but the emergence of this little group found them unprepared, inert. They filed out in descending order by altitudes, the father first, out through the sunlit doors in a sextet of calico isotropes and into the street, the elder smiling, along through the crowds and down the road toward the river still single file and with deadpan decorum leaving behind a congregation mute and astounded.

He rowed out to visit. Coming about the end of the shantyboat in his welded skiff and singing out at the woman where she sat on the porch shelling beans.

Howdy! he called.

She sprang like a wounded moose and came up against the rail at the far corner of the catwalk with her eyes walled and her fallen bosom heaving beneath the rag of a shirt she wore. He didnt seem to notice, sitting there with his impassive smile in the center of his suicidal boat with the FORD in chrome letter across the bow and the homemade paddle laid dripping across his knees. Right purty day, aint it? he said.

Lord God, she said, I knowed the law had me. Dont you never come up on me thataway, you hear?

Yes mam, he said, his face a flower in the warm sunshine.

She looked down at him. He just sat there smiling. She took her seat on the box she'd vacated and fell to shelling beans again.

I live crost the river yonder, he said. I seen ye'ns at church Sunday.

She nodded.

Thought I'd come on down and say hidy.

She looked at him with her caved eyes.

So, he said, toying with the paddle. So hidy.

Hidy, she said.

Where's the rest of the family at today?

Gone on over in town.

Left ye by your lonesome huh?

She didnt answer.

He looked about and he eyed the sun's progress. Looks like it's goin to be another warm'n, I'd say.

Perhaps she didnt hear.

Wouldnt you? he said.

She looked down at him. Flushed, her lank hair matted about her sweating face. I reckon, she said.

That's the biggest thing about this here boat. It gets hot as a two-peckered . . . it gets hot as anything. And it settin in the water where you'd allow it'd cool.

Yes, she said.

I like to of drownded in it once.

Uh huh.

It wont float atall.

He took a dip with his paddle to recover the current.

What time you reckon they'll get back?

I dont know.

Does that boy go to school?

He does sometime. He aint now.

I just despise a school. What kind of hides is them?

Coon hides. Or they was.

Harrogate leaned and spat into the river and raised up again. How old's that boy of yourn anyway?

She looked at him. She looked at the contraption in which he sat. She said: He aint old enough to ride in that.

What, this here? Shoot. Why you couldnt sink it with dynamite.

She tilted a paper of shucked beanpods overboard. Harrogate watched them drift away.

Old Suttree's a friend of mine. You know him dont ye?

No.

He et with ye'ns here the other evenin. Runs trotlines. He said he knowed ye.

She nodded her head and tilted the beans in the pan and rose and dumped the debris from the folds of her skirt.

He's a friend of mine, Harrogate said.

She bent and picked up the pan of shelled beans and tossed her hair back from her face.

He's rid in it, said Harrogate. In this here boat. Suttree has.

They were walking along the tracks with the city rat at Suttree's off elbow taking legstretcher steps over every other tie, his hands crammed in his hippockets gripping each a skinny buttock. He watched the ground and shook his head.

What do you say to em?

Say to them?

Yeah. Say.

Hell, say anything. It doesnt matter, they dont listen.

Well you gotta say somethin. What do you say?

Try the direct approach.

What's that?

Well, like this friend of mine. Went up to this girl and said I sure would like to have a little pussy.

No shit? What'd she say?

She said I would too. Mine's as big as your hat.

Aw shit, Sut. Come on, what do you say to em? Boy she's got a big old set of ninnies on her.

Yes she has. You dont think she's too old for you?

She's same age I am.

Well.

How do you get em to take off their clothes. That's what I'd by god like to know.

You take them off.

Yeah? Well what does she do while you're doin that? I mean hell, does she just look out the winder or somethin? I dont understand it at all Sut. The whole thing seems uneasy to me.

They swung off the right of way and went along a dogpath, Suttree grinning. Tell her she sure has got a big old set of ninnies on her, he said.

Shit, said Harrogate. She's liable to smack the fire out of me.

It was midsummer before they went back up the river. They left the crazylooking shanty in Knoxville and went by bus with their bedding and housegoods baled up. Suttree saw them off with promises he'd long regretted.

A week later he got a tow to the forks of the river and began rowing up the French Broad. After nine hours at the oars he pulled into the bank and crawled out with his blanket and slept like a dead man. He had reason to think of the old Bildad up on the Clinch who used to flood his skiff and sleep under water in it to keep the insects off.

When he woke in the smoky dawn he felt alien and tainted, camped there in a wilderness with his little stained boat and his weariness. As if the city had marked him. So that no eldritch daemon would speak him secrets in this wood. He ate two of the sandwiches he'd packed and drank a grape drink, sitting there on the bank and watching a wood duck that floated on the river like a painted decoy block mitered to its double on the pewter calm.

He rowed on upriver until he came to the landing at Boyd's Creek. His hands were puffy and clawed and he wished the skiff at the bottom of the river. He went into the store and drank two cold drinks and got a third one to sip on. Coming back out into the glaring sunlight he saw a thermometer hung in a tin coughsyrup sign on the storefront. The red line in the glass ran from bottom to top and out of sight. He eyed it with baleful bloodfilled eyes and turned and spat a grape-stained clot of mucus at the cooking world. Not even a fly moved.

It was early afternoon when he came upon them. He passed a huge and stinking windrow of shells on the south bank and struggled upstream through faster water, towing the boat up shoals with a rope over his shoulder, clutching and fending among the shore bracken, the water very cold and clear. They were camped like gypsies under a slate bluff and smoke rose among the trees. The skiff at the bank bore a strange rigging of uprights and crosspoles and a travis bar with lines and hooks hanging from it. The boy squatted on a stump watching him. The womenfolk were boiling wash in a big galvanized tub and the old man was asleep under a tree. When she saw Suttree tying up, the woman called Reese, Reese. Two dry flat birdnotes he'd heard all his life. He didnt move.

Suttree came on up the bank. Howdy, he said.

They all nodded. They were shrouded in steam and they looked limp and half fainting. The old woman's long white goat's udders hung half out above the tub and the flesh of her upper arms swung as she wound the water from a pair of jeans. The girl gave him a sort of defeated smile.

Daddy, she called.

Reese opened one eye tentatively from beneath his tree. Yonder's my partner, he sang out.

Hey, said Suttree.

Come set down. Boy we really into em up here. Looky yonder.

Suttree looked. A black slagheap of riven shellfish lay along the riverbank exuding a greenish vapor and quaking gently with flies.

And looky here.

The musselfisher lifted out the little foxcod purse and tilted into his palm a single pearl.

Suttree picked it up and looked at it. It looked a bit lumpy.

What's it worth? he said.

Caint tell. They's lots they go by. He took it and rolled it in his palm and dropped it back into the purse. They aint no tellin what it might be worth, he said.

How many have you found?

Well. That's the only really good'n. I got some others.

Suttree stared bleakly at the levee of shells.

We'll really get into em now though, what with two boats and all.

Suttree turned and looked down at the old man. He was squatting on his heels, having risen that far by way of greeting. Smiling. Optimistic. A pale and bloated tick hung in his scalp like a pendulous wen.

We got to get your boat rigged. I done hunted up some poles and stuff.

Have you got a hammer and nails?

I got some nails comin out of them boards yonder quick as I burn em. We'll get some more. They's plenty of old boards got nails in em.

Suttree was kneading his bloated palms. How do you aim to drive the nails, he said.

Just knock em in with a rock.

Suttree looked at the river. If you just get in your boat you can stretch out and sleep and barring snags wake up sometime back in Knoxville like you'd never been away.

I guess we'll manage, he said.

Why hell yes, said the old man.

Suttree wandered off to the skiff to get his blankets and gear. He took the two cans of beer he had stowed under the rear seat and tied them to a string and lowered them over the side.

The family had put up a rude lean-to against the wall of the bluff. Old roofing tin and random boards and a plywood highway sign that said Slow Construction Ahead. It all looked like it had washed up there in high water. Under the overhang of the bluff were thin home-sewn ticks and quilts and army blankets. Suttree didnt think it would rain anytime soon so he went on down past the camp with his gear to a little knoll that overlooked the river and where there were some small pines and a wind to stand the insects off. He fixed a smooth place on the ground and fluffed up the pineneedles and spread a blanket and sat down. He lay back and stretched out. The river chattered back a querulous babbling from the limestone shoals below the camp. The trees fell and fell down the lightly clouded summer sky.

Reese woke him kicking his foot. Hey, he said.

Suttree rolled over and shaded his eyes.

What you doin?

I was sleeping.

The old man squatted and eyed the river through the trees. We might's well get your boat rigged this afternoon, he said.

Suttree rose heavily. He was hot and sweaty and worn out.

You aim to bed down out here?

If it doesnt rain.

You can sleep up in the camp with us.

I snore, Suttree said.

The old man stood up. Snore? he said. Hell fire, son, you aint never heard a snore. I'll put my old lady up against any three humans or one moose.

Suttree went on up the bank.

He studied the brail rig in the old man's skiff and went into the woods to cast about for suitable saplings to make the uprights. He'd set the boy to straightening nails, beating them out with a rock. The old man had wandered off somewhere.

He sat in the stern of his skiff and trimmed the poles he'd cut, dressing the forks, shaving the lower ends flat to be nailed to the sides of the skiff. The white waxy woodpeelings coiled up cleanly under his knife and he watched them spin and drift on the river. With the point of the knife he bored holes partway through the flats on the butt end so that the wood would not split when it was nailed. The old man had come down the bank and was sitting on his heels nodding at Suttree's work and making encouraging talk. He always expected everyone to be out of heart.

By evening they had the skiff rigged with a ramshackle and barbarous facsimile of a brailboat's gear. Suttree carried the brails aboard and stowed them in the trees of the uprights and Reese eyed the sun.

You want to make a run this evening?

I dont think so.

You and the boy might make just a short run and see how she does.

Suttree stood up in the skiff and stepped ashore. And we might not, he said.

Well. We can get an early start of the mornin.

Suttree didnt answer. He went on toward the camp where smoke was rising from the supper fire.

Hidy, said the girl with studied boldness.

Hey, said Suttree. She was white with flour to her elbows, bent above a breadboard kneading biscuit dough. The two smaller girls were standing behind her and the old woman was at the fire. One of the girls poked her head around and said something and the older girl slapped at her and they fled shrieking with giggles.

Oh you all . . . Mama, make her quit.

You all quit, said the woman. She was stoking the fire and fixing the sheet of tin laid over the rocks. Flames licked from under the edges. There was a kettle and an iron pot on the tin and it sagged badly under the weight.

Is there any coffee? Suttree said.

Is there any coffee Mama?

You know there aint no coffee.

I dont guess there is none, said the girl.

What time do we eat?

In about a hour. It wont be long.

Suttree scratched his jaw and looked about. There was an old mattress in the lean-to and a packingcrate with an oil lamp on it and a miscellany of junk stored along the dark stone wall at the rear. He went down to the river again and stretched out on a cool rock in the shade and looked down into the water. On the rippled silt floor of the eddy a small turtle shifted with uncertain bowlegs. Small bits of wood, twigs, lay furred with silt and a muddog lay inert with its obscene gills branching like bright fungus. Suttree's face shifted and dished. A waterspider crossed on jointed horsehair legs and the river gave off a cool metallic smell. He spat at his trembling visage and sat up and took off his shoes and socks and lowered his feet into the water.

They ate on what looked like an outhouse door. A weathered wooden trestle propped on poles. Suttree was afraid to lean on it. They sat on planks and cinderblocks, the smallest girl's chin just clearing the boards. Suttree was lightheaded with hunger.

The iron pot came aboard and the kettle and pan of biscuits. In the kettle were some rough and hairy greens he'd never met before. In the pot whitebeans. He stirred them but no trace of fat meat turned up. He eyed the boy across the board and began to eat faster.

After supper they sat around the fire while the girls washed the dishes. The old man brought a soft and greasy leather bible from the lean-to and opened it on his knees. When the dishes were done the girls gathered around and the old man commenced to read aloud from the text. Suttree had gone to the river and fetched the two cans of beer. He opened them at the table and carried them to the fire and handed one to the old man. His eyes brightened in the firelight when he saw it. Lord have mercy looky here, he said.

Suttree gestured with his can and drank. The beer was cold and slightly bitter and very good. The old man tilted his beer to drink.

Dont you read scripture and drink that, the woman said.

What?

You heard me. Dont you read scripture and drink that.

Why hell fire, said Reese.

Nor cuss neither. You put that up or finish that beer one.

He looked around to see if anyone might be on his side. Suttree went off down to his little knoll above the river.

They went to sleep like dogs, curling up in their bedding on the ground until they were a scattering of dark shapeless mounds beneath the bluff. The fire had died. Suttree shucked off shoes and trousers and lay in his blanket. The river talked all night in the shoals. Some dogs in the anonymous distance beyond set up a clamor but they were far away and their barking muted by the river fell lost and dreamlike on his ears.

In the morning they were about and breakfasting almost with the first light. Thin cakes of fried cornmeal with sugar syrup. There was still no coffee.

The old man took the girl and went upriver and left Suttree and the boy to themselves. Suttree bailed the boat and stowed the can back under the seat and looked out downstream. A thousand smokes stood on the gray face of the river. After a while the boy emerged from the woods buttoning his trousers and came down the bank and climbed into the skiff.

You ready? he said.

Suttree looked at him. He was sitting in the bow of the skiff with his hands on his knees.

How about casting off for us.

Do what?

How about untying us.

He climbed out and got the rope loose from the stump and threw it into the skiff and knelt in the bow and shoved them off. Suttree let the oars into the river.

The skiff nosed downstream through pales of vapor. A small heron rose clacking from the reeds. The boy swung on it with an imaginary gun. Blam, he said.

I saw ducks on the river coming up, Suttree said.

Boy I bet if I had me a gun I'd kill everthing up here.

He was watching downriver, picking absently at one of the yellow pustules with which his chin was afflicted. After a while he said: What was you in the workhouse for?

Suttree leaned on the oars and looked behind him. They were in faster water and there were little weedy islands in the middle of the river. I was with some guys got caught breaking into a drugstore.

What did you break in for?

They were trying to get some drugs. Pills. They got some cigarettes and stuff. I was outside in the car.

I guess you was keepin the motor runnin and lookout and all.

I was drunk.

The boy looked at him but Suttree had turned to study the water. Across the river a tractor was plowing in the black and fallow bottoms and over the plowed land rim to rim lay a serpentine of mist the course and shape of the river itself like a ghost river there. The sun was a long time coming. In the graygreen light the midsummer corn moved with the first wind and the countryside had a sad and desolate look to it.

Did you go to college? the boy said.

Why?

I just wondered. Gene says you're real smart.

Who, Harrogate?

Yeah.

Well. Some people are smarter than others.

You mean Gene aint real smart?

No. He's plenty smart. You have to be smart to know who's smart and who's not.

I never figured you to be just extra smart.

There you are, said Suttree.

He looked puzzled. Old Gene used to come sniffin around after Wanda, he said. Mama run him off. You got a girl?

No. I used to have one but I forgot where I laid her.

The boy looked at him dully for a minute and then slapped his knee and guffawed. Boy, he said, that's a good'n.

How far down do we go?

We'll run the Gallops first and then go on down to the Wild Bull Shoals.

The Gallops?

That's the next shoals down. Taint far. You say you aint never musseled afore?

No.

Taint nothin to it. Yonder goes a mushrat.

Suttree turned. A dark little shape forded the dawn, a black nose in a wedge of riverwater.

Quick as furs primes I'm goin to be back up here with me some traps.

Suttree nodded, pulling along easily, the oarlocks creaking and the lines of the brail swinging behind the boy's head like a bead curtain. The sun came up. It bored up out of the trees in a greengold light and Suttree's silhouette lay long and narrow down the river among the brail line shadows like a rowing marionette.

He swung the skiff more shoreward. The boy was bent peering down into the water. In the clear shallows suckers trailed by their whiterimmed mouths from the rocks like soft pennants fluttering.

The boy took an empty rubber flashlight from his hippocket and dipping the lens in the river looked down through the gutted barrel at the piscean world below.

Do you see any mussels? Suttree said.

We aint into em yet, the boy said. They godamighty what a catfish. How deep is it?

Yonder goes a old mudturkle.

Suttree leaned on the oars. How about letting me look, he said.

The boy lifted his head.

I said how about letting me look.

Well. Sure.

Suttree shipped the oars and took the tube from the boy and bent over the side with it. A high sheer rock veered past wrapped in bubbles. Moted panels spun down deeps of dusky jade where dim shoals of fish willowed and flared and drifted back over the cold slate floor of the river. A braided cable among the rocks trailed rags of soft green slime in the current.

I dont see any mussels, he said.

The boy looked out downriver. Keep a lookin, he said. They'll be some directly.

He bent again. A whole tree lay on the bottom of the river, deep in a pool, a murky bole with filaments of moss swaying and a heavy black bass that waited on below. A sandy floor sloped away. Fat suckers sculled. A cloud of bubbles rolled up in the glass and cleared and a green cold slick faired over paler rocks, round river stones and ledges of slate gently sculpted. A seam of black shellfish lay beneath.

Here come some.

He heard the splash of the brail going overboard. The boat rocked and recovered with the boy's standing and Suttree's face dipped in the water. He raised his head and shook the water from the glass and bent to look again. Long greenbrown weeds swung in the current and dimly through the moving water he could see the mussel beds, a slender colony of them dark and quaking among the rocks with their pale clefts breathing, closing, folding slowly fanwise, valved clots of flesh in their keeps of cotyloid nacre. The shadow of the skiff like a nightshade passing swept them shut.

Is they lots?

A few.

The bottom fell away into an opaque green murk. The boat spun slowly.

Suttree raised up and took the oars and straightened the skiff out.

It deeps off here, the boy said.

Yeah.

We'll just go on down.

Okay.

How about lettin me have my looker?

Okay.

They ran downstream a quarter mile, the boy watching the bottom, Suttree at the oars. They swung into a long ropy glide and went rocking down a chute into fast water. The boy raised his head, his forelock dripping. We'll get em now, he called.

Suttree steadied the boat with the oars.

When they drifted out into the slow water at the foot of their run amid flotsam and tranquil spume the boy stood at the transom and hauled the brail aboard and hung it dripping in the uprights with a couple dozen black mussels clamped to the lines. They swung and turned and clacked and the boy took out an enormous brass cookspoon and began to pry them loose. Within minutes they lay like stones in the floor of the skiff and the boy had cast the brail overboard again. He turned to Suttree who was backoaring to stand in the current. His face was flushed and his breath short. That's how we do it, he wheezed.

Is that a pretty good batch for a run?

It aint no more'n average. I've seen em to come up solid with em. Me and Daddy has dredged messes we couldnt lift.

What's the other brail for?

You swap off. You hang up the full brail and thow out the othern.

Well why didnt you throw out the other one?

The boy was watching the river bottom again. He waved one hand in the air to dismiss the subject. I just wanted to show you how to strip the lines, he said.

Suttree edged the boat away from a dimpled suck in the river and they went rocking down the shoals, the sun well up now, the day warming. His hands were like claws on the oars.

They washed out in a slackwater where a gravel bar ran almost to midriver and the boy raised up the brail again and hung it dripping and clicking with mussels in the trees. He and Suttree looked at each other.

These is some jimdandy'ns, the boy said.

Suttree nodded. There were some big as your hand.

Let's swing up and run that bed one more time.

Suttree looked upriver dubiously.

You wont find em much better'n these here.

He swung the skiff and braced his feet and dug into the river. They went up along the inside shore. When they had gained the head of the glide he stood the boat in the current and swung back obliquely across the run while the boy cast over the empty brail.

I thowed one one time a hook got me behind the ear and like to took me with it.

How far down do we go? said Suttree.

You mean this evenin?

Yes.

We'll go on down to the Wild Bull. What Daddy said.

Who the hell is going to row back?

The boy squinted at him there in the sunshine, the spoon poised over the mussel in his hand, the mussels in the skiff floor drying in the sun to a gray slate color. You aint give out are ye? he said.

I've been rowing this damned thing for two days. What do you think?

Well shit, I'll swap off with ye comin back. It aint all that far.

They reached the shoals in the early afternoon. The boy boated the last rackful of mussels and shucked them from the hooks wet and clattering onto the pile in the boat and Suttree stood on one oar to turn them toward the bank. The boat would hardly move it lay so deep in the river with its cargo.

There was but one shovel and it had an old handmade tang about a foot long but no handle other at all. Suttree set the boy to shoveling the mussels out of the boat onto the bank and he himself went up through the woods until he found a good shade tree and he lay flat on his back beneath it and was soon asleep.

He was awakened by cries down toward the river. It occurred to Suttree that he and the boy didnt even know each other's names. He got up and went down through the woods.

Hey, called the boy.

All right, all right.

Hell fire, where'd you get to? I aint shovelin all these here by myself.

Suttree took the shovel from him and stepped into the boat.

I thought you'd run plumb off, the boy said.

My name's Suttree.

Yeah, I know it.

What's yours?

Willard.

Willard. Okay Willard.

Okay what?

Suttree heaved a shovelful of mussels up and looked at the boy. It was hot in the sun. The boy standing there in his rancid overalls looked pale and pitiful and slightly malevolent. Just okay, Willard, he said.

They rowed into camp at dusk sitting side by side on the seat of the skiff each with a sweep in two hands. Suttree staggered up the bank with the rope and tied up and went to the fire and sat and stared into it. Reese emerged from the lean-to in his underwear. Is that you all? he said.

Yeah.

Where you been?

Suttree didnt answer. The boy had come up and was looking around. Where you all been? the man asked him.

Where's everbody at? the boy said.

They've done gone to a social. Where you all been?

Is there anything to eat? Suttree said.

They's some whitebeans and cornbread in the pan.

Is they any onions? the boy said.

No they aint, said Reese. He came over to where Suttree was sitting on a board with his feet stretched out before him. Did you all do any good? he said.

Ask him, said Suttree.

How did you all do?

We done all right. Aint they no milk?

No they aint.

Shit, said the boy.

What?

I said shoot.

You better of.

Did ye'ns get a pretty good mess?

We got about all the boat would hold. How did you all do?

We done all right.

Suttree had taken up a plate and was spooning beans from the pot. Is there any coffee? he said.

No they aint.

He stared sullenly into the fire. No they aint, he said.

He was lying in his blankets out on the knoll when they came back. They came down through the woods by the river swinging a lantern and singing hymns. He lay there listening to this advancing minstrelsy and watching the moon ride up out of the trees. He was hungry and his shoulders ached. His eyelids felt like they were on springs, he couldnt get them to stay shut. After a while he got up.

One of the girls was going toward the river and he called to her. Hey, he said. Is there anything to eat up there?

It was quiet for a minute. The fire had been built back and the flames looked hopeful up there under the rocks. No they aint, she said.

In the morning they were up at some misty hour and were at donning the crazy calico churchclothes. They did not wake him. He raised the edge of his blanket and peered out. Among the slats of the lamplit shed he could see thin flashes of white flesh, birdlike flurryings. The girls emerged in their carboncopy dresses and the boy came out of the woods stiffly and looking churlish and sullen and strange, like a child pervert. They set off upriver through the woods and Suttree sat up in his blanket to better view the spectacle.

They were gone all day. He stirred out and searched through the kitchen things and through the jumble of stuff in the lean-to but he could find nothing to eat other than the cornmeal and a handful of whitebeans that had been left to soak. He made a fire and put the beans on and went off down to the river to look at the skiffs. He squatted on his heels and threw small stones at waterspiders skating on the dimpled river.

In the afternoon he sat in the cool under the bluff. Summer thunderheads were advancing from the south. He leaned back against the rock escarpment. Jagged blades of slate and ratchel stood like stone tools in the loam. Tracks of mice or ground squirrels, a few dry and meatless nuthulls. A dark stone disc. He reached and picked it up. In his hand a carven gorget. He spooned the clay from the face of it with his thumb and read two rampant gods addorsed with painted eyes and helmets plumed, their spangled anklets raised in dance. They bore birdheaded scepters each aloft.

Suttree spat upon the disc and wiped it on the hip of his jeans and studied it again. Uncanny token of a vanished race. For a cold moment the spirit of an older order moved in the rainy air. With a small twig he cleaned each line and groove and with spittle and the tail of his shirt he polished the stone, holding it, a cool lens, in the cup of his tongue, drying it with care. A gray and alien stone of a kind he'd never seen.

He took off his belt and with his pocketknife cut a long thin strip of leather and threaded it through the hole in the gorget and tied the thong and put it around his neck. It lay cool and smooth against his chest, this artifact of dawn where twilight drew across the iron landscape.

He was sitting on a log carving a whistle from willow wood when the family returned from service. He watched them come down through the woods, the six of them indianfile. When they had passed and gone on to the camp he rose and folded away his knife and went after.

Yonder he comes, sang out Reese.

Yeah, said Suttree.

We seen ye was asleep when we left out of here this mornin. Didnt want to bother ye.

The women were gone to the shed to change out of their clothes and Reese had taken a seat under his tree in his suit. Suttree squatted on one knee in front of him and pinned him with a hungry stare.

Look, he said, I dont want to be a bother to anybody but when the hell do we eat around here?

I'm glad you ast me that, said Reese. Somebody has got to go to the store and I was wonderin if you could maybe take the boy and run on over there.

You all just came from over there.

Yes we did. But I'll be danged if I didnt get over there and come to find out I didnt have no money on me. I thought of it quick as we got up to the church there. I'd meant to . . .

All right, said Suttree. He was holding out his hand. Let me have some money.

Reese eased himself up a little bit and leaned forward from the tree. He spoke in a low voice. I wanted to talk to you about that, he said.

Suttree stared at him a minute and then rose and stood looking off toward some brighter landscape beyond them all. Listen, Reese was saying. He tugged at Suttree's trouserleg. Suttree took a step away.

Listen. What it is, we've had so much expense settin up camp and gettin everthing ready, you know. We been up here two weeks now and aint had nothin but outgoes, bound to be a little short, and you a partner, regular partner you know, I thought we could share expense a little until we sold us a load and I could settle with ye. You know.

What the hell would you of done if I hadnt come up here when I did?

Why, somethin would of turned up. Always does. Listen . . .

Suttree had turned out his pockets and was putting together what money he had. A couple of dollars and some change. He dropped it on the ground in front of Reese. How long do you reckon we can eat on that? he said.

We can get something. He looked at the crumpled money lying there. He poked at it, as if it were something dead. It aint a whole lot, is it? he said.

No, said Suttree. It sure as hell aint.

That all you got? Reese squinting up at Suttree.

That's it.

He scratched his head. Well, he said. Listen . . .

I'm listening.

Why dont you and the boy go on over there and get us some bread and some lunchmeat. They's cornmeal and some beans here. Ast the old lady what all she needs real bad. Get a quart of milk if you can. You know.

Suttree stalked off to find the boy.

I just come from there, the boy said.

Well get your ass up cause you're going again.

They aint no need to cuss about it, the boy said. It Sunday and all.

They went off up the path through the woods. She'd written him a list, a pinched scrawl on a piece of paper sack. He balled it in his fist and pitched it into the weeds.

They went through the woods for a half mile and came out onto an old macadam road half grown back in patches of grass, small saplings. They followed it with its tilted slabs of paving through a countryside warped and bleared in the steamy heat. They passed the ruins of an old motel, a broken paintworn sign, a clutch of tiny cabins quietly corroding in an arbor of pines. When they came out onto the highway Suttree could see the little crossroads community at the top of the rise. A handful of houses and a stuccoed roadside grocery store with a gaspump.

He crossed the graveled forebay and entered the store. Old familiar smells. He got a pint of chocolate milk from the cooler and drank it.

You goin to set us up to a dope? the boy said.

Get one.

Let's get us a couple of cakes too and we wont say nothin about it.

Suttree looked at him. He was rummaging among the bottles in the drink case. These here R C's cold? he called out. Suttree went on to the meatcounter.

What for ye? said the storekeeper, appearing behind the case and taking down an apron from a nail.

Slice me a couple of pounds of that baloney, said Suttree.

He hung the apron back.

Slice it thin, said Suttree.

He got some cheese and some bread and a drum of oatmeal and two quarts of milk and some onions. When the merchant had totted up these purchases there was forty cents left. Suttree looked at the rows of coffee in their bags above the merchant's head. The merchant turned to look with him.

What's the cheapest coffee you've got?

Well, let's see. The cheapest I got is the Slim Jim.

Slim Jim?

Slim Jim.

How much is it?

Thirty-nine cents.

Let me have it.

The merchant lifted down a bag of it from the shelf and set it on the counter. It was dusty and he blew on it and gave it a little swat before he lifted it into the grocery bag.

Right, said Suttree. He scooped the bag off the counter and handed it to the boy and they left.

It was evening when they got back. Suttree went down and sat in the dark by the river until supper was ready, the light of the cookfire composing behind him on the high bluff a shadowshow of primitive life. He pitched small round pebbles at the river as if he were feeding it.

They ate sandwiches of fried baloney and bowls of whitebeans. Suttree came to the fire with his cup and held it out. The old woman lifted the potlid and sniffed. Suttree watched her. The plaited hawsers of hair that bound her thin gray skull. She took up her apron in one hand to grip the pot and tilt the hot black coffee out. Suttree went back to the box where he'd been sitting and stirred the coffee and put the spoon in his cuff for safekeeping and lifted the cup and sipped.

He sat very still, then he turned and spat the coffee on the ground. Good God, he said.

What is it? said Reese.

What's happened to this coffee?

I aint drunk none of it.

Suttree swung his nose across the rim of the cup and then pitched the coffee out on the ground and went on eating.

Reese wiped his mouth on his knee and rose. He came back with a cup of the coffee and stood over Suttree blowing at it and then he took a sip.

What is this shit? he said.

Damned if I know. Slim Jim, that's the name of it.

Reese took another sip and then tipped it out on the ground. I dont know what it is, he said. But it aint coffee.

The girl was sitting on the far side of the fire. She flung her black hair. What'd you do to the coffee, Mama? she called.

Reese had gone back to the fire. They had the package up trying to read it. Reese poured the coffee out on the ground. A squabble ensued.

Suttree what is this shit?

I dont know. I bought it for coffee.

It dont even smell like coffee.

They done emptied the coffee out and filled the sack back with old leaves or somethin, said the woman, nodding her head and looking about.

Bring me a cup of it, Willard, the girl called.

Reese cut his eyes about. It might be poison, he said.

Put eggshells in it, Mama, the girl called. That'll rectify it.

Where's she goin to get eggshells at, dumb-ass? They aint no eggs.

The woman reached and swatted the boy in the top of the head with her hand.

Ow, he said.

You mind how you talk to your sister.

Something woke him in the small hours of the morning. Things moving in the dark. He took his flashlight and trained it out along the trees until it ghosted away in the dark fields downriver. He swept it toward the woods and back again. A dozen hot eyes watched, paired and random in the night. He held the light above his head to try and see the shapes beyond but nothing showed save eyes. Blinking on and off, or eclipsing and reappearing as heads were turned. They were none the same height and he tried his memory for anything that came in such random sizes. Then a pair of eyes ascended vertically some five feet and another pair sank slowly to the ground. Weird dwarfs with amaurotic eyeballs out there in the dark on a seesaw sidesaddle. Others began to raise and lower.

Cows. He agreed with himself: It is cows. He switched off the flashlight and lay back. He could smell them now on the cool upriver wind, sweet odor of grass and milk. The damp air was weighted with all manner of fragrance. You can see it in a dog's eyes that he is sorting such things as he tests the wind and Suttree could smell the water in the river and the dew in the grass and the wet shale of the bluff. It was overcast and there were no stars to plague him with their mysteries of space and time. He closed his eyes.

In the morning they took the womenfolk downriver to shuck the mussels there, the girls giggling, the old woman clutching the sides of the boat nervously and staring with her hooded eyes toward the passing shore. That evening after supper he went down to the river with a bar of soap and sat naked in the water off the gravel bar. He washed his clothes and he washed himself and he hung his clothes from a tree and got his towel and dried himself and sat among his blankets. After a while Reese came down through the woods on tiptoe, calling out softly.

Over here, said Suttree.

He crouched in front of Suttree. He looked back over his shoulder toward the camp.

What is it? said Suttree.

We got to go to town.

Okay.

I figure we ought to just go on in the mornin and get done with it.

Suttree nodded.

I started to let Mama and Wanda go, but you caint depend on no women to do business. What do you think?

It suits the hell out of me.

Reese looked toward the fire and looked back. It suits the hell out of me too, he hissed. If I dont get shitfaced drunk they aint a cow in Texas. You ever been to Newport?

Not lately.

Lord they got the wildest little old things runnin around up there. It's a sight in the world.

They have?

You daggone right. The old man checked the camp again and leaned to Suttree's ear. We go up there, Sut, we'll run a pair or two down and put the dick to em. He winked hugely and set one finger to his lips.

They left in the early morning two days later. It had rained all night and the cars came down the long black road like motorboats and passed and diminished in shrouds of vapor. After a while an old man stopped in a model A and they rode on into Dandridge. The old man did not speak. The three of them hunched up like puppets on the front seat watched the summer morning break over the rolling countryside.

They got a ride from Dandridge to Newport on a truck. There was a tractor on the truckbed and it kept shifting in its chains so that the travelers stood back against the stakesides with their hair blowing in the wind lest the thing break loose. They reached Newport around noon and descended blinking and disheveled into the hot street.

The jeweler was sitting in a wire cage at the front of the store and he had what looked like a snuff jar screwed into his eye. The two of them stood there at the window and waited. Yes, the jeweler said. He didnt look up.

Reese laid a pearl on the counter.

The jeweler raised his head and sniffed and took the glass from his eye and donned a pair of spectacles. He reached and picked up the pearl. He rolled it between his thumb and forefinger and looked at it and put it back. He took off his spectacles and put the glass back in his eyes and bent to his work again. I cant use it, he said.

Reese gave Suttree an uneasy wink. He delved up another jewel from his little changepurse and laid it by the first. Larger and more round. Hey, he said.

The jeweler set aside a small pick with which he was sorting something in a boxlid. He looked at the two pearls before him and he looked at Reese. I cant use it.

Reese had fished out meantime his best pearl and this he brought forth and held out in one grimy hand. I guess you cant use this one either, he said in triumph.

The jeweler removed the glass and fitted the spectacles again. He didnt reach for the pearl. He seemed to simply want a better look at these two.

Go ahead, said Reese, grinning and gesturing with the pearl.

Fellers, said the jeweler, those things are not worth anything.

They're pearls, Suttree said.

Tennessee pearls.

Hell, they've got to be worth something.

Well, I hate to say it, but they're not worth a nickel. Oh, you might find somebody that wanted them. Keepsake or something. I've known people to pay three or four dollars for a really nice one that they wanted made into a pin or something, but you might have a shoebox full and I wouldnt give a dime for them.

Reese was still holding out the pearl. He turned to Suttree. He thinks we aint never traded afore, I reckon.

The jeweler had taken off his spectacles and was preparing to look through his glass again.

We may look country, but we aint ignorant, Reese told him.

Let's go, Reese.

You aint never seen no nicer a one than that there.

The jeweler bent with his monocle to his work again.

Suttree took the old man's arm and steered him out the door. Reese was looking over the prize pearl for some undetected flaw. In the street Suttree turned him around and got him by the shoulder. What the hell is going on? I thought you said that big pearl was worth ten dollars?

Shit Sut, dont pay no attention to him, he dont know the first thing about it.

Suttree pointed toward the windowglass. He's a goddamned jeweler. Cant you see the sign? What the hell do you mean he doesnt know?

He's just outslicked hisself is what he's done. He wants us to give him the goddamned pearls. I've traded with these cute sons of bitches afore, Sut. I know.

Let me see those things.

Reese handed him the pearls. Suttree looked them over in the hard light of midday. They looked like pearls. Somewhat gray, somewhat misshapen. Hell, they must be worth something, he said.

Reese took the pearls from him. Course they are, he said. Goddamn, you think I dont know nothin?

How many have you ever sold?

That's all right how many I sold. I sold some.

How many?

Well. I sold one last year for four dollars.

Who to?

Just to somebody.

Suttree was standing looking at the ground and shaking his head. After a while he looked up. Well let's try somewhere else, he said.

They canvassed the three jewelers and two pawnshops and were again on the street. Shadows were tilting on the walk, the day'd grown cooler.

What now? said Suttree.

Let me think a minute, said Reese.

That's all we need.

We aint tried the poolhall.

The poolhall?

Yeah.

Suttree turned and walked away down the street. Reese caught him up and was at his elbow with plans and explanations.

Suttree turned. How much money do you have on you?

He stopped.

Come on. How much?

Why Sut, you know I aint got no money.

Not a dime?

Why no.

Well I've got fifteen cents and I'm going over here and have coffee and doughnuts. You can sit and watch if you like. Then we'd better get on the goddamned road before it gets dark and try and get a ride out of here.

Hell Sut, we caint go back emptyhanded.

But Suttree had already stepped into the street. Reese watched him cross and enter the cafe on the other side.

Suttree borrowed a paper from a stack by the till as he went in and he sat at the counter. A fat man asked him what he would have.

Coffee.

He wrote on the ticket.

Do you have any doughnuts?

Plain or chocolate.

Chocolate.

He wrote that. Suttree craned his neck to see the price.

The fat man went down the counter and Suttree opened his paper.

He drank three cups of coffee and read the paper from front to back. Finally he folded the paper and went to the front and paid his bill and put the paper back and went out. He stood in the street picking his teeth and looking up and down. He waited around for the better part of an hour. The stores were closing. He eyed the failing sun. That son of a bitch, he said.

He was passing a small cafe when something about a figure within stopped him. He stepped back and peered through the glass. At a booth in the little lunchroom was Reese. He was buttering up large chunks of cornbread. Before him sat a platter of steak and gravy with mashed potatoes and beans. A waitress shuffled down the corridor toward him with a tall mug of coffee. Reese looked up to say some pleasantry. His eyes wandered from her to the scowling face at the window and he gave a sort of little jump in his seat and then grinned and waved.

Suttree threw back the door and went down the aisle.

Hey Sut. Where the hell did you get to? I hunted everwhere for you.

Sure you did. Where did you get the money? I thought you were broke.

Set down, set down. Honey? He raised a hand. He pointed at Suttree's head. Bring him what he wants. Boy, I'm glad I found you. Here, tell her what you want.

I dont want a goddamned thing. Listen.

They aint no need to cuss about it, the waitress said.

Suttree ignored her. He leaned to Reese who was loading his jaw with a forkful of steak. You're driving me crazy, he said.

Honey, bring him a cup of coffee.

I dont want a cupping fuck of coffee. Look Reese . . .

Reese lowered his head and gave Suttree a queer clown's wink and nod. Sold em, he whispered. Looky here.

Look at what?

Down here. Looky here.

Suttree had to lean back and look under the table where this grinning fool was holding pinched in his hand so just the corner showed a twenty dollar bill.

What the hell are you hiding it for? Is it counterfeit?

Shhh. Hell no son, it's good as gold.

Who'd you hit in the head?

Old buddy, we goin to take this to the tong games and come off with some real money.

We better get our ass down to the bus station is what we better do.

Honey, bring him a cup of coffee.

He said he didnt want none.

Suttree slumped back in the booth.

Bring him some, said Reese, waving a piece of cornbread. He'll drink it.

They stood in the street under the small lamps. A deathly quiet prevailed over the town.

I wisht it wasnt summer and we could go to the cockfights, Reese said. He sucked his teeth and looked up and down the street. Got to find us a goddamned taxi. He patted his little paunch and belched and squinted about.

Let me have a nickel and I'll go in and call one.

Reese doled the coin easily. Suttree wore a look of dry patience. He went in and called the taxi.

When it arrived Reese opened the front door and hopped in and was whispering loudly to the driver. Suttree climbed in the back and shut the door.

Let me just take you fellers on up to the Green Room, the driver was saying. You can get anything you want up there.

What do you say, Sut?

Suttree looked at the back of Reese's head and then he just looked out the window.

Course you can go anywhere you want, said the driver.

Daggone right you can, said Reese. When ye got the money to do it with. He turned and favored Suttree with a sleazy grin.

What kind of whiskey you boys want? You want bonded or some real good moonshine?

Is it real good sure enough?

Bonded, said Suttree from the back.

They were going by narrow back streets in the small town suppertime dark, by curtained windowlights where families sat gathered. Suttree rolled down the window and breathed the air all full of blossoms.

The driver took them up a gravel drive to the back of an old house. A yellow bulb hung burning from the naked night above them. The driver got out and a man came from the door and the two of them went across the yard and behind a garage. When they came back the driver was holding a pint of whiskey down by the side of his leg.

He got in and palmed the whiskey to Reese. Reese held it to the light and studied the label professionally as he unscrewed the cap.

They went back down the driveway with Reese's head thrown back and the bottom of the bottle standing straight up.

Get ye a drink, he wheezed, poking the bottle over the seat at Suttree.

Suttree drank and handed it back.

Reese held the bottle up and eyed it and held it under the driver's chin. Get ye a drink old buddy, he said.

The driver said he didnt drink on duty.

They drove out through the small streets and struck the highway, Reese and Suttree passing the bottle back and forth and Reese giving the driver a history of himself no part of which was even vaguely true.

Say you all never been to the Green Room? said the driver.

We aint been up here in a long time, said Reese.

They got some little old gals up here will do anything. They'd as soon suck a peter as look at ye.

Reese was elbowing the dark of the cab behind him vigorously. You hear that, Sut? he said.

They went out the highway several miles and turned onto a sideroad that had one time been the highway. At the top of the hill stood a squat cinderblock building with neon piping along the roof. The windows were painted black and one of them was broken and fixed back with blocks of wood stovebolted through the holes. There was an iron pole in the drive with a beersign hung from the crosstrees and perhaps half a hundred cars parked in the gravel. The cabdriver switched on the domelight and looked at Reese.

What we owe ye, old buddy?

Let me have five. That'll get the whiskey and everthing.

Reese paid and they stepped out into the gravel. The taxi slewed about in a cloud of dust and flying stones and went back out to the highway. Reese tucked in his shirt and hitched up his trousers and seized the doorhandle to make his entrance but the door was locked.

Ring the buzzer, said Suttree.

He pushed the button and almost immediately the door opened and a man looked at them and stepped back and they entered.

A concrete floor, a horseshoeshaped bar upholstered in quilted black plastic, a gaudy jukebox that played country music. A few sloe-eyed young whores in stage makeup and incredible costumes, ballroom gowns, bathing suits, satin pajamas. They lounged at the bar, they sat in the booths by the wall, they danced with clowns dressed up like farmers wooden clown dances in the shifting jukebox lights. Through a door to the rear Suttree could see thicker smoke yet and the green baize of gaming tables.

Godamighty damn, said Reese reverently. Looky here.

Suttree was looking. He'd been in places like this but not quite. A whole new style seemed to be seeking expression here. They crossed to the bar and were immediately set upon by whores. A blackhaired girl in a chiffon dress with a train that followed her about the floor sweeping up the cigarette butts had Suttree by the elbow. Hidy cutie, she said. Why dont you buy me a drink? Suttree looked down into a pair of enormous painted eyes dripping a black goo. A pair of perfectly round white tits pushed up in the front of her gown. You'll have to see this man here, he said. He's the last of the big spenders.

She immediately turned loose of Suttree and got hold of Reese's arm even though there were two other girls hanging onto him. Hidy cutie, she said. Why dont you buy me a drink?

I'll buy ye'ns all a drink quick as I get done at the tong table, cried Reese.

The bartender was standing at the ready and Suttree held up one hand and caught his eye. He raised his chin to know what Sut would have.

Bourbon and gingerale, said Suttree.

Where you all from, honey? said a blonde who appeared out of the smoke.

Suttree looked at her. Web City, he said.

You're a smart son of a bitch, aint ye?

He watched Reese at the cardtable until he became bored and went back out to the bar. But the whores had thickened and he got another drink and went back into the gambling room again. Reese seemed to have won some money and Suttree tapped him on the shoulder to get some quarters and dimes for the slotmachines. The dealer raised up and eyed him narrowly and told him to back off from the table if he wasnt playing. Reese handed him two dollars over his shoulder and Suttree took the money and went into another room and got change from a lady at a cardtable by the door. There were eight or ten slotmachines along the walls and several young men in dark gabardine shirts and their heads almost shaven were feeding money to the whores and the whores were operating the machines. Suttree won about seven dollars and went back out to the bar and got another drink. He was beginning to feel a little drunk. He bought the blackhaired girl a drink and she took him by the arm and they sat in a booth at the far wall and she immediately ordered two more drinks from a waitress dressed in a swimsuit and black net stockings. The black-haired girl put her hand on Suttree's leg and got him by the neck and ran her tongue down his throat. Then she stuck her tongue in his ear and asked him if he wanted to go out in the back.

Reese came reeling through the smoke and the din with a painted childwhore on his arm. She had an eyetooth out and smiled with her cigarette in her mouth to hide the gap.

Looky here, Sut.

Hidy.

Aint that a purty little old thing?

Suttree smiled.

Reese had her by the hand. He leaned toward Suttree. Listen, he said, you wouldnt tell on a feller would ye?

Maybe not. Where's the whiskey?

Here. Hell fire, get ye a drink. He brought the bottle forth from his overalls and handed it over.

You raise tobacco too? the girl said.

Sure, said Suttree.

Reese was making peculiar faces and jerking his shoulder at Suttree. Suttree spun the cap back on the bottle and slid from the booth. I've got to talk to my partner here a minute, he told the girl.

They conferred a few feet from the table. Let's hear the bad news, said Suttree.

Bad news's ass. Looky here.

He was cupping his hand at the mouth of his pocket, a roll of bills crouched there like a pet mouse. Old buddy, I strictly slipped it to em in yonder, he said.

The whore on his arm leaned across to whisper in Suttree's ear. You ought to get with Doreen yonder, she said, nodding toward a puffy blonde at the bar. She's real sweet.

We got to get us another bottle of whiskey, said Reese. Both she and Reese had taken to hoarse stage whispers and Suttree had to bend his head forward to hear them at all what with the howl of electric guitars from the jukebox. As he did so the old man seized him by the head and pulled him close and rasped in his ear: Go on and get her Sut. We'll strictly put the dick to em.

When he woke a light had come on in the cabin and a man and a girl were standing in the door. That goddamned Doreen leaves her goddamned dates in the cabins all the time, the girl said. Suttree groaned and tried to put his head beneath the pillow.

Hey, said the girl. You caint stay here.

His head was at the edge of the thin mattress. He looked down at the floor. The floor was pink linoleum with green and yellow flowers. There was a glass there and a halfpint bottle with a drink in the bottom. He reached down and got the bottle and held it against his naked chest.

Hey, said the girl.

Okay, said Suttree. Let me get my clothes.

He wandered off through the weeds in the dark. Out on the highway the sound of trucktires whined and died in the distance. He fell into a gully and climbed out and went on again.

When he woke it was daylight and he was lying in a field. He rose up and looked out across the sedge. Two little girls and a dog were going along a dirt lane. Beyond them the sunhammered landscape veered away in a quaking shapeless hell. A low gray barn, a fence. A fieldwagon standing in milkweed. Yonder the town. He rose to his feet and stood swaying, a great pain in his eyeballs and upon his skull like the pressure of marine deeps. He tottered off across the fields toward the roadhouse.

He found Reese asleep in a wrecked car behind the cabins. Suttree shook him gently awake into a world he wanted no part of. The old man fought it. He pushed away and buried his head in one arm there on the dusty ruptured seat. Suttree could not help but grin for all that his head hurt so.

Come on, he said. Let's go.

The old man moaned.

What? Suttree said.

You go on and I'll come later, tell em.

Okay. You comfortable?

I'm all right.

You want a sip of this cold lemonade fore I go?

An eye opened. The musty gutted hulk of the car stank of mold and sweat and cheap whiskey. Wasps kept coming in the naked rear window and vanishing through a crack in the domelight overhead.

What? said Reese.

I said would you like a sip of this cold lemonade?

The old man tried to see without moving his head but he gave it up. Shit, he said. You aint got no lemonade.

Suttree pulled him around by one arm. Come on, he said. Get your ass up from there and let's go.

A bloated face turned up. Ah God. Just leave me here to die.

Let's go, Reese.

Where are we at?

Let's go.

He struggled up, looking around.

How you feeling, old partner? said Suttree.

Reese looked up into Suttree's grinning face. He put his hands over his eyes. Where you been? he said.

Come on.

Reese shook his head. Boy, we a couple of good'ns aint we?

You dont have a little drink hid away do you?

Shit.

Here.

He lowered his hands. Suttree was holding the almost empty bottle at him. Why goddamn, Sut, he said. He reached for the bottle with both hands and twisted off the cap and drank.

Leave me corners, said Suttree.

Reese closed his eyes, screwed up his face and shivered and swallowed. He blew and held the bottle up. Goddamn, he said. I dont remember it bein that bad last night.

Suttree took the bottle from him and let the little it held fill up one corner and then he tilted it and drank and pitched the empty bottle out through the open window into the weeds. Well, he said. Think you can make it now?

We'll give it a try.

He pulled himself painfully from the doorless car and stood squinting in the heat little pleased with what he saw. Where do you reckon they sell beer on Sunday up here?

Right here probably, Suttree said, nodding toward the roadhouse.

They passed among the cabins and staggered across the dusty waste of gravel and trash with their tongues out like dogs. Suttree tapped at a door at the rear of the premises. They waited.

Knock again, Sut.

He did.

A slide shot back in the side of the building and a man peered out. What'll you have, boys? he said.

You got any cold beer?

342

It's all cold. What kind?

What kind? said Suttree.

Any goddamned kind, said Reese.

You got Miller's?

What you want, a sixpack?

Suttree looked at Reese. Reese was looking at him blandly. Suttree said: Have you got any money?

No. Aint you?

He felt himself all over. Not a fucking dime, he said.

The bootlegger looked from one to the other of them.

Where's that pearl? said Suttree.

The old man raised his foot and put it down again. He leaned against the side of the building and raised his foot and reached down in his sock. He held up his purse.

How come you to still have that, said Suttree. Did you not get any poontang last night?

You daggone right I got me some. But I never took off my shoes. He undid the mouth of the thing and rolled out the pearl and held it up. Looky here, he said.

What's that supposed to be? said the bootlegger.

A pearl. Go on. Take a look at it.

You sons of bitches get on away from here, said the bootlegger, and slammed the little window shut.

They looked at each other for a minute and then Suttree squatted in the dust among the flattened cans.

Shit, said Reese.

Suttree palmed his knees and shook his head. We're hellatious traders, he said.

Boy I hate a dumb son of a bitch like that that dont know the value of nothin.

Let's get the hell out of here. It's a long way home.

Coming over the Pigeon River Bridge into Newport a county police cruiser passed them. The old man saw them coming. Wave like they know ye, he said.

Fuck that, said Suttree.

The cruiser went by and Reese waved real big. The cruiser turned at the edge of the bridge and came back and pulled up alongside. A fat deputy looked them over. Who you think you wavin at buddy?

Suttree groaned.

Reese smiled. I thought you was somebody I knowed, he said.

Is that right? Maybe you'd like to come uptown and get a little better aquainted.

He didnt mean anything by it, officer.

The deputy eyed Suttree up and down, little joy in the beholding. I'll be the judge of that, he said. Where you two goin?

Both reckoned one more wrong answer would be all that the law allowed. They looked at each other. Suttree could hear the river beneath them. He saw himself in a swandive, heedless, lost. Under gray swirling waters. He could hear the cruiser's motor idling roughly with its high camshaft. Home, he said.

The driver had said something to the deputy. The deputy looked them over again. Well, he said, you'd better be gettin on there.

Yessir, Suttree said.

Much obliged, your officer, said the old man.

They pulled away and turned at the end of the bridge and came back. The driver glanced at them in passing but they were both looking at the ground.

Bastards, Suttree said. I thought for a minute there we were gone.

I knowed how to handle it, Reese said.

I told you not to wave, goddamnit. And what the hell is your officer supposed to mean?

I dont know. Shit, my head hurts.

He was stumbling along holding the top of his head with both hands. Suttree looked at him in disgust. We'd better get the hell out of here, he said.

We better not go through town.

Dont worry, said Suttree. We're not.

They turned down along the river and Suttree took bearings by the sun and plotted a course crosscountry that should bring them out on the highway on the other side of town. They went wandering mournfully down little dirt tracks and across fields. They went through a shantytown strung out along the edge of a branch, all grass and growing things about the creek and the encampment gone, a land of raw clay strewn with trash, with chickens and scabrous dogs. A cadaverous and darkeyed people watched mutely, furtive and dimly defined in their doorways. Such squalid folk as not even a weed grew among. Reese nodded and howdied to them but they just stared.

They crossed a pasture where grackles blue and metallic in the sun were turning up dried cowpats for the worms beneath and they went on past the back side of a junklot with the sun wearing hard upon them and upon the tarpaper roof of the parts shack and upon the endless fenders and lids of wrecked cars that lay curing paintlorn in the hot and weedy reeks.

They ended up lost in a big alfalfa field. On three sides were woods and on the fourth was where they'd come from.

Which way? Reese said.

Suttree squatted and held his head. Will some son of a bitch please tell me what I'm doing here?

I got to get out of this sun fore my old head pops, said Reese. He looked down. Suttree had tilted forward onto his knees. They looked like castaways. Dont lay down, said Reese, or ye never will get up.

Suttree looked up at him. You would absolutely pull the pope under, he said.

He probably dont even drink. Which way, do ye reckon?

Suttree struggled up and looked around and struck out again.

They crossed into heavy woods and began to climb. The ground was covered with random limestone and there were sinkholes to be fallen into.

You take poison ivy, Sut?

No. Do you?

No. Thank the Lord. I believe this here must be under cultivation.

They went on. They rested more and more going up the ridge. Just sitting in the undergrowth like apes eyeing one another with little expectation of anything and breathing hard. When they got to the top they looked out and they could see below them through the trees a piece of black highway about two miles away.

I dont think I can make it without a drink of water, Suttree said.

Dont drink no water, Sut. It'll make ye drunk all over again.

Suttree glared at him.

When they reached the highway they were staggerfooted and crazy-looking. As far as you could see in either direction there was not so much as a billboard. Suttree sat down by the edge of the road with his feet spread and began to pick at gravels and little straws and things.

Here comes a car, Sut.

Thumb it.

Well get up. He wont stop with somebody setting down.

They watched the driver's eyes. He looked like a skittish horse the way he rolled them and the car swerved out as if he'd keep from being leapt upon by these roadside predators who possibly fared on the flesh of motorists in lonely places.

An hour later they were still standing there. Three cars and one truck had passed. They looked at each other and at themselves. The old man fell to combing his hair with his hands.

We better start walking, Suttree said.

How far from home you reckon we are?

I dont know. Twenty miles. Thirty maybe. Suttree's eyes looked burnt and a crusty paste had formed over his lips.

What time do you reckon it is?

Suttree looked at the sky. Gently quaking like a vat of molten cobalt. Past noon. Maybe two oclock. Let's walk on down around this next curve. Maybe there's a store or something.

The old man shaded his eyes and looked down the hot and smoking road to where it dissolved in a distant haze. The landscape subsequent seemed to shift and veer so that he batted his eyes and made little gestures with his hands as if to shape things right again. I reckon we can try for it, he said.

They set off, stumbling along the roadway with their eyes down. If you keep from looking up for a long time you can surprise yourself with how far you've come. Suttree fell to counting the bottlecaps in the dusty roadside gravel. Then he ▮▮▮an to divide them into the rightside ups and the upside downs. Before they reached the curve he called for them to stop.

Reese when he looked at him seemed almost in tears. We nearly to the curve, Sut, he said.

I know. I just want to get rested a minute so that when we look down that next stretch of road and there's nothing there I wont faint.

How long you reckon a feller can sweat like this and nothin to drink without dryin up?

Suttree didnt answer. He was looking back up the road, the accrued flat of the surface making mirages of standing water on the heat-bleared black macadam. A truck was coming down. A phantom truck that augmented itself out of the boiling heat by segments and planes, an old black truck that rode down out of a funhouse mirror, coalesced slowly in the middle distance and pulled to a stop alongside them.

Shithouse mouse, cried Reese, staggering toward the truck.

Suttree thought that if he reached for the vehicle it would resolve itself back into the cooking lobes of his skull from whence it came.

But the old man was climbing up, jabbering mindlessly to the driver. Suttree followed. He pulled the door shut after them and it bounced open again.

Raise up on it, said the driver.

He raised up on it and it shut and they pulled away. As bad as they looked, bad as they smelled, this saint seemed not to notice.

How far are you going? Suttree asked.

Sevierville. How far you all?

He was a young boy, hair almost white, a light down at his chin and side jaws. We'll ride on in with you if you dont mind, Suttree said.

You more'n welcome.

Whew, said Reese. We was about give out.

Around the bend of the road was a store. An orange gaspump standing atilt. Suttree almost croaked out for a brief halt and Reese watched the building go past with sadder eyes yet.

Where you all from? the boy said.

Down around Knoxville. You from up here?

Naw, the boy said. I'm from down around Sevierville. He looked them over. I just come up here to mess around some last night, he said.

They watched the road in silence. Reese looked at the boy. He was wearing clean overall pants and he was leaning up over the wheel and he was chewing tobacco. You ever been to that there Green Room? said Reese.

The boy looked at him sidelong slyly. Shit, he said. Aint that the dangdest place?

You wasnt in there last night was you?

We come in there about three oclock this mornin.

Reese looked at him again. He shook his head. Well, he said. Be proud you wasnt there no earlier. That first shift is pure hell. Aint it Sut?

When they stumbled back into the camp on the river the four women and the boy were waiting for them with grim set mouths.

Boy if you aint a couple of good'ns, she said. Where's them groceries you was goin to bring?

I can explain everthing, Reese said.

Where they at? Hey? Boy if you aint a couple of good'ns.

Reese turned to Suttree. I told you she'd say that. What'd I tell ye?

Standing there with her hands on her hips and that stringy hair and her face a mask of bitterness she looked fearful and Suttree turned away. Reese tried to detain him to verify various lies but he went on toward the lean-to and got his bedding and slouched off toward the river with it. He could hear the debate rising behind him. Suttree'll tell ye. Ast him if you wont believe me.

He lay down in his blankets. It was growing dark, long late midsummer twilight in the woods. He wanted to go down to the river to bathe but he felt too bad. He turned over and looked at the small plot of ground in the crook of his arm. My life is ghastly, he told the grass.

The girl woke him, shaking him by the shoulder. He'd heard his name called and he rose up wondering. The boy was coming up out of the darkness downriver with a load of pale and misshapen driftwood like scoured bones from a saint's barrow. At the fire the woman bent and stooped and placed the blackened pots about and the old man squatted on his haunches and rolled one of his limp wet cigarettes and lit it deftly with a coal and watched. All this with a quality of dark ceremony. Suttree walked with the girl to the fire. One of the younger girls came up from the river with the coffeepot dripping riverwater and set it on the stones. She gave him a slow look sideways and arranged the pot with a studied domesticity which in this outlandish setting caused Suttree to smile.

They ate almost in silence, a light smacking of chops, eyes furtive in the light of the lantern. The meal consisted of the whitebeans and cornbread and the boiled chicory coffee. There was about them something subdued beyond their normal reticence. As if order had been forced upon them from without. From time to time the woman awarded to the round dark a look of grim apprehension like a fugitive. When Suttree had finished he thanked her and rose from the table and she nodded and he went off toward the river.

He woke once in the night to the sound of voices, a faint lamentation that might have been hounds beyond the wind but which to him as he lay watching the slow procession of lights on a highway far across the river like the candles of acolytes seemed more the thin clamor of some company transgressed from a dream or children who had died going along a road in the dark with lanterns and crying on their way from the world.

It was the boy came down with poison ivy. First between his fingers, then up his arms and on his face. He'd rub himself with mud, with anything. I seen dogs like that, said the old man. Couldnt get no relief.

His eyes is swoll shut, the woman said at breakfast next morning. The boy came to the fire like a sleepwalker. His arms puffed like adders. He tilted his head a bit to one side to favor the eye he could still see from. The skin of his upper arms had cracked in little fissures from which a clear yellow liquid seeped.

The old man shook his head in disgust. I aint never seen a feller swell up thataway with poison ivy. What all do you reckon's the matter with him?

Just keep him away from me, said Suttree.

I thought you didnt take it, Sut.

I think he's found a new kind.

Shoo, said Wanda. You're a mess.

He came toward her, arms flailing stiffly in a fiend's mime, and she ran screaming.

Well, the old man said. You wont get it just bein in the same boat with him.

I aint goin in no boat, the boy said.

You aint, aint ye?

I caint bend my arms.

Reese had a knife and spoon up in his hands, holding them like candles, waiting for the food. The boy was standing rigidly at the end of the table. You what? Said Reese.

Caint bend my arms, said the boy loftily.

The old man laid down his silver quietly. Well hell's bells, he said. He looked at Suttree. I reckon you and Wanda will have to take it today.

I've got a better idea, Suttree said.

What's that?

You and Wanda.

Well, I thought I'd make the downstream run by myself. I thought I'd let you take the upstream with Wanda on account of she knows it.

The woman swung a bucketful of oatmeal onto the table and the old man seized the ladle and loaded his bowl. Suttree looked downtable at the boy. He was still standing with his arms out at his sides. Wanda was sitting at the table across from him. She did not look up. She seemed to be at grace. Suttree took the ladle and dolloped out the oatmeal. Reese was blowing on his, holding the bowl in both hands and watching Suttree across the rim. Pass the milk, said Suttree.

She sat with her knees together in the stern facing him as he rowed, her hands in her lap, the brail drops swinging behind her from the poles. Suttree seeing new country and asking about things along the shore, which side of an island to take. Her pointing, her young breasts swinging in the light cloth of her dress, turning in the boat, caught up in a childlike enthusiasm, a long flash of white thighs appearing and hiding again. Her bare feet on the silty boards of the skiff's floor crossed one over the top of the other.

She said: Holler when you get tired and I'll spell ye.

That's all right.

I row for Daddy all the time. I can row good.

Okay.

You like to work with Willard?

He's all right.

I dont. I worked with him last summer some. He's a smart aleck.

I guess you got to practice up on your rowing with him.

Shoot. That thing wont do nothin. You know he tried to get me to hide out what pearls we found cleanin shells and we'd slip off and sell em and keep the money?

Suttree grinned. Well, he said. I'd guess old Willard probably doesnt have much luck finding pearls. I'd say that everybody else would find about five to his one.

Shoot, I bet he keeps what good ones he does find and hides em somewheres. Looky yonder at that old snake.

A watersnake was weaving his way upriver by the shore reeds, his sleek chin flat on the water.

I just despise them things, she said.

They wont hurt you.

Shoot. What if one was to bite ye?

They wont bite. They're not poison anyway.

She watched the snake, the tip of her thumb between her teeth.

Let's just row over there and get him and I'll show you, said Suttree, taking a hard turn on the larboard oar.

She squealed and jumped, grabbing at the oars. Suttree could see down the front of her dress all the way to her belly, the skin so smooth, the nipples so round and swollen. Buddy! she said, high and breathless and laughing. She was almost in his lap. You stay away from that thing.

The boat rocked. She steadied herself with a hand on his shoulder, she touched the gunwale and sat down, a shy smile. They looked toward the shore for the snake but the snake was gone. The sun was warm on Suttree's back. He let one oar trail and wet his hand in the river and put it against the back of his neck. You scared the snake off, he said.

You scared me.

Maybe we'll see another one.

You stay away from them things. What if one was to climb in the boat?

I guess you'd be climbing out. Suttree suddenly looked down over the side. Why here he is, he said. Right alongside the boat.

She squealed and stood up, holding her wrists together in front of her, her hands at her mouth.

Suttree shook and jostled the oar. He's coming up the oar, he said.

Buddeee! she wailed, climbing onto the seat in the transom. She peered down into the water. Where? she said.

Suttree had let go the oar and was laughing like a simpleton.

You quit that, she said. You hear? Buddy?

Yes? he said.

You promise me. You hear? Dont do that no more.

Okay, he said. You better sit down before you fall in.

She stepped down and sat, holding the gunwales at either side as if to be ready for rough water. He stood his feet against the struts in the skiff's side and pulled into the current.

They ate their lunch on a grassy knoll above the river. A cool wind that bore an odor of damp moss coming off the water. Reese had gotten credit at the store and there were baloney sandwiches on white bread with mayonnaise and little oatmeal cakes. She sat with her bare feet tucked beneath her and brought these things from a paper grocery sack and laid them out. When they'd eaten he lay back in the grass with his hands behind his head. He watched the clouds. He closed his eyes.

She took the oars as they went back down and Suttree handled the brail bars. She would help him haul the filled brails in, smelling of soap and sweat, her body soft and naked under the dress touching him, the mussels dripping and swinging from the lines and clacking like castanets.

They coaxed the loaded boat through the shallows, walking alongside it on the gravel floor of the river. Suttree raised the front of it by the ring in the prow and ran the water to the rear and grounded the bow of the skiff on a rock. Them leaning over the boat from either side, their heads almost touching, scooping out the water with bailing cans.

Drifting downriver in the lovely dusk, the river chattering in the rips and bats going to and back over the darkening water. Rocking down black glides and slicks, the gravel bars going past and little islands of rock and tufted grass.

When they reached the camp there was no one about. Suttree took the axe and went for wood while she built the fire back.

He came up dragging some dead stumps and found her sitting in front of the fire on a tarpaulin she had spread there. She looked up quickly and smiled. He set one of the stumps in the flames. Hot sparks rose and drifted downwind in the dark. Where is everybody? he said.

I reckon they're at church.

You think Willard went with them?

Mama makes him go. She puts him to work if he tries to lay out.

Suttree sat down on the tarp alongside her.

They could hear the river running on in the dark. He heard her breathing beside him, her breast rising and falling, eyes watching the fire. Suttree rose onto his knees and reached across the flames and jostled the stump forward into a better place. He looked back at her. She had her knees up and her arms locked about them. Her full thighs shone in the firelight, the little wedge of pink rayon that pursed her cleft. He leaned to her and took her face in his hands and kissed her, child's breath, an odor of raw milk. She opened her mouth. He cupped her breast in his palm and her eyes fluttered and she slumped against him. When he put his hand up her dress her legs fell open bonelessly.

This is nothing but trouble, he said.

I dont care.

Her dress was around her waist. Incredible amounts of flesh naked in the firelight. She was warm and wet and softly furred. She seemed barely conscious. He felt giddy. An obscene delight not untouched by just a little sorrow as he pulled down her drawers. Struggling one-handed with buttons. Her thighs were slathered with mucus. She put her arms around his neck. She bowed her back and sucked her breath in sharply.

Hers was a tale of bridled lust. He made her tell him everything. Never a living man. When he rose from between her thighs the fire had died almost to coals. She sat and smoothed her skirt and swept back her hair. She got up and took up her fallen underclothing and went to the lean-to. Suttree saw her go with a basin toward the river and when she returned she had bathed and changed her dress and he had mended back the fire and she came and sat by him and he took her hand.

She came to him again in the night where he slept above the river, waking him with her hands on him and her warm breath. She wanted to sleep with him but he sent her away. She came back again toward the morning and Suttree faced the day on buckling knees. He saw her coming from the river with a pail of water, smiling. He went up to the fire and found Reese squatting there with his arms folded on top of his knees.

Hot nights filled with summer thunder. Heat lightning far and thin and the midnight sky becrazed and mended back again. Suttree moved down to the gravelbar on the river and spread his blanket there under the gauzy starwash and lay naked with his back pressed to the wheeling earth. The river chattered and sucked past at his elbow. He'd lie awake long after the last dull shapes in the coals of the cookfire died and he'd go naked into the cool and velvet waters and submerge like an otter and come up and blow, the stones smooth as marbles under his cupped toes and the dark water reeling past his eyes. He'd lie on his back in the shallows and on these nights he'd see stars come adrift and rifle hot and dying across the face of the firmament. The enormity of the universe filled him with a strange sweet woe.

She always found him. She'd come pale and naked from the trees into the water like some dream old prisoners harbor or sailors at sea. Or touch his cheek where he lay sleeping and say his name. Holding her arms aloft like a child for him to raise up over them the nightshirt that she wore and her to lie cool and naked against his side.

She sat in the bow of the boat going upriver. She traced her cool fingertips along his nape and he turned and squinted at her. Sunlight swarmed on the water. That's going to get you screwed, he said. She knelt forward and ran her velvet tongue between his lips. She smelled of soap and woodsmoke. Tasted of salt.

He turned the skiff toward shore and he spread her naked in the grass, her grave and slightly smiling face pooled in black hair, her perfect teeth, her skin completely flawless, not so much as a mole. The nipples tulipshaped and full and her navel just a slit in her flat little belly. Her smooth thighs, her childlike shamelessness, her little hands dug into his buttocks. Her whimpering like a puppy's.

They swam in the river and slept in the sun. They woke in the hot forenoon and laughed at the hurry with which they worked. Reese came down in the dark to help them moor the loaded skiff and ran his flashbeam over the piles of shellfish and the three of them went up through the trees to the fire.

She sat across from him and watched him and she brought his coffee and pushed a soft young breast against his ear in taking away his empty plate.

I believe that gal's a better cook than her mother, said Reese. What do you think?

Suttree stopped chewing and looked sideways at Reese and then went on chewing again.

That little old gal is special to me, Reese said. She'll just do a man's work.

Suttree spat an insoluble wad of gristle at the dark. The women were laboring up the slope with a washtub of water between them, the girl laughing, the water licking over the sides.

You want some more coffee, Sut? Holler there and tell her to bring the pot.

And across the fire her hot eyes watched him and she seemed half breathless in the things she did. He walked off down by the river with his flashlight, along the path, flicking the light into the dead water by the shore where suckers lay on the bottom, old bottles furred with silt, pale mooneyed shad in catatonia. He turned off the light and sat in the easy dark and listened to a rip in some rocky shoal, a gentle whispering in the reeds where the river ran. A figure came down from the fire and squatted in the grass and rose and went back. The willows at the far shore cut from the night a prospect of distant mountains dark against a paler sky. Halfmoon incandescent in her black galactic keyway, the heavens locked and wheeling. A sole star to the north pale and constant, the old wanderer's beacon burning like a molten spike that tethered fast the Small Bear to the turning firmament. He closed his eyes and opened them and looked again. He was struck by the fidelity of this earth he inhabited and he bore it sudden love.

In the morning the boy helped them unload the mussels, sullen face filled with suspicion, a potential spy. The woman and the younger girls came up the river path with their shelling tools, the woman with her air of habitual rigidity and the girls in lockstep behind. At supper that night Reese said he thought the boy was well enough to work and the boy glared at Suttree across the table.

Two mornings later he was looking at Willard in the rear of the skiff. Willard wore a dark blue hat he'd come by somewhere made of imitation felt and maybe paper. Suttree rowed with his head averted watching the shore. They hardly spoke all day. By the time they'd unloaded the mussels downstream it was getting on toward evening.

Daddy's got a hole baited down here, the boy said. Said for us to run his thowlines.

Suttree leaned on his shovel. You go run them, he said.

Willard clambered ashore and disappeared whistling down the river path. He was gone the better part of an hour and when he came back he was lugging a goodsized spoonbill catfish, relict of devonian seas, a thing scaleless and leathery with a duck's bill and the small eyes harboring eons of night. Suttree shook his head. Some like spirit joined beast and captor. Looky here, called the boy. Suttree sat in the boat with his head in his hands. Darkness settled on them before they'd rowed halfway back to the camp.

They spent the last hour rowing upstream with the boy in the bow sounding with a pole, going up shoals where the oars grated on the gravel bottom and rocks passed along the planks with a slow dull wrenching, fighting off treelimbs that kept boarding them in the dark.

She came down to him at some hour before dawn and lay by him. She put her head against his chest.

We've got to stop this, he said.

Why.

We'll get caught.

I dont care.

You'll get pregnant.

She didnt answer. After a while she said: We could be careful.

There's nothing careful about us.

What are we going to do?

Suttree lay staring up through the trees at the night sky.

Do you not want me to come anymore?

He didnt answer.

Buddy?

No, he said. His voice sounded strange.

She lay there for a long time. They didnt speak. Then she rose and went back up the hill.

He thought she would come the next night anyway but she did not. He woke once and heard a rustle, night wind, a dog in the dark. One of the girls went down to the river and back. He got up and walked down the path and waded out and crouched there looking across the dark current to the darker shapes of trees on the farther shore and the faint shoals of mist.

In the third week of August it began to rain. He and the boy were on the river when it started and the rain was very cold and they tucked their necks against it and put toward shore. Not drops but whole glycerinous clots of water were falling in the river, raising great bladderlike weals that exchanged with constant hissing pops. The boy's hat came slowly and darkly down about his face like a flower in an inkbottle until he looked out from a soggy cowl, his back hunched and his eyes planing about in deep suspicion. Suttree at the oars grinned. The boy half grinned back. His whole head was turning pale blue with hatdye. I aint never seen it rain no harder, have you? he said

What?

I said have you?

No.

They sidled into the bank and Suttree boated the oars and took the rope in his hand and leaped for the bank. He went headlong and slid feetfirst back into the river, his hands dragging up great clawfuls of mud. When he came up he was in water to his chest. The first thing he saw was the boy hugging himself dementedly. He slogged over to the boat and hung his elbows over it. What the fuck are you laughing at, he said.

Whew, gasped the boy. You looked like a big springlizard slippin off into the river.

You simple shit. How about getting that oar and pushing us in.

The boy staggered up still shaking his head and took up the oar. They had drifted under some willows and Suttree was holding to the boat with one elbow and pulling on them. The rain was falling so hard it hurt. He got the boat tied and crawled through the willows and up the bank. There was a thick stand of cedars some little distance up the river and he made for that. Crawling under the trees, driving small birds forth into the weather. Within the copse the day was darker yet but the thick brown compost under him was almost dry and he took off his shoes and emptied out the water and fetched the wadded socks from the toes of them and wrung them out. He took off his shirt and twisted the water from it and put it on again. He heard his name called off down by the river. He heard his name called in the woods. Water was beading down through the cedars and dropping all about him. He parted the boughs and saw the boy going up the river path with his hat hanging about his ears and his face a mottled blue and his arms flailing like an idiot wandered from a pesthouse.

It rained for three days while they sat along the narrow strip of dry earth under the bluff and played cards and while they mended their clothes and Reese whittled first a flute from river cane and then a snake with seedpearl eyes and last a basswood bear he stained with shoeblack for the youngest girl.

It cleared a little on the fourth day and they tried to run their boats in the snarling yellow flood but were glad to give it up. That evening it began to rain again and it never did stop. They laid up in the camp for two weeks and watched the river bloat and swell until it was screaming through the trees below the bluff and the fields crossriver were flooded far as you could see.

The first of these days Reese had kept a watcher posted in the skiff to set forth should anything of value come down but soon the waters grew too treacherous for this commerce. They accumulated a strange collection of goods which he sorted and divided among them guided by inscrutable rules of equity. He'd squat for hours and watch the river pass, pointing sadly at valuables hurtling past with the speed of a train. He'd come back dripping and sit by the fire and shake his head.

They spent three days shoveling at the mussels upstream where the river was sucking away at the edge of the pile and taking back the shells. When they hiked downriver to see about things there they found part of the bank washed out and a great crescentshaped bite gone from their stacks.

At night she watched him with eyes full of questions. All were brought into such close and constant communion by the rain that the configuration of the family seemed to alter. A frailly structured matriarchy showed itself in these latter days, and Suttree reckoned it had always been so. Crouched there under the ledge in the wind's lee while the flames of the small fire lapped back the dark and all around and ceaseless fell the rain in the forest they could have been some band of stone age folk washed up out of an atavistic dream.

In the office of the old motel on the pike Suttree had found a stack of moldering books and he read through them one by one without regard. Lying with his blanket for a laprobe, propped against the rocks. He read *Tom Swift and His Motorcycle* and he read *The Black Brotherhood* and he read *Mildred at Home*. There were about a dozen titles and when he had finished them all he started over again. She read *Mildred at Home* and a story about nurses. She said that she would like to be a nurse. He looked at her. She smiled thinly.

When all were asleep in their places she rose with her blanket folded about her and came from the lean-to and went down the bluff toward the woods. Suttree watched. When she was gone he raised up and looked around. Then he pushed back his blanket and followed her.

He caught her up just beyond the edge of the trees. She was all over him. It was raining lightly and they were both wet. She was naked under her blanket. It fell in a dark pool about her feet. In which he knelt, rain dripping from her nipples, runneling thinly on her pale belly. With his ear to the womb of this child he could hear the hiss of meteorites through the blind stellar depths. She moaned and stood tiptoe, her hands holding his head to her.

These lovers lay crumpled in the dripping wood and listened to the fall of the rain heart on heart. Her wet hair lay across his face like black seaweed. She said his name. He moved as if to rise but she held him.

You'll catch cold, he said.

I dont care.

In their last week on the river two possumhunters came upon their camp. They'd heard hounds coursing on the ridge behind them and the hunters hallooed from the dark before they came up. Two figures shambling in from the night like bad news, bearing a lighted lantern by its long bail, a shotgun held together with tape. They squatted on their haunches side by side like buzzards and smiled around. Suttree looked at them. He looked at one and then he looked at the other. They were alike to the crooks in their stained brown teeth. The creases about their eyes, the quilting of their dry bird necks. They squatted there and bobbed their heads and smiled and spat at the fire and said howdy howdy.

Set and warm, said Reese. Hey old woman. Need some coffee cups over here.

Howdy howdy, said the possumhunters.

We heard ye'ns dogs a while back. Did they not tree?

Naw. Fernon here is got this young bitch keeps a treein flyin squirrels. He's kicked her till she's flat on one side but she dont want to give it up.

Quick as I can see one to shoot I'm goin to tie it round her neck and let her wear it till it rots off. That'll break em ever time. You all got dogs out?

Naw. We just camped up here gettin mussels. Danged if you fellers dont favor one another about as much as anybody I ever saw.

The possumhunters looked at each other and guffawed. Their chins jerked forward as if tied together to a wire and they spat into the fire. We're twins, one of them said.

I allowed maybe ye was.

Most folks caint tell us apart.

Boy you can pull some capers on folks when you look much alike as me and Vernon does.

Reese took cups from the woman and set them on a flat rock by the fire and took up the old blue enamel coffeepot. He gazed at the possumhunters from one to the other. You all aint got the same name have ye? he said.

The possumhunters guffawed and the one with the shotgun elbowed the other one in the ribs. Naw, he said. I'm Vernon and this here is Fernon.

Reese grinned. Suttree was leaning back against the slate of the bluff watching them. They were thin and longboned and squatting there their knees came almost to their ears and their hands lay palm up on the ground before them in the manner of apes.

Lots of folks thinks we got the same name, said the one with the lantern. Their bein so much alike. Dont that coffee smell good.

Just drink all ye want, said Reese, pouring carefully.

They hung their lean faces in their cups and peered over the rims. Reese was full of admiration and kept looking from one to the other of them and shaking his head and looking about at various members of his family to see what they thought.

We dont rightly know which one of us is which noway, said the one with the shotgun. Mama never could tell us apart. They'd just kindly guess. Up till we was long in about four or five years old and could tell our own names. Fore that they aint no tellin how many times we might of swapped.

We had little old bracelets had our names on em but we kicked them off first thing. I caint stand to wear nothin like that nor Vernon neither. I just despise a wristwatch.

One time we was eight year old I fell out of a tree and broke my arm Vernon was at Grandaddy's. They wouldnt let me go for somethin I done. I fell out of a black walnut tree in the back yard and laid there hollerin till Mama come and got me. Well, she run out in the road and stopped a car and they put me in it and took me in to Dr Harrison and we went up the steps to where his office was at and there set Vernon with his own arm broke.

The one with the shotgun grinned and nodded. We'd both fell out of black walnut trees at the identical same minute eight mile apart. I broke my right arm and Fernon his left'n and he's lefthanded and me right.

Pshaw, said Reese.

You dont need to ast us. It was in the papers. You can go look it up your ownself.

We had that piece from the paper a long time.

We can tell what one another is thinkin, said the one with the shotgun. He nodded toward the brother. Me and him can.

Reese looked at him and then he looked at the one with the lantern.

He can think a word and I can tell ye what it is. Or him me, either one.

Caint do it, Reese said.

The possumhunters looked at each other and grinned.

What'll you bet on it?

Well, I dont want to bet nothin. But I'd like to see it done.

They looked at each other again. They had a curious way of turning their heads toward each other, like mechanical dolls. Go on over there Fernon and I'll turn my back.

The one with the shotgun turned around with a lithe swiveling motion. He saw Suttree leaning against the rocks there and winked at him and put his hands over his ears and bent his head. The other one rose and went toward Reese and squatted by him and bent to his ear. Tell me a word, he said.

What kind of word?

Just a word. Whatever. Hush. Whisper it in my ear.

Reese leaned and cupped his hand to the possumhunter's ear and then sat back again. The possumhunter mouthed the word to himself, his eyes aloft. Downriver came the thin cry of hounds and across the flooded fields a yard dog yapped in the distance.

The man with the shotgun raised his head and took his hands from his ears. The boy had come to the fire and was squatting near Reese and the old lady and the girls were watching the hunter with the gun. You got it, Fernon? he cried out.

Yep, said Fernon.

The hunter opened his eyes. He squatted there motionless. His folded shadow skewered by the shotgun leaned across the slates. He looked at Suttree. *Brother,* he said.

Suttree stood up. The hunter spun about and faced his unarmed image across the fire, his sinister isomer in bone and flesh. They hooted like mandrills and pointed with opposing hands at Reese. Reese drew back, his hand to his throat. Suttree took up his bedding and went down the face of the bluff beyond the firelight and through the woods to the river.

In the morning he walked out through the rain to the highway and looked down the long black straight. There had been a high wind in the night and the wet macadam lay enameled up with leaves. He could have just walked off down the road.

The old woman and the girls came in about four oclock with some eggs and things from the farm upriver where they traded and the old woman cast about with her sullen eyes as she did her work, kneading out biscuits and placing them in the iron dutch oven and piling coals with care onto the lid. It was past dark when Reese and the boy came in. They ate supper in silence. The rain that had fallen so small and fine all morning had ceased and Suttree took his bedding off down to the river and lay there with his hands composed upon his chest. Watching up at the starless dark. The shapes of the trees rearing dimly in the lightning. A distant toll of thunder. The sound of the river. Each drift of wind brought rainwater from the trees and it spattered lightly in the leaves and on his face. He'd had enough of rain. The fire had died, he eased toward sleep. The next moment all this was changed forever.

Suttree leaped to his feet. The wall of slate above the camp had toppled in the darkness, whole jagged ledges crashing down, great plates of stone separating along the seams with dry shrieks and collapsing with a roar upon the ground below, the dull boom of it echoing across the river and back again and then just the sifting down of small rocks, thin slates of shale clattering down in the dark. Suttree pulled himself into his trousers and started up through the trees at a run. He heard the mother calling out. Oh God, she cried. Suttree heard it with sickness at heart, this calling on. She meant for God to answer.

Reese! he called. There was no light. He stumbled on a clutch of figures on the ground. A sobbing in the dark. The rain was falling on them. He had not known that it was raining. In a raw pool of lightning an image of baroque pieta, the woman gibbering and kneeling in the rain clutching at sheared limbs and rags of meat among the slabs of rock. One of the younger girls was pulling at her. The boy had come with a flashlight.

Dont, said Suttree.

God almighty, said the boy.

He snatched at the boy's hand. Get that damned light off of her.

Mama. Mama.

Oh God, said Reese.

Suttree turned to see him hobbling toward them holding one knee. He knelt by the woman. Where's that light, he said. I know I seen a light.

Suttree was kneeling by Reese. The cryptic lightning developed a rainveiled face stark and blue upon the ground. He took hold of a pale arm to feel for pulse. The arm was limp and turned the wrong way in his hand and there was no pulse to it. Reese was clawing at the rocks and the woman was moaning and pounding at them with her hand as if they were something dumb that might be driven off. Suttree took the light from the boy and cast it about. A havoc of old crushed signs and lumber. A pot, a mangled lantern. At the far edge of the slide the youngest girl sat dumb and bloody in the rain watching them. He reached and took hold of the topmost slate and raised it and slid it back.

They worked without speaking and when the stones were all shifted the old man got the girl's broken body up some way in his arms and began to stumble off with her. The flashlight lay cocked on the ground and the beam of it angled up toward ultimate night and the rain fell small and slant. He seemed to be making for the river with her but in the loose sand he lost his footing and they fell and he knelt there in the rain over her and held his two fists at his breast and cried to the darkness over them all. Oh God I caint take no more. Please lift this burden from me for I caint bear it.

He left downriver in the dark, the oars aboard, turning slowly in the current, jostling over the shoals. The cottonwoods went by like rows of bones. Come sunrise he was drifting through peaceful farmland upon a river high and muddy. He went along past grazing cows, their cropping in the grass audible above the clank of their bells. They looked up surprised to see him there. The fields were spatched with beds of silt and the shoreline brush wore shapes of wood and rags of paper all among the branches. He passed beneath a concrete bridge and boys fishing called to him but he did not look up. He sat in the skiff and held his hands in his lap with the dark blood crusted on the upturned palms. His eyes beheld the country he was passing through but did not mark it. He was a man with no plans for going back the way he'd come nor telling any soul at all what he had seen.

He lay for days in his cot, no one came. The drums under one corner were banjaxed and the shanty lay tilted in the water so that he had to shore up the legs of his cot on one side with bricks. He did not put out his lines again. The windows in the shanty were mostly broken but he did not turn out to mend them. The river filled with leaves. Long days of fall. Indian summer. He wandered up the hill one evening to look for Harrogate but he did not find him. The musty keep beneath the arches of the viaduct was barren of the city rat's varied furnishings and there was a dog long dead lay there whose yellow ribs leered like teeth through the moldy rug of hide.

He crossed the iron river bridge and went down the steep bank on the far side and came out on the railroad. Dry weeds among the ties, dead shells of milkweed, sumac and mimosa. The old locomotive was half swallowed up in kudzu and enormous lizards lay sunning on the tarred coach roofs.

He went past the high webbed iron wheels, the seized journals and driving rods and the fat coiled springs and past the tender and rotting daycoach with its sunpeeled paint and paneless carriage sashes to the caboose.

There was no one about. He climbed the steps and pushed open the door. The place was littered with trash and the little iron brakeman's stove had been kicked over and lay with the rusted sections of stovepipe in a tip of ash and cinder. On the table in the curious little baywindow lay a seal of yellow candlewax and two burnt matches. The old man's mattress was half off the bunk and there was little trace of his having ever lived there. Suttree kicked at the trash, the cans and papers and rags, and went back out. He followed the old railway trace downriver until he came to the bridge and here he called out the ragpicker.

Who is it?

Suttree.

Come on in.

Come on out.

The old man peered from his enormous vault. He came forth with reluctance. They sat on the ground and the ragman looked at him with his fading eyes. Unkempt baron, he ekes neither tariff nor toll. Where you been? he said.

I was up on the French Broad for a while. What's become of Daddy Watson?

I dont know. I aint seen him.

Well he's not living up here anymore. Dont you know anything about him?

The ragman shook his head. Here today and gone tomorrow, he said. He pointed vaguely toward the ground as if perhaps it were responsible.

Is he dead?

I dont know. I think they come and got him.

Who come and got him?

I dont know.

Shit, said Suttree.

Shit may be, said the ragman. I never took him to raise.

Was it the police?

It might of been any of em. I reckon I'll be next. You aint safe.

I'll agree with that.

What happened to your boatshanty?

It sprang a leak.

I seen it go down some ever day. I looked for it to go plumb in under.

Did he have any kin?

Did who have any kin.

Daddy.

I dont know. Who'd claim it if they was? I might have some myself but you wont see em runnin up and down hollerin it out.

No.

Nor yourn neither maybe.

Suttree smiled.

Aint that right?

That's right.

The ragman nodded.

You're always right.

I been wrong.

What about Harvey. Is he still alive?

You couldnt kill him with a stick.

Harvey's right too.

Drunk son of a bitch.

You're not the only one that's right.

The ragman looked up warily.

We're all right, said Suttree.

We're all fucked, said the ragman.

On a wild night he went through the dark of the apple orchards downriver while a storm swept in and lightning marked him out with his empty sack. The trees reared like horses all about him in the wind and the fruit fell hard to the ground like the disordered clop of hooves.

Suttree stood among the screaming leaves and called the lightning down. It cracked and boomed about and he pointed out the darkened heart within him and cried for light. If there be any art in the weathers of this earth. Or char these bones to coal. If you can, if you can. A blackened rag in the rain.

He sat with his back to a tree and watched the storm move on over the city. Am I a monster, are there monsters in me?

He took to wandering aimlessly in the city. He ate at Comer's hot plates of roast beef or pork with vegetables and gravy and rounds of fried cornbread, Stud jotting down each day the new account and never asking for a dime.

On the streets one day he accosted a ragged gentleman going by in an air of preoccupation. Streets filled with early winter sunshine. Suttree had smiled to see him and he tipped an imaginary cap. Morning, Dr Neal, he said.

The old tattered barrister halted in his tracks and peered at Suttree from under his arched brows. Who'd been chief counsel for Scopes, a friend of Darrow and Mencken and a lifelong friend of doomed defendants, causes lost, alone and friendless in a hundred courts. He pulled at his shapeless nose and waggled one finger. Suttree, he said.

Cornelius. You know my father.

For many years, quite honorably. And his father before him. How is he?

He's well. I see him seldom.

Of course. And what line of work are you yourself in now?

I'm a fisherman.

Into it commercially, is that it?

Yessir.

Now that is interesting. Yes indeed. I'd say a lad with your head on his shoulders should be able to put a wrinkle into it that would make it pay.

It does all right, said Suttree. He was swinging subtly about to recover the wind of the reeking figure he confronted. Studying the patterns of gravy and food on the old lawyer's shirt and tie, his belt of balingtwine. Which had broken one day in the line at the S&W cafeteria leaving him standing there with his tray in his hands, his feet hobbled in his old trousers, his thin old man's shanks the same dirty white as his shirt and as wrinkled.

Always had a warm heart for the outdoor life myself, he said. All sedentaries I suppose. Often wished I'd gone to sea. Have a brother in the navy, lives in the Philippines. He scratched at his unshaven cheek and looked up at Suttree. You stick to your guns, he said. Follow the trade that you favor and you'll have no regrets in your old age.

Suttree wondered what regrets the old lawyer had but he didnt ask.

He took a turn down through the trainyard. He'd a mind to see the station with the fireplaces and the inscriptions from Burns on the mantels, remembering his grandfather stepping down to the platform among the wheeltrucks and the steam and the smiling black porter with the red cap. The old man's cheeks new shaven and the fine red veins like the lines in banknote paper. His hat. His stogie. But when Suttree reached the station it was closed, had long been so. In the fine waiting rooms boxes and cartons piled, great crates in storage. A few abandoned coaches and one pullman stood on a siding and old handbills hung bleached and all but wordless on the notice board. The yard beyond was rafted up with reefers and flatcars, tared hoppers, the romantic stencils broken over the slatted sides of cattlecars, Lackawanna, Lehigh Valley, Baltimore and Ohio, the Route of the Chiefs. He turned on down the tracks toward McAnally.

Where he spoke one day with an old man in a rocking chair. Old man watching out over Grand Avenue from his collapsing porch, taking the sun, a small dog in his lap. Save that he was thin and the dog fat they looked a lot alike. The dog was a drab brown the color of shit and it seemed to have been inflated with a tirepump. Its eyes bulged and it bared its teeth. The old man held the dog and rocked. He claimed that it had saved him from terminal asthma. Suttree regarded the bloated dog doubtfully.

I wouldnt take a war pension for this dog, said the old man.

The dog looked sideways across its shoulder and snarled at Suttree.

When I die he's goin to come to sleep with me. We're to be buried together. It's done arranged.

It is.

I want him just like this. The old man held the dog up in his arms.

What if the dog dies first?

What?

I said what if the dog dies first?

The old man regarded him warily.

I mean if the dog dies first are they going to put you to sleep?

Why hell no that's crazy.

I guess maybe you could just have him frozen. Keep him till the time came.

The old man hugged the crazy looking thing to him. Of course I could, he said.

The blind man at Suttree's elbow in the seeping dusk kept close with his mincing blind man's walk and his hands wove images in the air to prove the things he said. They went down by steep little streets and took a trodden path through the winter fields. The blind man to read his way through the thin soles of his old man's kidskin boots, stepping like a heron among the gravelstrewn ties and down the slight embankment.

Inside Jones's shanty he nodded and smiled in the soft archaic lamplight and the smoke. A scene from some old riverfront doggery where cutthroats' eyes swang in the murk as if in appeal from their own depravity. Richard tottering woodenly in these strange surroundings, his hands outheld. Doll closed the door behind them and looked at the blind man and shuffled away. Suttree showed him to a chair and went to the cooler and raised the lid and dredged up two bottles from the water and opened them and went back to the table. The players' eyes flicked, some nodded gravely. Oceanfrog dealt the last card and tightened the deck in his hand and laid it on the table and looked his way and winked. In the yellow pool of light from the lamp overhead the crumpled bills fell like leaves.

When the bottles clicked on the stained stone Richard looked up and smiled and reached and seized his beer with great accuracy. Suttree eased himself into the folding wooden chair, the varnish peened up in little black blisters along the back where it had been salvaged from a riverside revival tent burnt years ago. The sun lay on the water behind them and thin blades of light played through onto the far wall, dicing the smoke, casting the poker table behind frail and luminous bars. Richard felt the shack tilt on the river and said so. He tested the air with his nose like a rabbit. Smokehouse spoke his name passing to the rear with empty bottles clutched in his hands and Richard smiled and raised his bottle and drank.

See if you can cipher the names under the table, Richard.

Richard looked at Suttree or almost at him. Names? he said.

Under the table. He tapped with his knuckle.

Richard ran a yellow hand beneath the marble slab, up among the twobyfours in which it sat. It's a gravestone, he said.

What does it say?

Richard smiled nervously, the paleblue clams in his eyesockets shifting under the useless lids, his ears tuned like a fox's to the world as he hears it. He slid his palm beneath the table and fished a cigarette from his shirtpocket with the other hand. Eighteen and forty-eight, he said. Nineteen ought seven.

Two of the cardplayers raised their hooded eyes to regard the blind man but he minded them not. Williams, he said.

It doesnt say who Williams?

No Sut, it dont.

Is that all it says?

Richard felt along the underside of the table. That's all, he said. He lit his cigarette and plumed two soundless streams of smoke from his nostrils.

Let's move to another table.

They rose and fumbled their way to the next table and sat again, Suttree steering him by the elbow through the chairs.

Who are they? said Richard.

They're just stones. They came off an island down the river before it was flooded.

Richard shook his head. Thisn dont say who.

It must say something.

He read the stone again, he shook his head. It's wore, he said. Near naked. His face wrinkled.

What is it?

Danged old chewin gum.

Let's try another one.

We ought not to be doin this. Drinkin off folks's gravestones.

Why not?

I dont know.

Would you care?

If it was some of my kin I would.

What if it was you?

I aint dead.

If you were dead. And me and Callahan drank off it. Your stone.

I dont know. I'd be dead. I'd drink off Billy Ray's.

I would too, said Suttree.

I'd drink off of it in a minute.

Suttree grinned.

Course maybe if you was dead you'd think different. I mean, if you're dead and all why I expect you got to be pretty religious.

We'd drink you a toast. Have a good time.

Richard smiled wanly. Well, he said. I like a good time well as the next feller.

I'll get us another beer.

But Richard was fumbling in his pockets and he stopped Suttree with his hand. Let me get em Bud, he said. What do they get for a beer down here?

Thirty-five.

Richard frowned. He's high, aint he? I reckon it's on account of the gamblin.

He doesnt have a license.

For gamblin?

For anything. For living.

I never see him uptown he dont say hidy, said Richard. They dont make em no whiter.

He doled the change into Suttree's palm and Suttree went to the box and got two more beers and came back to a new table. He took the blind man by the hand and led him to it. Doll raised her one eye from where she slept in her shapeless chair, her heavy arms folded across her bosom. One of the poker players jacked his chair back and reached for the stove door and opened it and looked in and she rose heavily and made her way across the floor to the coalscuttle. When she came back from tending the stove she wiped the tables that they'd read and eyed them curiously. Richard had his eyes closed and the smoke from his cigarette rose alongside his thin nose. Something had passed out on the river and the shanty lifted and settled in the swells. Richard suddenly placed his hands flat on the table. Then he lifted them off again as if it were hot. He took up his beer in both hands and held it like that. I aint readin no more, he said.

What is it? said Suttree.

The blind man sucked on his cigarette and shook his head. The thin gray webs of flesh in his neck trembled.

What is it? said Suttree.

There was an oil lamp sconced in the wall above the table and the blind man beneath it sat clearly lit. Suttree looked at his dead eyes but there was no way of seeing in. What is it? he said again.

You knowed what it was, didnt ye?

No. I dont know.

You aint done it for meanness?

I swear I dont know what it says. He was running his own hand under the table but he could not read the stone.

Will you keep it to yourself? said Richard.

Yes. What does it say?

Tween you and me?

Yes.

It says William Callahan.

He woke early with the cold and sat in his cot crosslegged swaddled up in his blanket and looking out the small window. The sun kindled the haze into a salmoncolored drop against which the brittle trees stood like burnt lace. Charred looking sparrows japed and chittered on the rail. Suttree parted back the sackcloth curtains to better see downriver and the birds flew. He was still sitting there when someone came aboard and knocked at his door. He leaned and reached his shirt up from the floor. The knocking came again, someone called his name softly as if he ailed.

When he went to the door Reese was standing there. He carried a new cap in his hands and smiled thinly.

Come in, said Suttree.

I aint got but a minute. I come to give ye your shares.

Come in.

He stood in the little room holding his cap, one foot wide to shore himself against the tilted floor. Suttree sought his shoes under the bed and stepped into them sockless and turned and sat on the couch. Sit down, Reese, he said. Sit down.

Reese sat at the little table and took his pocketbook from the bib of his overalls and opened it. He lifted out a sheaf of bills tied with a dirty string and laid them on the table and folded the pocketbook and put it away again.

What's that? said Suttree.

That's your shares. We never got sold till last week. We had a awful lot of trouble.

I dont want it, said Suttree. Put it back in your pocket.

Reese set his lips and shook his head. It's yourn, he said.

Well let me give it to you.

No.

Suttree looked at the money and shook his head. Where are you living now? he said.

We're back up in Jefferson County. Willard run off.

How are you?

I'm okay. I never did understand that boy. I never would just get to where I could talk to him but what he'd up and do some hatefulness and it not a bit of use in the world in it.

Suttree ran his hand through his hair. The old man seemed small and older yet sitting there.

I never did blame ye for leavin out. Poor luck as we had I reckon ye'd of done better never to of took up with us to start. Did you ever know anybody to be so bad about luck?

Suttree said he had. He said that things would get better.

The old man shook his head doubtfully, paying the band of his cap through his fingers. I'm satisfied they caint get no worse, he said.

But there are no absolutes in human misery and things can always get worse, only Suttree didnt say so.

In the afternoon he went uptown. He bought a thick army sweater at Bower's and he paid Stud twenty dollars on his lunch tab and he went to Regas and ate a steak dinner. When he got home he still had forty dollars left. As he let himself in at his door he thought he heard his name called somewhere like those sourceless voices that address our dreams. He went in and shut the door and lit the lamp and sat on the cot. As he was taking off his shoes he heard it again. Thin and far, somewhere in the night. He sat with a shoe in one hand listening.

He put his shoe back on and went out. Blind Richard was hailing him from the bridge.

What is it? the fisherman called.

The blind man on the bridge raised his thin arm into the lamplight like a supplicant to the chalice of God's bright mercies. A ghost of a voice fell.

Suttree couldnt hear what it said but he cupped his hand to his mouth. No, he called.

His name drifted down from the steel span hung in the night.

Go home Richard. It's late.

The blind man called again but he could not find his way down to the river and Suttree turned his back on him and his cries and went in and shut the door.

Billy Ray Callahan labored for a while as a tilesetter but was fired for drinking. The crewchief stopped him coming from his lunchbreak and confronted him.

You cant drink on the job and put in a day's work. You want to drink you can get your time now.

The crewchief's name was Hicks. Callahan grinned at him. Why Hicks, he said, if I was you I wouldnt be caught without a drink of whiskey on my breath.

Hicks looked suspicious. What do you mean? he said.

Why, so people would think I was drunk instead of just so damned ignorant.

He went to Atlanta looking for work but he didnt find any. He fought two boys from Steubenville Ohio in the alley behind the bus station and left one senseless in the well of a cellar window and went into the men's room and washed his swollen fist with cold water and crossed the station to the gate and boarded the bus back to Knoxville.

Where he worked what jobs he could find, tracking by night his isobar of violence through the streets and taverns. Suttree saw him whip a boy from Vestal named George Holmes, a tall boy who used to like to shoot people. All along the wall by the B&J folks from McAnally and Vestal stood dangerously together and Suttree saw pistols gripped in pockets and out. Callahan hit Holmes twice and Holmes went down. He'd have let it go at that but the crowd called out for more.

Stomp him Red. Stomp his ass.

He gave Holmes a few kicks but Holmes only doubled himself up on the sidewalk. When the police cruiser rounded the corner and came up the hill Callahan took off up Commerce and lay in the parking lot under Junior Long's car. The cruiser went back down the hill with Holmes in the back of it crying and cursing and the crowd had already begun to move away. Holmes had shot a dentist in Vestal not long before this and not long after he shot and killed a man across a cardtable at Ab Franklin's and was sent to the penitentiary. Years later he got out and went back to Franklin's and was shot dead himself over the same table.

The last job Callahan had was running a bootleg joint for a man named Cotton down off Ailor Avenue. Suttree saw him in Comer's and he looked subdued.

I seen ye the other day and you didnt know me, he said.

Bullshit, said Suttree. I never saw you. Where at?

Callahan put his arm around Suttree's shoulder and patted him on the belly. These old summer rabbits, he said. You can set on em and they wont hardly even squeal.

At the woodshed in McAnally they bought whiskey and rolled lightless out the far end of the alley passing the bottle about in the brown paper bag. They drove up Gay Street where Comer's was closing and the hustlers stood about the stairwell, Callahan leaning from the window of the car to hoot at them, and they drove past the little cafes and restaurants where dishwashers were cleaning up in the dim back light and they passed folks coming from the last movie who seemed almost unhinged by what they'd seen or were seeing.

At the West Inn Callahan routed an outland troupe from the premises. And aint they got no beerjoints where you come from? And dont let the door hit ye in the ass goin out. Suttree in the washroom stood slightly drunk and read the legends on the weeping wall. Advised that he was pissing on his shoes. Untrue. Wanted to trade: two blind crabs for one with no teeth. He looked up at the clotted bulb overhead. He buttoned and pushed open the plywood door and went out.

It ended on the Clinton Highway at the Moonlite Diner. Billy Ray smiling and going among the tables while the band played country music. He had his hands in his pockets when the barman confronted him. Small, vicious, quiet. He said: Red, you been stealin money out of them girls' purses.

Callahan rocked back on his heels with his hooligan smile and looked down at his assassin. His pockets were full of the stolen change spoken, he'd drunk their drinks. You're a damned liar, he said goodnaturedly. In the act is wedded the interior man and the man as seen. When he was shot he had his hands in his pockets. The last word came out lie. The roar of the pistol in his face chopped it off and the size of the silence that followed was enormous. Billy Ray was standing there with a small discolored hole alongside his ruined nose. A trickle of thin blood started down his face. The band had finished their set and the people going to the tables paused and looked toward the bar where a small cloud of pale smoke hovered above Billy Ray's shaggy head. They saw him lurch and topple.

Curious the small and lesser fates that join to lead a man to this. The thousand brawls and stoven jaws, the clubbings and the broken bottles and the little knives that come from nowhere. For him perhaps it all was done in silence, or how would it sound, the shot that fired the bullet that lay already in his brain? These small enigmas of time and space and death.

He was lying on his back with one leg doubled under him. He was bleeding from the ears and from the nose and from the hole in his face and he was breathing deeply and regular and he was looking up at the ceiling. The murderer had put the gun back in his pocket and stood looking on like any other spectator. A number of people had already started for the door and when Suttree came up Gary was squatting down looking at Billy Ray as if he did not know what to make of his lying there like that.

Oh my God, said Suttree. Callahan's eyes closed slowly. His whole face was blue and he closed his eyes so that you could not see death come up in them like a face at a window. Suttree pushed through the people and ran for the telephone at the back wall.

They pulled a blanket over him but Suttree drew it back from his face.

Cover him up, said the ambulance attendant.

He's not dead.

They gave Suttree a look much like a shrug and lifted the gurney into the rear of the ambulance and Suttree climbed in and sat on the little banquette at the side and the door closed after him.

Shrieking through the streets of Knoxville, the red domelight sweeping the near walls in narrow places, the windows, faces in cars. Billy Ray turned his head once and arched his neck. The pad beneath him grew black with blood. All through the town tonight are folks lie dying. Sirens in the city like the shriek of jackal birds.

They wheeled him through the emergency room door and into a small white room. There was a steel lamp in the ceiling and a steel table beneath it and there were steel cabinets along one wall. The orderlies lifted Callahan onto the table and wheeled the gurney out again. A nurse looked at him lying there, his chest rising and falling. Someone had put a patch of gauze over the hole in his head and the blood around his ears had blackened and dried. A great rugheaded lout lying there with his heavy hands composed alongside him. She shook her head and closed the door.

Later an orderly came in and looked at him and went out again. He returned with a doctor. The doctor carried a clipboard under his arm and he entered the room and pulled the gauze away from Callahan's face and looked at the hole. He lifted the eyelids and looked in and he lifted the shaggy head and let it back again. The orderly was watching the doctor. The doctor pursed his lips and made a little casual gesture with one hand. He felt Billy Ray's pulse and looked at his watch and raised his eyebrows. He said something to the orderly and then went out again, the orderly behind him, the orderly closing the door.

Suttree and Callahan's older brother Charlie rose from their chairs.

There's nothing we can do for that man, said the doctor.

He's not dead, said Suttree.

No, said the doctor. He's not dead.

The last visitor was an old black orderly, a gentle man who washed the stricken and the dead. He pulled back the gauze and unscrewed the top from a bottle of alcohol and poured it slowly down the hole into Billy Ray's brain.

He lived for another five hours and died sometime before daybreak unattended. They hadnt even taken off his shoes. Charlie had gone home and Suttree and the mother sat in the little waiting room. When the doctor came out and told them he was dead Billy Ray's mother began to cry very quietly. She sat there with her chin quivering and she shook her head slowly from side to side over her dead warrior. Suttree touched her shoulder but she waved him away and she did not look up.

He walked out of the hospital and across the wet grass toward the road. Very slowly the lights of the city were going out, the billboards, the streetlamps. He crossed the river by the high iron bridge, past the orchards in the dark, lights in the water upstream and the sky paling and the night and its disciplines draining away leaving the barren trees as black as iron and a paper city rising in the dawn. A great stillness had fallen. He walked through the dead gray streets. A newspedlar was opening his bale of papers at the corner. The streetsweepers had passed and in the black gutterwater the lights from the polelamps lay like pietins among the darker neon bleedings.

He leaned against the viaduct rail. Spat numbly at the tracks down there. At the dreams implicit in their endless steel reachings. Sectionhands were slouching toward work in the switchingyard. The Watkins man pushed his little trundlecart of nostrums across the bridge, humped between the cart tongues in the wan daybreak. Suttree went down the narrow back path at the end of the bridge. He passed beneath the house of the madman but he was not about at such an hour. Suttree stooped and scrabbled up a half a brickbat and slammed it off the curling clapboards high under the eaves. A crazed putty face slobbered up against the glass, a wild eye cocked there. Suttree turned and went on down the path toward the river.

He spent his days in the poorer quarters of the town seeking out some place with steam heat where he could winter cheaply. The season had grown cold and sunless and a mean wind was in the streets. He found at last a room in the deeps of McAnally. A graylooking woman regarded him sourly through the screendoor.

I came to see about the room, he said.

She sorted a key from among clotted tissues in her apron pocket and unlatched the screendoor and handed it out.

It's around the back, she said.

How much is it?

Five dollars a week.

He thanked her and went around the house by a brick walkway past old gray bushes clogged with leaves and down steps into an unpaved alley. The door was open and he walked in and stood in a dim and musty cellar. A furnace with upflung ductwork like a fat and rusty medusa, a dead iron grin in the doorgrate. He crossed to a painted blue door and peered in. A small cubicle with a concrete floor, an iron cot. He looked back into the furnace room. Some stairs materialized out of the deeper gloom and he crossed to them and mounted upward to a door at the top. Long nailed to. A dead lightbulb hung from a flyspecked cord. He turned in the dark of the landing and came back. The frayed and rotting stair carpet wore blooms of pale blue mold.

In a corner of the cellar was a zinc laundrytub. He tried the taps. A brown liquid spat into the sink and lay there. He went back into the room. There were two small windows let into wells high along one wall, the glass covered with rainspattered sand and hung with spiderwebs. Suttree looked out at the brambly undercarriage of a hedge, some whitestalked grass perhaps wild onions. In the wells dry leaves and papers. A weathered wooden firetruck.

He sat on the cot and looked around but there wasnt much to look at and after a while he went back out and around the house to the front door again.

She stood veiled behind the screen holding out her hand for the key.

I'll take it, he said.

Is it just yourself?

Yes mam.

That'll be five dollars.

He had his money out. Crossing the serried palm with wilted green.

Is that everything there is? I mean you dont have an extra rug or something do you?

I'll see if I do. She folded the bill into her apron pocket and faded away down the lightless hall.

He brought his blankets over and things for coffee. He lay in the little room in the dark a long time listening to the noises and he woke all night to the passing of cars in the street. In the gray dawn he felt alien and not unhappy and lay staring up at the pipes in their hangers on the ceiling, wrapped in burlap or canvas and leaking kapok or a white plasterlike substance. What woke him was a clanging of iron from the outer chamber and when he went to the door and looked out there was a small black hunchback with enormous orange teeth gleaming in the firelight at the furnace door.

Hey, said Suttree.

When the black saw him he turned and began to bow and smile and shuffle and make mows until Suttree thought he dealt here with a wandered idiot.

Are you the furnaceman?

Yazzuh yazzuh yazzuh, said the black, removing his coachman's hat with the lacquered black wickerwork vents.

Shit, said Suttree.

Yazzuh.

What time is it? What's your name?

The furnaceman was winching up a watch enormous from the pocket of his trousers. Ten oclock Nelson, he said, holding the face of the watch toward Suttree should there be any question.

Okay Nelson, thanks.

Yazzuh yazzuh, said Nelson.

Suttree pushed the door shut. He held his hand to the ventilator overhead. A faint breath there. He lit his little kerosene stove and took his kettle out to the sink. Nelson was loading scoops of coal through the iron door into the furnace where a sulphurous smoke swirled. He turned and offered up his ape's grimace all teeth and eyes wedged shut and Suttree nodded at him and turned the tap. The water coughed and spattered clots of iron scale into the sink and finally cleared to a silty dun color not unlike the river's and Suttree filled his kettle and clopped in sockless shoes back across the gritty concrete floor to his room again.

The only piece of furniture other than the cot was a small table with threadspool pulls to the one drawer. It was painted blue and in the drawer lay last year's someday news already foxed and yellow. A few silverfish scuttled away. Suttree had set his little burner on the table and he sat on the bed and read the lacy scrap of newsprint while the water boiled. It was dark enough to want a light of some kind but there was no bulb in the ceiling. He heard the fireman clank shut the door and leave and he poured the coffee and stirred in milk from a can and sipped and blew and read of wildness and violence across the cup's rim. As it was then, is now and ever shall. He was dressed and out by eleven oclock feeling very much a resident of the city, which made him smile to himself as might Harrogate. On whom his thoughts ran this brisk November morn.

He carried off scouring powder and soap and brushes from the men's rooms of restaurants. A broom and a mop from a backporch. Get the bucket too. He swept and scrubbed and in the afternoon went into town and bought cheap muslin for curtains and a wall lamp from the dimestore.

That evening he carried up everything from the shanty, toting his boxes aboard the Euclid Avenue bus and kicking them into the empty space behind the driver's seat while he rummaged his pockets for a dime. And went a figure among the figures through the chill and broken lamplight over the old streets, down Ailor Avenue to the Live and Let Live Grocery where he bought eggs and sausage and bread for a latenight breakfast.

Anybody seeing him all that forewinter long going about the sadder verges of the city might have rightly wondered what his trade was, this refugee reprieved from the river and its fishes. Haunting the streets in a castoff peacoat. Among old men in cubbyhole lunchrooms where life's vagaries were discussed, where things would never be as they had been. In Market Street the flowers were gone and the bells chimed cold and lonely and the old vendors nodded and agreed that joy seemed gone from these days none knew where. In their faces signature of the soul's remoteness. Suttree felt their looming doom, the humming in the wires, no news is good.

Old friends in the street that he met, some just from jail, some taken to trades. Earl Solomon studying to be a steamfitter so he said. They look through his books and manuals there in the cold wind and Earl seems uncertain, smiling sadly at it all.

He'd sit on the front bench at Comer's and watch through the window the commerce in the street below, the couples moving toward the boxoffice of the theatre in the rainy evening, the lights of the marquee slurred and burning in the wet street.

There was a letter for him, the stamp canceled by a vicious slash of dried birdlime. He read a few lines backward candled against the light at the window and wadded it and put it in the trash.

One day coming up Market he caught sight of a crowd among which the maddest man of God yet seen had appeared electrically out of the carbonic fog. He was some two thirds of a man tall and heavily set and red all over, this preacher. He had red curly hair on the back of his balding and boiled looking head and his skin was pale red and splotched with huge bloodcolored freckles and he was delivering the word in such fashion as even the oldest codgers on this street long jaded to the crop with crazed gospelarity could scarcely credit. Hucksters left their carts and vans untended. The pencil vendor crouched in his corner came crawling and growling through the crowd. The red reverend had hardly begun. He tore out of his coat and rolled his sleeves.

This aint goin to get it, he said. No. He made a sweeping gesture down Market and toward the markethouse. No. This just aint goin to get it. Friends, this aint where it's at.

The watertruck had passed on Union and a creek came curling down the gutter black and choked with refuse. The preacher scooped a bobbing turnip from the flood and held it aloft. He provideth, he said. He knelt, oblivious to all, offering up the turnip, the water boiling about his thighs and sucking down the storm sewer. He washed the turnip like a raccoon and took a great bite. Here's where it's at, he said, spewing chewed turnip. On your knees in the streets. That's where it's at.

An old man mad as he knelt beside. The preacher passed him the turnip. He give out the loaves and the fishes, he howled. Therefore ast not what shall I put on.

The turnip was going from hand to hand in search of communicants. The old man had crawled into the flooded gutter among the sewage and was demanding baptism. But the preacher had risen with his red hands joined in a demented mudra above his glowing skull and begun a dance of exorcism. In the marketplace, he screamed. But not this buyin and sellin. He had begun to rotate with arms outspread and his small feet mincing like a revolving parody of the crucifixion. His eyes had swiveled back in his head and his lips worked feverishly. He went faster. The old man had arisen dripping and he tried to emulate this new and rufous prophet but he tilted and fell and the preacher had begun to rotate with such speed that the crowd dropped back and some just stayed their hands from clapping.

Suttree went on. A mute and shapeless derelict would stop him with a puffy hand run forth from the cavernous sleeve of an armycoat. Woadscrivened, a paling heart that holds a name half gone in grime. Suttree looked into the ruined eyes where they burned in their tunnels of disaster. The lower face hung in sagging wattles like a great scrotum. Some mumbled word of beggary. To make your heart more desolate.

In the evening he would cross Vine Avenue hill on his way homeward, past the old school he'd attended in his infancy, morguelike with its archives of bitterness, past the church with her pawnshop globes of milkglass lightly decked each with a doily of coalsoot and past old brick apartments where in upper windowcorners a white hand might wipe the glass and glazed in the sash a painted face appear, some wizened whoreclown, will you come up, do you dare? He never. Maybe once. Crossing the Western Avenue viaduct he'd stop and lean upon the concrete balustrade where polished riverstones lay in the cracks and gaze down at the broad sprawl of tracks in the yard and the tarred roofs of railcars, a lonely figure framed against the gray pales of the city's edges where the smokestacks reared against the squalid winter sky like gothic organpipes and black and tuneless flags of soot stood down the wind.

One night he came upon a house aflame and took a seat beyond harm's way to watch. People coming to the front door like ants out of a burning log. Carrying their effects. One struggled with an old man in a nightcap who seemed bent upon incineration, tottering about and mouthing gummed curses backward at the fates so long familiar.

Lights appeared up and down the street. Neighbors in their flannel robes came out to watch. An upper window sagged and buckled and collapsed. Sheets of flame ran up the clapboards and they blistered and curled in the heat. A hot blue light crackled through the orange smoke.

How'd it start?

Suttree looked down. A little man was leaning to him with the question.

I dont know, said Suttree. How all things start.

He rose and went on.

A police cruiser must ask his name, where is he going. Suttree proper and wellspoke, bridling the malice in his heart. Pass on. Down alleyways where cats couple, rows of ashcans and dark low doors. This pane of dusty light.

Suttree stood in a kitchen among fugitives and mistried felons. A stout woman doled beers from a cooler and made change out of an apron pocket in which hung the shape of a small automatic pistol. An emaciated whore eyed him as he entered, a stringy sloe-eyed cunt with false teeth and a razorous pelvis beneath the thin dress she wore. Wallace Humphrey stood in one corner with his eyes half closed and his hands dangling. In his oldfashioned suit he looked like one of those western badmen photographed hanging from barndoors or propped up in shopwindows shot full of holes.

Let me have a Redtop, Suttree said.

She handed him a bottle and held out her wet red hand. Suttree placed a halfdollar in it and got his change and went past the whore toward the living room.

Hey sweetie, she said.

Hey, said Suttree.

Through the smoke he saw friends among the drinkers and he made his way toward them.

Here's old Suttree, called Hoghead.

Welcome to the Buffalo Room, said Bucket.

Where's old J-Bone, Sut?

He's still up in Cleveland.

When's he comin back?

I dont know. I had a letter from him said he was working as an assembler. He said every morning he assembles his ass in a corner and watches the proceedings for eight hours.

Old Richard Harper is back from Chicago, him and Junior. Harper was supposed to get em staked up there and Junior said he like to got em burned at the stake.

Junior said the windy city wasnt ready for Harper. He said they had enough wind as it was.

Get ye a drink here, Sut.

Bucket pulled a pint bottle from behind him and handed it to Suttree and he unscrewed the cap and drank.

Bobbyjohn's old crazy uncle was in here a while ago, Bud, he was goin on about haulin whiskey back in the prohibition. Said they come into Knoxville early one mornin with a load, wasnt daylight yet. Old Tip said he was asleep in the front seat and they was a car backfired and he raised up and shot a woman waitin on the bus. Said he seen her feet stickin out of a hedge.

Suttree grinned and drank from his beer. Figures slouched through the smoke like ghosts and there was about the room that eerie reverence felt in places where great crimes have been done. He stayed till the last cup was drained. Leaning in a doorway in the small hours watching a fat whore humping on a bed that bore the black shoetracks of many a traveler. Drifting with the last customers down the alley toward the street. Giggles and catcalls. The plastic purses of the whores cutting garish curves in the milkblue light of the streetlamps. Plates of white ice broken in the chuckholes. A small coalcolored owl trilled from a lightpole and Suttree looked and saw him fluff against the sky. He called again, called softly. Suttree sat on an old stone curb with his back to the pole, a silent dweller in a singing wood. Newsboys were putting forth with wagons through the murk, old feral fathers wading in the surf of older dawns to launch their tarred boats on some dark and ropy shoal.

An empty beercan rolled in a light tin clank down the street before the dawn wind. Wind cold in his nostrils. He watched the graying in the east, a soiled aurora. The city's fabled salients rising through the mist.

Sunday morning Suttree shuffled down a dim stairwell in the clothes in which he'd slept. Across the street the markethouse stood gaunt and dark in the easy rain. Hunched in front of the hotel in an uncanny silence he sucked his coated teeth. Old awnings covered the barren truckbeds and barrows. You could hear the small heeltaps of an idle whore receding in the streets. Claustral landscape of building faces even to the sky. The heelclicks sing with a stinging sound. Suttree looked upward. The baroque hotel front flaking a peagreen paint. A church clock tolling. Pigeons reel and flap in the bellpeal. In the gutted rooms sad quaking sots are waking to the problem of the Sunday morning drink.

It seemed to rain all that winter. The few snowfalls turned soon to a gray slush, but the brief white quietude among the Christmas buntings and softlit shopwindows seemed a childhood dream of the season and the snow in its soft falling sifting down evoked in the city a surcease nigh to silence. Silent the few strays that entered the Huddle dusting their shoulders and brushing from their hair this winter night's benediction. Suttree by the window watched through the frosted glass. How the snow fell cherry red in the soft neon flush of the beersign like the slow dropping of blood. The clerks and the curious are absent tonight. Blind Richard sits with his wife. The junkman drunk, his mouth working mutely and his neck awry like a hanged man's. A young homosexual alone in the corner crying. Suttree among others, sad children of the fates whose home is the world, all gathered here a little while to forestall the going there.

He spent a lot of time in the library reading magazines. An assortment of wildeyed freaks used to frequent the upstairs reading room, glancing furtively about, their cocks hanging out of their trousers beneath the tables, eyeing the schoolboys. One evening coming out of May's cafe and heading toward the B&J he passed two women sailing along in the other direction. He turned around and followed them back in. They spoke with yankee accents a jivy kind of talk he thought he'd listen to and he took the booth behind them and ordered a beer. Before he'd taken a sip of it one of them turned and fixed him with an up and down look of brazen appraisal. What's happening in this town? she said.

Suttree hung his arm over the back of the booth and looked at them. Not much, he said. Where you all from?

Chicago.

How long you been here?

Off and on for a couple of months.

Off and on is right, sweetie, said the older one. The other one smiled at Suttree. We're hustlers, she said. But we wont hustle you.

Suttree liked her.

Well, he said. There's usually something going on at the Indian Rock.

You want to go out there with us?

He rubbed his jaw. The clock hanging from the ceiling turned on its gilt chain. 11:20.

I'm Joyce and this is Margie, the nice one said.

Hi Joyce. Hi Margie.

What do you think?

Okay, he said. I guess so.

They went in a cab, the three of them in the back and him in the middle. They were all a little drunk.

She pulled out a handful of money to pay the cab with but he pushed it back and paid himself. The cabdriver hissed at him to bend and hear.

Them old gals is hustlers.

Suttree patted him on the arm.

When he danced with her she pressed her thigh between his legs and breathed against his neck. Hard impress of her pubic bone. She smelled very good. The older one kept cutting in on them and Suttree would have to dance with her. He saw no one he knew except Roop the drummer who kept winking huge hobgoblin winks at him.

You never told me your name, she said.

Bud.

Bud.

Yeah.

Okay Bud.

They'd been drinking whiskey and he found the floor a bit unmanageable but she didnt seem to notice. She nibbled his jugular with crimped lips. I like you, Bud, she said.

How do you know.

I can tell.

Can you feel it in the marrow of your bones?

That's not exactly the spot.

How long are you going to be around?

I dont know. A while. I cant go back to Chicago.

Why not.

A little indictment.

Ah.

I travel around. I'm in and out of Knoxville.

In and out and off and on.

She bit his neck.

Do you want another drink?

I'd love one. Let me get them.

I've got them.

He walked her back to the table and called the waitress.

That girl that was here said to tell you she had to go, the waitress said.

They looked at each other. Suttree ordered ice and drinks and the waitress moved away, writing on her pad, her lips moving.

You didnt say anything to her did you? said Suttree.

No. You know I didnt.

They watched each other over the rims of their half empty glasses. They started giggling.

When they pulled up in the mouth of the alley she put her hand on his leg, apprehensive as a young girl.

It's all right, he said.

What's here?

I live here.

There's no lights.

It's all right.

Why dont we go to my hotel?

Suttree was already out. He had one hand extended to help her out and the other lay on the cold steel top of the taxi. He looked up at the dim and midnight shadowworld of shapes above McAnally, dark nightscape of lightwires and chimneypots. He reached down and took her hand. Look, he said. I'm not Jack the Ripper. I live just down here. It's not much but it's clean and I've got something to drink, a couple of beers I know and a little in the bottom of a bottle of whiskey I think. Come on.

She emerged cautiously from the cab and Suttree held her hand while he paid the driver. He slammed the door shut and the cab pulled away and he took her down the little cinderpath alleyway, taking his key from his pocket, showing her the way.

He opened the door and turned on the light. She stood in a cellar. Fire showed in the slotted mouth of the furnace and a wild melee of piping reeled away over the ceiling, their own shadows dipping in the slight swing of the lightbulb from its cord. A deep musty smell. She turned and looked at him. I must be crazy, she said. Will someone tell me what I'm doing here?

He crossed to the door of his room.

What's that, the coalbin?

He turned the light on in his cubicle and ushered her in. She leaned in the doorway with one hand on his shoulder. Well, she said.

Go ahead.

He closed the door. They sat on the bed and kissed. They fumbled with each other. Mmm, she said. She leaned and licked his ear and whispered in. What you dont do right, she said, you're going to have to do over.

Winter sunlight parried from an upper wall fell over them from the high window. He lay awake in the narrow cot, one hand dangling on the floor. He turned to look at her. Pull back these covers from her chin. Is she gross? Is she horrid? Is she old?

She lay slackmouthed in sleep and not unlovely. He laid his face against her full breasts and slept again.

When he woke she was sitting on the edge of the bed in one of his shirts smiling down at him, her ashblond hair tumbled about her face. She was holding a cup of coffee for him.

Hi, he said.

Hello lover. Are you ready for liquids?

Mggh.

Yes, I know. Just sit up a bit. She fluffed the pillow with one hand and then held the cup to his lips.

What time is it?

Noon.

Do you have to go?

Yes. She brushed back his hair.

He drank the coffee.

I copped one of your shirts, she said.

You wont leave those bumps in it will you?

No, she said, taking the cup. She leaned over him. I wont leave anything messed up or marked on except you. She kissed him. She tasted of mint. She ran her hand down his belly. Oh my, she said.

What do you want? said Suttree grinning.

When he woke again she was dressed and sitting at the table combing her hair. He watched her. She put the comb in her purse and snapped it shut and turned around and came over to the bed.

I've got to go, baby.

Well.

Is that laundry tub what you bathe in?

Yes. Such as it is.

I was stripped off out there washing my pussy when some spade came in. An old guy. He almost fainted.

Marvelous, said Suttree. What did he say?

Well, he had on this crazy hat and he took it off and began to bow and to back out the door saying: Scuse me mam, scuse me mam.

God help him. He'll be more peculiar than ever.

She brushed his hair back. When will I see you?

I dont know.

What are you doing tonight?

Nothing. Are you asking for a date?

Do you mind?

No.

May I see you this evening?

It'll have to be someplace cheap.

I've got some money. Baby dont. I've really got to go. Baby.

She left in midafternoon. He lay in the bed a depleted potentate. He felt very good.

A wan midwinter sun hung low and oblong under the leeward fishshaped clouds. A sun hotjowled and squat in the seeping lavender dusk. Down this narrow street where the chinese sign glows green. She is waiting, cupboarded in one of the high booths. A congenial oriental to bid good evening. Suttree saw her smile from a far corner.

No. With the young lady there.

The waitress smiled.

Hello baby.

Hello.

He slid into the seat opposite but she took his hand. Come sit by me.

He stood up again. Come over here, he said. So we dont bump elbows.

You're a southpaw.

Yes.

She rubbed past him. Nice, she said.

She was wearing a pale yellow knit dress that fit her all over and she looked very good. They sat and looked at each other and she leaned and kissed him.

How long have you been here? he said.

I dont know. Half hour.

I didnt know I was so late.

I dont care. I dont mind waiting for you as long as you come.

Did you get wet?

No. I got a cab. Is it still raining out?

No. What shall we eat?

Do you want me to make a suggestion? She was smiling at him and she had taken his elbow in both hands.

No, he said.

They sat together in the booth looking over the newspapersize menu.

The butterfly shrimp are good.

Why dont you order for us.

Okay. What about the combination platter.

That sounds good. Does it have the sweet and sour pork?

Yes. And let's get some eggrolls.

With hot mustard.

You like hot mustard?

Yes. Do you?

I love it. They have some here that will completely remove your sinuses.

I'm hip.

There was no one else in the restaurant. It grew dark outside the window and she held his arm and they sipped tea and waited for the food to come.

They went to a movie. He smiled at the memories induced. Sitting rigid and frightened alongside some girlchild trying to muster the courage to take her hand.

The two of them whispering sexual slanders concerning the actors into each other's ear, vying to elaborate the most outrageous perversions. They had coffee at the Farragut coffee shop and they walked through the streets in the small rain and muted lights and looked in the shopwindows, wrapped in their coats and huddled close and the smell of her good perfume and her hair. And she who had not stopped smiling like a happy cat the evening long took him by the arm down Gay Street to her hotel and through the steamed glass doors into the lobby, the old white tiles and potted plants and polished brasswork. She sauntered to the desk and got her key and came back and took him by the arm and they went to the elevator with a small tancolored bellhop who had been reading the paper at a table in the lobby.

The old brass lattice door clicked shut and they began to rise. A dim hum of mechanisms, cables that slithered in a steep brick well.

You getting any of this white pussy, James? she said.

James shook his head that he wasnt.

She held Suttree's arm. They got off at the fifth floor and went down a long corridor, a black rubber rug. Past door and door alike with metal numbers nailed on them or missing or askew. She put the key in her door and opened it and held out her hand for him to enter.

Go ahead, he said.

He followed her in and she shut the door and took off her coat and hung it on the back of the door and turned to him and began to unbutton his peacoat. The room was neat and orderly with a great sprawl of cosmetics across the dressing table and bureau top and a portable hairdryer and curlers and some expensive looking clothes hung from the walls. A great stuffed ape with long arms and orange hair sat on the bed.

That's Og, she said.

Who named him that, you?

My girlfriend. She gave him to me.

Margie?

No. Chick in Chicago. Christ, this thing weighs a ton.

Let me get it.

I've got it. You're not wet are you? Your head's wet.

It's all right.

She had a towel and was tousling his hair with it. You look like a little boy, she said. Here. Sit down. Let me see if there's any music on the radio.

Suttree unzipped his shoes and kicked them off and scooted back on the bed and crossed his feet and lifted one of the ape's arms and let it fall again.

You like hillbilly?

Anything.

I used to hate it.

Find something else.

There was a knock on the door and she went to answer it. The elevator man stood with a tin bucket of ice and a pint of whiskey in a paper bag.

Baby, she said, do you want a Coke or something? I didnt think to ask you.

I dont need anything.

She paid the stolid yellow James and shoved the change back at him and shut the door with her elbow. She set the bucket and the package of whiskey on the bedside table and took a pair of glass tumblers from the shelf above the sink and brought them over and filled them with ice. She sat on the edge of the bed and started peeling at the seal on the bottle until Suttree took it from her and twisted the cap loose with his teeth. He poured the drinks and they sat on the bed opposite each other and sipped and looked at each other and smiled.

I wonder if I'm already hungry again or if it's something else, she said.

They say that's the trouble with chinese girls.

What?

An hour later and you're horny again.

She smiled and sipped from her glass. There was altogether too much of her sitting there, the broad expanse of thigh cradled in the insubstantial stocking and the garters with the pale flesh pursed and her full breasts and the sootblack piping of her eyelids, a gaudish rake of metaldust in prussian blue where cerulean moths had fluttered her awake from some outlandish dream. Suttree gradually going awash in the sheer outrageous sentience of her. Their glasses clicked on the tabletop. Her hot spiced tongue fat in his mouth and her hands all over him like the very witch of fuck.

He woke later in the night alone in the bed. She was sitting at the dressing table engaged in alchemic rituals with creams and lotions, she was at brushing her hair. In the dark window and partly obscured by the old lace drapes a red pulse of watered light bloomed and faded and the sound of the rain and the traffic in the wet streets made him sprawl deliciously in the sheets. She was watching him in the glass. She winked. Hi lover, she said.

Hello baby. What time is it?

She bent to see her watch. It's quarter to one, she said. Did you have a good nap?

Mmm.

Would you like a drink?

Yes. I can get it.

No.

She rose and came over to the bed. She was wearing a pale blue negligee that flowed lightly behind her. She came and bent and kissed him and he stroked her breasts and she propped him up with both pillows and fixed the drink and sat on the bed for a moment.

What was all that racket a while ago?

Goddamned Ralph came up here trying to get room rent. You wouldnt believe it. Said you were supposed to be in the date room.

Did you get him straightened out?

She smiled. I told him you were no goddamned date. I think I called him a nigger cocksucker.

How did he go for that?

He didnt say. That fucking James has got a big mouth too.

Was that Margie in here?

Yeah. She's jealous.

What, of you or me?

Silly. Her old man put her down I think. She's jealous of me, sure, but that chick is almost fifty years old for Christ sake.

I dont see how she makes it.

She's a hundred dollar a night girl.

Her?

Sure. All she has to do is turn fifty tricks. That's mean isnt it?

What brought you down here?

Money what else. Anyway I cant go back to Chicago for a while.

You said you were under indictment. What for?

Selling my pussy.

Her impish grin. Watching him. He sipped the whiskey. Where's Og? he said.

Oh, he's over here on the floor. I guess his nose is out of joint too. She tucked the covers about Suttree's naked chest and went back to her things at the dresser. He had finished the drink and almost drifted into sleep half sitting there in the sagging bed when she turned off the light and climbed in beside him, her warm soft scented body length to length against his own and her breath in his ear whispering obscene endearments.

The hammering of steampipes woke him in the small hours of the night and he lay in the strange room with the red neon flicker of the hotel sign silent at the window. Silence in the streets. She sprawled like a child, one hand loosely clutched by the side of her sleeping face.

In the morning it was still raining or raining again. Alone in the room, brailed in the soft and springshot bed he listened to the traffic below the window, the muted slicing of tires in the wet. Looking up at the ceiling, the petals of wallpaper hanging, the old and ornate gas fixture with brass cherubs. He eased himself up. Gray rain leaned past the window. There was some sort of horrendous foundrywork going on about the hotwater pipes and a little poppet valve on the radiator was hissing like a kettle. He crossed the cold buckled linoleum with puckered feet and stood naked by the window and watched the Monday morning traffic in the streets below. A different slant on life here. Old whiskey bottles with their bleached labels lying on the wet tar of the rooftops. A glass skylight covered with chickenwire. The cold winter rain falling everywhere over the city.

He put on his clothes and went down the hall to the bathroom. A door with MEN stenciled across it. A tall narrow hall of a room in domino tiles. A yellow tub on clawfeet, a sink and a toilet. Suttree pissed long and loud, peering out through the patterned glass of the window at the winter day.

When he got back to the room it was still empty. He took a towel and a bar of soap and went back down the corridor and had a hot bath. When he returned to the room he tried shaving himself with her electric razor. He looked through her things, careful to leave each as it had been. An eclectic tale of gewgaws, the fine with the shoddy. He borrowed her toothpaste and brushed his teeth with his fingers.

She came in smiling and bearing packages and smelling of perfume and rain. She took off the plastic babushka she wore and shook out her hair and came to him unbuttoning the belted raincoat and looking like a movie whore. She kissed him and said hello.

You havent eaten? I brought you some coffee and the paper.

What time is it?

It's about eleven. Why dont we go over to Regas and have lunch.

Okay.

I'm starving, arent you?

I'm about to faint. What time did you stir out this morning?

I dont know. Nine. Here. Be careful, it's hot.

Thanks.

She took off the coat and shook it and laid it on the bed and went to the dressing table to repair her makeup. She seemed ladylike and efficient in her spikeheeled shoes and her tweed suit. Suttree sat on the bed and sipped the coffee and looked at the paper. She watched him in the mirror. She gave him a big sexy wink.

They went down in the elevator with a young black who kept his eyes averted and she made obscene signals above the back of his small neat head. They crossed the lobby arm in arm like a honeymoon couple and she spoke cheerily to the lolling porter and turned up her collar and they crossed the wet street and ducked into Regas.

The next day they got thrown out of the hotel. Suttree hadnt been back to his room in McAnally and they had bought him new clothes to wear and she had picked out a pigskin shavingbag for him and fitted it with all manner of things that he hardly knew the use of, the powders and colognes and lotions and little chrome tools for the care of the nails. They packed all their things down and into a cab and went to the other end of Gay Street where she talked and gestured by the desk with the black bellcaptain and he sat in the back of the cab half buried in dresses and boxes.

She's wavin you on in, the driver said.

Suttree got out of the cab and entered the little dingy lobby that he'd passed a hundred times or more. The cadaverous keeper of the place knew him from the Huddle across the street. Suttree nodded to him and went over to the bellcaptain.

Bud, this is Jesse, she said.

Hello Jesse.

Jesse's head moved very slightly.

Listen baby, do you want to stay here?

What do you mean?

I mean move out of that cellar and stay here. Look, Jesse is an old friend. He knows me and he knows I'm not interested in turning five dollar tricks with these brokendown whores he runs in here. He's got a room up on the top floor we can have if you want. I think I'm going to Athens tomorrow.

Athens?

Yeah. I talked to the guy down there this morning. He said I could come for two weeks at least. Baby, I could come away from there with a grand if I had someone to take care of it for me.

Suttree, who wasnt all that sure what she was talking about, said that he would.

She was very businesslike. She gave him five dollars and he went out and he and the cabdriver carried in their things and stacked them on chairs and on the desk and draped clothes over the banister rail. The driver fumbled around for change but she waved him off and they went up the stairs with armloads of varied finery.

This place is a real rat trap, she said, wheezing back at him from the third landing. But they dont hassle you.

Suttree muttered into a mound of perfumed garments. They were going past gaping fist holes in the stairwell walls and places in the balustrade ripped bare and mended back with raw twobyfours. Down a narrow ill lit hall to a door where she leaned and held the key for him to take.

It looked like the room they'd left, somewhat smaller, a bit more shabby. They piled everything on the bed and went down to get the rest of it. They strung a piece of wire across a corner of the room to hang the clothes on, fastening one end to the doorhinge and the other to the curtainrod bracket above the window. Suttree looked out on the street below.

She woke him in the cold dark of morning among the pipeclang and the stridence of whores passing in the hallway drunk and she was whimpering with fright. He stroked her naked back while she breathed out a dream in the darkness. We were in a car and they dragged you out, they were taking you away it was awful.

You dont have any little friends I should know about do you?

She stroked his face. It was just a dream, baby.

In the morning he put her on the bus, kissing her there at the steps where the driver stood with his tickets and his puncher and the diesel smoke swirled in the cold, Suttree smiling to himself at this emulation of some domestic trial or lovers parted by fate and will they meet again? She went along the aisle with her overnight bag and sat by the window and made elaborate gestures of enticement at him through the glass like a whore mute or in such outland port as christians reck no word of speech there. Until he blew her a kiss and hunched his shoulders to say that it was cold and went up the steps.

Now at noon each day he wakes to the gray light leaking in past the gray rags of lace at the window and the sound of country music seeping through the waterstained and flowered walls. Walls decked with random flattened roaches in little corollas of oilstain, some framed with the print of a shoesole. In the rooms the few tenants huddle over the radiators, flogging them with mophandles, cooking ladles. They hiss sullenly. The cold licks at the window. In the bathrobe and slippers she has bought for him and carrying his pigskin shavingcase he goes along the corridor like a ghost through ruins, nodding at times to chance farmboys or old recluses with skittish eyes emerging from assignations in the rooms he passes. To the bathroom at the end of the hall that no one used save him, the yellow bowl spidered with cracks, the paintstained tub, the diamond panes in the window looking out on a ledge where pigeons crouched in their feathers lee of the wind. A gravel roof where a rubber ball lay rotting. The city a collage of grim cubes under a sky the color of wet steel in the winter noon.

Down the half wrecked stairs to the lobby where he'd get the morning paper from a rack and nod to the dayclerk and with his coatcollar up step into the brisk street with the wind cool on his shaven cheek and down to the Tennessee Cafe where for thirty cents you could get a stack of hotcakes and coffee cup on cup.

J-Bone was still in Cleveland. Others from McAnally gone north to the factories. Old friends dispersed, perhaps none coming back, or few, them changed. Tennessee wetbacks drifting north in bent and smoking autos in search of wages. The rumors sifted down from Detroit, Chicago. Jobs paying two twenty an hour.

The neon rigging went up early, wan ornaments adorning the bleak afternoon. From the hotel window he watched the traffic and he could see through the shelled brickwork of the Cumberland Hotel half razed across the street the rain falling on the dim jungled shacks of the black settlement along First Creek. The sound of the factory whistles in the long dead afternoon seemed sad beyond all telling. Suttree a sitter at windows, a face untrue behind the cataracted glass, specked with the shadow of motes or sootflecks, eyes vacuous. Watching this obscure and prismatic city eaten by dark to a pale electric superstructure, the ways and viaducts and bridges remarked from gloom by sudden lamps their length and the headlights of traffic going through the plumb uncloven rain and the night.

To come in half drunk at a late hour from the Huddle or what worse place and lie suspended in the bed in this house of derelict pleasures where half the night all through the cardboard chambers doors exchanged and brief ruts spent themselves in the joyless dark and the only sounds ever of desire the sometime cries of buckled tribades in the hours toward dawn when trade was done.

In the middle of the week Dick gave him an envelope postmarked Athens with a loveletter from her and two naked hundred dollar bills inside. He took from behind the cashregister the section of broomhandle the key was tied to and went to the toilet and took out the money and looked at it, such exotic tender with the values printed bold and green. He folded them and put them in his pocket. Tuesday she sent three more. He would lay out the five bills on the bed and he and the stuffed ape would look at them without really understanding them at all.

She arrived in the dark of early Sunday morning in a taxi she had taken from Athens and she was wearing a pair of flannel pajamas and a trenchcoat and she had the plastic overnight bag filled with money. She was slightly drunk. She pushed open the door and stood there framed against the orange and burntlooking hallway in a classic hooker's pose and said: Hey big boy. Suttree rolled over in the bed to see what was happening, and she said: How would you like to get fucked?

Not tonight, honey. I'm expecting her back.

She came across the room shedding her raincoat as she went. You son of a bitch, she said, laughing.

Watch out, you'll bend the tentpole.

You'll think tentpole when I get through with you.

Young lady try to control yourself.

Hello baby.

Hi.

They talked all morning. She told him everything. She was from Kentucky, which surprised him. She liked girls, which didnt. And all the towns and cheap hotels and a couple of lockups and a few sadistic pimps and tricks and the cops and the jails and the nigger bellhops while beyond the window dawn unlocked the city in paling increments of gray.

They went out to breakfast before the day had even well begun, going up to the corner through the fog and the coalsmoke and the smell of roast coffee to hail a cab, Suttree scrubbed and aromatic and pleasantly tired and hungry and her holding his arm.

What am I supposed to do with all this money? he said.

Well. You can buy my breakfast.

Seriously. I feel like every heist artist in town is watching me.

How much do you have?

The five bills you sent.

I didnt mean for you not to spend any of it.

I had some money.

Well, put it in the bank. I've got another three something. I thought maybe, I dont know . . . get an apartment. What do you think?

It's up to you.

No it's not.

Well.

They took a cab to Gatlinburg and stopped at a service station to have chains put on the tires. Suttree got two paper cups of ice and poured the ice from the cups into the glasses she had brought and poured the whiskey over the ice and they settled back with the blanket over their laps and drove into the winter mountains.

The silent cabman carried them through a white silent forest by caves in the roadside cliffs all toothed with ice and the only sound the trudge of the shackled tires in the dry snow of the road. Suttree cozied up with his trollop and his toddy, she looking out with child's eyes at this wonderland. It's fucking beautiful, she said.

They stopped for icicles to cool their drinks. Suttree clambered over a low stone wall and dropped into deep snow. Down the slope the firs stood black and brambly in their white shrouds and a fine mist of snow was blowing with a faint hiss like sand. He pissed a slushy yellow flower in the landscape, standing there with his drink in one hand, looking out on a wild white upland world as old as any thing that was and not unlike it might have looked a million years ago. Just when he would have said that nothing lived in these frozen altitudes two small gray birds flew. They came from a clump of snowbroken heather below and crossed the slope in a loping flight like carnival birds on wires and vanished in the forest.

He walked up the road, his shoes crunching in the packed snow. Under an overhang of icebound rock where sheer palisades of opaque crystal walled up the black forests above and he could hear the wind suck and moan in the trees. He reached to pluck small icicles from the rocks until he'd filled his glass with them.

Back in the cab she covered him with the blanket and rubbed his hands. You're icy cold, she said.

At Newfound Gap there were skiers, a bright group bristling with their poles and skis about the parked cars. They pulled in to watch them, goggled madmen in clouds of powder dropping down through the fir forests at breakneck speed. She clutched his arm, them standing there with their drinks and their breath swirling in the cold.

They went back in the early blue twilight, ghosting down the mountain with frames of snowy woodland veering inverted across the glass. They made love under the blankets in the back seat like schoolchildren and later she sat up and talked into the silent cabman's ear and made him promise not to tell what they had done and he said that he would not.

In the morning she took him shopping. Suttree in gray tweeds being fitted.

I love this, she said.

What, shopping?

For men's things. It's sexy.

They selected shirts and ties and cufflinks. They studied shoes in a glass case. A sleek attendant hovered.

Wednesday noon he appeared at Comer's in a pair of alligator shoes and wearing a camelhair overcoat. A pair of beltless gabardine slacks with little zippers at the sides and a winecolored shirt with a crafty placket requiring no buttons.

Fuckin Suttree's robbed Squiz Green's, said Jake.

Stud grinned and wiped the countertop before him. What'll you have, Sut?

I think I'll go for the steak and gravy.

Ulysses leaned on the counter and studied him. He took Suttree's lapel between his thumb and forefinger and eased the coat open to read the label, nodding sagely, a toothpick in his mouth. Fishing business has picked up a bit, has it? he said.

Fishy business, more likely, said Sexton, posed beneath his picture on the wall in flight gear, tapping his thigh with the wooden triangle and watching down the hall.

Let me have a chocolate milk, said Suttree.

She was gone to Asheville for ten days. He had a radio in the room now and a rug for the floor by the side of the bed for stepping out onto. In the afternoons he'd run down ads in the paper for apartments to let, stalking around in cold and barren corridors with half a heart and listening to the chatter of a graying landlord in houseshoes with his massive ring of keys like some latterday gaoler saying blah blah blah blah blah. When she came back he was still at the hotel.

He showed her the bankbook. It was in her name and there was eleven hundred dollars in the account. She gave it back to him and smiled and pushed his nose.

He watched her while she sat at the mirror and dried and set her hair, himself consumed in womby lassitude there in the sagging bed, watching her scoop great daubs of cream from a pot and slab it onto her arms and her breasts, her eyes turned to his in the mirror where he lay sipping his drink. She had smeared her face with a sizelike caulking that set up in a clown's alabaster mask, crumbling gently in the lines of her smile, a white powder sifting from the cracks. In this theatrical cosmetic she came to the bed and sat lotuslike clad only in her panties and dressed her heels with a stone, her full thigh arched, she bent intently.

He bathed and dressed in his new suit and shoes and the neatly folded silk tie and Suttree and his soiled dove descended the shabby stairwell and stepped into a cab at the curbside to take them to dinner. Later they went out to the American Legion and she won over a hundred dollars at the craptable and put it in the top of her stocking, giving him a big whore's wink while the patrons goggled at that outrageous expanse of flesh. She got a little drunk and they danced and she told him she wanted to make love right there on the floor, whispering in his ear and rubbing her cunt on his thigh until he had to take her home.

In the morning she came up with the papers, still in her nightwear under the raincoat, a jug of cold orange juice and a bottle of aspirin. They sat up in bed together and read the paper and went through the rentals with a pencil. They moved that afternoon.

Lugging stuff out of the taxi and up the cold high stairwell to the apartment on the second floor, Suttree poking around in the kitchen, looking in the empty refrigerator, the cupboards. Sitting in the airy front room above Laurel Avenue and staring into space, detached, a displaced soul musing on the hiatus between himself and the Suttree moving through these strange quarters.

The cabman stood fingering the brass snap on the leather change-pouch at his belt. Suttree looked up.

That's it aint it?

I hope so.

Well.

What do I owe you?

Two forty.

Suttree gave him three dollars and sent him down the stairs. She was hanging stuff in the closet. He stood in the doorway and watched her.

Imagine a closet, she said.

Imagine.

He got ice from the refrigerator and fixed them drinks and came into the bedroom with them.

Is it five oclock yet? she said.

Of course, said Suttree, clicking the glasses.

She went in to the bathroom and he stood at the window looking out, the drink in his hand. He could see an old man washing at a sink, pale arms and a small paunch hung in his undershirt. Suttree toasted him a mute toast, a shrug of the glass, a gesture indifferent and almost cynical that as he made it caused him something close to shame.

Toward the middle of February it grew bitter cold. She went to Chicago and he didnt hear from her for ten days, he thought she'd gone back to her girlfriend. The plumbing froze. He spent long hours in bed, his head hanging over the edge of the covers watching how the purfling of scorpions on the raw and napworn carpet went head and tail. Blue and dusky rose, dirtdulled, a center pattern esoteric and obscure. After a chemical dream, or the dried hand of some eastern adept.

One morning at Ellis and Ernest, sadly miscast among the scrubbed college children, sitting at the long pink marble counter he ordered coffee and flipped open the paper. There was Hoghead's picture. He was dead. Hoghead was dead in the paper.

Suttree laid the paper down and stared out at the traffic on Cumberland Avenue this cold bleak forenoon. After a while he read the piece. His name was James Henry. In the old school photo he appeared childlike and puckish, a composition of spots in black and white and gray. How very like the man. He had been shot through the head with a .32 caliber pistol and he was twenty-one years old forever.

It snowed that night. Flakes softly blown in the cold blue lamplight. Snow lay in pale boas along the black treelimbs down Forest Avenue and the snow in the street bore bands of branch and twig, dark fissures that would not snow full. He trudged home in a light fog of alcohol. A thin and distant bell was sounding and he stopped to listen. Something flew. Nameless bird. Suttree turned his face up to the night. The snowflakes came dodging out of the blackness beyond the lamps to settle on his lashes. Snow falling on Knoxville, sifting down over McAnally, hiding the rents in the roofing, draping the sashwork, frosting the coalpiles in the crabbed dooryards. It has covered up the blood and dirt and claggy sleech in gutterways and laid white lattice on the sewer grates. And snow has made cool bowers in the blackened honeysuckle and it has hid the packingcrates in the hobo jungles and wrought enormous pastry rings of trucktires there. Where the creek addles along gorged with offal. Upon whose surface the flakes impinge softly and are gone. Suttree turning up his collar. In the yards a switchengine is working and the white light of the headlamp bores down the rows of iron gray warehouses in a livid phosphorous tunnel through which the snow falls innocently and unburnt.

The Indian's used shoes creaked in the dry snow like chalk. Over his shoulders he wore a greasy tarpaulin stolen from a donkeyengine at a worksite and his skin was gray with the cold. The snow he stopped to knock from his shoes fell in two broken casts on the hallway floor with the print of the heels and the holes in the shoesoles intact. Leached lines of salt rimed the uppers like creeping frost. He shrugged up the tarp and mounted the dim stairs, a shadow batlike on the flowered wall, a muted creak and cry of tread, a thin clatter of teeth. At the door he breathed on his knuckles and tapped and bent to hear. He tapped again.

Suttree? he said.

But his voice was timid and the sleeper within slept deeply and after a while he descended the stairs and went away in the winter night.

Spring that year came early. There were sunny mornings sitting in the little kitchen drinking coffee and reading the papers. There were flowers in the dooryard, yellow jonquils tottering up through the cinders and loam. She was arrested in New Orleans in early May and he had to wire her five hundred dollars. She came back fat and unchastened. She said that if she ever started to work anywhere bigger than Knoxville would he please kick her ass and little as he liked to promise things he said he would.

He woke in the light of various hours to find her gone, or going, just returned. Sprawled in the heat with her heavy thighs agawp and sweat lightly beaded on her forehead like the dew of fevered dreams. Light tracery of old razor scars on her inner wrists. Her scarred paunch and peltlet of coiled black kid's hair. He tried the weight of her softly coppled rosebud teat in his palm and she shifted languorously, one foot trapped in a tourniquet of bedsheet.

Lying on his back he watched the day's shadows lengthen in the room, the blinds drawn, the muted perplex of traffic in the street below fading slowly. He'd rise from the bed and sit by the window like a fugitive and watch through the dusty slats the deepening eve and the wandlike colored lights come up. He'd shave and dress and go down for the paper, a walk in the streets. To come back and lie on the bed because this room was cooler. Reading the paper mindlessly and listening to the radio with its inane announcements. She seemed always bearing her douchebag about with the hose bobbling obscenely and the bag flapping like a great bladder. Her ablutions were endless. In her bright metal haircurlers she looked like the subject of bizarre experiments upon the human brain. And she was growing fatter. She said: How'd you like to live in a whorehouse? You'd eat too.

He'd go for walks, be gone for hours, come back to eyes huge and tearful or speckled with rage.

Follow now days of drunkenness and small drama, of cheap tears and recrimination and half-so testaments of love renewed.

In the secondbest restaurants of the small metropolis and beertaverns dim and rank with musk as brewery cellars. Where others kept their own counsel and nothing short of mayhem raised an eyebrow ever.

He surveyed the face in the mirror, letting the jaw go slack, eyes vacant. How would he look in death? For there were days this man so wanted for some end to things that he'd have taken up his membership among the dead, all souls that ever were, eyes bound with night.

Climbing again these stairs with their tacked runners of worn carpet, dark varnished wainscot panels finely veined like old paintings, the flowered paper, the light in the ceiling thirty feet above like some dim nebula viewed from the pit. An inexplicable picture in a gilt frame, two birds composed of actual feathers dyed bizarrely like hats and defying forever the orders of taxonomy. Down the hallway to the door with no name where he lived.

He passed the car almost every day going to and from town. It sat in the front row of Ben Clark's lot and it looked vicious and barbaric and feline crouched there among the family sedans. These warm days they had the top down and leaning on the wooden sill you could hang your head over the cockpit and drink in a heady smell of rich leather and admire the cluster of black dial faces in the dashboard like an aircraft and the fine red carpeting to match the hide of the seats and the polished burl walnut and the silver jaguar's head snarling from the center of the steering wheel.

Let me fix you up with that today, said the smiling salesman.

Suttree stood up and stepped back and ran his eye along the sleek cream lacquer flank of the thing. What year is it? he said.

Nineteen fifty. Just got twenty-two thousand on her. Spare's never been on the ground.

Suttree felt himself being slowly anesthetized. The silver wire wheels gleamed in the good spring sun.

Look here, said the salesman, lifting the decklid.

Inside the pristine tire so told. And little tools in a fitted case.

Next he had the long bonnet raised and they walked around it looking in at the polished aluminum camshaft covers and the neat little pots that housed the carburetor dampers.

Crank it up, called the salesman, holding open the little door.

Suttree deep in the leather cockpit turned the key, the fuelpump ticked. He put the gearstick in neutral and pulled the starter. It sounded like a motorboat.

He looked up. What do you want for it?

The little car will go for two bills, said the salesman, leaning confidentially on the door.

Suttree blipped the throttle a couple of times and shut it down. The salesman stood up. Take it for a ride if you like, he said. But Suttree was climbing out. He shut the door and turned and looked down into the car again.

The top's perfect, the salesman was saying, unbuttoning the canvas boot that covered it.

It's all right. Dont bother. I'm going to bring my old lady down to look at it.

It wont be here long my friend.

You may be right, said Suttree.

When she came back from Huntsville she had six hundred dollars. He put her in a cab and they went downtown. I've got something I want to show you, he said.

She walked around it and looked at it and she looked up at Suttree. Well, she said. It's beautiful.

We've got enough money to buy it.

Bullshit.

I'm serious.

She looked at him and at the car and at him again. Well, she said. Let's buy the fucking thing then.

He sought out the salesman while she looked it over. He found him in the little wooden box of an office where a fan stirred the humid air about. He was shuffling through papers and talking on the telephone. He nodded to Suttree and held up a finger. Suttree leaned in the door.

Right, said the salesman, hanging up the telephone. Okay. You ready to take the little car today?

Suttree eased himself into a chair. Look, he said, I've got a little over eighteen hundred dollars. Can we do business?

How much over?

Maybe eighteen and a half.

Eighteen and a half.

Yes.

You want the car?

Yes.

My friend, the little car is yours.

They drove to Asheville North Carolina and spent four days at the Grove Park Inn, a cool room high in the old rough pile of rocks and lunch each noon on the sunny tiled terrace overlooking the golf course and the mountains beyond in range on range of hazy blue. They went about the premises leisurely, these apprentice imposters, or sat by the pool while she told outrageous lies to the other guests. In the cool evenings they cruised through the mountains in the roadster and came back to have drinks in the lounge where a small orchestra played music from another era and older couples twostepped quietly over the dimlit dancefloor.

The summer passed in monotone, days run on days. The apartment was hot and unventilated. Lying in the damp sheets with sweat trickling coldly in the folds of his sated skin he fell victim to a vast inertia. She came naked through the room bearing glasses of iced tea and they sat in the barred and tepid gloom behind drawn blinds and sipped and held the cold glass to their faces. She lay there pale and streaked with sweat, wearing a dreamy cat's look, one leg cocked obscenely, the dark foiled hair below her belly matted, dewbeads nesting there. She placed a cool hand across the nape of his neck. A car started up in the street below and pulled away. In the distance a radio. They lay like fallen statuary. Suttree held a piece of ice against his tongue till it was numb with cold, then leaned and licked her nipple.

You son of a bitch, she said, smiling down at him.

Sunday they drove down to Concord, walked by the lake, scaled slates over the brown water. They came upon a fisherman who showed them his small catch of sauger. The water before him floated with amorphic patches of ambergris where he'd spat. They spoke of fish and weather and the old man looked them over and slyly brought forth a whiskeyjar and offered it. Suttree wiped the rim with his sleevecuff and drank. The fisherman looked at her and gestured slightly with the jar but she smiled no. He nodded gravely, spat and shifted his chaw and drank and hid the jar back beneath his raincoat.

I like a drink, he said, I aint no drunkard.

Suttree nodded.

I's married to one would suck the bottom out of the jar. Looky here.

He showed them a limp photograph of a bureau in a cheap room where five empty fifth bottles stood. I carry it daily, he said. Whenever I get to wishin her back I take it out and look at it. You'd be amazed at what you can learn to yearn for.

He turned to his lines and spoke no more. The floats rode serenely in their half shadows. An osprey was going down the lake. They wished the old man luck.

He showed her cores of flint jutting from the mud and he found an arrowhead knapped from the same black stone and gave it to her. Out there on a mudspit white gulls. Mute little treestumps on twisted legs where the shore had washed from their roots, darkly fluted, waterhewn, bulbed with gross knots. Their grotesque shadows fell long upon the silty water of the bay and down the beach each rock and pebble lay in its own dark lick of shadow so that the strand looked spattered with thrown ink.

I've never seen one before, she said, turning the arrowhead in her hand.

They're everywhere. In the winter when the water is down you can find them.

In the last of the day they walked out on the sandspit, their shoes sinking in the dry loam. He fetched up from among bonewhite driftwood and beachwrack a huge blue musselshell wasted paper thin. She carried it carefully, cradling inside the arrowhead and a strangely veined pebble she'd found that looked back like an eye. The gulls rose by ones, by pairs, all flew, bursting upward and wheeling overhead with the sun white on their cupped underwings and their feathers riffling in the breeze they rode. They went down the lake, balanced on dipping wings, necks craned.

Suttree knelt in the sand and skipped a stone. A curving track of ringshapes. The far shore lay deeply shadowed. The siltbars delicately sutured with the tracks of wharfrats. She had knelt beside him and nibbled at his ear. Her soft breast against his arm. Why then this loneliness?

On Simm's hill they stood looking down at the lights of the city. While the stars scudded and the sedge writhed all about them in the dark. A niggard beacon winked above the black and sleeping hills. In the distance the lights of the fairground and the ferriswheel turning like a tiny clockgear. Suttree wondered if she were ever a child at a fair dazed by the constellations of light and the hurdygurdy music of the merrygoround and the raucous calls of the barkers. Who saw in all that shoddy world a vision that child's grace knows and never the sweat and the bad teeth and the nameless stains in the sawdust, the flies and the stale delirium and the vacant look of solitaries who go among these garish holdings seeking a thing they could not name.

At midnight the fireworks went up. Glass flowers exploding. Slow trail of colors down the sky like stains dispersing in the sea, candescent polyps extinguished in the depths. When it was over he asked her if she was ready to leave. He could feel her breathing under the sweater she wore and he thought she was cold. She turned and put her face against his chest and he held her. She was crying, he didnt know why. Down there the city seemed frozen in a blue void. Senseless patterns like the tracks of animalcules on a slide. After a while she said yes and took his hand and they started down into Knoxville again.

Before cold weather came this all was ended. She had not been out of town for two months, then three. The figures in the savings account book began to unreel backwards. She spoke of getting a job. She drank. They argued.

One drunken Sunday morning at Floyd Fox's, a bootleg shack on a deserted stretch of Redbud Drive, she was taken with what seemed a kind of fit. She screamed at him half coherently and made weird gestures in the air, some threatening, some absurd. He tried to get her into the car. It had rained and they slid about and feinted in the slick red clay while drinkers from McAnally or Vestal sat on crates or rusty metal chairs and watched.

I didnt know they had dancin out here at the Redbud Room, called out a wit from the crowd.

He got her into the car, feet globed with mud. They swerved out of the driveway through deep ribbons of mud and onto the mud-stained blacktop road. She sat silent and sullen, an occasional eerie smile crossing her lips.

They were driving up Island Home Pike toward town when she grabbed the gearstick and tried to force it into reverse. The motor whined, gears ratcheted unmeshed with a thin squawk. Suttree grabbed her wrist and held it and she raised one foot and kicked the knobs off the radio.

You crazy bitch, he said.

But now she slumped in the seat for leverage and kicked out with both feet. The righthand windshield went blind white. She kicked again and it fell out onto the hood and slid off into the street.

He wheeled in to the curb. She was screaming at him something senseless.

You dizzy cunt, he said.

She looked at him almost soberly. It's just a car, she said. It can be fixed.

Across the street old faces at windows watching. Suttree stared at the windshield wiper hanging inside across the dashboard. The twisted stumps of the radio knobs. He looked at her. You're a pain in the ass, he said.

She raised her foot, a huge petulant child, and kicked the rearview mirror askew.

He grabbed her ankle. Quit it, he said.

She was sobbing drunkenly. You son of a bitch, she said. You couldnt say: It's okay honey, or say, or say . . . I guess you're so fucking perfect goddamn you anyway.

A police car pulled up without a sound. Two officers got out, one from either side.

What's the trouble here, said Suttree to himself as they approached, wishing a fissure to open beneath them and swallow all.

The officers looked down at Suttree and his whore.

What's the trouble here?

Suttree gestured helplessly. She got mad and kicked out the windshield, he said.

One of the officers was leaning on the roof, Suttree could see the shape of the elbow in the canvas inches above his head. The other was standing with his arms folded. They didnt say anything. Nor Suttree. All seemed to be waiting for another party to arrive.

Finally the officer leaning on the roof said: You got papers on this car?

Suttree leaned and opened the little wooden glovebox door. He shuffled through papers and handed the title to the policeman. The policeman said: Let me see your license.

He got out his billfold and offered the little card up. The officer inspected these documents and handed them back and straightened up. Is that the windshield back there?

Suttree stuck his head out of the window. Yessir, he said.

Well get it out of the street. Then you'd better get off the street yourself.

Yessir. I will.

They glanced at the car again and shook their heads and got into the cruiser and pulled away. Suttree went up the street and fetched the glass from where it lay limp and shattered in the gutter and brought it back and put it in the trunk and got in and started the motor and pulled away. They were going out Cumberland when she began to tear up the money. He heard a handful of it rip and looked in time to see a green confetti swirl away in the slipstream.

Shit, he said. He cut the wheel and went gliding into a fillingstation. There in the Sunday morning boredom old men were watching out through the plateglass window for something to occur. Here came an exotic automobile coasting in with tattered greenbacks blowing from the window and fluttering in the street, whole handfuls of it, who knows what denominations.

She was sitting there ripping it up and crying and saying that this money would never do anybody any good. The old faces were pressed against the glass, flat bloodless noses. Two small boys were coming across the street at a dead run. Suttree was out and gathering up pieces of tens and twenties from the paving. She had climbed from the car and stood with her hair disarranged, swaying slightly, smiling. The boys were scrabbling in the gutter and watching him like cats. Suttree went around and took the keys out of the car and started to close the door and then he stopped and put the keys back in the car and walked on out across the tarmac to the street. She was shouting at him some half drunken imprecations, all he could make out was his name. He seemed to have heard it all before and he kept on going.

It was still early morning when he made his way down the steep path by the ruins of an old wall. Some ancient city overgrown here. In a sere field worn clothes the wind has tattered hung from a hatted cross. Down there the littoral of siltstained rocks, old plates of paving and chunks of concrete sprouting growths of rusted iron rod. He'd even seen old slabs of masonry screed with musselshells here in the weeds. Coming down the concrete steps with the mangled iron handrail and past old brick cisterns filled with rubble. Past the stone abutment of an earlier bridge on the river and the last ramshackle house and the brown curbstones that had once lined the main street and the old cobblestones and pavingbricks and blackened beams with their axed flats and their mortices, all this detritus slid from the city on the hill.

He had passed the madman's house without regard and the old man must have slacked his vigil for he'd almost reached the street before he heard him cry.

Ah he's back, God spare his blackened soul, another hero home from the whores. Come to cool his heels in the river with the rest of the sewage. Sunday means nothing to him. Infidel. Back for the fishing are ye? God himself dont look too close at what lies on that river bottom. Fit enough for the likes of you. Ay. He knows it's Sunday for he's drunker than normal. It'll take more than helping old blind men cross the street to save you from the hell you'll soon inhabit. Suttree went on toward the street with his fingers in his ears.

Howard Clevinger raised one eyebrow at his appearance in the store. Thought you'd left town, he said.

I'm back.

A thin and fragrant arm descended on Suttree's shoulder in a taffeta whisper, a cufflink coined from a bicycle reflector. An African mask in meretricious harlequinade and ivory teeth beset with gold. Hey baby, where you been so long?

Hello John. Just around.

I been out of town myself.

Where've you been?

I's in Lexington. I seen James Herndon. Sweet Evenin Breeze. She just beautiful, for her age.

Who's the oldest?

Oldest what?

You or her. Him. It.

Hush. That thing is sixty.

How old are you, John?

Trippin Through The Dew ignored the question. He said: You know what they goin to put in the paper when she die? Big headlines.

What's that.

They done got it all ready. Sweet Evenin Breeze Blows No More.

Suttree grinned. The invert was bent double holding himself, his face squinched. He whinnied like a she horse.

What are they going to say about you John?

Sheeit. I aint goin to die.

Maybe not, said Suttree.

The houseboat lay half sunken by one corner and the windows were stoned out and the front door was gone altogether. He entered a scene of old memories and new desolations. Torn playing cards and halfpint whiskey bottles broken in the floor, the stove crammed tight to the maw with trash. He crossed the tilted floor and righted the foodlocker from where it lay on its face among broken glass and rags.

By afternoon he had the place swept out and the mattress on the roof for airing, he sat on the veranda in the sun with a glasscutter and shaped old panes purloined from an empty warehouse and with them glazed the naked sashes of his house. In the days that followed he tarred the seams in the roof and carried on his back a door from a razing beyond First Creek and sawed it down to fit and hung it.

Lastly standing off in the skiff on a warm October morning he fended off from the sheer wall of the dredger's hull and reached down the fireaxe handed him. The drums when he stove them filled and wheezed and sputtered and went slowly from sight in the river. He jostled the new ones into place and called up to the pilothouse. The winch creaked and the houseboat corner settled. Suttree unhooked the cables as soon as there was play enough and they went swinging up toward the deck.

What do I owe you? he called, passing up the axe.

The deckman jerked his thumb toward the pilothouse where the captain watched from his high window.

What do I owe you?

The captain spat. I dont know, he said. What's it worth?

I dont know. I dont want to make you mad.

Would you say five dollars?

I'd say that was fair enough.

He handed up the money to the deckhand. The dredger began to back. Great boils of muddy water churned and broke. Suttree raised a hand and the old pilot rang a small bell. Rafts of straw rose and fell and the ratholes in the bank sucked and popped and the dredger moved out, the deckhand leaning on the rail smoking a cigarette and watching toward the shore.

He bought three five hundred yard spools of nylon trotline and spent two days piecing them with their droppers and leads and hooks. The third day he put out his lines and that night in his shanty with the oil lamp lit and his supper eaten he sat in the chair listening to the river, the newspaper open across his lap, and an uneasy peace came over him, a strange kind of contentment. Small graylooking moths orbited the hot cone of glass before him. He set back the plate with the dimestore silver and folded his hands on the table. A beetle kept crashing into the windowscreen and dropping to the deck below to whirr and rise and crash again.

A clear night over south Knoxville. The lights of the bridge bobbed in the river among the small and darkly cobbled isomers of distant constellations. Tilting back in his chair he framed questions for the quaking ovoid of lamplight on the ceiling to pose to him:

Supposing there be any soul to listen and you died tonight?

They'd listen to my death.

No final word?

Last words are only words.

You can tell me, paradigm of your own sinister genesis construed by a flame in a glass bell.

I'd say I was not unhappy.

You have nothing.

It may be the last shall be first.

Do you believe that?

No.

What do you believe?

I believe that the last and the first suffer equally. Pari passu.

Equally?

It is not alone in the dark of death that all souls are one soul.

Of what would you repent?

Nothing.

Nothing?

One thing. I spoke with bitterness about my life and I said that I would take my own part against the slander of oblivion and against the monstrous facelessness of it and that I would stand a stone in the very void where all would read my name. Of that vanity I recant all.

Suttree's cameo visage in the black glass watched him across his lamplit shoulder. He leaned and blew away the flame, his double, the image overhead. The river spooled past dark and silent. A truck droned on the bridge.

All that season on the river he had warrant to remember in the toils of his trade old days of rain on the window and warmth in the bed with her body and how her eyes rolled back in her head like a turkish beggar's with just the bluish whites shining under the slotted lids and her tongue protruding while she seized her knees and cried out and fell back. Lying there on the drenched sheets like a suicide. Till she could flutter back to life and slur sweet lies into his ear or tell the spinebones in his back with such cool fingers.

In the toils of orgasm—she said, she said—she'd be whelmed in a warm green sea through which, dulled by the murk of it, pass a series of small suns like the footlights of a revolving stage, an electric carousel wheeling in a green ether. Envy's color is the color of her pleasuring, and what is the color of grief? Is it black as they say? And anger always red? The color of that sad shade of ennui called blue is blue but blue unlike the sky or sea, a bitter blue, rue-tinged, discolored at the edges. The color of a blind man's noon is white, and is his nighttime too? And does he feel it with his skin like a fish? Does he have blues, are they bridal and serene, or yellows, sunlike or urinous, does he remember? Neural colors like the fleeting tones of dreams. The color of this life is water.

In the morning he set off down the river to run his lines. A cool morning with mist still rising. Crossriver the cries of hogs in the slaughterhouse chutes like the cries of lepers without the gates. He sat in back of the skiff and sculled it slowly down beneath the bridge. As he passed under he raised his head and howled at the high black nave and pigeons unfolded fanwise from the arches and clattered toward the sun.

A season of death and epidemic violence. Clarence Raby was shot to death by police on the courthouse lawn and Lonas Ray Caughorn lay three days and nights on the roof of the county jail among the gravels and tar and old nests of nighthawks until the search reckoned him escaped from the city. What dreams did he have of the lady Katherine? Suttree saw her one evening in the Huddle with Worm Hazelwood. She had no need to travel about the country robbing people. And news in the papers. A young girl's body buried under trash down by First Creek. Sprout Young, the Rattlesnake Daddy, indicted for the murder.

Suttree found people out of doors that would as soon stayed in. A family of aged black folk sitting in the dark among their furnishings in total silence. Their figures swaddled up in old quilts against the cold and the old man's cigarette rising and falling in slow red arcs. When he passed there in the morning they were all gone to seek help save an old woman who sat in a chair on the sidewalk among the piled and grimy household goods. She watched the passers in the street but none watched back. A starling landed on the old yellow icebox and she struggled up to shoo it away.

The junkman lay among sleeping sots in the jungle nor did he stir when the thief who dropped from the dark of a boxcar door went among them. A hominid composed of smoke sucking out the pockets socklike and boarding loose change and half empty packets of cigarettes. Through dark bowerpaths in the honeysuckle where newsprint crouched like ghosts and smokehounds lay so drunk the flies had shat eggs in their earholes. Pausing here to take some shoes. Emerging from the jungle and disappearing into the dark of the car again and the train shunting into motion again as if it had been waiting him. A dog crossed the tracks and paused to sniff at the old man's feet and moved on.

And in the dawn a female simpleton is waking naked from a gangfuck in the back seat of an abandoned car by the river. She stirs, sweet day has broken. Reeking of stale beer and dried sperm, eyes clogged, used rubbers dangling senselessly from the dashboard knobs. Her clothes lie trampled in the floor. They bear bootprints of mud and dogshit and her cunt looks like a hairclot fished from a draintrap. She sees on rising two black boys crouched on the car fenders like gibbons purloined from the architraves of an old world cathedral. She folds her hands across her breasts and they leap to the ground and scamper hooting through the weeds. In the distance cars are rifling along a highway. She bends moaning to sort among her clothes.

Uptown one evening in the Huddle Suttree found Leonard fresh from the workhouse. Leonard had a job as dishwasher and he had gonorrhea of the colon and was otherwise covered with carbuncles. He hobbled over to Suttree's table and sat uneasily. He told how he had seen the lies run down the lawyer's tongue. Vague but of a substance, they came down like mice and looked about a moment before scuttling off. Leaning over Leonard and wagging a long finger, and is it not true that you sought to conceal the death of your father for the purpose of extorting monies unlawfully from the state? Wild in the eye, thrusting his sweating face into Leonard's smaller one and fixing him with a lidless look of triumph until Leonard half rising from his chair seized the lawyer's cold skull in his two hands and pulled his face down and parted those thin lips with a smoking kiss.

He come up, Sut. Draggin all them chains with him.

Fathers will do that, said Suttree.

I hunted you everwheres.

Suttree didnt ask what for.

The catamite tucked his chair closer and leaned in confidence. I need to ast ye somethin Sut.

Okay.

If you buy somethin and dont pay for it can they take it back?

Sure. Of course they can.

I mean no matter what it is?

Well. I dont know. I guess there are some things it would be hard to repossess. What is it?

Well this guy's been comin to the house . . .

Okay.

Well. You know after they found the old man and we had all that trouble with the law.

Okay.

Well, the old lady went and bought this plot out in Woodlawn so they wouldnt bury him down here in the whatever thing it is here and she bought this whole deal, this guy come out to the house, and he sold her this deal, this plot with anothern alongside of it for her and it had this pet, pet . . .

Perpetual care.

Petual care and got her to sign for it all and she didnt have to pay nothin down nor for the first sixty days I think it was and now she's three months behind on her payments and she owes em sixty-two fifty . . .

Leonard.

Yeah.

Are you trying to tell me they're going to repossess your old man's grave plot?

Can they Sut?

I dont know.

Well I know a guy one time they come and got his teeth he never made the payments.

I'll check on it for you. Did they really say they were going to repossess it?

What they tell me, Sut, if she dont make a payment by the tenth up he comes.

Suttree looked at the earnest pinched face. He shook his head in wonder.

Times been rougher'n a old cob, said Leonard. At our house they have.

What's become of Harrogate? said Suttree.

Leonard grinned. I dont know. I seen him uptown about a month ago he had some old country girl on his arm was about a head taller'n him. I hollered at him was he gettin any of that old long stuff but he didnt know me.

Maybe it was his sister.

May be. She favored him some.

Suttree closed his eyes as if he were trying to picture such a person. He opened them to see Leonard watching him. He looked about him as if he could not place how he came to be there.

And this was Harrogate. Standing in the door of Suttree's shack with a cigar between his teeth. He had painted the black one and it was chalk white and he had grown a wispy mustache. He wore a corduroy hat a helping larger than his headsize and a black gabardine shirt with slacks to match. His shoes were black and sharply pointed, his socks were yellow. Suttree in his shorts leaned against the door and studied his visitor with what the city rat took for wordless admiration.

What say Sut. How in a big rat's ass are ye?

I was okay. Come on in.

Harrogate pinched his hat up by the forecrown and swept it to his chest and entered, ducking slightly as he did so though the lintel of the doorframe was two feet above his head. He laid the hat on the table and hitched his trousers and tucked in his shirt with his thin little hands and puffed on the cigar and grinned and looked about. Good God, said Suttree.

I seen old Rufus said you was back down here.

Suttree shut the door. Sit down, he said.

I hunted you up at Comer's. They said you was into the tall cotton.

Yeah. Well, the market collapsed. Sit down, sit down.

Harrogate pushed his hat to one side to make room for his elbow and sat. You fishin again? he said.

Suttree leaned back on the cot. Fishing again, he said.

I thought you'd give it up.

I did too.

I come by a time or two. Your old boathouse was about in under.

What are you doing, Gene?

Hmm?

I said what are you doing.

Harrogate grinned. I got me a few little routes, he said. He turned the cigar in his teeth and gave Suttree a look of fey cunning. Got me a few little routes.

Suttree waited. The story must be elicited with care. It is that the city rat has a telephone route. With small dimestore sponges through which he's fastened wire loops. He runs his routes with a special hook taped to his forefinger, fetching down the blocks from inside the coinreturns of the telephones, a few nickels clattering into the slot, the sponge poked back.

I dont see how that would pay very much, said Suttree.

Harrogate grinned slyly.

How many phones do you have?

He took the cigar from his teeth. Two hunnerd and eight-six, he said.

What?

I had a twenty-six dollar day Saturday. I just barely could walk for the fuckin nickels in my pockets.

Good God, said Suttree. You've got half the telephones in Knoxville plugged up.

Harrogate grinned. It takes me all day to run em. I put on a few new ones ever day. You get away from uptown they's a lot of hard sidewalk tween telephones. I done wore out two pair of brand new Thom McAn shoes.

Suttree shook his head.

Harrogate tipped the ash from his cigar into his palm and looked up. Listen, he said. You ever lose any money in a telephone why you just let me know. I'll make it back to ye. You hear?

Okay, said Suttree.

Or anybody you know. You just tell me.

All right.

You the only other son of a bitch in the world I'd tell. I mean anybody could get on my route and run it if they knowed about it. They aint no way for me to protect myself.

No.

I got some other deals in mind too. There'll be a deal for you if you want in, Sut. You aint never been nothin but decent to me. I dont mind takin a buddy with me on the way up.

Gene.

Yeah.

You're on your way up to the penitentiary is where you're on your way up to.

Shit, said Harrogate. I have me another day like Saturday I'll buy the goddamned penitentiary.

It's not like the workhouse. They have these coalmines up there for you to work in.

Harrogate smiled and shook his head. Suttree watched him. Smiling a sadder smile.

I saw Leonard the other day and he said he saw you uptown with some girl on your arm.

Shit, said Harrogate easily. Man has a little money about him he can get more pussy than you can shake a stick at.

Suttree tapped at the dosshouse door. The keeper shuffled along the hall and unlatched the door and peered out. He shut one eye, he shook his head. No ragman here. Suttree thanked him and descended into the street again.

It was still raining a cold gray rain when he eased himself down the narrow path at the south end of the bridge and made his way over the rocks to the ragman's home. As he came about the abutment and entered the gloom beneath the bridge three boys darted out the far side and clambered over the rocks and disappeared in the woods by the river. Suttree entered the dim vault beneath the arches. Water ran from a clay drain tile and went down a stone gully. Water gushed from a broken pipe down the near wall and water dripped and spattered everywhere from the dark reaches overhead.

Hello, called Suttree. An echo echoed in the emptiness. He shaded his eyes to see. Hey, he called. He could make out the shape of the old man's bed dimly in the cool dank.

He stood at the foot of the ragpicker's mattress and looked down at him. The old man lay with his eyes shut and his mouth set and his hands lay clenched at either side. He looked as if he had forced himself to death. Suttree looked about at the mounds of moldy rags and the stacked kindling and the racks of bottles and jars and the troves of nameless litter, broken kitchen implements or lamps, a thousand houses divided, the ragged chattel of lives abandoned like his own.

He moved along the side of the bed. The old man had his shoes on, he saw their shape beneath the covers. Suttree pulled a chair up and sat and watched him. He passed his hand across his face and sat forward holding his knuckles. Well, he said. What do you think now? God, you are pathetic. Did you know that? Pathetic?

Suttree looked around.

These boys have been at your things. You forgot about the gasoline I guess. Never got around to it. Did you really remember me? I couldnt remember my bear's name. He had corduroy feet. My mother used to sew him up. She gave you sandwiches and apples. Gypsies used to come to the door. We were afraid of them. My sisters' bears were Mischa and Bruin. I cant remember mine. I tried but I cant.

The old man lay dim and bleared in his brass bed. Suttree leaned back in the chair and pushed at his eyes with the back of his hand. The day had grown dusk, the rain eased. Pigeons flapped up overhead and preened and crooned. The keeper of this brief vigil said that he'd guessed something of the workings in the wings, the ropes and sandbags and the houselight toggles. Heard dimly a shuffling and coughing beyond the painted drop of the world.

Did you ask? About the crapgame? What are you doing in bed with your shoes on?

He passed his hand through his hair and leaned forward and looked at the old man. You have no right to represent people this way, he said. A man is all men. You have no right to your wretchedness.

He wiped his eyes with the heel of his hand.

There's no one to ask is there? There's no . . . He was looking down at the ragman and he raised his hand and let it fall again and he rose and went out past the old man's painted rock into the rain.

She unscrewed the threaded halves of a wooden darningegg and took from inside a single piece of pale brown bone. Her hand closed up about it like a burnt spider and she turned slowly to Suttree where he sat at the table. The specter of things sings in its own ashes. Who has ears to hear it? She let shut her nutshell eyelids. A pair of fat black candles dripped and spat, the wax a gray grease congealing in the saucers where they stood. Her tiny hands with their yellow nails looked like the mummied hands he'd seen crossed on the breast of a dead slave in a wormfluted barrow at the rear of a secondhand furniture store. She had before her an ageblackened box of boardhard leather and now she opened it and began to set out her effects. Much like a priest with his deathbed kit. The candleflames lurched in the shadow of her movements and their own shapes reeled briefly on the wall.

Merceline Essary that they said would not never walk on this earth again by men was doctors come under me and I rewalked her in three days. She originally died in October of last year and she walked to that day.

I can walk, said Suttree.

You can walk, she said. But you caint see where you goin.

Can you?

To know what will come is the same as to make it so.

Suttree smiled. Somewhere in the house clockgears clacked.

She lifted from the hide box a castiron jar and set it on the table in a little stand. She took out a small alcohol burner and filled it from a bottle and lit it and set it beneath the pot. She unrolled and spread a black cloth and put things out upon it and seemed to puzzle over them. A blood agate bored with a small hole, a cracked and yellow tooth that may have been a boar's tusk, a tin box too small to hold anything of christian use. She touched each of these in turn. She looked at Suttree. He sat loosely in his chair with his hands resting on the insides of his thighs. He felt an easy peace settle in his spine. Studying the apposition of these effects for hidden systems, waiting for her to fetch down her purse of bones to see what construction they might have for him, their rorschach text, pattern in a carpet. A figure lifted from a cave floor wherein old fossils lay anachronistically conjoined, taxonic absurdities and enemies of order. But she had taken out an old bottle handblown that held an oily unguent and seemed gone on to philters now, spooning some grim powder from the tin into the pot where the oil began to smoke and sputter with a stench like frying dung.

Suttree seemed unalarmed. She unfolded the hand that held the piece of bone and she put the bone under her tongue and she placed her tiny palm against Suttree's eyes, one, the other. He felt a light tingling in his nape, his eyes lost focus. He leaned back in his lassitude and watched the shapes of the candleflames on the ceiling. She was at her triturations. Spooning to death in a salver a speckled slug, marked like an ocelot, viscous and sticky. A whitish paste. Crooning a low threnody to her pawky trade. She said: Aint no common fire can cruciate a groundpuppy. Fetching the smoking mess from the burner she stirred it with her spoon and she blew out the small blue flame and set the pot within the rack again. Her hands unmindful of the heat. Her movements rapid and sure. She spat through a ringbone into a watchglass and mixed with her finger a paste of something drear and leaned with her thumb to anoint his eyelids. Then she took up the pot again and she spooned out the mess within and swung it toward him.

Open you mouf, she said.

That's hot.

Under his hand the arm he stayed was like a piece of black meerschaum. Aneroid bones, birdhollow. To read the weathers in your heart.

Look here at me, she said.

Cold bloodwebbed globes. Wens clung along the dark and weighted lids.

Open you mouf.

He did. She thrust the spoon against the back of his throat and capsized its cargo down his gullet. A tasteless slime impacted with a harsh grit. He swallowed. She sat back to watch. Nodding her head. Suttree felt himself go queasy. He watched her eyes and her mouth but the words seemed detached. She spoke of a boarcat, black through. Find the bone that will not burn. Suttree had half forgotten the paste on his eyelids and he reached to wonder what had clogged them but she stopped his hand. He shuddered in the grip of grue. Scorpion dust, frogpowder in sowsmilk. Ye'll shit through the eye of a needle at thirty paces. Pieces of a dream unreeled down the back of his brain. He pulled himself up and looked at the old woman. She watched him as if he were a thing in a jar.

What? he said.

She did not say, nor was there any news at all in those faded eyes.

What do I do?

You dont do nothin. You will be told.

Will you tell me?

No.

A wave of nausea swept through him. He was going to comment on it but it was gone. And then came another. A shuddering sickness that brought his stomach up tight against his diaphragm.

I dont feel good, he said.

Dont you puke.

I think I might.

She took his wrist in her spider's hand and leveled her eyes at him. Dont you puke, she said.

I need to lie down.

She pushed back her chair without speaking and rose and took his arm. He stood woozily. He wanted mightily to vomit.

She took him across the room to a small cot. He looked like some medieval hero led by a small black gnome. He sat on the cot and lay back with his feet on the floor. She took down a lamp and lit it and put back the glass and turned to watch him. On the mantel a small brass amphora held a dark crepe rose and there was a mounted grackle with dull glass eyes and there were small objects, a box, a pincushion. In the lamplight the glass of the mirror in which these things lay doubled was the color of rhenish wine and it was streaked with mauve and metal blue, with petals of peeling spectra. She stepped from the hearth and crossed the room and went out. In the corner stood a coattree hung with celluloid birds green and yellow, and when the door closed they turned silently in the wind and dark flowers in the old coalscuttle swayed like paper cobras. Suttree stared at the fire within the iron teeth of the grate. She was gone for a long time. When she came back she stooped to look at him. He lay as before. The nausea had passed and he felt more and more removed from all that was. He said: Should I go home?

It dont make no difference where you go.

He went to raise himself up from the cot but when he was half sitting he became unsure as to whether he should walk about. There seemed no purpose to it. He lay back down. After a while he lifted his feet into the cot and stretched out his legs. The shifting of the flames in the coalgrate bloomed on the wall like the pulse of distant lightning. Suddenly the fire seemed to be far away and he seemed to be in another room. He seemed to be somewhere else. He looked at the old black woman. Her eyes were closed but when he looked at her she opened them. She was whispering something silently to herself like one in prayer but it was not prayer.

What is that stuff?

She didnt answer. She turned her face in profile, a black androgynous silhouette.

He felt hollow inside and there seemed to be a cool wind moving through him like wind in a street. A door closed on all that he had been. Look at me, he said.

Hush boy. I dont need to look at you.

Suddenly he realized that this scene was past and he was looking at its fading reality like a watcher from another room. Then he was watching the watcher. He was aware of the light in the room and his hands on the iron of the cot under his thighs but he could not determine where he was. And then he was somewhere else.

He had begun to move. He was wheeling in a vast brown circle and he was moving in a helix outward and each few minutes he would pass again the place where he had been. The shape of the fire in the grate would wheel past and the twin cups of light from the black candles on the table in the corner and the old hag's sere and shrunken face. And pass again.

He felt a laying on of hands, dry claws divesting him. A clammy fear clogged his heart. Unknowing if his eyes saw or saw not. They seemed lidless and opened or closed beheld things all the same. His own hand put out to save him seemed to sink in a nameless mucilage and he lay like a moth in a web. Dust fell from her, her eyes rolled wetly in the red glow from the fireplace. A dried black and hairless figure rose from her fallen rags, the black and shriveled leather teats like empty purses hanging, the thin and razorous palings of the ribs wherein hung a heart yet darker, parchment cloven to the bones, spindleshanked and bulbed of joint. Black faltress, portress of hellgate. None so ready as she. Her long flat nipples swung above him. Black and crepey skin of her neck, the plaguey mouth upon him. A gray and handstitched scar flickered in the light. Where she'd survived some murder. Tin figures, the toadstone, dragged on his chest where they hung from her neck by plaited horsehair strands. In the yard he heard a bird scream. They are not rooks in those obsidian winter trees but stranger fowl, pale lean and salamandrine birds that move by night unburnt through the moon's blue crucible. Suttree craned his neck to breathe. Dead reek of aged female flesh, a stale aridity. Dry wattled nether lips hung from out the side of her torn stained drawers. Her thighs spread with a sound of rending ligaments, dry bones dragging in their sockets. Her shriveled cunt puckered open like a mouth gawping. He flailed bonelessly in the grip of a ghast black succubus, he screamed a dry and soundless scream. In the pale reach of firelight on the ceiling spiders were clambering toward the cracks in the high corners of the room and his spine was sucked from his flesh and fell clattering to the floor like a jointed china snake.

The fire had died in the room, the candles burned to pools of grease in their dishes. Suttree saw with perfect clarity a parade he'd watched through the legs of the crowd like a thing that passed in a forest, the floats of colored crepe and the band with its drum and horns and the polished wine broadcloth and gold braid and the majordomo in a stained shako wielding a baton and prancing and farting like a brewery horse. He saw what had been so how a caravan of pennanted cars wound through the rain on a dark day and how Clayton in corduroy knickers and aviator's cap marched with his sisters in a high ceilinged room where the paneled doors were drawn and a nurse in a white uniform called closeorder drill and tapped out the time with a cane and he could remember the stamped brass grapes of an umbrella stand cool and metallic under his tongue and he knew that in that house some soul lay dying.

He saw a pool of oil on a steel drumhead that lay shirred with the pounding of machinery. He saw the blood in his eyelids where he lay in a field in a summer noon and he saw young boys in a pond, pale nates and small bald cods shriveled with the cold and he saw an idiot in a yard in a leather harness chained to a clothesline and it leaned and swayed drooling and looked out upon the alley with eyes that fed the most rudimentary brain and yet seemed possessed of news in the universe denied right forms, like perhaps the eyes of squid whose simian depths seem to harbor some horrible intelligence. All down past the hedges a gibbering and howling in a hoarse frog's voice, word perhaps of things known raw, unshaped by the constructions of a mind obsessed with form.

He saw white swans flying over a house he'd known as a child, enormous shapes laboring above the chimneypots like farm stock flying in a dream, apparitions of such graceful levity quartering on the winter wind with their long necks craned seaward, shouldering the thin and bitter air. And a mechanical victrola and the bitter taste of the cracked varnish and the small dull tiles in a victorian bathroom and the footed castiron standards of the tub and the smell of toothpaste and excrement and the languid amber kelp that rose and fell in the swells of a cold gray sea.

And he saw what had been so how the lilies leaned in the hall glass and a door closed and the candleflames trembled and righted again and he could smell the lilies and some other musty smell and he could feel the wirelike plush pricking the undersides of his legs in their short trousers where he sat in a chair with his elbows cocked high as his ears to rest on the dark oak chairarms. He saw a small boy in a schoolyard with a broken arm screaming and how the children watched like animals.

He saw shellfish crusted on the spiles of a wooden bridge and a salt river that ran two ways. Buoybells on a reef where the bones of a schooner broke the shallow surf on the out tide and the sound of the parlous and marbled sea and the seethe of spume and the long clatter of pebbles in the foam. He saw a jar in a garden with mousebones and lint and old sashweights stacked like ingots under a woodshed and the mortised shape of a wagonhub, spokestripped, weatherbleached, oaken, arcane. He saw a dead poodle in a street like a toy dog with its red collar and flannel tongue.

He saw what was so how his sisters came down the steps in their black patentleather shoes and he rode in the car with his mouth on the molding of the rear window and how the cold metal tasted of salt and hummed against his lips and he remembered the attar of rose and candlewax and the facets of a glass doorknob cold and smooth on his tongue.

And he saw old bottles and jars in a row on a board propped up with bricks in a field of sedge and the mixtures of mud and diced weeds within and round white pebbles wherein lay basilisks incubating and secret paths through the sedge and a little clearing with broken bricks, an old limecrusted mortarbox, dry white dogturds. He saw a mooncalf dead in a wet road you could see through it, you could see its bones where it lay pale and blue and naked with eyes as barren as lightbulbs.

And he saw what had been how that old lady who had sat in the stained and cracked photograph like a fierce bird lay cold in state, white satin tucked or quilted and the parched claws that came out of the black stuff of her burial dress looked like the bony hands of some grimmer being crossed at her throat. Black lacquer bier trestled up in a drafty hall and how the rain swung from the rims of the pallbearers' hats.

The coals in the grate had died to the faintest pulse and he lay staring at the ceiling in almost total darkness. He listened for some sound in the house but there was none. He could hear organ music trammeled up out of an old black record on a gramophone somewhere and the slow shuffle of feet over the polished floors and he could see how the wind from the open door raised the figured runner in the hall and he was lifted in his father's arms to see how quietly the dead lay. Suddenly Suttree sat upright. He saw in a small alcove among flowers the sleeping doll, the white bonnet, the lace, the candlelight. Come upon in their wanderings through the vast funeral hall. And the little girl took the thing from its cradle and held it and rocked it in her arms and Clayton said you better put that thing up. She took it through the halls crooning it a lullaby, the long lace burial dress trailing behind her to the floor and Suttree following and a woman saw them pass in the hall and called softly upon God before she ran from the room and someone cried out: You bring that thing here. And they ran down the hall and the little girl fell with it and it rolled on the floor and a man came out and took it away and the little girl was crying and she said that it was just lying in there by itself and the little boy was much afraid.

Suttree rose from the cot and stumbled from the room. He went down the hall in the dark and unlatched the door at the end of it and stepped outside. The rind of a moon lay cocked in the sky and the world looked cold and blue. He could see the stalks of dockweed dead in the yard and beyond them the barren and pestilential locust wood and the trashpapers and newsprint among the boughs like varied birds illshapen pale and restless in the wind. He wandered through the wood as if he meant to read the old bleached news spiked there, the artless felonies, the murder in the streets. His tongue lay swollen in his mouth and his skull vised his brain. He could see figures moving in the woods greenly phosphorescent. He thought he might hear singing and he stood in the dark a long time listening but there was no sound, not even a dog barked. He made his way through a world unreal, through causeways in a darkened town, a gray light moving in the east, past dark brick walls and windows kept by steel grates, their panes opaque with soot. He wandered in the night murk by the river, in the cold damp of dead weeds, the lights on the far shore marking orders he had never seen before.

He lay in his bed half waking. He knew what would come to be that the fiddler Little Robert would kill Tarzan Quinn. A barge passed on the river. He lay with his feet together and his arms at his sides like a dead king on an altar. He rocked in the swells, floating like the first germ of life adrift on the earth's cooling seas, formless macule of plasm trapped in a vapor drop and all creation yet to come.

In the madhouse the walls reek with the odors of filth and terminal ills they've soaked up these hundred years. Stains from the rusted plumbing, the ordure slung by irate imbeciles. All this seeps back constantly above the smell of germicidal cleaning fluids.

A cold and brittle day. The iron gate open and the trees like bare black fossils rising from the dead leaves on the lawn. Walking the long drive, the dark brick buildings on the hill looming dire against the winter sky.

Old scarred marble floors in a cold white corridor. A room where the mad sat at their work. To Suttree they seemed like figures from a dream, something from the past, old drooling derelicts bent above their basketry, their fingerpaints or knitting. He'd never been among the certified and he was surprised to find them invested with a strange authority, like folk who'd had to do with death some way and had come back, something about them of survivors in a realm that all must reckon with soon or late.

In the center of the room sat a nurse at a desk. She read the morning paper where the news was madder yet.

McKellar, Suttree said.

She took off her glasses and rubbed her eyes and pushed the paper back. She opened a ledger and held a pencil above it. Your name, she said.

Suttree. Cornelius Suttree.

You are . . . What?

I beg your pardon?

The nurse looked up at him. What, she said. A nephew?

Yes. Nephew.

You've been here before then.

Not in some years.

She put her glasses on again and laid down the pencil and turned in her chair. That's her with the other lady sitting by the far wall. The two by themselves.

Thank you.

Eyes watched him cross the floor. A lone pacer in a strange knitted cap paused and raised a cautionary finger. Suttree nodded, agreeing as he did on the need for care. The old women sat like almstresses on the floor in their hodden cloaks. He knelt before them and they regarded him mildly. He thought that he might know her in some way but age and madness had outdone all the work of likeness there had ever been and he could not guess. Aunt Alice? he said.

The older lady moved. She made a little motion of gathering the hem of her gown and she looked at him with no change of expression. Yes, she said.

I'm Buddy.

Oh yes. How have you been?

Do you know me?

Are you Buddy?

Yes.

Grace's son.

Suttree smiled, son of Grace. I didnt think you'd know me.

She reached out and took his wrist. Her hand cool and firm. He covered it with his own. She had her eyes fixed on him and would not look elsewhere. They were a pure cold gray and something feral in them but there was no malice there. He looked down at their hands. Hers was trembling, just gently. The old woman sitting by her reached over and put her hand with theirs and nodded her head solemnly. The three of them squatting there on the floor like conspirators pledging themselves.

How have you been, Aunt Alice?

A hollow croak of a voice in the drafty dayroom. He cleared his throat. He turned to see had he attracted attention. An old man in a wheelchair cringing by the wall watched. Chanting to himself some silent doxology.

I'm fine, the old woman said.

Do they treat you well?

Oh, a body ought not to complain.

Does Mother come?

Why she died in twenty-seven.

Does Grace come to see you? Or Helen?

Oh well. She shook her head and smiled. No. They dont come a whole lot.

Does Martha?

No. John comes much as anybody. He took me out. He took me out in his motorcar.

The old woman with them nodded her head. He did, she said. Her John did. Come in a car and fetched her.

The aunt leaned toward Suttree in confidence. He'd been a drinkin some. But I'd rather for him to of come drunk as for nobody to come sober.

Suttree smiled. They were speaking in hushed tones like people in church. The room was enormously silent. He could hear labored breathing, the rattle of osiers among the basketmakers. The clink of a bucket bail out in the hall somewhere. He looked around at the old room, the pale midwinter light that carried the windows tall and slant to the opposite wall and the plaster banded with the bones of lathing.

I never thought to end my time in such a place as this is, she said. If Allen had lived he never would of let no such a thing happen. He was always so good to me. I was like his little girl almost. I was just little when Daddy died.

What was his name? Your father. I never knew his name.

It was Jeffrey. My brother Jeffrey was Jeffrey Junior. Daddy was old when I was born. I know he'd been too old for service in the war between the states. He was a . . . He was wild. Pretty wild. They always said about him anyways. He was shot in a fracas of some kind. Long fore he married. Come near dyin. So I always wondered about that, had he died none of us would never have been at all and I never could . . . Well, that's a funny thing to think. Maybe we would have just been somebody else. But they said he was, that he had been in trouble, I dont know. I reckon it was so and I reckon Jeffrey must of took after him. I never knew Jeffrey. I was just a baby when . . . When he died.

He was hanged in Rockcastle County Kentucky on July 18 1884.

She didnt answer. She said: Allen always said that Robert favored him. But of course Robert never come back from the war. Lord he wasnt but eighteen poor baby. Allen never got over it. They say he died of cancer and that may be but he never had hardly a well day after they brought Robert home. I believe it killed him as much as anything did. They was nine of us you know. Me and Elizabeth outlived all the boys and now she's gone and I'm in the crazy house. Sometimes I dont know what people's lives are for. She looked at Suttree. Her eyes moved and she smiled.

Daddy kept store you know, and we had this horse his name was Captain and he used to pull the wagon delivered the groceries and he was my pet. He'd foller me around, just foller me around like a dog would. We lived in Sweetwater then. And they was hard times then and we had to sell the store and Daddy had to sell Captain. And they took me up to Nanny's because the man was comin to take him, you see. I was just a little thing. Years later when I was a young girl I was in Knoxville one Saturday and I seen this horse standin in front of a feedstore hitched to a wagon and it was Captain. I run over to him and thowed my arms around him and kissed him and I reckon everbody thought I was crazy, me about full growed standin there in the street huggin a old horse and just a bawlin to beat the band.

She pushed the palm of her hand hard against one cheek. She looked up at Suttree and smiled and she looked at the woman by her side who now was weeping and she gave her a great nudge with her elbow. Lord amercy, she said. You're the silliest thing in here.

The woman shook her head and snuffled and Suttree's aunt smiled at him. I want you to look at this old crazy thing, she said. She dont even know what all she's bawlin about.

Do too, said the woman.

It wasnt the first word she'd said but it was the first Suttree'd heard. She had her hand across her forehead and was rubbing it as if she'd have the skin off. She wore a faint mustache and her gray hair stood about her head electrically. Aunt Alice looked down at her with soft amusement. She brushed her cheeks again and turned to Suttree. Her eye was bright and her expression full of sauce. You're a good lookin somethin, she said. I believe you favor E C. You dont have a motorcar do you?

Suttree said he didnt. He felt himself being drawn into modes for which he had neither aptitude nor will. They were both watching him. The tears were gone. Their eyes seemed filled with expectation and he'd nothing to give. He'd come to take. He pulled away from them and they leaned toward him with their veined old hands groping at the emptiness. He rose. Casting his eyes over this wreckage. What perverted instinct made folks group the mad together? So many. He was the only person in the room standing and now they were watching him, eyes vacant or keen with suspicion or incipient hatred. Or eyes betrayed of any earnestness at all. An air of possible insurrection in the room, wanting just the cue to set these wretches clawing at their keepers. He looked down at the old ladies at his feet. They had their hands to their mouth in identical attitudes. I have to go, he said. I cant stay. He tore his look from theirs and wheeled off through the room. An old man in a striped railroader's hat was holding a huge watch in his hand and following Suttree with his eyes as if he'd time him. Their eyes met across the dayroom and Suttree's face drained to see the old man there and he almost said his name but he did not and he was soon out the door.

He was going from phone to phone in the booths of the Park National Bank and he was whistling to himself when a heavy hand dropped across his shoulder. He stopped and looked down, placing the nearest black wingtip shoe. He leaped up and came down on the shoe with his heel, his knee locked. Small bones cracked under the leather. The hand went away. Harrogate never even saw the man. He crossed Gay Street in the noon traffic over the actual hoods and decklids of idling cars, faces white behind the glass, sounds of buckling sheetmetal.

Suttree sought him out under the viaduct among the debris. Gene? he called. There was no fire, no sign of having been one. Cars rumbled distantly overhead. Hey Gene.

Harrogate crawled out of the concrete pillbox and squatted in the dirt. He was ragged looking and shaking with the cold and he had shaved his mustache off.

Suttree squatted beside him. Well, he said. What are your plans?

The city rat hunched his shoulders. He looked frail and wasted with defeat.

You cant stay down here, you'll freeze.

He shook his head slowly from side to side, staring at the raw ground. I dont know, he said. I been in there all day. I figured the law would of done had me by now.

Suttree stirred the dust with his forefinger. They will, he said. This is no place to hide out.

I know it. How'd you find me?

I didnt have any place else to look. Rufus told me you'd been up there.

Yeah. You caint depend on a nigger for nothin. I didnt know where else to go. All them sons of bitches. Many a time as I drunk whiskey with em. They didnt hardly know me.

Suttree smiled. A fugitive's life is a hard one, he said. What happened to your mustache?

Harrogate rubbed his lip. Shaved it off, he said. Maybe they wont recognize me without it. I dont know. Shit.

Well what are you going to do?

I dont know. I was ashamed to come to you.

Maybe you ought to get out of town for a while.

Where to?

Anywhere. Out of town.

Harrogate looked up at him vaguely. Out of town? he said.

If you stay around here they'll nail your ass.

Hell, Sut. I aint never been out of town. I wouldnt know where to go. I wouldnt know which way to start.

Just get on a bus and go. What difference does it make? You've scuffled in this town for three years, hell, you could make it somewhere else.

I dont have no friends somewhere else.

You dont have any here.

Harrogate shook his head. Shit, he said. Bus? I aint never even been on a goddamned bus.

All you do is get a ticket and get on.

Yeah yeah, sure sure. I'd get on the wrong damned bus or somethin.

There's not any wrong bus. Not for you.

Well how the hell would I know where to get off at? And where would I be when I did?

They'd tell you.

He looked at the ground. Naw, he said. I'd never make it. I'd get lost and never would get home again ever. He shook his head. I dont know, Sut. Seems like everthing I turn my hand to. Dont make no difference what it is. Just everthing I touch turns to shit.

Have you got any money?

Not a cryin dime.

What did you do with all that money you were making?

Spent it, naturally.

You could go on the train.

Do they not charge?

You can sneak on. Get in an empty car over in the yards. I can let you have a few dollars.

Train, said Harrogate, staring off toward the creek.

You could go south for the winter. Someplace where it's not so fucking cold. Hell, Gene. You've got to do something. You cant just sit here.

The city rat made a little shivering motion and drew up his feet but he didnt answer.

Who was it nailed you?

Fuck if I know.

Was it a detective? Plainclothes?

I dont know, Sut. I never seen nothin but his feet. I reckon it was the telephone heat. They tell me when them sons of bitches get on your trail you're completely fucked. They wont rest till they get ye.

Telephone heat?

Harrogate looked up warily. You fuckin ay, he said. Them bastards take it personal. He looked at the ground. I knew that, he said. I knew it, but I went and done it anyways.

Dark was falling over the creek and a cold wind was moving in the dry weeds. On the hill among the shacks a dog had begun to bark. They sat quietly under the viaduct in the deepening chill. After a while Harrogate said: They wouldnt be a soul there that I knowed. I'd bet on it.

Where?

In the workhouse.

There wasnt anybody there you knew the last time.

Yeah.

You're not there yet, anyway.

Me and old crazy Bodine used to have some good times racin scorpions in the kitchen. That was after you'd done left.

Scorpions?

Lizards I guess you call em.

Lizards?

Yeah. We'd get the yard man to get em for us. We'd race em on the kitchen floor. Get a bet up. Shit. I had me one named Legs Diamond that son of a bitch would stand straight up with them old legs just a churnin and quick as he'd get traction he was gone like a striped assed ape. Never would touch down with his front feet.

The city mouse shook his head, deep in the fondness of these recollections like a strange little old man there in the blue winter twilight under the bridge. Remembering the sunlight on the buffed floor and the broomhandles laid out and the chalk marks. Lying like the children they were on the cool floor with their fragile reptiles, the small hearts hammering in the palms of their hands. Holding them by their tiny pumping waists and releasing them at a signal. The lizards rearing onto their hind legs as their feet slipped on the smooth waxed concrete, strange little saurians. Harrogate has tacked the hinder toes of his with syrup and it scampers through the barry light to soundless victory.

Old crazy Leithal King worked in the kitchen after that. I believe he was the biggest fuck-up in the workhouse. Shit. I got tired takin stuff off of him he was so dumb. I used to race lizards with him I'd let him take his pick, we'd have upwards of half a dozen in a kettle. I'd have me some chili pepper in my hand and when I got my lizard I'd rub a little of that in his ass. He'd go like he was on fire. Old Leithal'd get em and wouldnt know how to hold em or nothin, half the time he'd pull their tails off. He raced one one time that son of a bitch stood straight up and went right on over backards, feet just a churnin.

They sat in blackness. Lights were coming on across the cut, blooming among the barren vines like winter fireflies there.

Come on, said Suttree. You can stay at my place till you get sorted out what you're going to do.

I dont want to put nobody out.

Hell with that. Let's go.

He rose reluctantly.

What happened to your cat? said Suttree.

Shit if I know. Seems like when the shit hits the fan they all clear out. Even the goddamn cat.

Suttree never locked his door and the city mouse would come and go at hours convenient to his obscure purposes. He wandered through the wastes like a jackal in the dark, in the keep of old warehouse walls and the quiet of gutted buildings. He was enamored of the night and those quiet regions on the city's inward edges too dismal for dwelling. Down alleyways of flueblack brick. Through a gate unhinged to a garden of gloom.

In the dawn when cold trucks cough and lumber over the cobbles and black men in frayed and partly eaten greatcoats of their country's service stand about the fires in empty trashdrums and spit and speculate and nod there'd shoulder in among them a paler derelict who held his small hands to the flames without a word.

At night sometimes he'd sit by the right of way where the rails go so surgically in the slack gloss of the quartermoon. Curving away to some better land where strangers sit freely without being asked. Among alien shapes in the honeysuckles watching the train pass chuffing and clacking down the cut between the high banks, leaving in the smoke and leaf swirl such utter loneliness that he, who'd come from hiding to see it go, knelt sobbing on the crossties among the lightly whispered collisions of the leaves with a hot and salty sorrow in his throat, his hands dangling and his stained face wretched, watching the barnred hinder carriage shuttle gently from sight beyond the curve.

He was caught at his first robbery. White lights crossed like warring swords the little grocery store and back, his small figure tortured there cringing and blinking as if he were being burnt. He dove headlong through a plateglass window and fetched up stunned and bleeding at the feet of a policeman who stood with a cocked revolver at his head saying: I hope you run. I wish you would run.

He rode handcuffed through the winter landscape to Nashville. It is true that the world is wide. Out there the open ends of cornfield rows wheel past like a turnstile. Dark earth between the dead stalks. The rails at a junction veering in liquid collision and flaring again silently in long vees. His forehead to the cold glass, watching.

They went on through the long afternoon twilight with the old carriage rocking and clicking and a rain that blew down from the north cutting long tears in the dust on the windows. Barren fields falling away desolate and small flocks of nameless birds flaring over the land and against the darkening sky like seafans stamped from black sheet iron the shapes of winter trees against a winter sky.

They passed a house and a woman came from the door and tossed a dishpan of water into the yard and wiped her hand on her apron. He pressed his face to the window, watching her recede quietly in the dusk. The train hooted for a crossing and they passed a little store squatting in the coke and dust beyond the yard and they passed a row of empty coaches, the dead windows clocking by and dicing the scene beyond and the long wail of the engine hanging over the country like a thing damned of all deliverance. Harrogate eased the steel bracelet on his wrist and rested his head against the harsh nap of the seat and slept.

He woke in the night with the train's slowing. Stale smell of smoke and an antique mustiness from the old woodwork of the carriage. The man he was manacled to slept slackjawed. He looked out the window. A long row of lighted henhouses on a hill went by like a passing train itself, row on row of yellow windows backing down the night and drawing off into the darkness. They went through a small town in the mountains, a midnight cafe, empty stools, a dead clock on the wall. As they moved on into the country again the windows became black mirrors and the city rat could see his pinched face watching him back from the cold glass, out there racing among the wires and the bitter trees, and he closed his eyes.

Somnolent city, cold and dolorous in the rain, the lights bleeding in the streets. Cutting through the alley off Commerce he saw a man huddled among the trash and he knelt to see about him. The face came up and the eyes closed. An oiled mask in black against the bricks.

Suttree took him by one arm. Ab, he said.

Can you get me home? A voice from the void, dead and flat and divested of every vanity. Suttree raised up one of the great arms and got it across his shoulder and braced his feet to rise. Sweat stood on his forehead. Ab, he said. Come on.

He opened his eyes and looked about. Are they huntin me? he said.

I dont know. Come on.

He lurched to his feet and stood there reeling while Suttree steadied him by one arm. Their shadows cast by the lamp at the end of the alley fell long and narrow to darkness. As they tottered out of the mouth of the alley a prowlcar passed. Ab sagged, swung back and slammed against the building.

Goddamnit Ab. Straighten up now. Ab.

The cruiser had stopped and was backing slowly. The spotlight came on and sliced about and pinned them against the wall.

Go on, Youngblood.

No.

I aint goin.

You'll be all right in a minute.

With them I aint goin. Go on.

No damnit. Ab. I'll talk to them.

But the black had begun to come erect with a strength and grace contrived out of absolute nothingness and Suttree said: Ab, and the black said: Go on.

All right, said the officer. What's this?

I'm just getting him home, said Suttree. He's all right.

Is that so? He dont look so all right to me. What are you doin with him? He your daddy?

Fuck you, said Ab.

What?

There were two of them now. Suttree could hear the steady guttering of the cruiser's exhaust in the empty street.

What? said the officer.

The black turned to Suttree. Go on now, he said. Go on while ye can.

Officer this man's sick, said Suttree.

He's goin to be sicker, said the cop. He gestured with his nightstick. Get his ass in there.

Bullshit on that, said the other one. Let me call the wagon. That's that big son of a bitch . . .

Jones lurched free and swung round the corner of the alley at a dead run. The two cops tore past Suttree and disappeared after him. The flat slap of their shoes died down the alley in a series of diminishing reports and then there was only the rough drone of the idling cruiser at the curb. Suttree stepped to the car, eased himself beneath the wheel and shut the door. He sat there for a moment, then he engaged the gearbox and pulled away.

He drove to Gay Street and turned south and onto the bridge. The radio crackled and a voice said: Car Seven. He turned left at the end of the bridge, past the abandoned roller rink, a rotting wooden arena that leaned like an old silo. He went down Island Home Pike toward the river. The radio fizzled and crackled. Calling any car in area B. Area B. Come in.

We've got a report of some kind of disturbance at Commerce and Market.

Suttree drove along the lamplit street. There was no traffic. The lights at Rose's came up along his left and the lights from the packing company. The radio said: Car Nine. Car Nine. Suttree turned off down an old ferry road, going slowly, the car rocking and bumping over the ground, out across a field, the headlights picking up a pair of rabbits that froze like plaster lawn figures. The dead and lightly coiling back of the river moving beyond the grass. The sparsely lit silhouette of the city above. The headlights failed somewhere out over the water in a gauzy smear. He brought the car to a stop and shifted it into neutral and stepped out into the wet grass. He pulled the hoodlatch under the dash and walked to the front of the cruiser and raised the hood. He came back to the car and sat in the seat and removed his shoelace. He looked out at the river and the city. One of the rabbits began to lope slowly through the light ground mist toward the dark of the trees.

The radio popped. Wagner? What's the story down there?

Suttree got out and walked around to the front of the car and bent into the motor compartment and pulled back the throttle linkage. The motor rose to a howl and he tied the linkage back with the shoelace, fastening it to the fuel line where it entered the pump. Live flame was licking from the end of the tailpipe. He climbed in and pushed the clutch to the floor and shifted the lever hard up into second in a squawk of gearteeth. The rabbits were both gone. He eased off the seat and stood with one foot on the ground and the other on the clutch. Then he leaped back and slapped the door shut.

For a moment it didnt move. The tires cried in the grass and smoking clods went rifling off through the dark. Then it settled slightly sideways, dished back again, and in a shower of mud and grass moved out across the field. It went low and fast, the headlights rigid and tilting. It tore across the field and ripped through the willows at the river's edge and went planing out over the water in two great wings of spray that seemed pure white and fanned upward twenty feet into the air. When it came to rest it was far out in the river. The headlights began to wheel about downstream. Then they went out. For a while he could see the dark hump of it in the river and then it slowly subsided and was gone. He squatted in the damp grass and looked out. There was no sound anywhere along the river. After a while he rose and started home.

Jones came to bay with his back to a brick wall, standing widefooted and gasping while the officers approached. A bloody dumbshow and no word spoken. The first policeman swung at him with his club and Jones slapped at it, a dead smack of meat in his palm. He swung again and this time the black's hand folded over the club. The policeman had the leather lanyard looped about his wrist and Jones swung him sideways and slammed him against the bricks. Then he jerked him to his knees and was strangling him when the other officer fell upon him and forced him to give it up. Jones kicked them back and the first officer staggered toward the center of the alley and dropped to his knees groaning. A cry of sirens was nearing in the streets. The able officer stepped back in alarm but Jones seized him like some huge black pervert. He struggled to reach for his revolver. By now a patrol car was coming down the alley in a blinding spray of lights. The seized officer gave up trying to loosen his pistol and was hammering away with his billy at the cropped skull above him and his hand and arm were slick with blood.

Men were running in the alley. Jones turned and started off lumbering and huge in the lights like a movie monster. The revolvers in that narrow space crashed like mortars and the bullets caromed and whined and skittered. But before they could get a true aim his knees went under him and he collapsed flailing among the trashcans at the alley's mouth.

The officer who opened the rear door of the paddywagon just closed his eyes. He had no time to fend or hide. Jones's boot caught him in the throat and he went to the pavement without a cry. The other officers received him with billies and slapsticks, his eyes huge and crazed and his jacket spongy with blood launching himself upon them like some unshackled wild man and taking them to the ground with him.

They dragged him bleeding and senseless down the corridor to the tank, his feet scuffing behind. His bearers were bleeding and torn and they cursed every step they took. They pulled him into the empty iron cage and let him fall face down on the concrete. Tarzan Quinn came from the dayroom with a cup of coffee in one hand. The jailer was locking back the hall door, a great ring of keys fastened to him with a chain.

Duck, said Tarzan.

The jailer turned. Yeah, he said.

You let me know when that son of a bitch wakes up.

Sure will, Tarzan.

Tarzan nodded and sipped his coffee. He worked his right fist open and shut and rubbed his palm on the side of his trousers.

She was a long time coming but when she saw him she opened the door and motioned with her head for him to enter. She had a lamp in her hand and she wore an old chenille robe and she had some sort of a nightcap on her head that looked vaguely orthopedic. She shuffled wearily into a chair and put her face in one hand.

He shut the door and leaned against it, watching her. After a while she raised her head and wiped her eye and her mouth. She was looking at the lampflame.

He aint dead is he? she said.

No. I thought maybe he got away but he must be in jail.

Well.

What do you want to do?

Aint nothin to do. Aint no use in goin over there till in the mornin.

I guess not.

She shook her head. They aint no way, she said. Just aint no way.

Do you have any money?

Some. I dont know. Them bondsmens gets it all. I'll have to look and see.

I've got about thirty dollars if you need it.

That wouldnt get him started.

What will they charge him with?

What wont they. Two year ago they tried to get him for temptin murder. It costed me fourteen hunnerd dollar.

I cant go down there with you.

You dont need to go down there.

They may be looking for me.

Dont let em get on you, she said. They never will get off.

A dull glow of coals showed through the drafthole in the stove door but it was cold in the room. She must have followed his thoughts. Come over here by the stove and warm, she said. You want a beer?

No. I've got to go. I've got to figure out what to do.

She shook her head and looked up. Black shining face, those lunettes of flesh ridging the skin and the one webbed and blinking eye.

He fifty-six year old, she said. You know that?

I knew he was something like that.

He caint carry on like this. They'll kill him. You caint tell him.

Suttree looked at the floor.

Well, she said. I thank ye for stoppin.

Do you want me to try and get hold of Oceanfrog?

No. I'll see him.

Well. I'll come by tomorrow.

She rose from the chair and put both hands on the table. Then she sat down again. Suttree opened the door and went out.

He crossed the cold white tiles of the lobby floor and leaned at the desk. There was no one about. He palmed the little bell. Brass through the nickel plate. After a while Jesse came from the rear and nodded with that expression of constrained contempt with which he beheld all life forms not midnight in color.

He be out in a minute.

The clerk came out and went through the little gate and stood facing Suttree.

You got a room? said Suttree.

He reached and took a card from a slot and slid it across the marble counter and laid a pen across it.

Suttree wrote his name and pushed the card back. The clerk didnt look at it. Is it just you? he said.

Just me.

How long?

I dont know. Couple of weeks.

He laid out a key on its fiberboard fob. Twelve bucks, he said.

For a week?

Right.

I only paid fourteen for a double. Last time I was here.

It's twelve bucks.

Suttree counted out the money and took the key and crossed the lobby to the stairs and climbed upward into the gloom. He found the room and went to put the key in the door but it was already ajar. He pushed it open. The latch was smashed, broken hardware hung from the screws. The whole door was cracked through and wobbled sickly when he pushed it shut. He went back down the stairs and dinged on the bell.

The clerk gave him another room and he went up again. It looked out over the alley in the rear of the hotel. There were enormous holes caved in the walls and patched over with cardboard and masking tape. A small iron bed. An oak veneer dresser on tall castered legs. He lay hammocked in the soft mattress and stared at the ceiling. After a while he got up and turned off the light and kicked off his shoes and stretched out again. Cars passed in the streets below. Already a faint gray light from the day to come lay in the eastward windows. He slept.

It was late afternoon when he woke. He shuffled off down the hall to the bathroom. There seemed to be no one about. He went down and got the paper in the lobby and crossed the street and went up to the drugstore where he sat in a back booth and had coffee and doughnuts. He ransacked the paper for news of the night before but there was no word.

With dark he went down to the end of the street and to the river. There was no light at Doll's and no one answered when he rapped at the door. Ab's cat came down from the roof and rubbed against his leg but he had nothing to give it.

It was dark on the river and the only sound was the dripping of the oars and the light rasp of the locks. He foundered among the shore brush with his flashlight and finally located the stake where his trotline was fastened and he hooked the line through the lock in the transom and took the oars again, the flashlight propped on the seat and the line coming up very white from the black water. He stripped the bait from the hooks as they came up and when he reached the farther bank he cut the line. It rifled off into the river with a thin sucking sound and disappeared from sight. Then he rowed down and ran the other line and cut it. By the time he came back upriver with his catch in the floor of the skiff it was past midnight. He lit his lamp and sat on the deck and cleaned the fish, pausing from time to time to warm his stained hands at the lampchimney. He wrapped the fish in newsprint and put them in a box and he went down and drew the skiff ashore and turned it over. Then he went in and got his clothes and the few personal things he owned and blew out the lamp and went across the fields toward the town with these things piled atop the fishbox in front of him.

He went down every night but there was no one home. By day he kept off the streets. There was nothing in the papers. He asked for her at Howard Clevinger's but no one knew where she was. As he turned to leave he saw Oceanfrog going along the street.

Hey baby, the frog said.

What's happening, said Suttree. Where's Ab.

The man's in the hospital.

Is he bad?

I dont know. I aint been out there.

Where's Doll?

She out there with him. Frazer turned up his collar and looked off down the street. He turned back to Suttree. You goin out there? he said.

I dont know.

They got a cop on the door.

Ah, said Suttree.

Oceanfrog squinted at him and smiled. He tugged at his collar again and took a step backward preparatory to going on up the street. Thought you ought to know, he said.

Have they been down to my place?

They been there, baby. Hang loose.

He went up the street in his jaunty stride and Suttree looked toward the river and tested the air with his nose in a gesture of some simpler antecedent but the wind and the landscape alike remained cool and without movement.

He'd walk out at night to the end of the bridge and lean on the ironwork and watch the river and the squalor of the life below. He could hear the music from upstairs in the old frame house that Carroll King ran as a nightclub, Paul Jones at the piano full of gin and old offcolor songs. A black girl named Priscilla who worked by day in a laundry.

A few nights later he saw the faintest fall of light on the river from the rear of Jones's place and he descended the little path in the dark.

For a while he thought she wouldnt come to the door. He was almost ready to leave when it swung open.

Her hair lay about her head in greasy black clots as if she were besieged with leeches and her eye was bright and inflamed and swiveled up silently to see him. She crossed her arms and held her shoulders and her breath smoked in the cold.

How is he? said Suttree. Is he here?

She shook her head.

Is he not out of the hospital?

Yes. He's out. The Lord taken him out. She began to cry, standing there in her housecoat and slippers, holding her shoulders. The tears that ran on her pitted cheek looked like ink. She had her eye closed but the lid that covered the naked socket did not work so well anymore and it sagged in the cavity and struggled up and that raw hole seemed to watch him with some ghastly equanimity, an eye for another kind of seeing like the pineal eye in atavistic reptiles watching through time, through conjugations of space and matter to that still center where the living and the dead are one.

That spring he did not go to the river. The shadows of the buildings still harbored a gray chill and the sun sulked smoked and baleful somewhere above the city and in the sparsely weeded clay barrens wasting on the city's perimeter first flowers erupted drunkenly through glass and cinder and came slowly to bloom. The days grew warm and grackles returned, hordes of blue tin birds that weighed the shrieking trees. Small bodies that the cold has kept went soft with rot, a cat's balding hide that tautened and dried cloven to the meatless ribs, an upturned eyesocket filled with rainwater and for all weathers this lipless grin, these bleaching teeth.

He went out seldomer, his money dribbled away. The days grew long and he lay hourlong on his cot. The clerk came and tapped at the door and went away again. One day came an eviction notice.

Then he fell sick. First his nose began to bleed nor could he stop it. The floor lay strewn with wads of wet toiletpaper stained with watered blood. The clerk came and rapped again. Shadow of his shoes in the threshold light. And went away. Things had begun to go peculiar. Grainy underwater singing sounds in his head. He lay on his cot and watched the barren vinework of cracks in the ceiling. Old rags of lace lifted at the window. Cries of children at noon on the Bell House School grounds. Suttree lay naked in fever. Even his eyes were hot. He slept some of the afternoon, waking out of a dream fraught with the odor of a long forgotten blanket whose satin selvedge bore blue ducks. His father's weight tilting the bed, how do you feel son, I dont feel so pretty good. Under the slant ceiling, close by the eaves.

He opened his eyes. The room had a warped look to it. He watched arcana uncoil from out of the rough plaster. Something unseen possessed the troweler's hand. Shapes grimacing in a calcimine moonscape. Record of an old mason long dead it may be. He closed his eyes again. A huge and pulsing thumbwhorl hovered above his swollen lids. He steadied himself with one hand to the wall like a drunk.

The day expired in rose and ashen light. Blue dusk cooled in the room.

He lay in darkness.

After a long time he staggered to the wall and threw the switch. Under the stark bulblight he groped for a towel to wrap his loins and reeled out and down the corridor to the bathroom. There he knelt on the cold white tiles and vomited blood into the toilet. When he came back to his room he sat on the bed and looked at his toes.

Well, he said. You're sick.

A shoe salesman named Thomas E Warren found him shortly after midnight. He thought him drunk. Kneeling, he stirred him by the shoulder. Hey Bud, he said.

Suttree was lying naked on the bathroom floor where he'd come for the cool. Warren got him to his feet and Suttree stared back without comprehension, not having expected anyone from the world of the quick. Down a far wall of his smoking brain withdrew a ghastly company. He disengaged himself from the grip of the living Thomas and tottered to the toilet and sat.

You okay, man?

Yes, said Suttree.

He was alone in the narrow room. Water sluiced down a black pipe past his ear. His head had sagged forward and he was clutching his stomach. He shat a loose and bloody stool.

At the sink he laved cold water over his head. Ahh, he told the drainhole.

I know you're in there, said the clerk from beyond the door.

Suttree opened his eyes. He was lying on his cot and it was day. The door rapping faded. Footsteps in a corridor. He looked toward the window. Are there parades in the street? What is this roaring? Who is this otherbody? I am no otherbody.

He sat. The room reeled. He fell back and laughed briefly into the musty bedding.

All day he lay in a quaintly fevered world, nothing in the room but the sun and himself, making what construction he could of the sounds that carried to him, the hammering of a roofer, the long farting of airbrakes from a truck in the streets, screendoors banging, children called. A blank wall against which to elaborate his pantomimes. A less virulent cast of the grim had come to occupy his mind and there was a time in the early noon when he had hope of his own recovery. But the sounds he heard began to coalesce and rush and he no longer knew if he dreamt or woke.

In the long afternoon he fell prey to strange cravings of the flesh. Out of a pinwheel of brown taffy his medusa beckoned. A gross dancer with a sallow puckered belly, hands cupping a pudendum grown with mossgreen hair, a virid merkin out of which her wet mauve petals smiled and bared from hiding little rows of rubber teeth like the serried jaws of conchshells.

Suttree groaned in his sleep. He lay in a sexual nightmare, an enormous wattled fundament lowering slowly over his head, in the center a withered brown pig's eye crusted shut and hung with puffy blue and swollen lobes. A white gruel welled. He pressed his face against the cool wall. And who is this Mr Bones rising wreathed in pale and bluegreen gas? He comes about tottering and wooden like a dummy on a track and goes past with a slight smile and a bow. Lights run over his wetlooking bones and the feet of small rodents grip from within the chamfers of his eyesockets and in his pale blue teeth are cores of blackened silver packed. In a rattle and clang of wheels and pulleys Father Bones tilts out through saloon doors and is gone, old varnished funhouse skeleton. Suttree in his sleep smiled at such child's fancies. A gray crust broke at his mouthcorners. His eyes snapped open. He sat and reached for the towel. It fell from him and he went out and down the hall naked.

Clotted gouts of gore stained the water in the toiletbowl. Pink, magenta, burgundy.

He stretched himself on the tiles. A faint tang of urine there. Bird shadows on the whited windowglass. Water dripped in the sink. I saw her in an older dream, an older time, moving in an aura of musk, a breath of stale roses, her languid hands swaying like pale birds and her face chalk and lips pink and her nigh-blue hair upbuckled in combs of tortoise, coming down out of her chamber in my unhealed memory clothed in smoke.

Hey Bud. Hey.

It is my old J-Bone and no other.

What the fuck are you doing?

Sicky sick, James.

What the hell have you done to yourself? Can you get up?

I'm all fucked up, James.

I can see that. What is it?

Dear friend, it's checkout time.

J-Bone patted his shoulder. Hang on a minute. I'll be right back.

Suttree opened his eyes. In a minute I am going to have a drink of water. He licked his lips.

J-Bone arrived with a fat cabbie. They pulled Suttree up by the arms and began to work a shirt onto him.

I'd just let him sleep it off, said the cabdriver.

I cant leave him layin in here.

Suttree's arm dropped, his knuckles banged on the floor.

He aint sick is he?

Hold him here a minute while I button these. He just needs to get dried out.

Desist officer. I'll come peaceably.

He better not be sick. You hear?

I've seen him worse than this. Let him back down now.

Has he got any shoes?

I'll find him some. Help me lift him here.

What's this?

What?

Hell, he's bleedin out of his ass.

Maybe he's got piles.

Piles hell. Look at it.

A crimson stain was spreading about Suttree's pale and naked haunches. He lay buttoned up in a shirt with a pair of trousers bunched about his knees. The cabdriver backed toward the door. J-Bone looked like an assassin kneeling there. The cabbie turned and fled down the hall.

Go on then, you son of a bitch, J-Bone called.

Son of a bitch, said Suttree from the floor.

J-Bone pulled him sideways out of the blood and began to wrestle the trousers up around him. He fetched his shoes and got them on. He got him up under the armpits and dragged him out and down the hall and stood in Suttree's bed and pulled him up onto it.

Water Jim. A little old drink.

J-Bone was back in ten minutes with another cabdriver.

Can he walk?

No. Give me a hand with him.

Damn if he aint about as fucked up as anybody I ever saw.

He gets this way.

Suttree's toes left a faint wake in the scurfy warp of the hall carpet. His shoes fell down the stairs like toys. He watched the hard sunlight ascend the stairwell. His head banged something.

You goin with him aint ye?

Yes. I'll ride back here. Go ahead.

That's the drunkest human ever I witnessed, said the driver.

Whose house is this? said Suttree.

Take it easy Bud.

Why I'm all right.

They struggled with him. I was all right, he said.

Rank odor of caustic and drugs. Standing in a white room. He leaned in confidence toward an ear. I'm all right now, he lied. Someone has stole the pins from his kneehinges. He leaned heavily on a steel table. A wall placard listed regulations. In the center of the room the taut white linen of the emergency table. An orderly opened the door and looked at him.

To wish to lie down here is to entertain the illusion that kings may worship, said Suttree.

The orderly closed the door.

Another door closed, door closed, door closed softly in his skull. Light bloomed rose, lime green. He was going out by a long tunnel attended by fading voices and a grainy humming sound and going faster and past gray images that clicked apart in jagged puzzle pieces. Down a corridor that opened constantly before him and dissolved after in iron dark. While the dead wheeled past in floats of sere and faded flower wreaths with little cards on which the ink of the names had run in the rain. Callahan and Hoghead leering with their crazy teeth and little plugs stoppering the holes in their skulls and Bobby Davis on a slab with his torso peppered like a pox victim and Jimmy Smith with broken neck and Aunt Beatrice composed and sedate in grayblack gingham with candlewhite hands enfolding a rose and passing in a glass casket. She cracked one powdered eye, winked hugely and was gone. Suttree said I am going out of the world, a long silent scream on rails down the dark nether slope of the hemisphere that is death's prelude. Attended by ponderous and mercurial figures composed of colored gas and wrenching themselves slowly apart, pale green cerise and bottleblue butyljawed fools that galloped softly and cried out Powww and Boyyy, exulting into the breach with boneless cartoon mouths puckered and wapsy galligaskins, lumbering eternally toward the edge of all.

A quartermoon the color of a broken file lay far down the void. Likecolored figures crossed it. He no longer cared that he was dying. He was being voided by an enormous livercolored cunt with prehensile lips that pumped softly like some levantine bivalve. Into a cold dimension without time without space and where all was motion.

A nurse took Suttree's temperature.

Thank you nurse. Yes, that's fine.

You men can come around to the other side here. Yes. Clear the door there. Thank you.

Suttree opened his eyes. Solemn young men in scrubsuits stood about his bedside watching. He fell back laughing and was gone again. Down a cycloid in a sidecar, a streamlined dreamride through the eye of a poisoned kaleidoscope, cutting a helical course and yawing up the wall at speeds that drained his face and rifling through a hot drift of ether where his ears sang. Attending members appeared over and over, face and figure, a harridan with brown flame for hair reeling past, coming again, a cyclic procession shot through with fleering gas mosaics, and again, slightly mutant, slowly altered, until phased out to abstractions of color and form that severed in elastic parallax like colorplate ghosts in a printing and parted forever. Whereon new forms arose and wheeled all and along, good carousel of crazies. Suttree observed these phenomena with mild interest from his galactic drainsuck. An enormous white doctor crossed his vision and drew away, shrinking rapidly down the small end of a spyglass. Suttree realized his eyes were open. From his incredible heights he watched these bald bipedal mutants struggling down there on the raw and livid rim of consciousness with a sad amusement. His astronomical bias placed him beyond the red shift and he wondered at the geography of these spaces or how does the world mesh with the world beyond the world? A door closed. He eddied up in a backwash, wheeled, drew breath and was gone again.

A black cyclocephalic levered him up and withdrew a bowl of his bowels' blood and carried it out covered with a linen.

A medical cart wheeled in on rubber tires, a stench of sulphur and alcohol. A needle sank in his buttock. He rolled back. He thought he'd seen treebranches in a yard beyond the window. Filled with small figures waiting for he. Wizened and crouching, barbate and cateyed dwarfs with little codpieces of scarlet puce. Who could make them out? An old man lay in the bed next, a gray man sucking air feebly through a slack gray naked mouth. Like me like me. Have they trestled up my bones on a cold stone slab and are they honing small blades against my dismembrance?

Wheezing rubberoid oafs with pendulous girths kept lumbering down a slope one by one in a drifting vapor. Everyone was going on.

When they began packing Suttree in ice he felt an enormous sadness touched with rue. He heard someone say the time but he could not understand. He drifted in a morphine sleep.

Along a wet street, a freshened wind with spits of rain in it. Raw musky smell of the walks. He was in some kind of trouble. Clockshop. A fourlegged clock in a glass bell, a pending treblehook baited with gold balls revolving slowly. Coming to rest. The clock hands too. He looked at his face in the glass. On the wall beyond other clocks are stopping. Me? The shop is closed. A thought to ask. He will not ask, however. Clocks need winding and people to wind them. Someone should be told.

Will the accused please stand.

You have heard the charges against you.

Yes.

Yessir. I come in about eight like I usually do. Seen this feller lookin in the winder and never thought nothin about it. Well, I got in there and I looked at the clock and I seen it wasnt right and I went up to set it and it wasnt runnin. It was wound but it wouldnt run. Then I begun to look around and they was all kinds of peculiarness afoot.

And could you describe these things for us briefly.

Yessir. Well, I kindly hate to . . .

You may speak freely. The accused is securely fettered. Is the accused fettered? Aye, fettered.

Yessir. Well, I commenced lookin about and I seen straightaway they wasnt nary clock in the place knowed what time of day it was. And then I seen Tweetiepie's dead.

You seen Tweetiepie was dead. Were dead.

Yessir.

Let the record show that Tweetiepie is dead.

At the hand of person or persons unknown.

It was him done it settin over there feathered.

Will you identify these remains.

O lordy no I caint bear it I'm so tore up with grief.

Your bird sir?

The same.

Let the record show that the bird is the same bird.

Of course the bird is the same bird, called Suttree, lying thin, white, soft, in a tray of ice, curious tetrapod cooling.

Mr Suttree in what year did your greatuncle Jeffrey pass away?

It was in 1884.

Did he die by natural causes?

No sir.

And what were the circumstances surrounding his death.

He was taking part in a public function when the platform gave way.

Our information is that he was hanged for a homicide.

454

Yessir.

Are you aware of the penalty fixed upon conviction of lycanthropy?

Suttree moaned in the ice. It was never me, he called.

Who segued lithe as an eel from chancery to forest path, abroad by dark tarns in a deep wood where no sun shone and the reeds grew black and fish blind. Until he was stopped by a turtlepedlar bearing a sack of turtles and a rifle gun. Clad in burlap and unshaven he was and in brogans out at the toes and it cold weather.

Harkee stranger, cried the man. A turtle for your soup.

Stranger let me pass for I am weary.

Fifty cents and your choice of the best, ye'll not buy cheaper.

Outbound I am, beyond all wares.

It's hard else could bring you here.

This is no path of my choosing.

Nor mine.

Leeway and ease, the night is coming.

The turtlemonger held forth his sack. Fine turkles, fat turkles. Turkles for the stew.

The dreamer would pass but he has let fall the long dark lilac iron of his riflebarrel to bar the way. An outlaw tollsman reeking of woodsmoke and swamp rot and seeking some chiminage dearer than a path so dark could warrant. Or any path at all.

These be special turkles. Dont pass on without you've give em your consideration.

To this the traveler did consent. The vendor's face grew crafty. The wet sack collapsing aclatter on the ground. He turns back the mouth.

Those are not turtles. Oh God they're not turtles.

Suttree had half reared up in the bed, his swollen tongue gagging his cries. He fell back. Voices spoke beyond a wall. He saw with icy prescience the deathcart before the door, menials entering with a pallet to haul away his puling body and surely the stink of the unshriven dead is a dire stench rising to affront the nostrils of God. Impenitents snatched from the midst of their leprous revels, hard justice. Suttree saw the General pass atop his coalwagon, a paler horse in the traces. He lifted a hand. No fingers to the glove he wore, his cart made no sound. They receded into the vapors till there was just the orange light from the lantern where it swung by its bail from the tailboard.

Down Front Street streetlamps marked the way with measured rings of chromeblue light. The sleepfast shacks lay rotting, dusky sleepers lay within. The dooryard flowers half awake in the lamplight and the city's neon constellations emerging on the night, a pastel alpenglow in which the dust of demolition rose from the jagged ruins of the Cumberland Hotel, the Lyric Theatre.

At the door of the Huddle folk from the looms of McAnally are convened. First among these is a beardless Celt with spattled skin and rebate teeth. Three eyes in his head he has and he is covered over all with orange hair like unto a Cathay ape. At his elbow a stripling with a small and foxy face let into the lower part of a bulbous skull. His towcolored hair is cropped and stands wispily erect and seen from behind he most resembles an enormous dandelion. Suttree smiles to see such friends. The murdered are first to embrace him. Callahan's heavy arm about his shoulder, grinding the scapulae. He speaks through the flarey airholes of his boneless nose to the silverhaired and senatoriallooking barman.

Hey Hatmaker. Tell Hoghead and Donald and Byrd and Bobby and Hugh and Conrad and all of em that they aint barred.

They're dead.

Whoops of laughter among the watchers at the door.

Well you wouldnt bar a dead man would ye?

The tavernkeeper folded his towel and wiped the long mahogony bar. He said that he would not. Suttree among the rabble entered in. Outside the junkman stood alone.

Coin of the realm, coin of the realm, muttered Mr Hatmaker, unmaddened by mercurial bloodliens.

Coin, called Big Frig. Are you holding, fendervendor?

Harvey shuffles forward tugging at his changepurse. A few pieces of Denver silver. Avowing blind faith in deaf deities. He takes a stool at the bar. A fishbowl. He orders.

Big Frig nudges the junkman and leans with a huge horsewink. And make it light on the fish.

Blind Richard at the bar, his eyes batting in the beerlight and the clabbered matter in his sockets shining with a bluish cast leans forward and takes hold of his mug in both hands. His ears remark the voices in his shoreless void. Alice is eyeing the room with contempt. When the moon shines down upon my Wabash then you'll recognize your Indiana home. The whores at the oval table raise their steins. Names of a thousand malefactors and melancholics incised in the black formica there. Faye wears in her garter a glass syringe. I'd give a hog a rimjob to get high, she says. And have, says Shirley. On film, says Rosie.

The queers in the corner booth turn one to the other in shocked amusement. Their spectacles wink small semaphores. Above them in the gutted cage of an electric fan and trapped in a bias of smokegorged light the execrator crouches and drools and turns to and back.

I didnt do it they only said I did. Twas a little jewdoctor come in the night with tailor's shears.

Oh do hush, says a languorous faggot glancing upward.

Foul perverts one and sundry. Silkbedizen pizzlelickers. Roaming the world. Slaking their hideous gorges with jissom. Oh I shall not be loath to tell. I'll bewray the tribe of them to the high almighty God who ledgers up our deeds in a leatherbound daybook. With marbled endpapers, I'm told.

Harrogate in morningcoat stands easily upon the decked and buntinged bar. He wears a small flag in his lapel. Friends, he says. I come from humble circumstance and rose up in the world by my own efforts. And if I'm to leave my footprints in the sands of time let it be with a pair of workshoes.

Someone was tugging at Suttree's sleeve. A small nun with a bitten face, a smell of scorched black muslin and her dead breasts brailed up in the knitted vest she wore. She tugged with little soricine claws at the bones in his elbow.

Cornelius you come away from here this minute.

Mr Suttree it is our understanding that at curfew rightly decreed by law and in that hour wherein night draws to its proper close and the new day commences and contrary to conduct befitting a person of your station you betook yourself to various low places within the shire of McAnally and there did squander several ensuing years in the company of thieves, derelicts, miscreants, pariahs, poltroons, spalpeens, curmudgeons, clotpolls, murderers, gamblers, bawds, whores, trulls, brigands, topers, tosspots, sots and archsots, lobcocks, smellsmocks, runagates, rakes, and other assorted and felonious debauchees.

I was drunk, cried Suttree. Seized in a vision of the archetypal patriarch himself unlocking with enormous keys the gates of Hades. A floodtide of screaming fiends and assassins and thieves and hirsute buggers pours forth into the universe, tipping it slightly on its galactic axes. The stars go rolling down the void like redhot marbles. These simmering sinners with their cloaks smoking carry the Logos itself from the tabernacle and bear it through the streets while the absolute prebarbaric mathematick of the western world howls them down and shrouds their ragged biblical forms in oblivion.

An orderly was going along the outer hall with mop and bucket. He paused for feet to pass. Clicking down the corridor. Voices. And beyond these sounds like the natter and babble of the damned a muted bedlam of voices that were no right voices. Suttree's hands clutched the stenciled sheets.

Did you hear him a while ago?

Shoo. I never heard such stuff.

He's out of his head.

Your head, said Suttree from the depths.

Lord is he awake?

No. Help me turn him, we got to take his temperature.

A sepia crone darted out from under the lower corner of his right eye and cackled and ducked back. Suttree smiled. Dont pack me, ladies. I'm not gone yet.

Hairy aint it?

Oh hush, Wanita. I'd be ashamed.

Pussy, said Suttree from a new place. Weet pussy. Sweet giggling ensued. His penis rose enormous from between his legs, a delicious spasm and there unfolded from the end of it a little colored flag on a wooden stem, who knows what country?

Lightly tinctured, a flavor of sunlight lay in the room. Water dripped in a bowl. He could hear the flat detonation of tennis shoes along a pavement beyond a wall in a courtyard in another kind of kingdom.

Late in the afternoon he rose and wobbled about the room on naked bony legs, a coarse cotton shift just covering his shanks, some strings dangling. He found a sink in the corner of the room and hung by the taps with his face in the bowl and cold water running over his smoking skull. Blood hammered through bearing bad news. He raised up dripping and urinated a few drops painfully into the sink. He looked about the room. Two other beds, both empty. A steel cart with enameled bedpans. He had lifted his nightie and was palming water over his shrunken gut when a nurse entered the room. He turned. They made their way toward each other, reeling across the floor with outstretched arms.

I've got you, said Suttree.

What were you doing?

Bellycooling. Do I know you?

Be careful.

Listen, said Suttree. We were never promised that our flesh, that our flesh . . .

Hush now. Come on.

I have a thing to tell you. I know all souls are one and all souls lonely.

Here we go.

He paused with one knee in the iron bed. He looked up into an uncertain face. It crumbled away grayly, a dusty hag's mask. He lay back. Sheets clammy with salt damp. They clove to him like windings. She tightened the bed while he fanned his belly with the skirt of his gown.

Quit that, she said.

I will not, he said.

She covered him and went away. He lay half waking in the heat, floating like a vast medusa in tropic seas while at his ear he heard sometimes the curious invocations attendant to his case, two hundred milligrams, good deal of fluid in the pleura. . . .

His dreams were of houses, their cellars and attics. Ultimately of this city in the sea.

Some eastern sea that lay heavily in the dawn. There stood on its farther rim a spire of smoke attended and crowned by a plutonic light where the waters have broke open. Erupting hot gouts of lava and great upended slabs of earth and a rain of small stones that hissed for miles in the sea. As we watched there reared out of the smoking brine a city of old bone coughed up from the sea's floor, pale attic bone delicate as shell and half melting, a chalken shambles coralgrown that slewed into shape of temple, column, plinth and cornice, and across the whole a frieze of archer and warrior and marblebreasted maid all listing west and moving slowly their stone limbs. As these figures began to cool and take on life Suttree among the watchers said that this time there are witnesses, for life does not come slowly. It rises in one massive mutation and all is changed utterly and forever. We have witnessed this thing today which prefigures for all time the way in which historic orders proceed. And some said that the girl who bathed her swollen belly in the stone pool in the garden last evening was the author of this wonder they attended. And a maid bearing water in a marble jar came down from the living frieze toward the dreamer with eyes restored black of core and iris brightly painted attic blue and she moved toward him with a smile.

Suttree surfaced from these fevered deeps to hear a maudlin voice chant latin by his bedside, what medieval ghost come to usurp his fallen corporeality. An oiled thumball redolent of lime and sage pondered his shuttered lids.

Miserere mei, Deus . . .

His ears anointed, his lips . . . omnis maligna discordia . . . Bechrismed with scented oils he lay boneless in a cold euphoria. Japheth when you left your father's house the birds had flown. You were not prepared for such weathers. You'd spoke too lightly of the winter in your father's heart. We saw you in the streets. Sad.

The priest's lamptanned and angular face leaned over him. The room was candlelit and spiced with smoke. He closed his eyes. A cool thumb crossed his soles with unction. He lay aneled. Like a rapevictim.

I am familiar with the burial rites of the nameless and the unclaimed.

What is it? said the priest.

Well may he wonder, praetor to a pederastic deity.

The priest wiped his fingers with bits of bread and rose. By candlelight he put away his effects in a little fitted case and left bearing the candle and followed by a nun and Suttree alone in the dark with his death and who will come to weep the grave of an alias? Or lay one flower down.

He dreamed of a race at the poles who rode on sleds of walrus hide and rucked up horn and ivory all drawn by dogs and bristling with lances and harpoon spears, the hunters shrouded in fur, slow caravans against the late noon winter sunset, against the rim of the world, whispering over the blue snow with their sledloads of piled meat and skins and viscera. Small bloodstained hunters drifting like spores above the frozen chlorine void, from flower to flower of bright vermilion gore across the vast boreal plain.

Down the nightworld of his starved mind cool scarves of fishes went veering, winnowing the salt shot that rose columnar toward rifts in the ice overhead. Sinking in a cold jade sea where bubbles shuttled toward the polar sun. Shoals of char ribboned off brightly and the ocean swell heaved with the world's turning and he could see the sun go bleared and fade beyond the windswept panes of ice. Under a waste more mute than the moon's face, where alabaster seabears cruise the salt and icegreen deeps.

When he woke there were footsteps in the room. Shapes crossed between the light and his thin eyelids. He was going again in a corridor through rooms that never ceased, by formless walls unordered unadorned and slightly moist and warm and through soft doors with valved and dripping architraves and regions wet and bluish like the inward parts of some enormous living thing. A small soul's going. By floodlight through the universe's renal regions. Pale phagocytes drifting over, shadows and shapes through the tubes like the miscellany in a waterdrop. The eye at the end of the glass would be God's.

Suttree saw the faces of the living bend. He closed his eyes. Gray geometric saurians lay snapping in a pit. Far away stood a gold pagoda with a little flutterblade that spun in the wind. He knew that he was not going there. He was awake for days. No one knew. He touched a hand attending him and smiled at its withdrawing. The freaks and phantoms skulked away beyond the cold white plaster of the ceiling. A tantric cat that loped forever in a funhouse corridor. He'd see them again on the day of his death.

One morning the priest came. The bed tilted. Suttree's body ran on it saclike and invertebrate, his drained members cooling on the sheets.

Would you like to confess? said the priest.

I did it, said Suttree.

A quick smile.

I'd like some wine.

Oh you cant have any wine, said a nursevoice.

The priest bent and opened his little leather case and took out a cruet. You had a close call, he said.

All my life. I did.

He tipped winedrops from the birdtongue spout down Suttree's throat. Suttree closed his eyes to savor it.

Do you have any more?

Just a drop. Not too much, I dont think.

That works, Suttree said.

Are you feeling better?

Yes.

God must have been watching over you. You very nearly died.

You would not believe what watches.

Oh?

He is not a thing. Nothing ever stops moving.

Is that what you learned?

I learned that there is one Suttree and one Suttree only.

I see, said the priest.

Suttree shook his head. No, he said. You dont.

The days were long and lonely, no one came.

He watched birds come and go in the tree beyond the window, like a memory from some childhood scene, dim its purpose.

He was given no food. A strange sour potion to drink. A nurse who came to catheterize him. He'd lain for hours with his cock hanging down the cool throat of a battered tin pitcher.

Catheterina, he said.

My name is Kathy.

We've got to stop meeting like this.

Hush now. Can you lift up some? Lift up some.

Try to control yourself. Damn.

You dont even have a temperature so I know this is all put on.

I hear water running.

Hush.

I never saw a lovelier ass.

I never knew anybody to get sexy being catheterized.

Will you marry me?

Sure.

One night as he lay there he felt suddenly strong enough to rise. He thought he'd dreamed of doing so. He eased his feet over the edge of the bed and stood. He tottered across the room and rested against the wall and came back. And again. He felt giddy.

The next night he went down the corridor. I feel like an angel, he told an old lady with a bucket whom he passed. There was no one about. A porter nodded at the desk. Suttree went out the door.

Down the street in his nightshirt till he came to a phone booth. No coins blocked away in there. He had a tag with the name Johnson on it pinned to the front of him and he took it off and laid it on the little metal shelf beneath the phone and he straightened out the pin and lifted the receiver from the hook. He worked the pin through the insulation of the cord and grounded the end of it against the metal of the coinslot. After a few tries he got a dial tone and he dialed 21505.

Carlights washed across this figure in nightwear crouched in his glass outhouse. He dropped to the floor of the booth. A reek of stale piss. The number was ringing. Suttree wondered what time it might be. It rang for some time.

Hello.

J-Bone.

462

Bud? That you?

Can you come and get me?

As they descended into McAnally Suttree let his head fall back on the musty plush of the old car seat.

You want some whiskey, Bud? We can get some.

No thanks.

You okay?

Yeah. I'd just like maybe a drink of water.

Mr Johnson like to left us didnt you Mr Johnson?

So they say. Who put the priest on me?

They said you was dyin. I came up last week and you didnt know nothin. I had a little drink hid away too.

Suttree patted J-Bone's knee, his eyes shut. Old J-Bone, he said.

I think you're a lowlife son of a bitch for not bringin us one of them, said Junior.

He opened one eye. One of what?

Them slick little nighties.

Piss on you.

Old Suttree's thinner than Boneyard, said J-Bone.

Old Suttree's all right, said Suttree.

They seemed a long time going. Down over the pocked and gutted streets under random pools of lamplight, blue jagged bowls moth-blown that reeled along the upper window rim by dim strung light-wires. Pale concrete piers veered off, naked columns of some fourth order capped with a red steel frieze. New roads being laid over McAnally, over the ruins, the shelled facades and walls standing in crazed shapes, the mangled iron firestairs dangling, the houses halved, broke open for the world to see. This naked spandrel clinging some-way to sheer wallpaper and mounting upward to terminate in nothing-ness and night like the works at Babel.

They're tearing everything down, Suttree said.

Yeah. Expressway.

Sad chattel stood on the cinder lawns, in the dim lilac lamplight. Old sofas bloated in the rain exploding quietly, shriveled tables sloughing off their papery veneers. A backdrop of iron earthmovers reared against the cokeblown sky.

New roads through McAnally, said J-Bone.

Suttree nodded, his eyes shut. He knew another McAnally, good to last a thousand years. There'd be no new roads there.

At night in the iron bed high in the old house on Grand he'd lie awake and hear the sirens, lonely sound in the city, in the empty streets. He lay in his chrysalis of gloom and made no sound, share by share sharing his pain with those who lay in their blood by the highwayside or in the floors of glass strewn taverns or manacled in jail. He said that even the damned in hell have the community of their suffering and he thought that he'd guessed out likewise for the living a nominal grief like a grange from which disaster and ruin are proportioned by laws of equity too subtle for divining.

The destruction of McAnally Flats found him interested. A thin, a wasted figure, he eased himself along past scenes of wholesale razing, whole blocks row on row flattened to dust and rubble. Yellow machines groaned over the landscape, the earth buckling, the few old coalchoked trees upturned and heaps of slag and cellarholes with vatshaped furnaces squat beneath their hydra works of rusted ducting and ashy fields shorn up and leveled and the dead turned out of their graves.

He watched the bland workman in the pilothouse of the crane shifting levers. The long tethered wreckingball swung through the side of a wall and small boys applauded. Brickwork of dried bloodcakes in flemish bond crumbling in a cloud of dust and mortar. Walls grim with scurf, a nameless crud. Pale spongoid growths that kept in clusters along the damper reaches came to light and all day grimecaked salvagers with hatchets spalled dead mortar from the piled black brick. Gnostic workmen who would have down this shabby shapeshow that masks the higher world of form. And left at eventide these cutaway elevations, little cubicles giving onto space, an iron bedstead, a freestanding stairwell to nowhere. Old gothic soffits hung with tar and lapsing paintflakes. Ragged cats picked their way over the glass and nigger dogs in the dooryards beyond the railsiding twitched in their sleep. Until nothing stood save rows of doors, some bearing numbers, all nailed to. Beyond lay fields of rubble, twisted steel and pipes and old conduits reared out of the ground in clusters of agonized ganglia among the broken slabs of masonry. Where small black hominoids scurried over the waste and sheets of newsprint rose in the wind and died again.

When he went one morning to the river he found the houseboat door ajar and someone sleeping in his bed. He entered in a fog of putrefaction. A hot and heady reek under the quaking tin. So warm a forenoon. He screened his nostrils with his sleeve.

Suttree nudged the sleeper with his toe but the sleeper slept. Two rats came from the bed like great hairy beetles and went rapidly without pause or effort up the wall and through a missing pane of glass as soundlessly as smoke.

He went back out and sat on the rail. He watched the river and he watched the fishing canes wink in the sunlight at the point. Wands dipping and rising, an old piscean ceremony he'd known himself. Pigeons came and went beneath the arches of the bridge and he could hear the rattling whine of a bandsaw at Rose's across the river. Upstream at Ab Jones's no sign of life, he looked. After a while he sucked in a breath and entered the cabin again. He kicked away the covers. A snarling clot of flies rose. Suttree stepped back. Caved cheek and yellow grin. A foul deathshead bald with rot, flyblown and eyeless.

He stood against the wall as long as he could hold his breath. A mass of yellow maggots lay working in one ear and a few flies rattled in the flesh and stood him off like cats. He turned and went out.

A woman was trudging stoically across the fields toward his houseboat. She dipped into the swale on the far side of the tracks and rose up again, crossed the tracks and came on down the barren path toward the river. She was roundshouldered and slumped and she walked with a kind of mindless dedication like a circus bear. Suttree waited on her, pulling the door to at his back.

When she reached the river she looked up at him and shaded her eyes with one hand. Mr Suttree? she said.

Yes.

She looked at the plank doubtfully, then shifted into motion again and came plodding up to the deck. She was sweating and she blew the hair from her eyes and wiped her eyes against her shoulders, one, the other, as if she were used to having things in her hands and had forgotten somewhat the use of them.

I seen ye from over in the store, she said. They told me you come in over there. I was about give up on ye.

Who are you? said Suttree.

I'm Josie Harrogate. I wanted to see you about Gene.

Suttree looked at her. A big rawboned woman, her hair matted over her face. The armpits of her cotton housedress black with sweat. Are you Gene's sister?

Yessir. He's my halfbrother is what he is.

I see.

My daddy died fore Gene was born.

Suttree ran his hand through his hair. Have you been to see him? he said.

No. I allowed maybe you knowed where he was at.

You dont know where he is?

No sir.

Suttree looked off down the river.

Mama died back in the winter I dont reckon he even knows it.

Well. I hate to have to tell you. He's in the penitentiary.

Yessir. Whereabouts?

Petros.

Her lips formed the word but nothing came out. What was it again? she said.

Petros. It's the state penitentiary. Brushy Mountain, it's called.

Brushy Mountain. Where's it at?

Well. It's west of here. About fifty miles I think. You could probably get a bus out there. They could tell you up at the bus terminal.

What's he in for?

Robbery.

She stared fixedly into his eyes to stay his lying or to know it if he did and she said: They aint fixin to electricate him are they?

No. He's in for three to five years. He could get out in eighteen months.

Well how long has he done been in?

A couple or three months.

Well, she said. I sure thank ye. I knowed you was a friend to Gene.

Gene's a good boy, Suttree said.

She didnt answer. She had turned to go but she stopped at the rail. What was that name again? she said.

Brushy Mountain?

No. That othern you said.

Petros.

Petros, she said. She said it again, staring emptily upward. Then she started down the catwalk. There must have been a loose cleat somewhere because going down it she fell. Her feet shot from under her and she sat down. The plank bowed deeply and rose again, lifting her flailing figure. She managed to get a grip and steady herself and she stood carefully and went on, teetering along till she reached the shore.

Are you all right? called Suttree.

She didnt look back. She raised one hand and waved it and went on, stooped and heavy gaited, across the fields and the tracks toward the town.

Suttree went up the river path through dockbloom and wild onion to the old floating roadhouse and tapped a last sad time at the green door. He rested on the railing and he tapped again but no one came. After a while he descended the plankwalk and crossed the fields and the tracks to the store.

She's moved out, said Howard Clevinger.

Yes, said Suttree.

She had a brother in Mascot, I think she went to live with them. Did that woman find you that was huntin you?

She did.

I seen you over there.

Suttree went back out and crossed to the river and sat on a stone and watched the water pass for a long time.

It was just dusk. Hung in the darker wall of the hillside among kudzu and dusty vines a few pale windowlights. The porch at Jimmy Smith's with its yellow light and half shadowed drinkers above the slat railed balustrade. A broken portico not unlike the shorn wreckage in McAnally save pasted up with these small crazed faces peering out. Over the squalid littoral, the wasteclogged river and the immense emptiness of the world beyond. A garish figure was coming along, a hoyden that sallied and fluttered through the one cone of uncashiered lamplight down all Front Street. Trippin Through The Dew in harlequin evening wear. They half circled, regarding one another.

Well I see you're still around anyway, said Suttree.

Honey I'm always here. They cant do without me. He smiled, primlipt and coyly.

Where's your hat this evening?

Oh honey hats are out. They just are. I always thought they were tacky anyway. Except mine of course. He knit his hands and rolled his shoulders and a whinny of girlish laughter went skittering among the little gray shacks and along the quiet twilit riverfront. He sobered suddenly and cocked his head. Where you been? he said.

I was in the hospital. Typhoid fever.

Lord honey I thought you looked peaky. Let me see you. He turned Suttree toward the streetlamp and peered into his eyes with genuine solicitude.

I'm okay, Suttree said.

Sweetie you have just fell off to skin and bones.

I lost about twenty pounds. I've gotten some of it back.

You want to rest and take care of yourself. You hear?

Suttree held out his hand. Tell me goodbye, he said.

Where you goin?

I dont know. I'm leaving Knoxville.

Shoot. He slapped at Suttree's outstretched hand. You aint goin noplace. When? When you goin?

Right now. I'm gone.

The black reached out sadly, his face pinched. They stood there holding hands in the middle of the little street. When you comin back?

I dont guess I'll be back.

Dont tell me that.

Well. Sometime maybe. Take care.

Honey you write and let me know how you gettin on.

Well.

Just a postcard.

Okay.

You need any money?

No. I've got some.

You sure?

I'm okay.

Trippin Through The Dew squeezed his hand and stepped back and gave a sort of crazy little salute. Best luck in the world baby, he said.

Thanks John. You too.

He lifted a hand and turned and went on. He had divested himself of the little cloaked godlet and his other amulets in a place where they would not be found in his lifetime and he'd taken for talisman the simple human heart within him. Walking down the little street for the last time he felt everything fall away from him. Until there was nothing left of him to shed. It was all gone. No trail, no track. The spoor petered out down there on Front Street where things he'd been lay like paper shadows, a few here, they thin out. After that nothing. A few rumors. Idle word on the wind. Old news years in traveling that you could not put stock in.

He took the shortcut up the path behind the houses, avoiding any chance of other meetings in the street. Old broken Thersites would have called down from his high window but he was not well these latter days. Dried vitriol hung in glazen strings from a bush by the side of the house and Suttree even thought he heard muted sounds of grousing in an upper room. He cocked one eye up the high warped clapboard wall to the chamber kept by this old taperheaded troll but no one watched back. The eunuch was asleep in his chair and he stirred and mumbled fitfully as if the departing steps of the fisherman depleted his dreams but he did not wake.

The city ambulance swung down off Front Street and went bobbling over the ground and across the tracks and up the river path until it came to the houseboat. People were watching along the porches and there were people standing around in front of the store watching with grave faces. Two men went in with a canvas stretcher and a blanket and in a few minutes they came out with the body and slid it quickly into the rear of the ambulance. In backing around they got the ambulance stuck in the mud. One wheel shot reams of gouty mire out into the river. The men climbed down and looked. One pushed. The ambulance sank until it was resting on its differential carrier.

After a while three tall colored boys in track shoes came along and pushed the ambulance out.

Who sick? one said.

There was a man dead in there, the driver said.

They looked at each other. How long he been dead?

A couple of weeks.

Shoo, one said, wrinkling his wide nose. That's what that's been.

You dont know who it was do you?

No suh.

Dont know who lived here?

No suh.

Come on Ramsey, we got to go.

I heah you, man.

The driver closed the door and motioned with his hand and the ambulance pulled away. The boys watched them go. Shit, one said. Old Suttree aint dead.

He had a small cardboard suitcase and he came out of the weeds and set it on the edge of the road and straightened up and began combing his hair. He looked about his appearance, propping one foot on the case and bending to scrape beggarlice from his trousers with his thumbnail. New trousers of tan chino. A new shirt open at the neck. His face and arms were suntanned and his hair crudely barbered and he wore cheap new brown leather shoes the toes of which he dusted, one, the other, against the back of his trouserlegs. He looked like someone just out of the army or jail. A car came down the highway and he gestured at it with his thumb and it went on.

Traffic was slow along the road and he was there a long time. It was very hot. You could see his skin through the new shirt. Across the road a construction gang was at work and he watched them. A backhoe was dragging out a ditch and a caterpillar was going along the bank with mounds of pale clay shaling across its canted blade. Carpenters were hammering up forms and a cement truck waited on with its drum slowly clanking. Suttree watched this industry accomplish itself in the hot afternoon. Downwind light ocher dust had sifted all along the greening roadside foliage and in the quiet midafternoon the call of a long sad trainhorn floated over the lonely countryside.

A boy was going along the works with a pail and he leaned to each, ladling out water in a tin dipper. Suttree saw hands come up from below the rim of the pit in parched supplication. When all these had been attended the boy came down along the edge of the ditch and handed up the dipper to the backhoe operator. Suttree saw him take it and tilt his head and drink and flick the last drops toward the earth and lean down and restore the dipper to the watercarrier. They nodded to each other and the boy turned and looked toward the road. Then he was coming down across the clay and over the ruts and laddered tracks of machinery. His dusty boots left prints across the black macadam and he came up to Suttree where he stood by the roadside and swung the bucket around and brought the dipper up all bright and dripping and offered it. Suttree could see the water beading coldly on the tin and running in tiny rivulets and drops that steamed on the road where they fell. He could see the pale gold hair that lay along the sunburned arms of the waterbearer like new wheat and he beheld himself in wells of smoking cobalt, twinned and dark and deep in child's eyes, blue eyes with no bottoms like the sea. He took the dipper and drank and gave it back. The boy dropped it into the bucket. Suttree wiped his mouth on the back of his hand. Thanks, he said.

The boy smiled and stepped back. A car had stopped for Suttree, he'd not lifted a hand.

Let's go, said the driver.

Hello, said Suttree, climbing in, shutting the door, his suitcase between his knees. Then they were moving. Out across the land the lightwires and roadrails were going and the telephone lines with voices shuttling on like souls. Behind him the city lay smoking, the sad purlieus of the dead immured with the bones of friends and forebears. Off to the right side the white concrete of the expressway gleamed in the sun where the ramp curved out into empty air and hung truncate with iron rods bristling among the vectors of nowhere. When he looked back the waterboy was gone. An enormous lank hound had come out of the meadow by the river like a hound from the depths and was sniffing at the spot where Suttree had stood.

Somewhere in the gray wood by the river is the huntsman and in the brooming corn and in the castellated press of cities. His work lies all wheres and his hounds tire not. I have seen them in a dream, slaverous and wild and their eyes crazed with ravening for souls in this world. Fly them.